LA GRANGE
PUBLIC LIBRARY

10 West Cossitt Avenue
La Grange, IL 60525
lagrangelibrary.org   708.215.3200

THE
WRECKAGE

Also by Michael Robotham

The Suspect
The Drowning Man (aka Lost)
The Night Ferry
Shatter
Bombproof
Bleed for Me

THE
WRECKAGE

Michael Robotham

MULHOLLAND BOOKS

LITTLE, BROWN AND COMPANY

NEW YORK BOSTON LONDON

Mulholland Books/Little, Brown and Company
Hachette Book Group
237 Park Avenue, New York, NY 10017
www.hachettebookgroup.com

First Edition: June 2011

Mulholland Books is an imprint of Little, Brown and Company, a division of Hachette Book Group, Inc. The Mulholland Books name and logo are trademarks of Hachette Book Group, Inc.

The publisher is not responsible for websites (or their content) that are not owned by the publisher.

Library of Congress Cataloging-in-Publication Data

Robotham, Michael
  The wreckage / Michael Robotham. — 1st ed.
    p. cm.
  ISBN 978-0-316-12640-3
  1. Bank robberies — Fiction. 2. Baghdad (Iraq) — Fiction.
  3. Journalists — Fiction. 4. Ex-police — England — London — Fiction.
  5. Bankers — Fiction. I. Title.
  PR6118.O26W74 2011
  823'.92 — dc22
                                                           2011012657

10 9 8 7 6 5 4 3 2 1

RRD-C

Printed in the United States of America

For Ursula Mackenzie

BOOK ONE

During times of universal deceit, telling the truth becomes a revolutionary act.

GEORGE ORWELL

H*ave you killed?"*

"Many times."

"Were you scared?"

"No."

"Never?"

"It's not hard to take a life when a life has been taken from you. It is not about embracing revenge or nurturing hatred. And forget about taking an eye for an eye. Equality is for the weak and stupid. It's about pulling the trigger...simple as that. One finger, one movement..."

"Who was the first?"

"A schoolgirl."

"Why?"

"I can't remember, but I've never forgotten the warmth of the day, the blinding glare, the dust on the leaves of the apricot trees. It was apricot season. In that final instant everything slows down — the cars, the buses, voices on the street. Everything goes quiet and all you hear is your own heartbeat, the blood squeezing through smaller and smaller channels. There is no other moment like it."

"Why do they call you the Courier?"

"I deliver messages."

"You kill people?"

"People kill every day. Nurses push needles. Surgeons stop hearts. Butchers slay beasts. You're doing something good here. You and the others are going to be famous. You are going to create a day that will live forever, a date that doesn't need an explanation. History made. History changed. These things begin somewhere. They begin with an idea. They begin with faith."

"Why me?"

"The others will also be tested."

"Are you going to film it?"

"Yes. Here is the gun. It won't bite you. This is the safety. Pull back the slide and the bullet enters the chamber."

"Nobody will see my face?"

"No. Now walk through the door. He's waiting. Seated. He will hear you coming. He will beg. Don't listen to his words. Press the barrel to the back of his head and pull off the hood. Make him look at the camera's red light: the drop of electrified blood."

"Should I say something? A prayer."

"It's not what you say—it's what you do."

1

BAGHDAD

The most important lesson Luca Terracini ever learned about being a foreign correspondent was to tell a story through the eyes of someone else. The second most important lesson was how to make spaghetti marinara with a can of tuna and a packet of ramen noodles.

There were others, of course, most of them to do with staying alive in a war zone: Do not make an appointment to see anyone you do not trust absolutely. Do not go out before checking whether any suspicious vehicles are loitering outside. Do not assume that a place that was safe yesterday will be safe today.

These security measures were followed by all western reporters in Baghdad, but Luca had added a few of his own over the years — advice that came down to possessing three vital tools for survival: a natural cowardice; several US hundred-dollar bills sewn into his trouser cuffs; and a well-developed sense of the absurd.

The first call to prayer is sounding. Sunrise. Luca had been woken by the racket of washing machines, TV sets and air conditioners coming to life simultaneously. The government can only provide electricity during certain hours, which means the appliances trigger at random times, day or night, creating a strange symphony of music and metal.

Stripping off his T-shirt, he scoops water from a bucket with a ladle, pouring it over his head. Droplets pour from his short dark beard and down his chest over his genitals. It's already nearly ninety degrees outside and not even the shutters can keep the heat out once the sun hits the side of the building.

Drying his hair, he chooses a thin cotton shirt, something plain, cheap. He dresses like an Iraqi and tries to sound like an Iraqi. His shoes are not western. His sunglasses are not too foreign looking.

Sliding his hand beneath the mattress, he pulls out a compact semi-automatic 9mm pistol and tucks it into a holster in the small of his back. In his office, he unplugs his mobile, grabs his camera gear and opens the front door of his apartment, checking the corridor and then taking the rear stairs.

A security guard dozes behind a desk in the foyer.

"Sabah al-khair, Ahmed."

The guard jerks awake, reaching for his rifle. Luca holds up his hands in mock fear and the guard grins at him.

"Have you made the city safe, Ahmed?"

"I have defused two dozen bombs."

"Excellent. Just don't recycle them."

The guard laughs and gets to his feet. His belt is undone, his stomach bulging freely.

Luca opens his mobile and calls Jamal.

"Where are you?"

"Two minutes away."

Glancing through the taped windows, the street view is shielded by concrete blast walls that are fifteen feet high. There are checkpoints at the two nearest intersections, giving the illusion of safety. Just like his rules for survival, Luca has developed his own conflict metabolism, attuned to the violence. His heart no longer punches through his chest when a mortar explodes and he doesn't duck when a round zings overhead.

Most of his colleagues reside in secure hotel compounds or in the International Zone (formerly the Green Zone), seeking safety in numbers, which is another illusion. Clean sheets, cold beer, wireless broadband and satellite TV—modern tools for the modern reporter.

The bombings a month ago had provided a salutatory lesson. The first explosion targeted the Sheraton Ishtar, toppling the concrete blast walls and leaving a crater fifteen feet deep and thirty feet wide. Cars were torn apart by the spray of metal and glass, which littered the lawns and courtyards of the fish restaurants along the river.

Three minutes later, a bomb went off near the Babylon Hotel; and six minutes later at the al-Hamra, tearing off the façade. Four-teen people died at the Sheraton, seven at the Babylon and sixteen at the al-Hamra, including a policeman who once helped Luca find a new battery for his mobile.

Luca had arrived at the hotel when the plume of dust and smoke still drifted across the skyline and the scent of shorn eucalyptus trees mixed with the ugly, sweet stench of burning flesh. Two women were found beneath the rubble, one of them covered in dust with long streaks of blood running down her face. "May God kill the government," she shouted as they pulled her free.

Another ordinary day in Baghdad.

A text message on Luca's mobile: *Thirty seconds. Out front.*

Moments later a battered Skoda 130 pulls up outside the apart-ment block, a young man behind the wheel. A second vehicle is immediately behind—a Toyota HiLux—the "chase car."

Luca stays low as he runs. The moment the car door closes, Jamal jams down on the accelerator, swerving around the flat-faced concrete barricades. The HiLux is close behind, ready to intervene in case of an ambush.

The Skoda is a classic Baghdadi car with a windshield criss-crossed with cracks and a dash covered in an old strip of carpet and faded pictures of Shia martyrs. Beneath the bonnet is a V8 engine from a Chrysler 340 and slabs of iron welded inside the doors, bullet-proofing Iraqi style.

Jamal drives like he's at Le Mans and dresses like he's a gay cow-boy in plaid shirts and western-style jeans. He was studying to be a doctor before the invasion. In the chaos that followed, the univer-sity's computers were stolen and the files destroyed by fire. Now he can't prove he has a science degree or three years of medical training.

Jamal's cousin Abu is driving the HiLux. He's older and built like a battering ram, with a semi-automatic pistol beneath his shirt and a sawn-off shotgun on his lap. In the four years they have worked together, Luca has exchanged little more than a dozen words with Abu. Jamal does the talking. On a busy thoroughfare, the vehicles travel bumper to bumper, weaving between groaning trucks, vans, mopeds and cyclists.

"There was another robbery," says Jamal.

"When?"

"Overnight. They set the bank on fire."

"Where?"

"In Karrada."

"I want to go there."

"What about the media conference?"

"They still won't have formed a government." Luca mimics the voice of the former Prime Minister Iyad Allawi. *"Today we are a step closer to agreement. Old hatreds are being put aside and we are talking in good faith. I am committed to the constitution and believe Iraq will get the government it deserves."*

Jamal laughs. "One day they're going to kick you out of Iraq."

"Promises, promises."

He calls Abu in the HiLux. "We're going to Karrada."

"What address?"

"Follow the smoke."

The two vehicles circumnavigate Firdos Square and head south along the dusty dual carriageway past mud buildings and footpaths lined in places with drums and razor wire.

Baghdad used to feel foreign to Luca but he's no longer spooked by the strangeness of the place—the jangle of tongues, the confusion of smells and the thick honey-colored light. A bus has broken down. Passengers are standing on the pavement, arguing with the driver. The men draw on cigarettes, forming wraiths of smoke that are whisked away on the breeze. The women are delicate, unknown creatures swathed in black, with non-descript bodies and dancing eyes.

Jamal takes a stick of chewing gum from his pocket and turns on the radio, beating out a rhythm on the steering wheel as he listens to a local pop song. He and Luca have become friends over the years, but that friendship has boundaries. Luca has never been to Jamal's house, or met his wife or his two young sons. There are people who cannot know that Jamal and Abu are working for an American journalist. Sunnis. Shiites. Insurgents. That's where death lurks. Grudges are a national sport in Iraq.

A black plume of smoke rises into the white sky ahead of them. Normally Karrada is one of the havens, thrumming with street traders and gaudy shouts of greenery. Now police and fire engines have sealed off an intersection and hoses like black pythons twist across the asphalt, bulging and squirming. Some are so perished and worn they are spraying the concrete instead of the smoldering building.

The Zewiya branch of the al-Rafidain Bank has been gutted and the windows are ringed with dark shadows of soot that leak like a beauty queen's tears down the pale walls.

Jamal parks the Skoda and Luca takes his camera from his rucksack. He signals Abu, who waits with the cars, keeping watch from a distance.

"How many is that?"

"Six in the past two months."

"And this year?"

"Eighteen."

"Soon there will be no banks left to rob."

Across the street, a group of teenage boys are laughing and shoving each other, frantic to be noticed. They are admonished by older men and told to show some respect.

A siren. A convoy. Four military vehicles weave between the fire engines, escorting a white police car with blue doors. The car pulls on to the curb, scraping metal beneath the chassis. Luca recognizes the man in the passenger seat: General Khalid al-Uzri, Commander of the National Police. Two uniformed officers wrestle each other to reach his door.

Al-Uzri stands and stretches, cracking his vertebrae and rolling his head from side to side. Cigarette smoke hangs over him like a personal cloud. Dressed in black-and-blue camouflage with a beret and epaulettes of a crossed wreath and star, he waves dismissively at the offer of an umbrella and walks through the spray, pausing to appraise the bank building as though considering making an offer.

A senior fireman emerges from within. His uniform looks too large for him, like he's wearing his father's clothes. He shakes al-Uzri by the hand and kisses each cheek.

"What has been lost?" asks the general.

"Three dead."

"The money?"

"Gone."

The general brushes water from his jacket sleeve and glances at Luca.

"You're a photographer?"

"Yes, General," he answers in Arabic.

"Today you work for the police."

Luca exchanges a glance with Jamal, who shakes his head. Luca ignores him. He follows the general and the fireman down the ramp, stepping through oily black puddles and around piles of smoldering debris.

The large roller door has buckled and twisted in the heat. Two bodies lie inside. Security guards. They look like discarded mannequins with melted and blackened flesh. The smell pries open Luca's senses. Vomit rises. He swallows hard, coffee chewing at his stomach.

Al-Uzri crouches beside the corpses. "It's the protein," he explains. "When it burns it sticks to your clothes and the inside of your lungs."

Holding a skull, he turns it as if he's testing the firmness of melons at a market stall.

One of his aides speaks. "There were six guards rostered on last night."

"Where are the others?"

"We're looking for them."

"These men were shot. Take photographs of this."

The general stands and walks onwards, wiping his hands on the coat of the nearest fireman.

The concrete vault has a heavy metal door that has barely been singed by the blaze. It opens easily. Nothing remains inside except a single aluminum case, smashed open. A handful of US banknotes are floating in a grimy puddle.

The general leaves the vault, moving towards the internal stairs. Firefighters have erected ladders to the upper floors.

"Is that going to take my weight?" asks al-Uzri.

"Yes, sir."

He points at Luca. "You go first."

The journalist climbs the ladder and steps over a collapsed section of the floor. A toilet has come through the ceiling and landed vertically across a doorway. Glancing past it, he can see a long corridor with offices on either side. The desktop computers have melted into modern sculptures.

The senior fireman stops at one of the offices. It takes a moment for Luca to realize what he's supposed to photograph. A blackened corpse is seated at a metal desk with stiffened half limbs reaching towards the blown-out window. Charred beyond recognition, the skin of the face is shrunken and leathery, gripping the skull, and the mouth is wide open in a scream. A swollen tongue protrudes from between teeth that seem unnaturally white.

Al-Uzri circles the body, examining it from all sides, his wet brown eyes full of wonder but not horror. Luca is taking short breaths through his mouth.

"This is one of the ignition points," says the fireman. "Someone doused the body with petrol and poured a trail along the hallway to the door."

Al-Uzri has moved behind the carbonized body. He pulls a small Swiss army knife from his coat, unsheathing the blade. His hand steady, he holds the sharp edge against the corpse's neck and pulls something away, a wire thread embedded in the skin. A garrote.

He nods to Luca. More pictures are taken.

Closing the knife, he lights a cigarette, blowing smoke towards the ceiling.

Nothing shows in his eyes. Not surprise or sadness. Luca has seen that look before in soldiers who have witnessed such horrors that nothing is new under the sun or moon.

"A bad business," says the fireman. "Have you seen enough?"

The general nods. He addresses Luca. "Deliver the photographs to my office. They are the property of the Iraqi police."

Descending the ladders, he retraces his steps through the puddles and up the ramp, pausing only to blow cotton wool from his nostrils. Luca follows him outside where drivers scramble into cars, preparing to depart.

"Excuse me, General, I have a question about the robbery."

The commander turns.

"Your name?"

"Luca Terracini—I'm an American journalist."

"Your Arabic is very proficient, Mr. Terracini."

"My mother was Iraqi."

Al-Uzri lights another cigarette, shielding it from the spray. He takes a moment to study the journalist.

"Most of your colleagues wear Kevlar vests and travel in numbers. Do you think having an Iraqi mother will protect you?"

"No, sir."

"Perhaps you are very brave?"

"No, sir."

Water trickles down Luca's back. It might be sweat. "The bank manager was tortured."

"It appears so."

"Do you know how much money was taken?"

"No."

"What happened to the other security guards?"

"Perhaps they chased after the robbers."

"Perhaps they ran off with the money."

The leaking hoses have doused the general's cigarette. He stares at the soggy offering. "It is not a good idea to make accusations like that."

"This is the eighteenth bank robbery in Baghdad this year. Does that concern you?"

The general smiles, but the corners of his mouth barely move. "I find it reassuring that somebody is keeping count."

His car door is being held open, the engine running. He slides into the passenger seat and waves the driver onwards with a flick of his hand. The convoy moves off, weaving between fire engines, adding one more siren to a city that sings with them.

2

LONDON

Being measured for a new suit was not something Vincent Ruiz expected to happen until he was lying cold and stiff on an undertaker's slab. And if that were the case, he didn't suppose he'd care about an effeminate stranger nudging a tape measure against his balls. Maybe he's weighing them. Every *other* measurement has been taken.

Emile drapes the tape measure around his neck and jots down another set of numbers.

"Does sir want the trousers to touch his uppers or the top of the soles?"

"Call me Vincent."

"Yes, sir."

He holds the tape measure against Ruiz's hip and lets it fall before tugging it tight again. "Has sir considered cuffs?"

"Are they extra?"

"No. You have the height to wear cuffs. Short men should avoid them. I'd recommend about one and a half inches."

"Fine."

Next the tape measure is wrapped around Ruiz's upper thigh. "Does sir dress to the left or the right?"

"I like to swing both ways."

Emile's eyebrows arch like inflection marks.

"Just give me loads of room," says Ruiz. "I want to be able to hide a hard-on. My ex-wife is coming to the wedding and she's a lot hotter since we divorced."

"Very good, sir."

Ruiz sighs and gives up trying to get a smile out of Emile. Instead he ponders his daughter's wedding. Claire is getting married in just under a week and he is supposed to walk her down the aisle and "give her away." She rang him last night and threatened to ask someone else if he didn't start following instructions.

"That's just it," he told her. "I don't want to give you away. I want to keep you."

"Very droll, Dad."

"I'm being serious."

"I'm getting married whether you like it or not."

"I could have Phillip arrested."

"He's a lawyer, Dad, not a criminal."

"Is there a difference?"

Emile picks up his brocade cushion and retreats from the fitting room. Ruiz pulls on his worn corduroy trousers and heavy cotton shirt. As he buttons the front, he catches a glimpse of himself in the mirror. Turning sideways and sucking in his stomach, he straightens his shoulders and examines his physique. Not bad for a man who has hurdled sixty. Some mileage on the clock, but that's to be expected. His doctor wouldn't agree, of course, but *his* doctor is the sort of idiot who thinks people should live to be a hundred and fifty.

Slipping on a jacket, he pats the pockets and takes out a metal tin of boiled sweets. Unscrewing the lid he pops one into his mouth where it rattles against his teeth. He gave up smoking six years ago. Sugar is the substitute; calories as opposed to cancer.

As he steps out of the menswear shop, a hand slips through his left arm, pulling him close. He accepts Claire's kiss on the cheek, bending slightly so she can reach.

"Is it done?"

"It's done."

"That wasn't so hard?"

"A strange man has been weighing my balls."

"Emile is lovely."

"He's gayer than a handbag full of rainbows."

She giggles and skips to keep up with him. Dark-haired and pretty, she walks on her toes like a ballet dancer—her former career. Now she teaches at the Royal Academy, crippling prepubescent girls who look pregnant if they eat an apple.

"OK, now remember we have a dinner with Phillip's folks tomorrow night. They're catching the train from Brighton. Mr. Seidlitz has invited us to his club."

Ruiz's heart sinks. "What sort of club?"

"Don't worry, Daddy, he doesn't play golf."

Seidlitz is a Ukrainian name. Maybe golf isn't big in the Ukraine. Ruiz isn't looking forward to it—a table for six, small talk. Miranda will be his date. His ex-wife. Number three. She's the one who acts like they're still married. Ruiz knows there is something fundamentally amiss about this fact, but Miranda is the sort of ex-wife that most men dream about. Low maintenance. Self-sufficient. Classy. When they divorced she asked him for nothing except for a few souvenirs from the marriage and to be allowed to stay in touch with Michael and Claire. They still needed a mother, she said.

Over the past few years Ruiz and Miranda have periodically fallen into bed together—a perfectly satisfactory "friends with benefits" arrangement, offering companionship, a pinch of romance and the sort of sex that can fog the windows. Not love, it's true... not exactly—but closer to love than most relationships Ruiz had known.

Claire looks at her watch. "I'm meeting Phillip. He'll be early."

"Why?"

"He always is."

"That's another reason not to marry him."

"Oh, stop!"

Blowing him a kiss, she skips across the road, leaving him on the corner. He wants to call after her, to hear her sweet voice again.

Married…in a week. She seems too young. Thirty-two on her last birthday, yet Ruiz can still picture her in pigtails and braces. Her fiancé is a lawyer who works for an investment bank. Does that make him a lawyer or a banker? He votes Tory, but everybody does these days.

Ruiz wishes Laura were here. She would have loved all this— preparing menus, choosing flowers, sending out invitations— weddings are about mothers and daughters. The father of the bride just has to turn up, walk down the aisle and hand his daughter over like she's part of a prisoner swap.

Ruiz isn't even expected to pick up the tab. Phillip has everything covered. He earns more in a month than Ruiz used to make in a year as a detective inspector. He didn't even melt a little during the global meltdown, while Ruiz's retirement funds have halved. His investment advisor isn't answering his calls, which is always a bad sign.

Office workers are spilling out of buildings, their day ending, the commute ahead. Ruiz tries to avoid public transport during the peak hours. Lust, greed, sloth, envy, pride…the full pathology of human behavior is played out on the tube every morning and evening. It's like an experiment in overcrowding using humans instead of rats. Ruiz prefers to conduct his own scientific study, which involves a pint of Guinness and a table by the window where he can watch the office girls walk by in their tight skirts and summer blouses. Not a dirty old man but a lover of the feminine form.

The Coach & Horses in Greek Street used to be one of his favorite pubs, back in the days when Norman "You're Barred" Balon was still in charge. Norman was London's grumpiest publican, famous for abusing patrons. He retired a few years back. Regulars gave him a standing ovation and three cheers. Norman told them to shut up and "spend more fucking money."

Setting his pint on a table, Ruiz pulls out a notebook and reads over the sentences he wrote this morning. Stories. Anecdotes. Descriptions. Ever since he retired he's been making notes and trying to remember things. He doesn't see himself as a writer. He has no desire to be one. It's about finding the right words and sorting out his memories, rather than justifying his actions or leaving something behind.

Forty-three years as a copper, thirty-five as a detective, all he has left are the stories: triumphs, tragedies, mistakes and missed opportunities. Some may be worth reading. Most are best left alone.

Ruiz misses the camaraderie of the Met, the sense of purpose, the smell of cigarette smoke and wet overcoats. It was an unreal world, yet it was more real than real, if that makes sense. Important. Frustrating. Over.

Three empty pint glasses are sitting in front of him. It's growing dark outside, but the streets are still teeming with tourists and diners. London seems more foreign to him every summer — not just because of the influx of visitors, who are mainly Japanese, American and a generic kind of East European. The city is changing. Old haunts disappear. Safe streets become less safe. The heart beats to a different rhythm.

Ruiz notices a girl sitting on her own at a corner table. Her eyes are faded, almost transparent blue like his own and somehow even worldlier. Sullen-faced and pretty, she's wearing leopard-print leggings, lace-up boots and a white peasant blouse. Her coal-black hair is cut short and curled where it brushes her shoulders and swings when she turns her head, waiting for someone to arrive.

She's reading a newspaper with a pen in her hand. It's a copy of *The Stage* — the theater magazine, the auditions page, looking for work. Checking her watch, she folds the magazine and goes to the bar for another drink.

Her eyes, unnaturally wide, flick from face to face as if rapidly collecting details or assembling a jigsaw puzzle. There are two suits on stools at the bar, junior executive types with their ties at half-mast. They offer to buy her a drink. She declines. One of them motions to her with his forefinger. She steps closer.

"You see that," he says. "I just made you come with one finger — imagine what I can do with the rest of them."

A flush of embarrassment colors her cheeks, quickly replaced by anger.

Back at her table, she tries to ignore them, but they follow.

"Why won't you have a drink with us?"

"I'm waiting for a friend."

"Is she as pretty as you?"

"No, but he's *bigger* than you are."

One of them snatches the magazine from her and holds it out of her reach. She knows they want her to humiliate herself by trying to retrieve it but she simply waits until they grow bored and give it back to her.

Ruiz is watching, impressed. The little actress is a no-nonsense sort of girl.

Ordering another pint, he goes back to his notes and doesn't look up again until much later. A man has arrived and is talking to the actress. Perhaps he's her boyfriend. Tall and loosely strung, he's wearing a frayed turtleneck, dirty jeans and boots.

They're arguing. He grabs her by the wrist and tries to make her stand. In the next instant, his fist swings into the side of her head. The blow is so short, sharp and unexpected that nobody in the bar reacts. The girl is holding her face. Wide-eyed. Shocked. The boyfriend is standing over her with his fist clenched, ready to hit her again. Ruiz doesn't let it happen. Grabbing the upraised hand, he wrenches it backwards, twisting it up the boyfriend's spine.

"Maybe you should pick on someone your own size."

"What's your fucking problem?"

"Honestly? If she weighed another hundred pounds I'd call it even and watch her kick your arse."

"Fuck you!"

Ruiz twists the arm higher. The boyfriend grunts and rises on to his toes. The main door is only three paces away. Cool air. A wet pavement. Ruiz shoves the boyfriend against a parked car and waits for him to spin, knowing he's going to fight. At that same moment, one of the barmen makes an appearance, gripping a metal bar. The boyfriend steps aside. Mumbles something. A threat. An insult. Ruiz can't hear the words but he knows the odds have altered; the chemistry changed. The boyfriend points his finger at Ruiz as though marking him for future reference and then slinks off. Inside the pub someone has filled a towel with ice, which the actress has pressed to the side of her face. Ruiz buys her a drink. Scotch. Neat.

"This will settle your nerves."

He watches her throat move as she swallows.

"My name is Vincent."

"Holly."

"You want to call the police, Holly?"

She shakes her head.

"Show me your cheek."

She lowers the towel. One side of her face is a little swollen. There'll be a bruise. Her eyes shift past him, searching the floor.

"My bag!"

"What did it look like?"

"It's black . . . with buckles."

Ruiz helps her search. "What did it have in it?"

"Money. My phone." She groans. "My keys."

"Does anyone have a spare set?"

"My boyfriend."

Ruiz makes her put the ice-towel back on her cheek.

"Is there someone you can call?"

"I don't have any numbers."

"Maybe your boyfriend has cooled off by now."

Holly borrows Ruiz's mobile. The call goes straight to voicemail. She leaves a message. Apologizing. She shouldn't *have* to apologize.

Ruiz gets her another drink. She pushes the hair off her face, hooking it behind her ears. Her accent is from the north.

"So you're an actress."

Holly eyes him nervously over the rim of her glass. "What makes you say that?"

"I saw you reading *The Stage*."

She shrugs. "Someone left it behind."

Ruiz wonders why she would lie to him.

"I've been all sorts of things — a waitress, a receptionist, a dishwasher, a barmaid — I was even a badger."

"A badger?"

"I was supposed to be a beaver, but they couldn't find a beaver costume. It was for a building company at a trade fair. Beavers make stuff in wood, you know, like dams."

"I can see the connection."

"Good. You can explain it to me."

She smiles for the first time. Ruiz notices a small silver teddy bear on a chain around her neck; her piercings, one through her nose, more in her ears.

"Has your boyfriend ever hit you before?"

She shrugs ambivalently. "It's what unites all men."

"What does?"

"Violence."

"Not all men are violent."

She shrugs again and changes the subject.

"What happened to your finger?"

She points to his missing digit, severed just below the first knuckle on his ring finger, a pale stump where the flesh seems to have folded in on itself.

"It was bitten off by a crocodile."

"You're not a very good liar."

"It was shot off."

"How did it happen?"

"You believe me then?"

"Yes."

"Is being shot more believable than being attacked by a crocodile?"

"We live in England. There aren't many crocodiles."

"It's a long, boring story."

"It doesn't sound very boring."

"It was a high-velocity bullet. I took one in the leg and one in the hand."

"You were a soldier?"

"A detective."

Concern flashes across her eyes and just as quickly disappears. She starts a new conversation, jumping subjects. Ruiz feels as though he's being dragged behind a speedboat bumping over the swells. It's getting late. He has to make a decision.

"What are you going to do, Holly?"

She shakes her head.

"Do you have anywhere to stay?"

"No."

"You could come back to my place. Make some calls."

Holly ponders this for a moment. "You live alone?"

"Yes."

"You're divorced."

"Is it that obvious?"

"Yes."

Outside the temperature has dropped and a breeze sprung up. Holly pulls on a distinctive red jacket with wooden pegs as fasteners and a hood. Pulling it tight around herself, she waits while Ruiz hails a cab and then slides across the seat.

The driver is listening to the radio. Evening talkback with Brian Noble: "The Voice of the Lord."

Mersey Fidelity today announced a record profit while the rest of the economy continues to struggle. Isn't it nice to know that our banks are back in business again? We bailed them out, gave them half a trillion pounds in cash, loans, shares, lucre, dosh, quantitative easing—no strings attached—and now they're making hay while the rest of us shovel horse manure.

Now I know that Mersey Fidelity weathered the storm better than most of our banks, but I ask you this: Why hasn't there been one court case, one prosecution, one political resignation, or one apology from a banker? Too big to fail, now they're cashing in. The lines are open. What advice would you give our banksters?

The cab navigates through Piccadilly, Knightsbridge and along Old Brompton Road. Holly holds on to the side strap as the cab corners, occasionally glancing behind her through the rear window.

Ruiz lives in a three-storey terrace, open plan on the ground floor, bedrooms above and narrow stairs to a loft with his study. The house is too big for him. He should have sold up and moved years ago, but wasn't willing to abandon the memories.

There is a bicycle partially blocking the hallway. Brand new. Unused. His birthday present from Miranda. She expected him to keep fit by riding along the river. Good luck with that.

"You want a tea or coffee?"

"Anything stronger?"

He opens a bottle of wine and lets Holly do the pouring. He gives her the phone to use.

"I don't have any numbers," she says.

"What about your parents?"

"Dead."

"Friends?"

"I don't really know anybody in London."

Ruiz sits on the sofa. Holly prefers the floor. She nurses her wine glass in both hands.

"When you got shot—did you think you were going to die?"

"Yes."

"Is that why you limp when you walk?"

"It is."

"What would it take for you to kill yourself?"

"What sort of question is that?"

"It's just a question."

"I've seen too many suicides."

"What if you were in awful pain, dying of a terrible disease?"

"There are painkillers."

"What if your mind was failing? You had dementia and couldn't remember your own name?"

"If I had dementia it wouldn't matter."

"What if you were being tortured for top secret information?"

"I don't have any top secret information."

"What if someone had a grenade on a bus and they were going to blow it to the sky? Would you throw your body on the grenade?"

"Where do you get these questions?"

"I think about stuff all the time; how one decision, even a small one, can change your life. I have really weird dreams. I once dreamed I had a penis. Does that make me bisexual?"

"I have no idea."

She tops up Ruiz's wine and begins looking through his collection of DVDs stacked on a shelf. Old films.

"Oooh, I love this one." She holds up *Philadelphia Story*. "Katherine Hepburn."

"And Cary Grant."

"I loved him in *To Catch a Thief.*"

"Favorite old-time actor?"

"Alec Guinness."

"Mine is Peter O'Toole."

"Typical."

"What does that mean?"

She shakes her head. "Favorite old-time actress?"

"Ingrid Berman."

"I thought you'd say Grace Kelly. Men seem to prefer blondes."

"Not this one."

The room has warmed up. Holly unbuttons her jacket, letting it slip off her arms. Her blouse is edged with silver thread and beads. The fabric pushes out over her breasts and she looks more like a woman than a girl.

If Miranda could see him now, what would she say? She'd tell him to go to bed and to stop embarrassing himself.

Holly has poured him another glass of wine. How much has he had to drink? Four pints. A scotch. Three glasses of wine...

Ruiz is trying to shake the fuzziness out of his head.

"I could make a bed for you," he says, feeling his thoughts drifting. Sliding. Spilling down the mountainside, settling in the hollows. His legs are so heavy he can't move them.

Holly sits next to him on the sofa and puts a pillow beneath his head. He's watching her lips move. What is she saying? It might be goodbye. It might be sorry.

3

LONDON

Sunshine crashes through the lace curtains. Ruiz opens one eye. The ceiling comes into focus, dead moths in the domed light fitting. His right nostril is grouted closed. His mouth tastes like a small animal has crawled inside and died.

Rolling on to his knees, he groans and feels his stomach lurch and gurgle. The rug has a pattern. He hasn't noticed it before. Perhaps he's forgotten. Another convulsion and he stumbles to the toilet, holding on to the side of the bowl.

His stomach empty, he sits against the tiled wall. Shaking. Sweating.

The events of last night—the girl, the trip home, the bottle of wine—what's the last thing he remembers? She put a pillow beneath his head. She said she was sorry. What did she slip him?

Rinsing his mouth out under the tap, he scoops water on to his face, eyes stinging, the cold working. Looking in the mirror, he blinks through bloodshot eyes. The foul taste is in his mouth, the toxins in his system. The smell of urine in his hair, on his clothes... Someone pissed on him. The boyfriend wanted some payback.

He walks up the stairs. Drawers have been pulled out, up-ended, searched. The contents lie on the floor.

What's missing? His camera, a police medal, an iPod Claire gave him (still in its box), some euros, his passport...He flicks through his checkbook. Two blank checks are torn from the middle. They were clever. Practiced.

He should make a list. Not touch anything. Call the police. Then what? They'll send a car out sometime in the next two days. He'll have to make a statement. He can hear them laughing already. The jokes. The ribbing. Detective Inspector Vincent Ruiz, taken in by a girl he invited home. They'll suspect she was a hooker or a call girl. Ruiz is paying for sex now, they'll say, like some sad old pervert.

Another thought occurs to him. He climbs the stairs to the study. The desk has been swept clean. The pages of the manuscript are scattered on the floor. He didn't number them.

The drawers have been forced open. One of them had been swollen shut for twenty years. Ruiz remembers what it contained — Laura's jewelry, her engagement ring and an antique hair-comb that had been passed down through her family. When Laura knew she was dying, when disease swam in her veins and grew in her chest, she wrote a series of letters to the twins — to be opened when they turned eighteen, or when they married, or when they had children of their own . . .

One of the letters was for Claire on her wedding day. It contained the rings and the hair-comb. Now the torn envelope lies discarded on the floor. The letter screwed into a ball. The small drawstring bag with the jewelry has gone.

Ruiz picks up the crumpled letter and tries to smooth out the creases. Laura's handwriting had grown spidery as the chemo robbed her of energy, but none of her sentences are crossed out or corrected. Perhaps a person knows exactly what to write when the sand is trickling away.

Ruiz stops himself reading. The letter is meant for Claire. His eyes drift to the bottom of the page where Laura finished with hugs and kisses. A small circular stain has marked the porous paper — a fallen tear as a punctuation mark.

Anger rises. Burns. Most of the missing items can be replaced — the camera, the iPod and the money — but not the jewelry. He wanted Claire to wear the hair-comb on her wedding day. It was the "something old" to go with something new and borrowed and blue — just like the rhyme says. But it's more than that. The hair-comb is something that Ruiz has cherished. Laura was wearing it when they first met at a twilight ball in Hertfordshire in 1968. She looked like a proverbial sixties flower child with her hair braided and pinned high on her head.

Early in the evening she danced with him but then Ruiz lost her in the crowd and spent four hours trying to find her. It was after midnight. People were starting to leave. Buses were waiting to ferry them back to London. Ruiz saw Laura standing near the entrance. She pointed to him and summoned him with her finger. Ruiz looked over his shoulder to make sure she wanted him.

"What's your name?" she asked.

"Vincent."

"I'm Laura. This is my phone number. If you don't call me within two days, Vincent, you lose your chance. I'm a good girl. I don't sleep with men on the first date or the second or the third. You have to woo me, but I'm worth the effort."

Then she kissed him on the cheek and was gone. He called her within two hours. The rest is, as they say…

Picking up a notebook, Ruiz makes a list. First he contacts his bank and reports his cards stolen. The recorded messages give him six options and then another six. Eventually, a girl with an Indian accent takes the details. Checks his account. There was a cash withdrawal just before midnight and another one just after; a thousand pounds in total. There were two other online purchases. She won't give him the details.

"Someone from our fraud department will call you, sir."

Sunlight makes his head throb. He considers his options. How can he find the girl? The actress. The boyfriend either followed them home or Holly must have called him. Maybe both.

Ruiz picks up his phone and hits redial. The last number she dialed was a mobile — the boyfriend perhaps.

A man answers with a grunt.

"Listen, I don't know who you are. I don't care. But you took something of mine last night, something of great sentimental value. You can have the rest of my stuff. I don't care about that. But I need the jewelry — the rings and the hair-comb — they belonged to my wife. Give them back to me and I won't come looking for you. You have my word on that. If you don't give them back, I will find you and I will punish you. You have my word on that too."

He pauses. Listens to the breathing. The boyfriend clears his throat.

"Fuck off!"

Ruiz listens to the dead air.

"Who was that, babe?"

"Nobody."

Holly Knight is awake now. She won't go back to sleep.

"He sounded angry."

"Don't worry about it."

Zac rolls over and squashes a pillow beneath his head. Within half a minute he's asleep again, his nostrils barely moving as he breathes.

Holly examines his sleeping face, the angular jaw line, darkened with growth, his heavy lids hiding blue-green eyes. There were no nightmares last night. No silent screams or sobs.

Running her fingers across his exposed back, the scars look like ripples on a dried-up lake bed, pink and grey and dead looking. When she touches them in the dark it feels as though his skin has been eaten away by acid or dissolved by some sort of flesh-eating bug.

Slipping out of bed, she goes to the bathroom and sits on the toilet, staring at the discolored tiles and the rust stains in the bath. Finishing, she pulls her jeans over her panties, buttoning them on the flatness of her stomach.

Looking in the mirror, she touches the bruise on her face. Zac hit her too hard last night. Sometimes he forgets his own strength. She will say something to him when he wakes and is in a good mood.

The flat has peeling walls, mismatched furniture and different floor coverings in every room. Poverty in progress. An old arm-chair sits in the middle of the kitchen floor, because Zac likes to watch Holly cooking and doesn't like to be alone.

Smearing butter on the inside of a frying pan, she cracks two eggs. The smell of breakfast wakes Zac, who comes out of the bed-room in his boxers, scratching the line of dark hair below his navel.

Self-conscious about his scars, he pulls on a T-shirt, and brushes a finger across Holly's cheek.

"You hit me too hard last night."

"Didn't mean to."

"You might break me if you're not careful."

"I'm sorry, babe."

Holly sets his plate on the table.

"Do we have any...any...you know?"

"We didn't have any bacon."

"No, do we have any, ah, any...?" He begins shaking his hand up and down. "Brown stuff."

"Sauce?"

"Yeah."

Holly finds the bottle in the fridge. Zac eats with his head low and one arm curled around his plate. Yesterday he forgot the word for petrol. He kept saying he needed to get "stuff" for the bike, "to make it go." And before that he drove himself into a rage because he couldn't remember who played left back for Spurs in the League Cup final in 2008. That's one of the reasons he gets so angry—he can't remember things.

According to the doctors there was no sign of brain damage, but something got rewired in Zac's head when he was in Afghanistan. Now he forgets things. Not the big stuff, but small details—names and words.

There was a fire. Seven men were trapped inside a troop carrier, according to the commendation they gave Zac with his gallantry medal. He pulled three men from inside the carrier while it was under attack. That's when he got burned. That's when he started forgetting things.

Zac turns on the telly. A girl in a raincoat is giving the weather report, pointing to a map with cartoon clouds.

"How pointless is that," says Zac. "Look out the window and you can see the sun is shining."

Next comes a report on the stock market, the Dow Jones. Is that a person, wonders Holly; is there someone called Mr. Jones?

Zac picks up the near-empty bottle of Scotch.

"It's too early," she says.

"Hair of the dog."

He pours two fingers into a glass.

Holly leaves him to get changed.

"I've got to go and see Bernie," she yells from the bedroom.

"Why?"

"We owe the rent."

"Again?"

"Comes round every month. We don't have enough to pay Floyd."

Floyd is their landlord on the estate and also a local crack dealer.

"I'm going to sell that stuff we got last night."

"Don't let Bernie rip you off."

"I won't."

"And don't let him touch you. He's always trying to touch you."

"Bernie is pretty harmless."

"You want me to come?"

"No it's OK. I want you to fill out the form from the DSS. You need to get your pension sorted."

Holly has changed into her nicest clothes. She rinses Zac's plate in the sink.

"I'm going to sell Bernie the laptop and other stuff. Then I thought I might take the jewelry to Hatton Garden."

"Don't let them rip you off."

"I won't. I have my audition today."

"Can I come?"

"You know I get nervous when you're there."

He nods and goes back to watching an infomercial for a hair-straightening wand that features women with perfect teeth and lottery-winning smiles.

4

BAGHDAD

The queue outside the Ministry of Finance stretches more than a hundred yards, snaking between concrete blast walls that are decorated with political posters and daubed with anti-American graffiti.

Checkpoints are always dangerous. Anyone can approach— beggars, vendors, teenagers selling soft drinks or newspapers; fuel sellers carrying jerrycans and rubber hoses that are swung through the air making a whooshing sound. Any one of them could be carrying a grenade or wearing a suicide vest.

Luca produces his accreditation. The Iraqi soldier looks at both sides of the media pass, studying the English and Arabic versions. Then he consults a visitor's book in the plasterboard kiosk.

"Your name is not on the list."

"I made the appointment only an hour ago."

The soldier taps the pass against his cheek and slowly circles the Skoda, as one of his colleagues checks the boot and passes a mirror beneath the chassis.

They are waved through. Jamal pulls up outside the Ministry. Engine running. Luca opens the door.

"Are you going to wait?"

Jamal taps the dashboard. "I have to get petrol. The queues are long today."

"I'll give you money for black market fuel."

"I should queue like everyone else."

Luca smiles. "You're the only person in Iraq who doesn't buy on the black."

Jamal looks a little sad. "It won't always be this way."

The two men slap their palms together and their shoulders touch.

"Give my love to Nadia and the boys."

Luca jogs up the stairs, zipping up his jacket. There are more checkpoints inside, along with metal detectors and bag searches. He surrenders his pistol, which is placed in a strongbox, and asks for Judge Ahmed Kuther, the Commissioner of Public Integrity. The receptionist points to a row of a dozen plastic chairs, all of them taken.

Luca waits.

A cleaner is polishing the marble floor, running an ancient machine across the smooth slabs. Elsewhere workmen are peeling blast tape from the windows. Wishful thinking.

It has been more than a year since the Coalition Provisional Authority handed over control of Iraq to the Iraqis, but independence is still mostly a state of mind. The parliamentary elections were five months ago but no single party emerged with a clear majority. The level of violence has increased since then as various groups have tried to influence the outcome or scupper the talks completely. Uncertainty is the only constant in Iraq apart from the petrol queues and power outages.

One of the security guards begins telling a joke. Luca has heard it before. A young boy runs to his mother, sobbing, because his father has touched a live wire and been electrocuted. Throwing up her hands, she says, "Allah be praised—there is electricity!"

A convoy of four SUVs has pulled up outside, doors opening in unison. Six men in black body armor emerge from the vehicles, setting up a perimeter guard. Two others jog quickly up the stairs and scan the foyer before giving the signal.

Four passengers climb from the SUVs and are ushered up the stairs. Heads down. Moving quickly. The guards are civilian contractors. The passengers are westerners, dressed casually apart from the Kevlar vests.

One of them is a woman with a baseball cap pulled low over her eyes. Pretty. Hair bunched up in a ponytail, poking through the back of the cap. Dressed in a loose white shirt and cargo pants, she's wheeling a pull-along bag, looking like an off-duty airline hostess or a film star checking into the Betty Ford clinic.

Half the security team escorts her across the foyer, while the rest stay behind, making sure they're not being followed. Luca recognizes one of them. Shaun Porter runs one of the smaller American security companies. Big and bulked up, he looks like a surfer with his sun-bleached hair and brightly colored Hawaiian shirt beneath a Kevlar vest, but he was born and raised in New Jersey.

Shaun slings his weapon over his shoulder and gives Luca a high-five.

"Yo, my man, my man! Long time no see. How's it hanging?"

"I'm good. I'm good. How about you?"

"Same old shit—babysitting some IT geeks."

"Americans?"

"UN auditors—they're installing new software."

Luca watches the woman enter the lift. She turns and peers between the shoulders of her bodyguards. Their eyes meet for a moment and she glances away, taking in everything.

Shaun punches his shoulder. "Hey! What you doing tonight? It's my birthday. We're having a few drinks at the al-Hamra. Come along."

"How old are you?"

"Thirty-nine."

"You were thirty-nine last year."

"Fuck off!"

Shaun punches him harder. Luca tries not to grimace.

Most of the contractors are good old boys, former soldiers with shaved heads and softening bodies, who couldn't cut it in civvies. They have nicknames like "Spider," "Whopper" and "Coyote." Luca met Shaun when the latter was still a Marine and came walking into the bar of the al-Hamra one night asking journalists if they had any books they wanted to exchange. He and Shaun had been swapping novels ever since—mainly crime stories: McDermid, Connelly and James Lee Burke.

"You still living outside the wire?"

"Yeah."

"And you think *I'm* crazy!"

"Maybe just a little."

Shaun scratches his unshaven chin. "I lost money on you."

"How so?"

"Some of your colleagues in the pool ran a book on how long you'd survive outside the wire."

"I heard about that."

"Some guy had you down for six days. I gave you six weeks. Thought I was being generous."

"Bummer."

"You're one lucky SOB." Shaun looks at his wristwatch, which is big and silver with lots of buttons. "I got an airport run. Some new blood coming in."

"Don't let them shoot anyone on their first day."

"I'll try not to."

"How is the Irish route?"

"Safer than it used to be, but I miss the old days—we could fire first and ask questions later."

Luca shakes his head and Shaun laughs. "Got a mate coming in. Dave Edgar. 'Edge.' You'll like him. Edge was Third Infantry Division Armour, first into Baghdad in '03. Toppled Saddam all on his own."

"And he wants to come back?"

Shaun rubs his thumb and forefinger together. "It's all about the folding stuff."

The SUVs are ready. He nods to his colleague.

"Come to my drinks. You can meet him."

After Shaun has gone, Luca goes back to waiting. Iraqi bureaucrats operate on their own timetables and the idea of an independent media acting as a guardian of the public interest is a complete anathema to the culture.

Minutes pass slowly. Closing his eyes, his mind floods with images from the bank—the burnt corpses and empty vault; the manager's body, a macabre Venus de Milo dipped in tar, locked in a silent scream.

He opens them again. A secretary is standing in front of him; her body garbed in black and her head covered in a white scarf. She does not make eye contact with him in the mirrored walls of the lift or as she holds open the doors. Falling into step behind her, Luca is taken along wood-paneled corridors hung with tapestries.

Judge Ahmed Kuther isn't alone. Five of his colleagues are leaning over his desk, looking at photographs.

"Come in, Luca, come in," he says, waving him closer. "I'm just back from Moscow. I have pictures."

Someone passes him a photograph. It shows Kuther in Red Square, grinning widely, with his arm around a blonde wearing a short skirt and a slash of red lipstick.

"She had a younger sister. Another blonde."

"Double the fun," says one of his friends.

"For double the price?" jokes another.

Luca puts the photograph on the desk. "It's a nice souvenir. Not one for your wife to see."

Everyone laughs, including the judge. Kuther is wearing a well-cut suit and a blue tie rather than the traditional loose-fitting shirts and long cloaks. His only concession to his heritage is a kaffiyeh, a square scarf folded and placed over a white cap, which he wears on those rare occasions he risks appearing in public.

Twice tortured and imprisoned by Saddam Hussein, the judge is now tasked with the most dangerous job in Iraq. The Commission of Public Integrity is the country's anti-corruption watchdog and has issued over a thousand arrest warrants against corrupt officials in the past four years. Seven members of his staff have been killed during the same period, which is why Kuther travels with up to thirty bodyguards.

Clapping his hands together, he sends people back to their desks. Then he slumps in a leather chair, spinning it back and forth from the window.

"How was Moscow?"

"It's not Baghdad."

"Successful trip?"

"How does one measure the success of such a trip? I addressed a legal conference, while the Minister asked for money, shook hands and smiled for photographs." He circles his hand in the air. "But you didn't come here to talk about Moscow."

"There was another robbery."

"I heard."

"How much money was taken?"

"Even if I knew the exact amount, I could not comment."

"It was US dollars."

"Are you telling me or asking me?"

"It could have been an inside job. Four security guards are missing."

Kuther raises his shoulders an inch. Drops them. A cigarette appears in his hand, then between his lips. He lights it with a counterfeit Dunhill lighter.

"I cannot become too fixated on money, Luca. Do you know how many people die in this city every day?"

"Yes."

"No, you don't see all of them. You hear about the bombings, the big events that provide footage for your news bulletins." The judge points to a report on his desk. "This is from last night: seven bodies were found in Amil, three bodies in Doura, two bodies in Ghasaliyah, one body in Khadhraa, one body in Amiriyah and one in Mahmoudiyah. There were eight more bodies in Rusafa. None have been identified."

Luca looks at the file. "Why are they sending this to you?"

"Because the Interior Ministry cannot handle so many."

"You're supposed to be investigating corruption."

"I do what is necessary."

Kuther draws on his cigarette and exhales a stream of smoke that looks like his very spirit escaping from his chest.

"We are tearing ourselves apart, Luca: kidnappings, executions, house by house, family by family. The same people who celebrated the toppling of Saddam would today go down on their knees and kiss his feet if they could bring him back."

"You're losing hope?"

"I'm running out of time."

The judge crushes the cigarette. He's a busy man.

"Tell me exactly what you want, Luca."

"I want to know who's robbing these banks. These are US dollar robberies. Reconstruction funds."

"Money is money," says Kuther. "Green, brown, blue…any color."

"A platoon of US Marines captured an insurgent two months ago with a wad of hundred-dollar bills that had sequential serial numbers. The bills were part of a shipment from the US Federal Reserve in 2006. They were stolen from a bank in Fallujah four months ago."

Kuther bows his head and places his hands together as though praying.

"There is a war on, Luca. Perhaps you should ask the Americans where their money is going."

5

LONDON

The pawnshop is on Whitechapel High Street, squeezed between a Burger King and a clothing emporium that has "ladies, gents & children's fashion wear" spilling from bins and racks. Bernie Levinson's office is on the first floor, accessible via a rickety set of metal stairs at the rear of the building that are held in place by a handful of rusting bolts.

In the basement there is a clothing factory where thirty-five workers, most of them illegal, sit crouched over sewing machines that operate day and night. Two shifts of twelve hours, Bangladeshi and Indian women earning three quid an hour. It's another of Bernie's business ventures.

A dozen people are waiting on the stairs to see Bernie, mostly junkies and crackheads. They're carrying a selection of car stereos, DVD players, laptops and GPS navigators—none of them in boxes or with instruction manuals. Holly Knight waits her turn, clutching her shoulder bag on her lap.

Bernie sits behind a big desk next to an air-conditioning unit that takes up most of the window. A goldfish bowl rests on the corner of his desk, magnifying a lone fish that barely seems to move. Bernie is a short man with a doughy body, who favors baggy trousers and candy-colored shirts.

"Do a twirl," he tells Holly. "Show me what you're wearing, such a pretty bint. My daughter is the size of a cow. Takes after her mother. Bovine family. Built to pull ploughs."

Holly ignores him and opens her shoulder bag, placing the contents on his desk. She has a passport, three credit cards, a mobile phone, a digital camera, four collector's edition gold coins and some sort of medal in a case.

"What's this?" asks Bernie, flipping open the box.

"I don't know."

"It's only a police fucking bravery medal!"

"So?"

"You turned over a copper, you daft cow."

"He said he was retired."

"Yeah, but he's going to have friends, isn't he? Colleagues. Old Bill." Bernie is waving his hands at her. Wobbling his chins. "I don't want any of this stuff. Get it out of here."

Resting her hip on the desk, Holly leans closer, letting the front of her blouse casually gape open.

"Come on, Bernie, we look after each other. What about that gear I brought you the other day?" She points to a dark leather briefcase sitting on top of his filing cabinet. "That's top quality."

She and Zac had turned over a suit in Barnes and scored the briefcase, a laptop, two mobiles, passports and jewelry.

Bernie grunts dismissively. "You're getting sloppy. Taking too many risks."

"It won't happen again...I promise, but I'm really short this week. My landlord is going to give me grief."

Bernie hesitates. Contemplates. The pawnbroker is not a soft touch. He thinks the only true sin is to surrender. He lost most of his family in the ghettos of Warsaw and at Treblinka. They meekly surrendered and were led away, a fact that Bernie despises. That's one of the reasons he keeps a pistol in his top drawer, a shotgun downstairs and a bodyguard in the next room. Whatever happens, he's not going to simply disappear.

Glancing at Holly's cleavage, Bernie wets his bottom lip. "How much you short?"

"Eighty quid."

"And what does Uncle Bernie get?"

Holly thinks, if Zac were here he'd reach across the table and squeeze your head until your eyes pop out. But she needs the money and she'd rather owe Bernie than Floyd, who charges interest with a silver knuckleduster.

Holly walks to the door and locks it. Then she pushes back Bernie's leather chair and sits astride him, her knees on either side of his thighs, grinding her pubic bone into his groin. Her hand slides down his chest, unbuttoning his shirt so her fingers can slide across his chest.

Leaning forward she whispers something into his ear. Then she straightens and slowly undoes the buttons on her blouse, opening it a few inches. She's wearing a black lace bra. Bernie takes a wheezing breath, lust painted all over his face.

Motioning to the cashbox, Holly waits while Bernie fumbles with the key. She takes four twenties and slips the notes into her shoulder bag. Bernie begins to unbuckle his trousers but Holly starts moving again, bumping and grinding. She increases the pressure, whispering in his ear, letting her tongue trace the outline of his earlobe. He tries to stop her, to lift her off, but Holly keeps moving.

Bernie groans. "No, no, nooooo...!"

His eyes roll back into his head and his molars grind together, shuddering.

Holly buttons her shirt and swings her body off his lap. The wet spot on his trousers is starting to spread.

"I want my money back," he bleats.

Holly scoops the stolen goods into her bag and swings it onto her shoulder. Unlocking the door, she turns. "Here's what I'll do, Bernie, I'll sign you up for membership of the Premature Ejaculation Society. They got a strict dress code. You got to *come* in your pants."

She opens the door. Tommy Boyle, Bernie's bodyguard, is outside. "Everything OK, boss?"

Bernie has a tissue in his hand. "Just shut the fucking door."

6

LONDON

Late morning in Central London: Ruiz is waiting downstairs at Scotland Yard. He still has a few contacts in the Met — colleagues who have survived the shake-ups, shake-outs and new brooms. Some adapt. Some pucker up. Some bend over and brace themselves.

Detective Superintendent Peter Vorland is one of the good guys. Snowy headed, thinning on top, he has a powerful handshake and an Afrikaans accent. He came to the UK in the late seventies, escaping apartheid. Thirty-five years later and he's never been back — not even for a holiday.

Ruiz once asked him why, but Vorland wouldn't talk about it. Later, when they got drunk after a Twickenham test match, Vorland said he couldn't forgive Mandela for the Truth and Reconciliation Commission.

"It's not in my nature to exonerate torturers and murderers," he said.

A few years back Vorland had a heart attack. Thought he was dying. He told Ruiz he saw fireworks exploding above Table

Mountain and heard a black gospel choir singing. The crash cart and 300 volts brought him back.

Everyone thought Vorland should have retired but he wanted to come back. After six months recuperating, he was leaner, fitter, no longer drinking. Ten years younger and twice as miserable.

His office is on the fourteenth floor with a view across the rooftops of Whitehall to Westminster Cathedral.

"You want some crap coffee?"

"I'm good."

They spend the first few minutes talking about rugby, more out of habit than need. Finally Ruiz elaborates on a phone call he made earlier, telling the DS about "a friend" who was robbed after playing the Good Samaritan.

"Why didn't your friend report this crime?" asks Vorland.

"He thinks his wife might misinterpret what happened."

"Where did your friend meet this girl?"

"The Coach & Horses in Greek Street."

Vorland glances down at a yellow legal pad by his elbow. "I did a computer search and came up with five robberies in the past six months, same MO, two perps, one female, one male."

"Descriptions?"

"The girl is eighteen to twenty-five, Caucasian, five-five, blue eyes, dark hair, cut short, but it could be a wig. She's also been a blonde and a redhead. The boyfriend is six foot, close cropped hair and a northern accent."

Vorland taps a fountain pen on the pad. "I also checked out that phone number. The SIM card is registered to a fake address in Wimbledon. Pay-as-you-go. The police won't track the handset unless your friend reports the crime…" He raises an eyebrow. "Maybe you could convince him…"

Ruiz gives a non-committal shrug. "I'll have a word."

Vorland remembers something else.

"You could talk to the CCTV Control Centre at Westminster Council. They've got a hundred and sixty cameras in the West End."

"Big Brother is watching."

"They do a job."

"I preferred the cowardly old world to the brave new one."

Ruiz rises slowly and makes his way downstairs, dropping his visitor's badge at the security desk. When he steps outside the revolving door he exhales as though he's been holding his breath this entire time. Sometimes he needs a reminder that retirement was the right decision.

City Watch Security is in Coventry Street, up a narrow stairway from street level without any signage on the door. The reception area is a small windowless room with posters on the wall urging people to be eternally vigilant. The control centre is registered as a charitable trust, funded by Westminster City Council, the Metropolitan Police and private businesses.

The woman in charge, Helen Carlson, has white-grey hair and a head that looks slightly too large for her body, giving her a doll-like quality. Ruiz follows her to a separate building, around the corner in Wardour Street, where they enter a dark sub-basement with industrial bins and a caged lift. Ms. Carlson taps a number into a panel. The door opens. They wait for it to close behind them. Another panel, a different code and a second door opens into a large room where dozens of men and women watch the streets of London on vast screens, twenty-four hours a day, seven days a week, every day of the year.

There are images of pedestrians in Oxford Street, couples embracing on a park bench in Leicester Square, a bicycle courier weaving between buses at Piccadilly Circus, a tramp going through bins in Green Park, a delivery van blocking a street in Soho, three teenagers kicking a can outside Euston Station. Snapshots of London, viewed from swivel chairs in a darkened room—Orwell's imaginary world, twenty-five years later than expected.

Ms. Carlson taps a keyboard. Her pink nail polish stands out brightly against the keys.

"What time?"

"Between eight p.m. and ten p.m."

She swivels a joystick control. Fast forwards through archival footage. There are four views of Greek Street. One of them shows the Coach & Horses. The screen has a red square box in the top right corner.

"That signifies the street is an area of suspicion," explains Ms. Carlson. "We focus on hotels, nightclubs and alleyways."

"Must be riveting."

"If you have nothing to hide, you have nothing to fear."

"Did Stalin write that?"

The time code is running along the bottom of the screen. It slows as the footage decelerates. Ruiz sees the boyfriend walking towards the camera carrying two motorcycle helmets. He must have stashed them somewhere.

Fast-forwarding again, the time code says 21.24. Ruiz sees himself emerging from the pub and shoving the boyfriend into a parked car. The barman appears. The boyfriend walks away from the camera. At 22.08 Ruiz leaves the pub and hails a cab. The actress is wearing her red coat. The door closes and the cab pulls into the traffic. Moments later a motorbike passes the camera. The number plate has been obscured.

"Did you get what you wanted?" asks Ms. Carlson, clearly proud of the technology.

"Tell me something," asks Ruiz. "If your cameras see a crime being committed, what do you do?"

"We alert the police."

"And you keep filming?"

"Of course."

Ruiz grunts dismissively.

"We're fighting crime," she says defensively.

"No, you're recording crime. Your cameras can't intervene to stop a rape or a murder or a robbery, which makes you just another bystander, sitting on the sidelines, watching it happen."

The Coach & Horses is busy with a lunchtime crowd. Ruiz recognizes the Aussie barman. His name is Craig and he has freckles on his eyelids.

"You remember me?"

He nods and keeps stacking drinks.

"The girl who was in here last night, the one who wore a fist from her boyfriend; ever seen her before?"

"Nope."

"What about her charming fella?"

"You should have hit him harder."

"She was reading a copy of *The Stage*. You must get a lot of actors in here."

Craig grins. "You want to see my show-reel?"

"Maybe never."

Ruiz orders a steak-and-Guinness pie and a pint of ale. While he's waiting he ducks outside to a newsstand and buys a copy of *The Stage*. Turning to the listings, he runs a finger down the page. Most are by appointment only. She was looking for an open casting. His finger stops. Taps the page.

Speed Dating, a romantic comedy.

Alasdair has been dumped by his girlfriend and is convinced to go to a speed dating night. Rehearsals begin September 18.

We are looking for:

—Alasdair 25–35. Northerner. Slim, a little clumsy around women.

—Jenny 20–30. Confident and sassy with a bruised heart.

—Felicity 20–30. Jenny's best friend.

—Chris 25–35. Jenny's fiancé.

Casting at Trafalgar Studios in Whitehall, 3 p.m. to 5 p.m. (Please bring headshots and a brief resume.)

Ruiz looks at his watch. It's almost two now. Lunch first and then a look-see.

7

BAGHDAD

The helicopters are flying close tonight. Luca can hear the *whump whump* of the propellers concussing the air as they pass overhead. American troops are patrolling, searching for weapons and insurgents and "wanted" faces on playing cards.

They're early. Most of the raids don't happen until after midnight. The Apaches hover above convoys of armored Humvees that will seal off entire streets. The phys-ops vehicles are fitted with loudspeakers broadcasting messages in Arabic or Farsi or Kurdish, telling people to put their weapons next to the front door and walk outside. Few have time to comply.

Five soldiers will enter the house while five wait outside. They go upstairs first, grabbing the man of the house, dragging him out of bed in front of his wife and children, forcing him up against a wall. Other family members are corralled into the same room and made to kneel with their hands on their heads.

The interpreter will ask the head of the household if he has any weapons or anti-US propaganda. He will then ask if he is involved in any insurgent activity. The householder will say no, because that is normally the truth. If something is found, they will shackle and hood the men and teenage boys, tossing them in the back of a Bradley. If nothing is found, they will say, "Sorry to have disturbed you, sir. Have a nice evening," before moving on to the next house.

Luca spent three months embedded with the Third Brigade, First Armoured Division, and watched these "cordon and search" operations first hand. He saw Iraqi men humiliated in front of their terrified families and their homes trashed. He saw accidents because soldiers, wound up with fear, were convinced that people inside these houses were waiting to kill them. One wrong move, one mistaken gesture, and innocent people died.

Passing through the hotel security screening, he enters the foyer of the al-Hamra. Some of the windows still haven't been replaced since the bombing and are covered with plywood. People have taken to scrawling their signatures on the wood panels and leaving short messages.

The bar is crowded with security contractors, engineers, journalists and western NGOs. Luca knows most of the reporters, cameramen and photographers. Some of them are in the veteran class because a year in Baghdad can seem like a lifetime.

They're talking about a car bombing this afternoon in al-Hurriyah Square. Fifteen civilians died and thirty were injured in the marketplace. One of the Associated Press photographers has photographed the severed head of a small girl. Now he's drinking tonic water and showing the picture to anyone who wants to see it.

The security contractors are out by the pool because the al-Hamra doesn't like guns in the main bar. For the most part their weapons are hidden, tucked into shoulder holsters or socks. Their heavy artillery is at home in their apartments and hotel rooms.

"Hey, Luca, you made it!"

Shaun Porter waves from a deckchair. He's lying next to a pretty Iraqi girl who is sipping a fruit juice. Prostitution in Iraq is one of those hidden vices, outlawed under Saddam, but never stamped out. Now there are families that bring their daughters to the hotels for the enjoyment of the westerners.

Shaun pulls a beer from a bucket of ice and flips it open with the edge of a cigarette lighter. He hands it to Luca, who wishes him a happy birthday.

"You know most of the guys."

"I've seen them around."

Beer bottles are raised in welcome. A redneck from Texas is wearing a T-shirt that says, "Who's your Baghdaddy?" He starts telling a joke about why Iraqis have only two pallbearers at their funerals.

"Because garbage cans only come with two handles."

The men laugh and Luca wishes he were somewhere else. A big guy in a cut-off sweatshirt joins them. He has blue flames tattooed on his forearms.

"This is the mate I was telling you about," says Shaun. "Meet Edge."

Edge's grey eyes flick over Luca as though sizing up his fighting weight. Slightly older than the others, he has deep wrinkles around his eyes and a crushing handshake.

"You're that journalist living outside the wire."

"That's right."

"Does that make you crazy or fucked up?"

"Deluded, maybe."

Edge raises his margarita and sucks salt crystals from around the rim. Behind him, the pool lights glow an alien green beneath the water.

Two Filipino women shriek with laughter. They're wearing short denim skirts and skimpy tops, flashing midriffs and muffin tops to the group of contractors who keep plying them with drinks.

Edge is watching, amused. Sexual conquest is a local sport among the contractors.

"You were here in '03," says Luca.

"Saw the whole clusterfuck."

"So what made you come back?"

"I missed the place."

Edge drains his margarita and licks his lips.

"I got bored working for my father-in-law. America's fucked, man—people losing their houses, their jobs, factories going off-shore—the bankers and politicians screwed everyone over."

"You think this place is any better?"

"Here you can shoot the bad guys." He grins. "In America we give them corporate bonuses and promote them to Treasury Secretary."

He holds his glass aloft, signaling to the barman for another. "You know the moment I knew I was coming back to Baghdad?"

"No."

"Happened before I even left. I had to pick up a package from the Military Postal Service—it was a birthday present from my folks. This fat chick was sitting behind the counter painting her nails. She said it was her coffee break and she made me wait fifteen minutes while I watched her stuff her face with Twinkies. I was getting blown up and shot at for twenty-five grand a year while that fat chick, sitting on her fat ass, lifting nothing heavier than a pencil was making four times what I did. Tell me if that seems fair?"

"I'm not a great judge of fairness."

"Yeah, well, nobody twisted my arm to come here the first time, but now I'm gonna fill my boots."

Luca glances past Edge to a table on the patio. A woman is sitting with two men. Luca recognizes her from the Finance Ministry. She was part of the UN Audit team. Dressed in grey flannels and low-heeled shoes, she's wearing her hair down and nursing a glass of wine. Her high cheekbones look almost carved and her eyes are shining in the reflection from the pool. She doesn't seem to be listening to the conversation at her table.

"I wouldn't waste my breath," says Edge, following his gaze.

"Why's that?"

"I offered to buy her a drink and she treated me like I was contagious."

"Maybe she's sick of being hassled."

"Or she could be an uppity, better-than-everyone, super bitch."

Edge has the barman's attention. Luca slips away and stands beneath a palm tree, checking the messages on his phone. The woman is no longer at the table. She's standing by the pool, talking on her mobile, arguing with someone.

"It's only for two more weeks...I know...but you can wait that long. No, I'm not at a party. It's the hotel." She makes eye contact with Luca. Looks away. "I think you're being totally unreasonable...I can't talk to you when you get like this...I'm going to hang up..."

She snaps the phone closed and purses her lips.

"Problems at home?" asks Luca.

"That's not really any of your business."

"No, I'm sorry."

She has an American accent and large eyes with eyelids that pause at half-mast like a face from a da Vinci painting.

"I shouldn't have been listening. I'll leave you alone."

Luca walks away. She doesn't stop him. He goes to the bar and has a drink with a German journalist and his French colleague, who are both pulling out when the last of the American combat troops leave at the end of the month.

At nine o'clock Luca calls it a night. As he crosses the hotel lobby, he notices the woman again—this time she's arguing with the hotel receptionist. There is a problem with the room. The power points don't work. She can't recharge her laptop.

Luca is going to walk right by but stops and addresses the receptionist in Arabic—sorting out the problem.

"They're moving you to another room," he says. "It will take fifteen minutes."

"Thank you," she says, hesitantly, her mouth fractionally too big for her face. Luca nods and turns to leave.

"Where did you learn to speak Arabic?"

"My mother is Iraqi."

"And you're American?"

"I was born in Chicago."

She glances at her feet. "Can I buy you a drink?"

"Why?"

The question flummoxes her.

"Do I have to explain?"

"You could say loneliness, or guilt, or perversity..."

"I'm sorry for being so rude to you."

"In that case I'll have a whisky."

Rather than go back into the bar, they go into the restaurant. She's a foot shorter than he is, but carries herself very straight, her footsteps almost floating across the tiles.

"I'm Daniela Garner."

"Luca Terracini."

"That's an Italian name."

"My grandfather came from Naples."

"It's impressive to meet a journalist who speaks Arabic."

"I'm glad you're impressed. How do you know I'm a journalist?"

"Most of the people here are journalists or private contractors. You don't look like a mercenary."

"I saw you today. You were at the Ministry."

She shrugs. A waiter takes their orders. She's drinking white wine. Luca tries again.

"You're working for the UN?"

"Who told you that?"

"Shaun is a mate of mine. He called you an IT geek."

"I'm an accountant."

She shifts in her chair, recrossing her legs. Everything about her is dainty and refined, yet strong. The restaurant is dark apart from the table lamps.

"We're installing new software to audit government accounts and keep track of reconstruction spending."

"Sounds dry."

"Bone."

"How long will the job take?"

"They told us two weeks, but from what I saw today, it's going to be longer. I don't think anyone in Iraq understands bookkeeping."

"Good luck with that."

He drinks half his whisky but can't really taste it. Downs the rest. Orders another.

"How long have you been here?" she asks.

"Six years."

"Do you mind if I ask why? I mean, who would stay here...if they had a choice?"

"Most Iraqis don't have a choice."

"Yes, but you have an American passport. Do you have any family here?"

"No."

She motions over her shoulder towards the bar. "I mean, those guys out there—the mercenaries—they're here for the money or to play at being soldiers or because of their homoerotic fantasies; and most of the journalists are here because they have this romantic ideal of being war correspondents in flak jackets, appearing on the evening news. You don't strike me as being like the rest of them."

"Maybe I'm deranged."

"No."

"Or pumped full of drugs."

"It's something else."

Luca can feel a dangerous light-headedness coming over him, a trembling inside. He knows he should end the encounter. Draining his glass, he gets up from the table.

"Thank you for the drink." He gives her a tight smile.

Daniela looks disappointed. "Have I offended you?"

"No."

"I think I have. I'm sorry. Your friend in there—the one with the tattoos on his forearms..."

"He's not my friend."

"His first words to me were that we might get blown up tomorrow and did I fancy a fuck? I'm not interested in your life history, Luca. I was just making conversation because you were nice to me."

Silence.

Luca takes a deep breath. Relaxes. Manages a proper smile. "There are things you do to get by in a place like this. Masks you have to wear."

The way she looks at him, her silence, her detachment, it reminds him of a shrink he went to see after Nicola's funeral.

The hotel receptionist has crossed the restaurant. Daniela's room is ready.

She looks down at his hands and then up into his face. Her tongue touches her lower lip.

"Do you want to help me move my luggage?"

"They can send someone up."

She doesn't reply and turns away, leaving the restaurant. Luca walks outside, beyond midnight, making his way home to an unmade bed and sweat-stained sheets. He doesn't contemplate what it would have been like to sleep with Daniela Garner. He doesn't fuck any more. He's not a performer.

8

LONDON

Trafalgar Studios has crimson carpets, dusty chandeliers and an ageing splendor. Dozens of wannabes are milling in the foyer, pretending to ignore each other. Some are rehearsing soliloquies or listening to iPods or chewing gum. Multi-tasking in the modern age.

Holly Knight gives her name to a brisk young assistant wearing a headset and carrying a clipboard. She's handed a scene to read— a two-page dialogue between "Jenny" and "Alasdair," a young couple meeting for the first time.

"You'll be assigned a partner," says the assistant.

"But I've prepared my own material," says Holly.

"I'm sure your mother loves it."

The assistant is already taking another name.

Holly has to climb the stairs to find a square of carpet, beneath a window. She reads each line of her dialogue and closes her eyes, trying to memorize them.

After waiting an hour she gets bored. Pushing open a polished wooden door, she finds herself in a small theater with a brilliantly lit stage. Tiered seats rise into the darkness on three sides.

The director, dressed in a Che Guevara beret and fatigues, barely seems to pay attention as names are called and a new pair of actors arrives on stage. Candidates are whittled down. Holly watches them, some trying too hard, others battling nerves. Periodically, the director whispers something to his personal assistant, an unnaturally tall, thin girl with large eyes and a swan neck—a model with dreams of becoming an actress; not beautiful, just different.

It's almost five o'clock before Holly's name is called. Her assigned partner is an inch shorter than she is and seems to be channeling Hugh Grant with his flop of hair and nervous mumbling. Holly ignores his affectations and tries to relax, finding places in the dialogue to move and look away and back to her partner.

When she finishes, she waits. The director confers with his assistant. Then he tells Holly to leave her number. It's not a call back and it's not a rejection. She almost skips off stage.

Outside she runs along the street and descends the steps into Charing Cross Station. She needs to get to Hatton Garden before the jewelry shops close. Walking down the escalator, she follows the subterranean maze of passages until she reaches the Northern Line and takes a tube to Tottenham Court Road, before changing to the Central Line and surfacing again at Chancery Lane.

Stepping into a doorway on Holborn Road, she takes off her coat and pulls on a cashmere cardigan before brushing her hair. Using a small compact, she paints her lips and checks her make-up, pouting at her reflection. Finally she unwraps the delicate hair-comb from tissue paper, sliding it into her hair and looking at the result in a shop window. Satisfied, she turns into Hatton Garden and chooses a jewelry shop that is clear of customers.

An assistant is returning a tray of engagement rings to a display case.

"Can I help you?"

"I'm not sure. I haven't done this sort of thing before," says Holly, putting on a perfect Sloane Square accent. "My mother wanted a few pieces of jewelry valued. She's looking to sell them. They were gifts from Daddy, who isn't her favorite person."

Holly takes out a small velvet box and places it on the glass counter-top. The assistant fetches the owner, who emerges from the back room as though he's been interned there since the war. Blinking at her shyly, the old jeweler examines each stone and setting with an eyeglass.

Holly leans closer. She's wearing an expensive watch on her wrist. She wants the jeweler to notice.

"There's nothing here of particular value," he says. "Apart from the sentimental sort," he adds.

"Oh, Mummy will be disappointed. I think she was hoping…well, it doesn't matter. Thank you anyway."

As she's talking, Holly takes out the hair-comb and tosses her hair back before reinserting it again.

"That's a very interesting piece," says the jeweler. "May I see it?"

"What? This old thing."

Even before she places the hair-comb in the old jeweler's hands, she can see the hunger in his eyes. Desire is something Holly understands, particularly in men.

"It belonged to my grandmother."

"And perhaps to her grandmother," he says.

"Is it that old?"

"Indeed it is."

The jeweler motions to his assistant, who unfurls a dark velvet cloth. The hair-comb is placed carefully at the center of the fabric.

"Would you consider selling it?"

"But it's an heirloom."

"A shame." His fingers tap thoughtfully on the counter. "I could give you seven hundred pounds."

Holly has to stop herself from looking surprised. "Really? I didn't think…"

Opening the cash register, the jeweler begins counting out notes in front of her. "Perhaps I could go as high as a thousand."

"No, really, I couldn't."

The stack of notes has grown higher.

"What about these?" Holly motions to the velvet box.

"Fourteen hundred for the lot."

"If I change my mind?"

"By all means—come back. I am a reasonable man."

The door opens behind her and a man enters. Holly turns. She recognizes him but it takes a moment for her mind to put him in any sort of context. Then it dawns on her. The robbery…last night…the ex-copper!

Panic prickles on both sides of her skin and she hears a sad little squeak in the back of her throat.

"That's stolen property! She stole those from me," says Ruiz, pointing to the jewelry.

Holly blinks at him, shocked, telling herself not to lose control.

"Is there a problem?" asks the jeweler.

"Yes, there's a problem," says Ruiz. "This girl is a thief."

Holly clutches her bag to her chest. "Stay away from me, you pervert!" She turns to the jeweler. "This man has been following me. He's a stalker. There's a court order out against him. He's not supposed to come within a hundred yards of me."

The old jeweler looks alarmed. "Should I call the police?"

"Good idea," says Ruiz. "Let's do that."

Holly doesn't flinch. She scoops the hair-comb into her hand and jabs her finger at him. "Don't touch me! Don't come near me!"

The door opens. A security guard enters. Short and muscular, he's carrying a baton and every pie he's ever eaten around his waist. Holly takes one look at him and collapses in a dead faint, scythed down like a stalk of wheat.

Ruiz catches her before she hits her head on a display case. Her eyes are shut. She's unconscious. Out cold. Her arms flung wide.

"This man has been stalking her," says the jeweler.

"That's not true."

"Step back, sir," says the guard. "Did you hit her?"

"No, you moron, I caught her as she fell."

Holly's eyes open and she blinks at him.

"Did I do it again?" she asks.

"Just lie still," says Ruiz. "Someone call an ambulance."

She shakes her head. "I just fainted."

"You were out cold."

"It happens sometimes." She sits up. Pushes hair from her eyes. "Something about my blood sugar level."

"You're diabetic."

"No. I just sort of fall down. It's no big deal."

Someone has brought her a glass of water. She needs some fresh air. The security guard walks her out on to the pavement. Holly asks for more water. The guard takes the glass from her and turns his back. In that moment, she's gone, sprinting down the street, dodging pedestrians and shoppers.

The guard has no chance of catching her.

9

LONDON

Holly doesn't stop moving. Doesn't look back. When she reaches an intersection with a red "don't walk" sign, she turns left and heads down the road, trying to lose herself in the crowds of shoppers, tourists and commuters. Further along the street, she makes the crossing, skipping between cars and buses.

The Underground is just ahead. No, not the tube, she could be too easily cornered. She walks past the station entrance and heads south towards the Thames.

On Waterloo Bridge a jaundiced sun is setting through the haze. Finally she pauses, sweating under her clothes, cold on her face. For twenty minutes she studies the pedestrians and cars. How did he find her—the man from last night? The ex-copper. He said his name was Vincent. He looked harmless. Old. Crippled.

She calls Zac. He's not answering. He was the person who taught her about counter-surveillance: how to blend in with a crowd and lose a pursuer. For the next thirty minutes she continues south, occasionally doubling back and ducking into shop doorways where she can watch the street behind her. Her feet are hurting. She's thirsty.

The streets become shabbier as she gets closer to the Hogarth Estate. Shops give way to factories, railway yards and seventies tower blocks that rise above the rooftops like tree stumps in a nuclear winter.

It's almost dark on the estate. Children have been summoned indoors and TV sets drown out the arguments. Pushing through the entrance, Holly steps past old food containers and discarded Styrofoam cups.

Why isn't Zac answering his phone?

She doesn't trust the lift. Takes the stairs. A smell she can't place in the stairwell mingles with other odors that she doesn't want to name.

The door is open. The frame splintered. At first she thinks Zac has locked himself out and broken into the flat. She looks into the living room. The sofas have been disemboweled. Drawers pulled out. Furniture broken. Clothing scattered. A pressure band tightens around her skull.

Stepping across the threshold she can see through the partially opened door of the bedroom. The mattress is no longer on the bed.

Then she sees the chair. Zac sitting upright, his skin slick with blood, his arms bound behind him, his feet tethered together at his ankles. His eyes open at the sound of her cry. She wants to go to him, but he mouths a word through broken lips.

She stops.

He says it again.

"Run!"

As Holly turns she catches a glimpse of a hand reaching for her. She ducks, falling, scrambling on her knees. The hand comes again. She knocks it away, scuttling backwards, kicking with her legs.

"I don't like hurting a woman, but I have made exceptions," says the shadow.

Holly tries to scream. No sound comes out.

"Where is it?"

"What?"

"You took something that wasn't yours."

"I don't know what you're talking about."

He grabs her by the hair with both his hands and begins to spin, forcing Holly to run in circles. She grabs at his wrists to take pressure off her scalp. Faster and faster he spins, finally letting go, flinging her across the room where she ricochets off a wall and crumples. She tries to crawl away. He keeps coming. Amid the debris her fingers close around something cold and heavy. A saucepan. Cast-iron.

He grips her ankle and tries to drag her back to the bedroom. She kicks. He has her hair again. Lifting her. She swings the saucepan into his face. Blood sprays from his mouth. The man picks a broken tooth from inside his cheek and stares at it like he's found a penny in a Christmas pudding.

Twisting her wrist he forces Holly to her knees and the saucepan drops from her fingers. Holly bunches her fist and swings, driving her knuckles into his groin. He doubles over and groans. It's an animalist sound. Picking up the saucepan she hits him again across the side of the head. He staggers and raises his gun hand. Tries to focus. Pulls the trigger. The bullet hits the wall behind her.

Holly runs. She's small and agile. Four years of gymnastics. Seven years of running from her father. At the door, along the walkway, at the top of the stairs, letting gravity carry her down. Almost out of control. Zac's face in her mind, his body broken.

Reaching the ground floor, she hurls herself at the fire door, which bangs open. She's almost to the road. There are cars. Lights. People. Somebody steps in front of her. She can't stop. Her arms fold across her head, bracing for a collision.

"Gotcha!"

The girl is screaming hysterically, fighting at his arms, scratching at his face; her cheeks streaked with tears and snot.

Nothing Ruiz says seems to make any difference. Holding her firmly, he tells her to settle down. Getting rougher. He slaps her hard across the face and then holds her tightly, his arms around her chest, her feet off the ground.

"What's wrong? What are you so frightened of?"

Her eyes shoot behind him, looking over his shoulder.

"He's got a gun! Run!"

"Who's got a gun?"

She sucks in a breath. "Him. Upstairs. Please, let me go."

"Your boyfriend?"

She shakes her head and tries to pull away from him again. This is not another performance. She's terrified. Shaking.

Ruiz takes her to his car and puts her in the front seat.

"OK. Stay here."

"Don't leave me!"

"You're safe."

Ruiz crosses the road at a jog and pushes through the fire doors. Looks at the lift. It's on the third floor. He peers up the central staircase. Concrete. Cold. It's hard to move quietly. He climbs slowly. Counting the floors.

There is a long walkway, open at one side, overlooking a quadrangle. More concrete. Another set of stairs is at the far end. The flats are numbered, all beginning with "3."

Glancing over the railing, he peers into the darkness. The lights in the quadrangle float like yellow balls suspended from above. Something moves in the shadows, a hooded figure, head down, walking quickly. It could be anyone.

The flat is fifteen yards along the walkway. Edging along the wall, Ruiz stoops in a crouch and looks through the splintered door. He can only see one half of the entrance hall. Keeping his back to the wall, he steps inside. A darkened bedroom is off to the right. The place has been searched. Ransacked. Drawers pried open, yanked out, emptied. Wardrobes pillaged, clothes ripped from hangers and tossed on the floor.

The sitting room is another disaster. The sofa slashed, a bookcase overturned, the back smashed in. Dishes and cups have been raked from kitchen shelves and lie broken on the linoleum.

The boyfriend is sitting in a chair in the main bedroom. Naked. Rail thin. Covered in wounds. His forearms and wrists are thick and corded with muscles and veins; his thighs are slick with blood.

Ruiz tilts Zac's head, looking for signs of life. His eyes are open. The neat hole punched through his forehead is like a red bindi on an Indian bride.

Standing frozen for a moment, Ruiz drops his hands to his sides, his senses dulled, his mind deafened by the sound in his head like pounding surf. He backs out the door, not touching anything.

10

BAGHDAD

Luca works late. His body has an internal clock that will not let him sleep before the early hours. He sits at the kitchen table working on his laptop, answering emails and making notes for a story. On the wall above the table there is a map of Baghdad, already out of date because the areas of control have changed, along with the locations of the checkpoints.

Nothing about his apartment really belongs to Luca or couldn't be left behind if he had to evacuate, except for the photographs. Only one of them is of Nicola. The rest he gave to her family with her clothes and mementos.

Eight months have passed, yet he still imagines seeing her face in crowds or in cafés as he drives by. Once or twice he's caught a glimpse of someone with the same dark eyes or feminine walk and has wanted to shout out and wave and run to her. Luca doesn't believe in ghosts, but he understands how the dead haunt the living.

He looks at his emails. There are messages from commissioning editors and his publisher. The latest chapters of his book are due. He's also late delivering a feature for *The Economist*.

His mother has left six messages, most of them indecipherable. When Luca was last home he installed voice recognition software on her computer because she couldn't type. Now she just yells at the screen and the words get jumbled.

Her latest missive could be about his great-aunt Sophia or about his mother's cat Sophocles. One of them is dead. Run over. There's mention of a funeral. He's none the wiser.

Opening the paper cartridge on his printer, he takes out the sheets of blank paper and pinches one corner, flicking through the pages. Several printed sheets flash amid the white. Hidden notes. Retrieving them, he looks at the first page.

050707	Bank of Baghdad:	US$1.6m
062207	Rasheed Bank:	US$3.8m
070107	Dar Al-Salam Bank:	US$28.2m
081107	Middle East Investment Bank:	US$1.32m
030208	al-Warka Bank:	US$1.2m
061808	Industry Bank (ransom payment):	US$6m
072909	al-Rafidain Bank:	US$6.9m
092709	Bank of Iraq:	US$5.3m
020710	Rasheed Bank:	US$15.6m
021210	Iraqi Trade Bank:	US$1.8m

Luca adds another robbery to the list:

| 082310 | al-Rafidain Bank: | Amount Unknown |

Half a billion US dollars stolen in four years. This is on top of dozens of smaller robberies that netted Iraqi dinars. The amounts seem almost inconceivable, but so many things in Iraq defy belief. Billions have washed through the country since the invasion, funding reconstruction, repairing infrastructure, paying for security. The robberies have become so commonplace that banks have stopped using armored vans because they draw too much attention. Instead they use private couriers in ordinary cars loaded with sacks of cash, making high-speed dashes across the city.

Opening a file on the laptop, Luca continues writing a story, using two fingers to type.

IRAQ: Three bank employees are dead and four are missing after the latest armed robbery to rock Baghdad—the eighteenth this year in a city that has become the bank robbery capital of the world. The robberies and ransom demands in Iraq are escalating but nobody can say if this is the work of insurgents, criminal gangs or sections of the Iraqi security services...

Luca's mobile rattles on the tabletop. He catches it before it topples off the edge. It's Jamal.

"They found the missing bank guards in a village outside of Mosul."

"Are they under arrest?"

"Their bodies are in custody."

Luca takes a moment to consider the news. He closes his laptop. "I want to go there."

"Mosul is dangerous. The Kurds and Sunnis are killing each other."

"I can ask Shaun for security."

"No, it's best we use our own cars."

They make a plan. Jamal will call Abu. Civilian clothes. Concealed weapons. First light.

11

LONDON

Ruiz has been five hours at the police station. Five hours with another man's blood on his shoes. When he closes his eyes he can picture the scene in miniature, precisely detailed like a scaled down model built by a stage designer. A trashed apartment. A torture scene. A distraught girlfriend. Images he thought he'd left behind in a past life when he still worked for the Met and was being paid to care.

Someone flushes a toilet. The cistern empties and fills. Water rushes through pipes within the walls. The interview room doesn't offer a view or ventilation or natural light. Incumbents aren't supposed to be comfortable.

Ruiz looks at his shoes again, wanting to clean them.

The door opens and a detective enters. Tall and stoop-shouldered, Warwick Thompson has a beak-like nose and breath as stale as vase water. Their paths crossed once or twice when Ruiz was with the Serious Crime Squad, but they were never friends. Thompson was a churchgoer, one of the Christian mafia in the Met, who married a vicar's daughter. Her name was Jackie, a very charitable woman who spent her Sundays in church and the rest of the week delivering comfort to the needy, including two of her husband's colleagues in the drug squad.

Thompson survived the humiliation and the jokes. He even forgave Jackie and the marriage survived. Not long afterwards he busted a string of minor celebrities for drug possession. The tabloids had a field day. Unfortunately, during the subsequent trials it emerged that Thompson's snitch was supplying most of the stuff in the first place. The cases collapsed. Red faces all round. Thompson was transferred out of the drug squad. His career flushed. This is where he washed up.

"Tell me again how you know this girl?"

"I met her last night."

"And took her home?"

"I tried to help her."

"Did you give her one?"

Ruiz rolls his eyes. Was he ever this predictable when he was interviewing people?

Thompson hasn't changed much over the years — put on a few pounds, lost some hair, but his wardrobe is the same. He has a habit of tilting his head as though he's deaf in one ear. Maybe he is, thinks Ruiz. He's certainly not listening.

Going over the story again, he describes the argument in the pub, the sting, the robbery. Thompson doesn't seem any more convinced than the first time.

"Why didn't you report any of this to the police?"

"I decided to recover the property myself."

"By taking the law into your own hands?"

"I followed a lead."

"Did you kill Zac Osborne?"

"I didn't even know his name."

"Why is his blood all over you?"

"I checked to see if he was breathing."

"Was that before or after you put a bullet between his eyes?"

Ruiz holds out his hands. "You want to test me for gunshot residue?"

Thompson doesn't appreciate the sarcasm. "You see how it looks? They robbed your house. Took personal stuff. You were pissed off. So you followed this girl home..."

"You think I tortured this poor sod because he took some of my dead wife's things?"

"I think you know more than you're saying. What did you say to the girl? Why won't she talk to us?"

"Maybe you're not asking her nicely enough."

"Did you see anyone else leaving the flat?"

"There might have been someone on the far stairs. It was dark."

"Convenient."

"I've told you all I know. She set me up, stole my stuff and I went looking for her. Then I followed her home and found her boyfriend dead. That's the blood, guts and feathers of it. Maybe if you told me who this guy was, I could actually help you."

Thompson weighs up his options.

"Zac Osborne. War vet. Iraq and Afghanistan. Wounded twice, won the Queen's Gallantry Medal. After his second spell in hospital he became addicted to painkillers and the military discharged him. He was arrested eighteen months ago for breaking into a pharmacy in Kew. Given a good behavior bond because of his military record."

"What about the girl?"

"Holly Knight. Nineteen. In and out of foster care since the age of seven. She has two convictions for shoplifting and others for criminal damage, resisting arrest and anti-social behavior."

"What did she do?"

"Broke a shop window, threw fireworks at a police horse and wrestled with a police constable."

"Where is she now?"

"Next door."

"You keeping her in?"

"For as long as we can."

There is a knock. A familiar figure fills the doorframe. Commander Campbell Smith looks like he's been stitched into his uniform. Every button polished. Shoe leather gleaming. Ruiz has known him for forty years—ever since they did their training together at the Police Staff College, Bramshill. He also introduced Campbell to his wife Maureen at a barbecue—having slept with her first, a fact that didn't enamor him to either of them.

It's been four years since Ruiz last saw him. Campbell has been promoted. He was always on the fast track. Not so much nose to the grindstone as nose between the cheeks.

"Vincent."

"Campbell. You're a commander now. Congratulations."

They shake hands. Campbell smiles. He has a great smile. You can see the child in it before the wear and tear of a thirty-year marriage and a longer sentence with the Metropolitan Police.

"When they told me they had Vincent Ruiz in the interview room, I thought it must be a mistake. Had to come and see it for myself."

Ruiz opens his arms and does a slow turn.

"You've put on weight."

"Living the good life. How's Maureen?"

"She's gone on a cruise."

"Mediterranean?"

"Canada."

Campbell Smith leans closer. Motions him to do the same.

"How did you get mixed up in this?"

"I'm an accidental tourist."

The commander nods. His hat is tucked under the crook of his left arm. "You know why this guy was killed?"

"Nope."

He gives Ruiz a wry half smile and maybe a twitch of the eyebrow. Then he tosses his head towards the door.

"Do you know what I learned first day in this job, Vincent?"

How to brown nose, thinks Ruiz.

"I learned that the simple answer is nearly always the right one. The explanation is never that complicated. There's no mystery. The guy was a junkie. It's a drug deal gone wrong."

"So that's the official version?"

"You think there's more than one version?"

"There's *always* more than one version."

Campbell stares at him with his head cocked to one side. Turning to leave, he adds, "I've told the SOCOs you won't mind having your fingernails scraped and giving them some swabs."

"Anything to help."

"Maybe you could also do us another favor."

"What's that?"

"Make a statement and press charges against Holly Knight."

Ruiz can see where he's going with this. The police need a reason to hold her.

"Can I speak to her?"

"No."

"She stole something from me — pieces of jewelry that belonged to my first wife. My daughter is getting married next weekend. The jewelry was going to be a present."

Campbell sucks in his cheeks and puckers his lips reflectively. "If you lodged a complaint against Holly Knight, those items would be regarded as evidence."

"And I wouldn't get them back for months."

The faintest trace of a smile enters Campbell's eyes. "Sorry, old chap, I can't get involved. No hard feelings."

Ruiz isn't going to forget the feelings.

Campbell wants the final word. "Listen to me, Vincent, this whole 'don't fuck with me' act might have worked when you were still on the job, but you're a civilian now."

The commander turns and marches down the corridor, an ordered man with a disordered heart.

12

LONDON

The Courier watches a skinny black-haired girl in a G-string and high heels undulate around a pole, moving like there's an itch in her groin that she can't quite reach. He pulls a twenty from his wallet and tucks it into her G-string, brushing his fingertips along the fabric. She dances away, waggling her finger at him.

She has a pageboy haircut. Black. Straight. A wig. Painted eyes. Red lips. The red reminds him of his first hit, the schoolgirl, the blood that seeped from the corner of her mouth as she lay in the dust, one leg folded under her, her schoolbag still in her hand.

He can't remember if she was on her way to school or coming home, or if she was just visiting someone at another settlement. She was killed because she was *there* and not somewhere else. It was a test. His initiation. That was fifteen years ago on the West Bank near the city of Nablus.

He was told that the first killing would be the hardest — a leap of faith across a blood-soaked divide — but in that moment between the recoil and the bullet hitting the target, the blink of an eye, he felt nothing. Each killing since has been an exercise in trying to *feel* something, some sense of horror or satisfaction or completion.

The second person he killed was an Iraqi dissident, found hanging in a townhouse in San Francisco. Next came an Iranian defector who fell beneath a train in Amsterdam and a Syrian politician who died in a hit-and-run accident in Cairo. The most recent — an Iranian nuclear scientist — was killed by a booby-trapped motorbike, triggered by remote control outside his house in Tehran. State TV blamed "Zionist and American agents." A smokescreen. Masoud Ali Mohammadi had been leaking details of Iran's nuclear program to the US.

How many in total? More than a dozen but less than his enemies suspect. Defectors. Dissidents. Spies. Sympathizers. Rivals. Enemies. He does not judge—he carries out the judgment of others.

The girl on the pole has finished her dance. She clomps off stage, retrieving a wad of chewing gum from the edge of a glass. As she moves through the tables, a bouncer steps in to protect her. Later she emerges from her dressing room wearing a midriff top and low-slung jeans. A tattoo ripples across her lower back—the tramp stamp. Forty years from now there'll be tens of thousands of old ladies trying to hide the ink-pricked follies of their youth.

The Courier sends her a note. Offers to buy her a drink. She signals her interest. Five minutes. He waits.

Yesterday hadn't gone to plan. The soldier hadn't capitulated. The Courier had shown him the long-nosed pliers, drawn attention to them, demonstrated, but it made no difference. The soldier had simply smiled at him, a mad grin—that's what war does to a man, puts spiders in his head.

"I have no desire to kill you," the Courier told him, "but you took information that didn't belong to you. Now I must collect it. Just tell me what you did with the notebook."

The soldier grinned. Died that way.

Now it's up to the girl. He should never have let her get away. That was careless. He had underestimated her. Most women meekly surrender or go rigid with fear. This one knew how to fight. Survive. Now he can't get her face out of his mind—her smoky blue eyes and her nice white teeth, slightly overcrowded at the bottom. He remembers the heat of her skin and the smear of her saliva across the back of his hand.

They took her to the police station. There was someone with her, a much older man, solid, but quick on his feet. It didn't look like he lived on the estate. He was driving an old Mercedes. Should be easy to trace.

13

BAGHDAD

The new day is a bright orange line on the horizon but already the trees are sagging in the heat and the landscape has blurred to a shimmer. Driving at speed past barricaded shops and bawling vendors, Luca and Jamal cross the Greater Zaab River, withered and brown, into the province of Nineveh. Abu is in the vehicle behind them, never more than a car length away.

Soon the desert stretches out on every side with flat expanses of hardpan between brush-covered ridges and dry creek beds that look like old scars in the earth. Rural Iraq is like something from a Biblical story with men in dishdashas, boys herding sheep and simple mud-brick houses the color of sand.

The traffic is heavier than Luca remembers. Good news. Business is being done. Jobs created. Families fed.

Jamal's eyes dart back and forth to see if any vehicle has "picked them up." "Dickers" can be anywhere; sympathizers who punch a number into a mobile phone and summon insurgents to a "soft target."

Below them at the base of a ravine the remnants of a US Humvee lie twisted and blackened. Fresh tar covers the bomb crater at the edge of the road.

When they reach the outskirts of Mosul they turn east and cross the Tigris. After stopping twice to ask for directions they reach a village too poor to pave its stretch of road. It has one dusty street and a broken line of mud buildings. Four or five men sit outside a café, playing poker and drinking tea. Their faces are like the desert—old, worn and craggy. Watching.

Jamal asks about the bodies that were found. One of the men raises a weathered hand and summons a young boy from the kitchen. Barefoot and dressed in rags, the boy sprints ahead, his pink heels flashing in the dust. Jamal and Luca follow, while Abu stays with the cars. Their young guide waits for them to catch up. He runs again, zigzagging through a dusty yard full of half bricks and broken concrete.

Then he stops. Waits. He points at a collapsed house, rubble instead of walls, the roof in pieces; some sort of explosion or implosion. Luca moves closer, stepping gingerly into the debris. He pulls aside a twisted rectangle of tin, stained with rust. Not rust. Blood. Flies lift off and settle again.

Luca retreats, wiping his hands on his shirt. He questions the young boy in Arabic. There were four men inside the house. They were wearing uniforms. The police took their bodies away.

The nearest dwelling is across the street. Luca notices a young girl on the rooftop, sitting beneath a tarpaulin slung from three poles. She's wearing a scarf drawn across her mouth, peering from beneath the edge of the fabric, not quite looking directly at him.

"Did anyone see what happened?" he asks the boy.

"We were sleeping. My house is there," he points further along the street. There is a woman hanging washing on a clothesline. The wet clothes are piled in an aluminum case just like the one he saw in the bank vault. On the opposite side of the road an old woman is selling onions and peppers from another case.

"Where did you get this?" he asks her.

"It was not stolen."

"Where?"

The boy answers, "We found them."

"Show me."

Luca follows the boy again, walking between buildings that radiate heat, yet trap the cool behind thick walls. Goats bleat from the shade of a lone tree. Stopping at the edge of a ravine, Luca's feet have disturbed loose stones that bounce and slide down the steep slope, rattling against bags of household rubbish, discarded clothing, furniture and broken pottery. Scattered on top are more than a dozen aluminum cases. Luca counts them. Including those he saw in the village it makes sixteen. How much money did they contain?

Walking back to the destroyed dwelling, he begins taking photographs. Through the lens he notices the girl again, still watching him from the rooftop. Luca waves. She doesn't respond.

Crossing the road, he knocks. For a long while nobody comes. An old man opens the door, a yellowed bandage around his head. His eyes disappear in dark holes like burrowing animals afraid of the light.

Luca greets him with respect. He can smell the rotting flesh beneath the bandage. Infection.

"What happened to your head?"

The old man shrugs.

"Do you have antibiotics?"

"I cannot afford them."

Luca sends Jamal for the first-aid box in the car. The room has rugs on the floor and a few simple pieces of furniture. The old man sits down on a wooden stool.

"Did you see anything last night?"

"No."

"What about your granddaughter—did she see?"

"I don't have a granddaughter."

"The girl on the roof."

"That is where she sleeps." The old man blinks at him. "You are not an Arab."

"No."

"What is your religion?"

"I don't have one."

"Who is your God?"

"I have no God."

"What sort of man has no God? What does he believe in? Why does he live?"

He lives because he is a man.

"You are American?"

"I was born there. My mother is Iraqi."

"I like George Clooney and Arnold Schwarzenegger. How come Americans don't like football? Everybody in the world likes football."

"We have our own sort of football."

The old man grunts, unimpressed. The girl appears on the narrow stairs. Barely sixteen, her face still covered. She feels her way, pressing her palm against the wall. The old man calls her closer. She raises her chin. Her eyes are a dull and sightless white.

"She heard them," he says.

"What did she hear?"

The girl speaks softly in Arabic. "There was a truck and two cars. Men were arguing."

"How many men?"

"Seven or eight."

"What were they saying?"

"Some of them were told to go into the house. They were beating at the door, trying to get out. The other men loaded the truck."

"Did you hear any names?"

She shakes her head. "They were driving Land Cruisers."

"How do you know?"

The old man answers for her. "She can recognize different engines."

"Did they say where they were going?"

She hesitates. The old man barks, "Tell him, wife."

Not her grandfather!

"I heard them say Al Yarubiyah," she says.

It's a crossing on the Syrian border, eighty miles to the west.

"The men in the building were yelling and screaming," she says, covering her ears. "There was a big noise and then they stopped."

Luca leaves a bottle of antibiotics on the table and tells the old man how many to take. He steps into the brightness of the afternoon. A dozen men are watching him, their faces wrapped in kaffiyehs. Eyes empty.

Jamal and Abu are waiting at the vehicles. Abu is eating a homemade sandwich of bread and meat. He has a weapon slung across his chest.

"Time to go," says Jamal, glancing over his shoulder.

They leave the village in a cloud of dust but even before it settles Abu spots a vehicle tracking them, a battered pickup about two hundred yards away, travelling in the same direction, bouncing over ruts.

The driver is dressed all in white. He's not alone.

Jamal puts his foot down, swerving around potholes, his knuckles white on the wheel.

"How far to the dual carriageway?"

"A mile and a half."

Luca pulls a Kevlar vest from his bag. "Put this on."

Jamal shakes his head. "I'm fine. You wear it."

"We both wear one."

Jamal takes one hand off the steering wheel and puts it through the sleeve, then the other one.

Reaching beneath the seat, Luca pulls out a machine pistol. He cracks the car door, holding it partially open, keeping his weapon out of sight.

The pickup is still with them, the distance closing.

"They could be farmers," says Luca, not believing it. He raises the machine pistol and fires a warning shot. The pickup doesn't slow down or change course.

Ahead, lying discarded beside the road is a hessian sack. Jamal swerves violently, bouncing through a gutter and sending the Skoda rearing like a rodeo bull. At the same moment the sack explodes, blowing out the side windows and lifting the Skoda on to two wheels where it balances for what seems like the longest time, trying to decide whether to roll over or right itself.

Gravity is kind to them. Four wheels kiss the earth. Luca's ears are ringing. Jamal is yelling.

"He's coming in! He's coming in!"

The pickup has closed to within thirty yards. The passenger is firing on them, sending bullets pinging off the side of the Skoda.

Luca leans over the back seat and shoots through the rear window. Ejected cartridges, brass, red-hot, rattle on to the floor. Out of the corner of his eye he sees Abu in the Toyota HiLux, rearing over the dunes and the undulations. He has pointed the vehicle directly at the pickup, closing at speed.

The gunman in the passenger seat recognizes the danger and changes his aim but it's too late. The force of the collision sends the pickup spearing into an embankment. Its nearside bumper digs into the earth and the entire vehicle lifts off the ground and rolls once...twice...three times in slow motion before exploding. Black smoke rises and billows like a mushroom cloud, perfect in the heat and stillness of the afternoon.

Jamal and Abu pull up at a safe distance.

The cousins look at each other, breathing hard, wordlessly taking stock. Uninjured. Jamal runs his hand along the side of the Skoda, putting his finger through one of the many bullet holes.

"And you laughed at my armor plating," he says, with a hint of pride.

Abu glances at the burning wreck.

"They will have friends. We cannot stay here."

14

LONDON

Holly Knight stares at a spot on the wall, concentrating on a crack in the paintwork because it stops her thinking of Zac. The police took away her clothes for testing. She fought them at first and it took three female officers to undress her. Then she sat in her underwear, refusing to wear the prison overalls.

There was an argument outside her cell.

A man said, "I can't interview her if she's half-naked."

"She won't get dressed."

"Get her some proper clothes."

The voices went away and came back later. A WPC brought a pair of jeans, a sweatshirt and Converse trainers.

"They're not going to let you go unless you've been interviewed. You don't have to answer the questions, but you have to listen to them."

Holly could see her point.

Now in the interview room the questions are washing over her like background music in a shopping mall. Threats. Accusations. Abuse.

"When did you last see Zac Osborne?"

She doesn't answer.

"What happened in the flat?"

Silence.

"Did you see his attacker? What did he look like? Are you deaf? Your boyfriend is dead. He was murdered. You won't say a word. You're not crying. You're not upset. Maybe you don't care."

Holly doesn't react. She only turns her head when someone new enters the room, fixing her eyes on them, committing them to memory. Past experience has impressed upon her the need for silence. She has learned to analyze the consequences of co-operating with the police and has come to the conclusion that the best way to get out of her present circumstances is to say nothing at all so her words can't be twisted and used against her.

The detective quotes from her file. A history lesson. The foster homes, the past arrests, her alcohol and drug abuse. Her mind slips back over some of these events, but most have been forgotten or blocked out.

She has decided that she does not like DS Thompson, who is no longer polite or respectful. He has an undertaker's face and dandruff on his shoulders.

In Holly's experience, people tend to talk *at* her and not *to* her. They preach or they browbeat and they hear what they want to hear. But that's not the reason she doesn't answer. She doesn't trust the truth. The truth can be a lethal thing.

Her mother used to work nights as a nurse. Her father, Reece, would go to the pub every evening, dressed in his best jacket, smelling of aftershave, whistling as he walked up the street. He left

Holly in charge. Aged seven. Her brother Albie was five, epileptic, small for his age. One night Albie left the taps running when he filled the bath. It overflowed and flooded downstairs, coming through the ceiling in a torrent of plaster and dust.

When their father came home, Holly had tried to clean up but the wet plaster dust was like glue and she couldn't hide the hole in the ceiling. Albie lay mute and fearful in his bed. His cat was under the covers with him.

"It was my fault," she said. "I should have been paying attention."

She watched her father's large callused hand go up in the air and come down hard on the side of her face: harder than Zac had ever hit her. It knocked her across the room.

Albie lay transfixed, holding the cat against his chest.

The skin of Reece's face was tight against the bone. He dragged Albie out of bed by the neck and took him to the bathroom.

"You want to be clean? I'll show you clean."

He pushed Albie's head into the toilet bowl. Flushed. Did it again. Albie's socked feet scrabbled on the tiles. He couldn't breathe. Reece pulled his head from the bowl and bounced it off the cistern before flushing it again. He left Albie lying on the floor, toilet water dripping from his face.

That's when it happened. Albie's eyes began to flicker and roll back in his head. He was stuttering and his limbs were jerking like a fish pulled from the water. After a while he stopped moving. He had a blue ring around his mouth.

Holly thought time had stopped. It was like watching a DVD and someone had pressed pause, freezing the frame in a blurred snapshot. Reece tried to shake Albie awake. Gave him mouth to mouth. CPR. Called 999.

The ambulance took Albie to hospital but he was DOA. "What does that mean?" Holly asked, but nobody answered her.

Her mother came running down the corridor. Reece caught her. Held her. "He just collapsed, babe. He had one of his turns."

He was stroking her hair, whispering, muffling her sobs. Then he looked at Holly and there was a moment of chilling certainty that registered in her mind.

"Ask Holly, she'll tell you."

Holly remained motionless. Reece rolled his jaw like he was chewing on something hard.

"He killed Albie," she whispered. "He put his head down the toilet."

Her father's eyes narrowed like he was looking at her down the barrel of a gun.

"The little bitch is lying. It was an accident, babe, I promise you. I tried to save him. Gave him CPR, just like you taught me..."

"No, Mama, Albie overflowed the bath. Daddy got angry."

"You shut your mouth!" he warned.

"It's the truth."

Her mother had pushed Reece away.

"She's lying, babe, I'd never do anything to hurt Albie. He had one of his turns. Ask the doctors."

"Why would she lie?"

"I don't know. Maybe *she* flooded the bathroom. You know what she's like—always blaming Albie for things."

Holly's eyes grew hot and bright. She rocked from foot to foot.

This time her mother knelt in front of her, holding on to her shoulders. "This is really important, sweetie, you have to tell me the truth."

"I *am* telling the truth."

There was no fight. No more harsh words. That night Holly and her mother stayed at a women's refuge in Battersea. They shared a bed and Holly fell asleep listening to her mother's sobs.

It took Reece three weeks to find them. He came to the door of the refuge in his blue suit. Sober. Freshly shaven. He carried a bunch of carnations for her mother that he'd bought at the train station. He also had a present for Holly—a cheap pink Barbie rip-off with straw-colored hair. Her mother and father drove off together—just to talk things over, Reece said. Holly knew he was lying.

Later that night, Reece parked in a quiet street and put his hands around her mother's throat. They found her body next morning lying in the passenger seat with a blanket over her knees. Reece left a suicide note in his flat. He hung himself from a beam in his lockup garage.

A brother, a mother, a father, her entire family broken by the truth—she wouldn't make that mistake again. Holly dreamed that night of Albie waving to her from Heaven, signaling her to come.

DS Thompson is shouting in her face. She can feel the flecks of spit land on her eyelids and lips. She wipes them away with her sleeve.

"We can do this the easy way or the hard way," he says.

"There is no easy way," she replies.

"What?"

"People say there's an easy way, but there never is."

DS Thompson slaps the folder closed and mutters something to a colleague about her being "retarded." He leaves her alone for a few minutes. It might be longer.

Then he comes back into the room.

"Get up."

She's taken outside, along a corridor, down the stairs to a parking area. A police car is waiting. The doors open.

"Where are you taking me?"

"To identify a body."

15

LONDON

Ruiz splashes water on his face and tries to wash the coppery taste from his mouth. Leaning over the gutter, he empties the rest of the plastic bottle over his head. The police released him at three in the morning. Instead of going home, he drove to Westminster Public Mortuary in Horseferry Road.

Now it's just gone seven. The morning is bathed in a faint glow.

He's listening to the radio. Stories about Iraq and Afghanistan. A US Senate hearing into Goldman Sachs. Accusations of reckless greed. Claims and counter-claims.

A swinging door opens and a pale figure emerges. Gerard Noonan is in his sixties with short-cropped blond hair and no discernible eyebrows. His skin is so pale he seems to glow in the shadows, hence his nickname, "The Albino."

When Ruiz was heading the Serious Crime Squad he worked more than a dozen cases with Noonan, a veteran Home Office pathologist, who enjoyed far better relationships with the dead than the living. Unmarried. Childless. Noonan has always struck Ruiz as being borderline autistic because of his social ineptness. The only sentient creatures that he relates to are horses—the thoroughbred variety that run round in circles carrying brightly colored leprechauns.

Ruiz falls in step.

"Gerard."

"Vincent."

"All-nighter?"

"People don't die to a timetable."

"How thoughtless of them. Had breakfast?"

"Not hungry."

"Coffee then?"

"Are you going to follow me all the way home?"

"Depends."

The café is a family business run by Italians with an endless supply of "cousins" working the tables and a barista who seems to have four arms. There are paintings on the walls of fat little nymphs playing in a forest.

Noonan orders a coffee. Ruiz wants the full English with everything fried, including the bread.

"I do autopsies on guys like you."

"We keep you in work."

The pathologist pushes up his sleeves. Ruiz is amazed at how

Noonan has almost no color on his arms. It's like someone has drained his blood or replaced it with milk.

"You autopsied an ex-soldier."

"Might have done."

"I called it in."

"How much you want to hear before you eat?"

"Just get to it."

Noonan puts three sugars in his coffee. "Let's just say he was one tough bastard."

"Meaning?"

"There was a lot of penile and testicular damage. He had his genitals remodeled with a set of long-nose pliers."

"He was tortured?"

"Went every round. I don't know what information he had but I hope he begged to give it up. I hope that's what happened."

Ruiz can feel his testicles retract. He looks at the side of Noonan's face. The pathologist is gazing out the window at pedestrians, huddled beneath umbrellas, spilling from Victoria Station.

"How did he die?"

"Suffocated. The bullet was insurance."

"A professional hit?"

"Looks like it."

"Gangland?"

"Maybe."

"Did you do a tox screen?"

"Results will take a few days."

Ruiz scratches his unshaven chin, feeling the dirt between the hair follicles. "The police are saying it was a drug-related hit. What do you think?"

Noonan shrugs.

"Did they find any drug paraphernalia in the flat?"

"No."

"Any needle marks?"

"None."

"The guy was a war hero."

"I heard."

Noonan swallows the last of his coffee. "I'm too old for this shit."

"For what?"

"To understand what some people do."

———

Holly Knight sits in the back of the police car, letting the reflections of city buildings wash over her pupils. She's dirty and tired and her shoulder aches where she was slammed against the wall during the fight.

The police car pulls into a walled yard with iron gates and razor wire. Holly is escorted through a door and along a wide corridor with a polished floor. It smells like a hospital with something missing. Patients. Hope.

Thompson makes her walk quickly, hustling her along without touching her.

"Wait here," he says, leaving her in a room with two small sofas, a coffee table, water cooler and box of tissues. A curtain screens one wall.

Alone, Holly thinks about Zac. He had saved her. They had saved each other. Normally she didn't get close to people. It was safer that way. Never pat stray dogs or they'll follow you home. Her mother told her that.

She and Zac met at a rehabilitation center, which is a fancy term for a psych ward. Holly was undergoing tests. Zac was being treated for post-traumatic stress. Zac didn't treat her like the other men in her life. He didn't care about her history. That was a year ago. Long enough to fall out of love. It hadn't happened. Closing her eyes, she can picture his stretched angular face and the blur of big freckles on his shoulder blades.

DS Thompson joins her in the room. Without any fanfare or warning, he pulls open the curtain. Zac is laid out on a metal trolley covered with a white sheet from the neck down. Bruised. Pale. Changed. It's amazing what a breath can do. Fill a chest. Fire a heart. Bring color to a face.

"Can you confirm the name of the deceased?"

Holly whispers, "Zac Osborne."

The curtain is drawn closed. Holly sits on the sofa, feeling herself getting smaller and smaller like Alice in Wonderland. DS Thompson is talking to her. Something about Holly's grief has melted the ice within him and his attitude has changed. Mellowed.

"Do you have somewhere to stay?" he asks. "We can't let you go unless we know how to reach you."

A voice answers him from the doorway. "She can stay with me." Ruiz is holding a coffee for her. "I have a spare room."

Thompson looks at him incredulously. "Two nights ago you offered her a bed and she robbed you."

"That was two nights ago."

Ruiz addresses Holly. "You can't go back to your flat. And the police won't let you go unless you give them an address."

Thompson interrupts again. "Why are you doing this?"

"That's my business."

He sniffs hard, trying to get a handle on Ruiz, who is still focused on Holly.

"It's up to you. Stay here or come home with me. I don't bear grudges."

Words. Promises. Everything is happening too quickly for her. She nods but doesn't look at Ruiz. Then she follows him down the corridor, taking two steps to each one of his.

"You're asking for trouble," yells Thompson.

Ruiz doesn't answer.

"I'll need to talk to her again."

"You know where to find me."

The Merc edges out of a parking spot and joins a stream of traffic. Brake lights blink between passing cars. Ruiz glances at Holly. Her eyes are closed. Her hair is drawn back and she's wearing a man's coat because her own clothes are in the lab. She's a pretty thing, preposterously young. It's a shame about the piercings.

"You don't like the police very much?"

She doesn't answer.

"I'm not a copper anymore."

Silence.

"DS Thompson wanted to have you sectioned. Do you know what that means? He thinks you're a couple of channels short of basic cable."

Again he gets no response.

"You don't have to be frightened of me."

"I'm not frightened."

"I'm not going to cause you any trouble."

"Don't even try."

She is five foot five, weighs 125 pounds wringing wet, but something in her voice tells Ruiz that Holly wouldn't hesitate to fight.

"I'm not going to fuck you," she says matter-of-factly.

Ruiz glances at her in amazement.

"Don't give me that look," she says. "You're a man. You're all the same, unless you're gay, which you're not. Maybe you're too old."

"Somebody should scrub out your potty mouth."

She gets a look of alarm. "Don't even try it!"

They drive in silence through a hinterland of council houses and industrial estates, staying south of the river through Clapham and Wandsworth. The big old Mercedes has a soft ride. It's the sort of car Holly used to throw up in as a kid. She sits as far away from Ruiz as possible with one hand on the door handle, sneaking occasional glances at him, contemplating what sort of monster he would turn into. He doesn't look much like a policeman, even a former one. He seems big and slow, yet she saw how quickly he could move.

"Why are you doing this?" she asks.

"It's my good deed for the day."

"You're lying."

"I want my stuff back—the hair-comb you stole."

"I don't have it."

"Where?"

"I dropped it at the flat."

Ruiz nods. "Did you see the guy who killed Zac?"

Holly nods.

"Would you recognize him again?"

"Yeah."

"Describe him to me."

She mumbles, "Mid-thirties, dark hair, your height, but thinner."

"What color eyes?"

"It was dark."

They drive in silence for another while, pausing at red lights. Ruiz glances at Holly. Only half her face is visible. Goose bumps on her arms.

"Why?"

"Huh?"

"Why did this guy hurt Zac?"

She doesn't answer.

"Did you owe someone money?"

"No."

"The police think it was a drug deal gone wrong."

"They're lying! Zac didn't touch the stuff—not for a long while. He got clean. Went to meetings."

"Was he dealing?"

"No fucking way."

Holly brings her knees up to her chest, resting her chin on them. Looks even younger.

"Sooner or later you have to level with someone, Holly."

"I'm telling the truth." Her eyes float.

"So you're saying Zac wasn't using."

"Not for a long time."

Ruiz raises his voice but remains composed. "Why should I believe you?"

She doesn't answer. She's staring at the passing parade of Londoners.

"Are you using?"

"No."

"I saw you sniffling and snuffling."

"I got a cold." She tugs her hair back from her face, glaring at him. "You're not my father, so don't start lecturing me. Just drop me on the next corner. I don't have to put up with this shit."

"Why won't you talk to the police?"

"Been there, done that, bought the T-shirt."

"That bad?"

"Nothing good."

16

LONDON

The Courier wakes in a bed and breakfast hotel in Lancaster Gate. There is a girl sleeping next to him, snoring softly, hair a mess, eyes smudged.

He kicks her.

"What was that for?"

"Your wake-up call."

"You paid for the night."

"And now it's morning."

Scowling, she slips out of bed and pulls on a G-string, stuffing her bra in the pocket of her long black coat. She bends to buckle her sandals and notices a prayer mat in the corner.

"Are you one of those?"

"What would that be?" There's a jagged edge to his voice.

"Nothing."

"I'm a Muslim—does that bother you?"

"No."

He smiles and rolls on to his feet. She backs away, holding her jacket to her chest. He raises his hand slowly, palm spread, reaching for her face, tracing two fingers down her throat. Stops. Her windpipe pulses beneath his thumb. Rocking forward imperceptibly, adding pressure, he seals off her airway.

"Do you ever pray?"

She shakes her head.

"Maybe you should."

Hoarsely, "Please let go."

Releasing his fingers, he laughs. She ducks under his arm and out the door. He can hear her running down the hall and hammering the button on the lift.

Out the window he can see the Tai Chi class on a patch of ground in the park. People in tracksuits, moving like puppets in slow motion. Stopping. Moving again. Ignorant people. Fearful people. People who wake up every morning of their lives scared about something.

Chewing on a hangnail, he removes a piece of skin and spits it on to the floor. Then he looks into the mirror and fingers the bruise on the side of his head. The girl left it there. He thinks of her again, her dark hair and the pinkness of her lips.

His mobile rings. He listens rather than talks, letting his fingers slide over the tautness of his stomach. He closes the phone and goes to the bathroom, where he wets a towel and washes the smell of sex from his genitals, before splashing water over his face and neck. He will pray before he eats. He will eat before he kills.

17

BAGHDAD

Luca Terracini orders a beer and a whisky chaser. He downs the shot-glass in a swallow, feeling the alcohol hollow out his cheeks and scour his throat. He orders another whisky.

The TV is on above the bar. CNN. Footage of a US Senate hearing; Carl Levin, the committee chair, has wire-framed glasses perched on the end of his nose. He stabs his finger at an executive from Goldman Sachs, saying the firm's own documents show the bank was promoting investment products it knew would fail while at the same time betting against them.

Luca orders another drink and takes it outside. Most of the journalists are upstairs on their satellite phones, filing the story of the day: the US Ambassador in Baghdad, Christopher Hill, has finally commented on the fact that Iraq doesn't have a government five months after the elections. He called it the "growing pains of a nascent democracy," making Iraq sound like a pimply teenager whose voice would break soon.

Luca's hands have stopped shaking, but he can feel the gun oil between his thumb and forefinger when he rubs them together. Men died in the burning pickup; men who had wanted to see him dead; men with no reason to hate him, yet who did so completely and irrationally. Men with families; men who woke this morning and ate breakfast and washed and prayed and did all the normal things . . . yet before the day had ended their lungs were full of fire instead of air. What a waste.

Right now Luca's life doesn't seem worth very much. At some point in the evening he decides to go home, but changes his mind. He doesn't remember getting upstairs. He must have asked reception for her room number.

Now she is standing in front of him, wearing a bathrobe cinched tightly at her waist.

"Well?"

"Do you want a drink?"

"I think you've had enough already."

She doesn't shut the door. She doesn't open it any wider.

"Can I come in?"

"No."

"Do you want to go for a walk?"

"We're in Baghdad. I don't think it's very wise to go walking."

"No, you're right." He sways slightly. "We could walk around the pool."

"That's a very short walk."

"We could do it more than once."

Daniela hasn't taken her eyes off him. Her head tilts to one side, her face smooth as porcelain. He wonders how warm it would be to touch.

"What happened today?" she asks.

He doesn't want to lie. He's told too many lies to women. Instead he changes the subject and asks about that drink again. She should tell him to get lost. Sober up. Call her next time.

"Let me get changed. I won't be a minute."

He waits in the hallway, leaning on a wall, watching the lights on the ceiling blur and separate into pairs.

When she appears she's wearing a fitted blouse and jeans. They take the stairs. Luca uses the handrail.

It's a clear night, quiet except for the diesel generators. They walk in silence for a time, gravel crunching underfoot, along a path lit by garden lights hidden within the foliage. Each time they circle the garden they reach a point where the path narrows and Luca steps back to let Daniela go first. She knows he's checking out her figure.

"So you're an accountant."

"You make it sound like a disease."

She tells him the story of her father, a brilliant mathematician, David Garner, famous for his work on probability and risk.

"I always thought that was quite ironic because he's never taken a risk in his life."

"He doesn't gamble?"

"Never. Anybody who knows the slightest bit about probability would never gamble."

She describes him as a big, shambolic man, dressed in tweed or gabardine, with a New York Yankees cap that he wears everywhere. Constantly lost in thought. Living with numbers.

"He forgets appointments, anniversaries, shopping lists…

Sometimes he interrupts dinner and begins jotting down notes on the tablecloth. One day he gave me a lovely china tea set for my birthday before realizing it wasn't my birthday at all, but my brother's."

"How does your mother cope?"

"She accepts his foibles. That's what she called them. She can't understand his work, but consoles herself with the knowledge that few people can, perhaps only a handful in history."

"Where is he now?"

"In a home. Once or twice a year the children get summoned and he changes his instructions about his will and his funeral and threatens to leave us nothing. He has only debts, of course. For a math genius he was always lousy with money."

Without being asked, Daniela mentions a husband, estranged, living in Detroit.

"How long were you married?"

"Eight years."

"Another woman?"

"That's normally how it happens."

Beyond the perimeter walls, between the strands of razor wire, Luca can see a half moon hanging in the night sky.

"How long are you here for?" he asks.

"I don't know. A month. Maybe two. The incoming government—when they choose one—needs to know the state of Iraq's finances." Daniela's arm brushes against his. "We're using fairly standard software. Accounting with a few extras. It collates payments, expenses, insurance, that sort of thing." She hesitates. "I really shouldn't talk about it..."

She changes the subject. "Do you think about leaving?"

"All the time."

"Why?"

"People aren't interested any more. They're bored with hearing about Iraq and Afghanistan, just as they got bored with hearing about Vietnam, Watergate, the Iran–contra scandal, the global financial crisis and the oil spill in the Gulf."

Daniela tilts her head, studying him. "Did something happen today?"

"I took a drive to Mosul—following up on a story. It didn't go to plan."

"Meaning?"

"Two men died."

"Journalists?"

"Haji."

She shivers. Not from cold. They find a quiet corner of the lounge with armchairs and a sofa. Daniela wants a hot chocolate.

"I don't know if that's a house specialty."

"Maybe I'll be surprised."

He sits opposite her, his head clearer now.

"You won a Pulitzer Prize."

"You Googled me."

"I was curious. Nosey. I shouldn't have told you that. Are you sobering up?"

"Yes."

"Do you always drink so much?"

"No."

Tucking her legs under her, she leans on the side of the sofa, resting her chin on her hands.

"What made you come to Iraq?"

"I'm a war correspondent. This is a war."

The answer is too flippant. She lets him know it and he tries again, his voice a hoarse whisper.

"I guess I needed to understand why this mess was necessary in the first place. And why it's necessary now. Growing up, I heard so many stories about Iraq from my mother that I felt I might belong here."

"Is that because you don't belong anywhere else?"

The prescience of the observation rattles something inside him. He blinks twice, moving his mouth, but no words come out. A waiter arrives and delivers their drinks.

Daniela is holding her mug in both hands. Her pink tongue

appears, wetting her bottom lip, and disappears again. For the next hour they talk about Iraq, Afghanistan and other war zones in his career. As he tells her stories, Luca can feel himself being drawn into the scene like an actor who forgets that he's acting and the drama becomes his life—the journeys to sad, violent places; reporting on the best and worst of human beings.

"So much for me," he says, not liking the way she's looking at him, her neutrality, her silence, the way her eyes seem to be probing him for weaknesses—not to hurt him but to see where he's broken.

"Were you scared today?"

"Yes."

"You're not like any journalist I've ever met."

"How so?"

"You don't seem very excited about what you do or driven to make your mark."

"That's because I wonder if I make things worse by being here. I distort the outcome. The observation of an event alters the event itself."

"Heisenberg's uncertainty principle?"

"You know your physics?"

"My father was a mathematician, remember?"

"If people like me weren't here reporting the bombings and sniper attacks and sectarian killings, would they still be happening?"

"Yes."

"What makes you so sure?"

She shrugs. "We can't just look the other way."

"Why not?"

"Because the innocents are the first to suffer—the women and children."

Daniela has finished her drink. She runs her finger through the pale froth left on the rim of the mug.

Luca glances through the doors. "I should go home."

"It's dangerous out there."

"I know the back streets."

She opens her mouth, changes her mind. Tries again.

"You can get a room here."

"They're booked out."

"You could stay in my room."

He looks at her a moment too long.

"There are twin beds. You can use the shower."

The practiced womanizer in Luca wants to celebrate his success. The sexual historian within him reminds him of past mistakes. He's not a player, remember? She's too young, too earnest, she's been hurt before; he should go now, leave her be, wish her a long and happy life.

Sitting in silence he looks into her eyes, down to her breasts and then at his own hands, still covered in gun oil.

Daniela uses the bathroom first. She has cleared her papers and books from the spare bed. There are pages of handwritten notes in a neat, slanting hand. Luca sits in the cone of lamplight and stares at his reflection in the window, exhausted, half sober.

After he showers he borrows a robe and carries his clothes into the bedroom. Daniela is already in bed. Her eyes open. She notices the holster and weapon on his folded clothes.

"I didn't think journalists carried guns."

"I live outside the wire."

"Is that a reason or an excuse?"

He picks up the pistol and pushes a catch. The ammunition clip drops into his hand. He shows her the single bullet lodged in the spring mechanism.

She looks at him, expecting an explanation, fearing for a moment she might not get one.

"There are some groups who value me as a trophy or a hostage or a commodity that can be traded for money or weapons: Shiite death squads, Sunni insurgents, criminal gangs..."

"One bullet won't be enough."

"It only takes one."

A pulse seems to shiver in her eyes.

"I don't want anyone risking his or her life to save me," Luca explains. "And I don't want my mother watching my execution on the internet."

Daniela turns away from him, facing the wall, pulling the covers tight around her. She hardly seems to breathe at all.

Luca turns off the light and lies on his bed. Listening. Desiring. Wondering why every woman he touches seems to bloom and then wither like a cut flower. Sleep comes unexpectedly. It doesn't stay. He wakes in fright, fighting a pillow, the top sheet twisted around him. A hand on his chest . . . hers.

"You were having a nightmare."

She is sitting on the edge of his bed.

"I'm sorry I woke you."

"You don't have to apologize."

He knows the dream. It's the same loop he watches on the wrong side of every night — the unbroken litany of destruction and misery. And it always ends the same way, with Nicola's broken body almost buried beneath rubble. Only her head is exposed, her brown eyes open, blood on her lips.

Nicola once told Luca that he tried to distinguish between pain observed and pain shared. Pain observed is a journalist's pain. His role was to watch and report without getting emotionally involved. Nicola said those who watch brutality and do nothing are no better than those who inflict it. "They are the bad Samaritans," she said. It was a term that Luca had never forgotten. He was the bad Samaritan.

Daniela still has her hand on his chest. She looks into his eyes and leans forward, brushing her lips against his. Opening and closing her mouth, letting her lips move wider, her teeth nibble at his tongue and lower lip and her hands slide down his chest.

Pulling her down next to him, he presses himself against her, listening to her heart fluttering with the urgency of a damaged watch. Impatiently, she rolls him on top of her and he pauses with his penis resting at the entrance to her sex. He looks into her eyes, asking the question silently, *Is this what you want?*

Hooking her ankles around his waist, she presses him closer, sighing into his shoulder, and he begins moving, pulling the world forward beneath them.

18

LONDON

There are lights on inside the house. Ruiz doesn't remember leaving them on. He makes Holly wait in the car. Unlocks the door. Pushes it open with one foot.

Claire is standing in the hallway. She looks like her mother — not her hair or her build but her eyes and her high forehead. Unfortunately, she inherited Ruiz's temper. She's talking on her mobile.

"He's not dead — not yet anyway... I haven't asked him. I'll call you later."

Ruiz looks past her into the lounge. Phillip, her fiancé, is sitting on the sofa, resting his feet on the coffee table. Blond and blue-eyed, he has a touch of Boris Johnson about him, including the foppish hair. Acknowledging Ruiz with a nod, he almost looks sorry for him.

Claire picks up her coat. "We can go now, Phillip."

"Is something wrong?" asks Ruiz.

"Oh, nothing much," she replies, sarcastically. "You missed the dinner last night with Phillip's parents. We waited for over an hour."

"Shit!"

"I spent all night trying to call you. Phillip's parents caught the train back to Brighton this morning." She holds up her hand like she's a traffic cop. "Come on, Phillip. We're leaving."

Ruiz intercepts her at the front door.

"I was robbed. They took a lot of stuff. Personal things. Some belonged to your mum. I was trying to get them back before the wedding."

Claire studies his face.

"When was this?"

"The night before last."

"Did they steal your phone?"

"No."

"What about all your phone numbers?"

"No."

"So you could have called me?"

Ruiz hesitates. Claire keeps landing verbal blows. "You forgot, that's the truth of it. You missed dinner because you forgot."

"I didn't forget...I mean, I would have come. I was planning to, but they stole important things..."

She gazes at the ceiling. Sighs.

"I thought you'd been in some terrible accident. I started calling hospitals...the police..." Her eyes narrow. "Did you report the robbery?"

"No."

"Where did you sleep last night? I came round here looking for..."

Claire stops in mid-sentence. Holly is standing in the doorway, slightly pigeon-toed, holding a plastic bag against her chest. Claire looks at her as if unsure of the protocol and who should speak first.

"Holly, this is Claire, my daughter. Claire, this is Holly."

Neither woman speaks.

Ruiz turns to Holly. "There's a bath upstairs and you'll find some of Claire's old clothes in a wardrobe in the spare room. She's about your size. I'm sure she won't mind."

Claire looks bewildered. Holly steps past her and climbs the stairs.

"Who is she?"

"The girl who robbed me."

The look of confusion on Claire's face changes to one of disbelief.

"She doesn't have anywhere else to stay," says Ruiz, aware of how little sense he's making. "She took your mother's jewelry. I'm trying to get it back."

Claire shakes her head. "It doesn't matter, Dad. I don't know why I expect anything different from you. You didn't turn up at parent–teacher nights or at ballet recitals or Eisteddfods. When I auditioned for the Academy, when I had my car stolen, when Michael got himself arrested . . ."

"When did Michael get arrested?"

"He brought that bag of coca tea back from Peru."

Ruiz nods, remembering.

Claire hasn't finished. "You were always too busy or too selfish or too self-absorbed in your police work or rugby or your woman-izing. Michael and I raised ourselves."

"And look how you turned out."

"This isn't funny, Dad. The only smart thing you ever did was marry Miranda, and then you went and divorced her."

"*She* divorced me."

"And whose fault was that? You keep spouting the same tired old crap, Dad. Same excuses. Same jokes."

She pushes past him, pulling on a cardigan, ignoring his apologies. Ruiz can imagine her talking to a therapist ten years from now, recounting how her father was only a shadowy presence in her life. He didn't bake cakes on cake day. He couldn't put her hair in a bun. He didn't take photographs or home movies. He didn't under-stand ballet.

For a brief moment he contemplates telling her about Laura's letter to her and the importance of the hair-comb, but if he can't get the items back maybe it's best that Claire doesn't know.

Ruiz turns to Phillip. "Tell your parents I'm sorry. Maybe we can reschedule the dinner."

"Absolutely," he says, saying no without using the word no.

Claire is on the doorstep. She turns suddenly, kissing Ruiz on the cheek.

"Daddy."

"Yes, Claire?"

"Sometimes you make it very hard to love you."

19

BAGHDAD

Daniela Garner opens her eyes and finds herself alone. She listens for a time, thinking he might be in the bathroom. The digital clock reads 7:15. His semen has dried on her thighs and she can still feel his weight pressing her into the mattress.

She had seduced him. He hadn't objected. He had held her like a drowning man clinging to the wreckage. She should be full of regret. She should be cursing her stupidity. Instead, she feels a sense of empowerment.

Out of bed, she opens the curtains. A haze hangs over the city, softening the light.

Why had she let him come to her room, this troubled man, this good man? Is he a good man? She thought so last night. Maybe all men change when they get what they want. They put on a persona to attract a woman but after the sex it peels off like a bad paint job.

So what if he's gone? They would only have woken and made meaningless small talk, each being ultra-polite while wishing they were somewhere else.

Luca Terracini might call her later. He might not. The slight bruising between her labia will act as a reminder all day of last night's events. It will make her ovaries shiver and something soft and ripe inside her want to see him again.

Showered and dressed she meets her security detail downstairs. The man called "Edge" is doing close protection. Daniela prefers Shaun, who doesn't look at her like he wants to do a cavity search.

There is a young woman in the security detail, Hispanic looking, with dark hair pulled into a ponytail and her fatigues tucked into heavy boots. She smiles at Daniela and opens the car door. Shaun is behind the wheel of the lead SUV. Glover is already in the back seat. Sulking.

An effete twenty-something who dresses in stovepipe jeans and blue cotton shirts, Glover is from Hamburg but looks and sounds English because of his clipped English accent and the way he stands with an arched back as though someone is pressing a gun into his spine. A computer programmer and IT specialist, he has spent his entire time in Iraq complaining about the heat and the food.

The convoy moves off. Edge leans over the front seat.

"How are my favorite geeks today?"

Glover and Daniela don't acknowledge him.

"Did you sleep well, princess?"

"Very well."

Maybe he knows, she thinks. Maybe he can read the signs. When she lost her virginity at seventeen she was convinced her parents could see it in her eyes.

Edge belches. "I feel rougher than hessian underpants. That's the problem with Haji food."

They drive in silence, weaving at high speed between traffic and sometimes crossing on to the wrong side of the road. Daniela hates these transfers — the bullying and heightened sense of fear.

At the Ministry, the bodyguard ballet is repeated, this time in reverse. Daniela goes straight to the technology center in the basement of the building. Badly ventilated and poorly lit, the rooms are at least functional and the hardware is good quality.

She checks her emails and then looks at the results from overnight. The data-mining software has been running for forty-eight hours. Every ministry has provided details of spending, savings and revenue since 2006. What contracts have been awarded. Completion dates, compliance certificates, inspections, operating budgets, invoices, planned spending, cash flow, staffing levels and security. Millions of transactions are being crosschecked and tabulated.

A stream of green numbers fills a black screen. A second computer has black type on a white screen, listing projects and spending. Running her finger down the first screen, Daniela presses a button on a small digital recorder and makes a note to herself.

Nearly eight hundred suspicious transactions have been identified overnight, more than half of them duplicate payments ranging from a few thousand dollars to $2.1 million. There could be an explanation, but she won't know until she examines the documentation.

After noting the largest payments, she moves on. One name appears more than once—Jawad Stadium. She consults a satellite map of the city. The stadium is in south-east Baghdad, showing up as concentric rings of seating around a brown square. The image is six months old.

She looks at the clock. It's still early in New York. Alfred Nilsen won't be at his desk for another five hours. She sends him an email, requesting details about the stadium.

It was Nilsen who recruited her three months ago at a strange meeting in his apartment on the Upper West Side. She remembers it vividly because it was the first time anyone she knew had been invited to Nilsen's home. The invitation had been handwritten on a small, embossed card. *Saturday, 3 p.m. Afternoon tea.* He had used the words "cordially invited." Does anybody use language like that anymore?

Daniela feels a flush of embarrassment as she remembers Nilsen opening the door to her that day. She had cycled across Central Park and was wearing a fluorescent yellow windbreaker and Lycra leggings. Nilsen looked her up and down as though she had beamed down from another planet.

The softly spoken Norwegian was chairman of the United Nations Board of Auditors and a twenty-five-year veteran of the UN. He had worked in Saudi Arabia and Kuwait before spending four years in Iraq, where he headed the International Advisory and Monitoring Board (IAMB), overseeing the Development Fund of Iraq.

Tall and heavily built, he had suffered some sort of palsy in his fifties that had paralyzed one side of his face. It meant that his left profile was smiling and jovial, while the right side could appear almost cruel.

He had invited Daniela into a sitting room furnished in leather and dark wood and they sat at a small lamp-lit table. She was nervous about being alone with him. Not fearful, but wary of his intellect. Nilsen offered her tea. He had a special thermometer measuring the exact temperature of the water.

"Are you a connoisseur?" she asked.

"I'm a pedant."

The tiny china cups looked as though they belonged in a dolls house. "You are probably wondering why I invited you here?"

"Yes."

"I have a request — something that would require you changing your future plans. An audit must be done...a difficult one. Sensitive. After what happened with the Oil for Food program, nobody wants to be embarrassed again."

"Iraq?"

"Is that a problem? Normally I wouldn't bother to ask. I know you're leaving us, but I thought I might be able to convince you to stay on for another few months."

He smiled at her. A torn shred of tissue paper clung to his neck. It must be hard for him to shave, she thought. Strange seeing two faces in the mirror.

"I'm sure you've read some of the reports of waste in Iraq. I wish I could tell you that they are exaggerated. Nobody is sure of the true losses, but it will run into tens of billions."

He had paused, letting the figure wash over Daniela.

"I find it quite ironic when people get worked up over Bernie Madoff and his Ponzi scheme. What he stole was chicken seed compared to what's happened in Iraq." He meant to say chicken feed, but she didn't correct him.

"I met Madoff once or twice," Nilsen said. "He used to have an apartment in this building where he kept his mistress. I always thought if he could cheat on his wife, he could cheat investors."

Nilsen poured another cup of tea, using a silver strainer to capture the leaves.

"I was in Iraq a month after the invasion. George Bush had just declared mission accomplished and the US began airlifting planeloads of cash into Baghdad. That first payload was mainly small bills—fives and tens and ones—twenty million dollars in total, loaded on to a C-130 at Andrews Air Force Base and flown to Baghdad.

"Later airlifts had larger denominations—stacks of hundred-dollar bills packed into bricks and loaded on to pallets, forty in total, weighing thirty tons—the largest one-day shipment of cash in the history of the Federal Reserve. Twelve billion dollars in US banknotes were delivered to Iraq that first year. The aim was to hold the country together. Pay for basic services. Stop the country descending into chaos. The banks had been looted and the infrastructure destroyed. But once that money arrived, there was no oversight or control. I saw pay-offs in paper bags, pizza boxes and duffel bags. Cash was ferried around the city in private cars and funneled through middlemen, fixers, clerics and politicians. Fraud became another word for "business as usual." At one point more than eight thousand security guards were drawing paychecks but only six hundred "warm bodies" could be found. Halliburton charged for forty-two thousand daily meals for soldiers but served only fourteen thousand of them.

"I was heading the UN team of auditors trying to keep track of the spending. We were supposed to be looking over the Americans' shoulders, but they didn't let us anywhere near the accounts. I remember a BBC reporter asking the Coalition Provisional Authority's director of management and budget what had happened to all the cash airlifted to Baghdad. Do you know what he said?"

Daniela shook her head.

"He said he had no idea and didn't think it was important. The journalist said, "But billions of dollars have disappeared without a trace."

"Yes, but it is *their* billions — Iraqi money frozen in western bank accounts — so what difference does it make?"

Nilsen leaned back in his armchair, tired all of a sudden.

"Iraqis voted in elections in March but there still isn't a government. When the politicians stop posturing they will need to know the state of the country's finances. The UN wants to undertake an audit. That's why I'm offering you a job."

Cooling down after her ride, Daniela felt her nipples swell against the thinness of the nylon. The apartment was colder than she first imagined.

"Why me?" she asked.

"You understand the nature of the work ... the sensitivities."

"Is there opposition?"

Nilsen hesitated, choosing his words carefully. "The audit must be conducted within certain parameters."

"What parameters?"

"The government of Iraq and the reconstruction agencies are not interested in the mistakes of the past. The audit will only cover the term of the previous government, from May twentieth 2006 up until the present," explained Nilsen. "Any projects commenced prior to that date will be excluded."

"Whom would I be answerable to?"

"Me."

"Staff?"

"As many as you need — within reason."

Daniela had felt a sense of displacement that shifted and separated inside her.

"I'm not really interested."

"I can offer you five thousand a day or a guaranteed hundred thousand dollars if the job takes less than three weeks."

Daniela tried not to react. People who tell you that money doesn't matter are invariably the ones without large mortgages and credit card debts. Daniela liked nice things. Clothes. Art. Theatre.

This was a month's work for a year's wages. Nilsen gave her two days to decide. She took two hours.

There is a knock. Glover slouches against the doorframe with his shirttail hanging out.

"Have I told you how much I hate this country?"

"Yes."

"We need to replace one of the computers. A power surge fried the hard drive."

"What about the surge protectors?"

"Toasted."

"Did we lose anything?"

"No."

Daniela motions him to her desk. "Have you ever heard of Jawad Stadium?"

"Nope."

"It was rebuilt. The work was finished two years ago." She points to the list of numbers on the black screen. New drainage. Covered stands. Changing rooms. Seating for forty-five thousand. Turf imported from Sweden."

"Duplicate payments," says Glover.

"Nearly forty-two million dollars."

"Who was the contractor?"

"Bellwether Construction. Bahamas registered. It subcontracted the work to various Iraqi companies."

"What do you want to do?"

"Put a call in to the US Embassy. Find out which of the Provisional Reconstruction Teams approved the rebuild."

"I thought we weren't supposed to go back any further than May twentieth 2006."

"The dates aren't clear on this one."

Glover gives her a youthful grin, knowing she's overstepping her authority.

"You want me to mention this to Jennings?"

"Not just yet."

Jennings is the State Department's "man on the ground" who

has been complaining about the audit since day one. He calls Daniela regularly, offering to answer her questions and reminding her that "this is a war zone" and to "ignore the random," whatever that means. He also seems to be laboring under the misapprehension that she works for the US and not the UN.

Glover pauses at the door.

"Hey, your friend called."

"What friend?"

"He left his name."

There is a pause. "Presumably you wrote it down."

"It was Italian sounding."

"Luca?"

"That may have been it. He said he'd call back."

"Did he leave a number?"

"No."

He disappears down the corridor and she can hear his Converse trainers squeaking on the tiles like blind kittens.

20

LONDON

The small attic room has a sloping ceiling, a window and a skylight. It reminds Holly of her last foster home, where she had slept on a bed between steamer trunks full of old paintings and boxes of self-help books. The house is gone now. She burnt it down. The flames were fifty feet high. Old books and oil paints are good fuel. Holly had stood on the far side of the road and watched the great arcs of water being poured on the burning house, marveling at how the moisture evaporated in the heat, creating clouds of steam.

Some people put out fires, other people start them and the rest watch blissfully from the perimeter with flames dancing in their eyes. That's the power of the match. Struck against the side of a box, balanced between two fingers, given the right fuel, it can raze a house or fell a forest. Rome burned. So did Dresden. Holly's world burned that night.

She was sent to a psych ward and then to a children's home where she spent two years. When she turned eighteen she no longer had to answer to judges and social workers. She was free, but freedom didn't come with a safety net. That's why Zac was so important. Darling Zac.

Holly grips the edge of the mattress and feels her throat begin to close. Maybe this is what grief feels like. Suffocating. Paralyzing.

If Zac were here, he would tell her to cup her hands over her mouth and breathe deeply. Count slowly. Relax. After a time the anxiety passes. She pushes back the bedclothes and begins searching through the wardrobe, choosing clothes: jeans, a plaid shirt, a scarf, a leather satchel...

Ruiz is downstairs, sitting at the kitchen table reading a newspaper.

"You found some clothes."

Holly nods. "Is it OK if I take this?" She holds up the satchel.

"Sure. You want breakfast? There is cereal, bread, eggs, bacon..."

"I don't eat bacon."

"Eggs then?"

She doesn't answer.

Sitting opposite him, she stares at the back of his newspaper without reading the words. He pours tea and spoons sugar. Stirs. The spoon sounds loud against the rim of the cup. Without warning, Holly begins to speak.

"Were you really a copper?"

"Yes."

"Why'd you give it up?"

"It gave me up."

"You got fired?"

"I got retired."

Holly has tied her hair up in a scarf, which makes her look like a 1940s aircraft worker.

"Why are you being so nice to me?"

"Do I need a reason?"

"Well it doesn't happen very often. And people who are nice to me usually end up leaving or dying."

"Who else has died?"

"My brother…my parents."

"How old were you?"

"Seven."

"What happened to them?"

Holly shakes her head and changes direction. "I knew a guy at school, Scott Kernohan. He got hit by a train." She changes direction again. "How did your wife die?"

"Cancer."

"Did you remarry?"

"Twice."

Holly looks at a framed montage of family photographs on the wall beside the fridge. Snapshots of weddings, dinners, holidays, children's concerts, birthday celebrations, anniversaries.

"When is your daughter getting married?"

"On Saturday."

"I saw the invitation."

"When you were robbing me?"

Holly lets the comment slide. "Do you like the guy she's marrying?"

"Sure."

She smiles wryly.

"What's that look for?"

"You're lying." She points to a photograph on the wall. "Is that him?"

"No, that's my son Michael."

"He's cute."

"He's in Barbados."

"But he's coming home for the wedding, right?"

"We hope so."

Holly loses interest and begins opening cupboards. Ruiz can't concentrate on his newspaper because he wants to watch her. She opens a box of cereal and eats with her hand.

"I have bowls."

"It's OK."

He tries to read, but can feel her eyes upon him. Silence until he can stand it no more. He folds the newspaper. "Why do you rob people?"

"To pay the rent."

"You couldn't find another way?"

"I'm sure you're going to give me a list."

"Whoever killed Zac was looking for something."

"You don't know that."

Holly takes another handful of cereal.

"Who did you rob?"

"Rich horny guys, businessmen, suits, married, middle-aged."

"How many?"

"Nine, maybe ten," she says defensively. "We didn't do it all the time—just when we needed the rent. Zac wasn't getting his army pension. They lost his paperwork."

"I need names and addresses of everyone you robbed."

"Oh, yeah, I kept them on speed dial."

Sarcasm scratches her pretty face.

"What did you take?"

"Phones, cameras, computers, jewelry—stuff we could carry."

"What did you do with it?"

"Fenced it."

"Who with?"

Holly hesitates. "I'm not a grass."

"I just want to talk to him."

"That's another lie."

"What is it with you? You keep calling people liars."

"I can tell."

"Sure."

"It's true." Holly is staring into her mug as if reading the dregs. Tired. Wan. Resigned to being disbelieved. Ruiz thinks of his mother. Before her mind was scattered by dementia, Daj would often talk of people having "gifts" or a "third eye," seeing things that other people don't. A gypsy gift and a gypsy curse have little to differentiate them.

"Test me," says Holly.

"How?"

"Tell me something true or false. Anything."

"I'm not playing games."

"OK, don't do it." Holly shrugs and pushes back her chair.

Ruiz reaches into his pocket and closes his fist.

"OK, what's in my hand?"

"I don't know."

"I have a coin. Do you know which one?"

"No."

"It's a fifty-pence piece."

"No it's not."

"Why do you say that?"

"Because you're lying."

"What if I told you it was twenty pence?"

"You'd be a liar."

"What about a pound?"

"Yes."

"You sure?"

"I'm sure."

Ruiz uncurls his fingers. The pound coin lies flat in his palm.

"Lucky guess."

"If you say so."

She's challenging him. Ruiz knows he should let the subject go, but her cockiness irritates him.

"Let's do it again."

"Only if we play for money. I get a pound for every time I'm right."

"OK."

Ruiz takes a moment to plan his tactics.

"I'm going to tell you five things. Tell me which ones are true."

"That's five pounds."

Holly sits opposite him, looking at his face.

"I was once arrested on suspicion of murder."

"Wow, that's a bummer."

"You think it's true?"

"Yes."

"My middle name is William?"

"No."

"My middle name is Yanko?"

"What sort of name is that?"

"Is it true?"

"Yes."

"I have a brother but he doesn't live in London."

She hesitates. "That's two facts."

"So what?"

"He doesn't live in London."

"Are you saying I don't have a brother?"

"No, but there's something wrong..." Holly taps the table with her finger, thinking of the possibilities. "Is he alive?"

Ruiz's heart seems to lurch sideways in his chest. How could she possibly know that?

"This is ridiculous. I don't want to play anymore."

She holds out her hand. "I want my five pounds."

How can she...it's impossible...is he *that* transparent? Then he remembers that Holly has been in his house. She looked through his things. There are photo albums upstairs, marriage and birth certificates, pictures of Claire and Michael, Laura's letters...

"You really are a piece of work," he says, glaring at her, pushing up from the table.

Holly cringes as he passes, waiting for the blow to fall. The front door slams.

She has glimpsed the monster. There's one inside every man.

21

BAGHDAD

Luca has a long wait at the checkpoint into the International Zone. A soldier wearing reflective sunglasses examines his papers, while another walks around the Skoda and seems to be counting the bullet holes.

"You were lucky," he says.

"That's exactly what I thought at the time," replies the journalist. "I was dodging those bullets and thinking, How lucky am I?"

The sarcasm is lost on the guards, who are mostly Latinos or Nepalese working for private security companies.

The boom gate rises and Luca enters a different world—four square miles of air-conditioned, fully supplied comfort in the middle of a bombed city. There are juice bars, ice-cream parlors, beauty shops, cafeterias, clothing stores, swimming pools, gyms, a Pizza Hut, a Subway and a giant PX store.

Iraq took control of the zone in 2009 but little has changed in the fortified compound. The only difference is that now it's home to dozens of Iraqi politicians bickering with one another, oblivious to what's happening on the other side of the wire. They don't have to queue for petrol or worry about roadblocks, or suicide bombers or sniper attacks. They don't live in the same fear, which is the dangerous disconnect that skews all decision-making in the new Iraq.

Luca drives to the eastern edge of the zone and stops outside a gated compound protected by ten-foot-high electric fences, topped with razor wire. Inside, baking in the heat, are dozens of gleaming SUVs parked in rows.

He sounds the horn. Jimmy Dessai looks up from a deconstructed truck engine. Six foot plus, overweight, with a fringe of greasy black hair, Jimmy has a wide arse that causes him to waddle when he walks. Every time he sees Luca his face lights up like he's surprised that the journalist is still alive. Then he immediately starts working the angles, quizzing Luca on what he needs and what he'd pay to get. Jimmy is a fixer, a King Rat, a man who can source things that are hard to find.

He came to Iraq with the US Army Motor Pool, but later resigned his commission and opened up his own transport business. Now he's the Hertz, Avis and Budget of Baghdad, all rolled into one.

He glimpses the Skoda and walks around it slowly. Impressed.

"What happened?"

"We got shot at."

"No shit!"

Luca glances into the lot. "I need another set of wheels."

"I got nothing to spare."

"What about them?" He points to the SUVs.

"They cost two grand a day."

"I'm a freelance journalist."

"And I'm a businessman."

Jimmy takes him to the office where Johnny Cash is singing "Ring of Fire" from an iPod speaker and a dog is sleeping beneath his desk. Pitted with scars and eczema, the animal reacts to every visitor as though expecting a boot.

"You want a drink, Scoop?"

"No thanks."

Jimmy hammers a soft drink machine in the corner and a can drops into the tray. The dog jumps and then slinks into a corner, looking at him with rheumy, half-closed eyes.

Vehicles aren't Jimmy's only business. He also provides armed bodyguards and drivers. Armor plating is extra. The full package comes in at four thousand dollars a day, but he still bleats that insurance is killing him.

His two regular mechanics are Iraqis, half his size. Brothers. Jimmy calls them sand niggers, camel jockeys and ragheads, but the mechanics seem totally unfazed.

"You can still drive the Skoda," he suggests.

"It's rather conspicuous."

"I could swap a few door panels."

"It's leaking oil."

"Might need a new engine."

"How much will that cost?"

"Seven grand."

"Three."

"You got to be kidding. Six."

"We're mates."

"Mates are going to send me broke."

"Make it five and we're done."

They shake hands. "That's how to do a deal," says Jimmy. "These camel jockeys want to serve you tea and fondle their worry beads, telling you how poor they are and how you're stealing food from their children's mouths."

A helicopter thumps the air overhead. Luca has to wait for the noise to pass.

"I have a question about trucking."

"Stick to journalism."

"If someone had a large amount of cash they wanted to smuggle out of Iraq, where would they take it?"

"So we're talking hypothetically?"

"Of course."

Jimmy crushes the can and sends it arcing over Luca's head where it rattles into a bin. "Take your pick — Turkey, Jordan, Syria, Saudi, maybe not Iran — they're all within reach and porous as hell. I've never met a border guard who couldn't be bought."

"What about the Syrian border, by way of Mosul?"

"That's a pretty busy crossing. On any given day maybe a thousand trucks go through carrying everything from sheep to shit-rolls."

"Who are the drivers?"

"TCN's mostly." Third Country Nationals, the bottom of the food chain. Pakistanis, Indians, Filipinos, Afghans, Sri Lankans... most of them working for less than ten dollars a day. "It's a rat run."

"Meaning?"

"Some of them are running passengers, six at a time in SUVs, charging about twenty bucks per person. They take people out and come back with boxes of stuff that's hard to get in Iraq—laundry powder, dishwashing liquid, that kind of thing.

"Others are still smuggling oil. They take old station wagons and turn them into fuel tankers carrying five hundred liters of diesel. Mad fuckers."

"Why do you say that?"

"The TCNS travel without protection, unlike the military convoys. One stray bullet or errant spark and boom, they're decorating the desert with body parts."

"If I wanted to talk to some of these drivers, where would I go?"

"The trucking camps," says Jimmy. "That's where they live when they're not driving. They get food and water; live behind barbed wire; compare bullet holes."

Luca asks Jimmy if he can make a few enquiries—ask about drivers who might be prepared to make a border run carrying cash.

"And if I find someone?"

"Let me know."

Luca hitches a ride to the Republican Palace, which has been renamed the Freedom Building. Within the walls it is like a small city with tree-lined boulevards, shops and offices—a small corner of Iraq that will be forever American.

After changing some money, he gets a haircut. Then he calls Daniela Garner. This time she picks up.

"It's me," he says.

"Hello."

"About last night—"

"I've never done that before."

"No you haven't, I would have remembered."

"It was a random act."

"Of kindness?"

"Of lust."

"Which you now regret?"

"I always regret things. It's my automatic response to almost every decision I make."

"You've come to the right place. This is a country full of regrets."

Silence. He should say something.

"Well, I don't regret a single moment of it. I was sort of hoping it might happen again some time…in the future…which could mean tonight."

"*That* soon?"

"Strike while the iron is hot."

"Is it that hard."

"Like a crowbar."

"Now you're just boasting."

She feels her face flush and blood rush to other places.

"I have a question and it's not about the thing you do with your pelvic floor muscles."

"The thing?"

"Yes."

"What's your question?"

"You remember the story I was following up."

"The bank robberies."

"There was another one a couple of days ago in the financial district of Baghdad. Seven people are dead including six bank guards. They took US dollars in aluminum boxes, larger than briefcases."

"How many cases?"

"At least sixteen."

"You're sure?"

"Yes."

"Cases like that can hold up to four million US dollars each, depending on the denominations."

There is a pause. Both of them have done the calculation.

"No bank branch should hold that sort of cash. There's no need," she says.

"Iraq is still a cash economy."

"Even so."

"It was the eighteenth bank robbery this year."

"You're going to ask me to do something."

"The cash must have been provided by the Central Bank. There must be a record of the transfers."

"I don't know if I can help," says Daniela, typing as she speaks. She calls up information on cash deliveries to banks. The list runs to six pages. She narrows the search by including only US dollar deliveries.

"What were the dates of the robberies?"

"I can text them to you."

"No promises."

"I understand. I still want to see you later."

"You want my body."

"We could eat first . . . or not."

She laughs. "You know that second dates are trickier."

"How so?"

"Traditionally, they're about getting to know each other better. You might discover I'm a selfish, controlling, overbearing and difficult woman."

"Are you?"

"Yes. And I think you've seen enough of me already."

"There are places I haven't seen yet."

"Now you're just being dirty."

22

LONDON

Ruiz walks alongside the river, smelling the briny stink of low tide. Fat-bellied boats, canted drunkenly to starboard, are stuck fast in the mud. When he first came down to London from Lancashire he was posted with the Thames River Police. On average they pulled two bodies a week from the river, mostly suicides. Rivers seem to draw people to them, cleansing souls, christening them, or dragging them to the bottom.

Holly Knight fascinates and appalls him. Full of fuck-you apathy and repressed anger, she lies almost compulsively yet recognizes when people are deceiving her. An actress. Intense. Volatile. Disconcerting. She trusts nobody and treats every question like it's wired to go off.

Taking out his mobile, he searches for a familiar name in the directory. Calls. Waits. Joe O'Loughlin answers.

"Hey, Professor, how does a cow know it's not a butterfly dreaming of being a cow?"

"It can't fly."

"Makes sense."

The professor is a clinical psychologist who spends too much time in other people's heads. He looks exactly like you'd expect an academic to look — slightly disheveled, unkempt, undernourished — only he has Parkinson's which means he shakes it like Shakira when he's not medicated.

Ruiz met him eight years ago, when he was investigating the murder of a young woman in London, one of O'Loughlin's former patients. The professor was a prime suspect until he proved that another patient was setting him up. That's what happens when you deal with psychopaths and sociopaths; it's like trying to hand-feed sharks.

"How are things?"

"Good."

"The girls?"

"Fine."

"Julianne?"

"We're talking."

A posse of thin androgynous cyclists sweeps past him in a blur of latex and brightly colored helmets.

"Claire is getting married at the weekend."

"Congratulations."

"You want to come to the wedding?"

"Why?"

"I can bring someone."

"Don't you want to bring a date?"

"I'm too old to bring dates."

"What's the real reason?"

"There's someone I want you to meet. She's nineteen. Damaged. Angry. Her boyfriend was killed two nights ago but she won't talk to the police. Doesn't trust them."

"What's her name?"

"Holly Knight. D.O.B. twelfth December 1992. You still got any contacts in the DHSS?"

"One or two. Where is she now?"

"Staying with me. I'll explain when you get here."

"You're assuming I'll come."

"Of course."

The conversation hits an air pocket and lurches into silence. The professor is an expert at reading the pauses. "Something else on your mind?"

"She says she can tell when people are lying."

"Why does that bother you?"

"I think maybe she can."

Ruiz walks back to his Merc and pauses for a moment, considering how he got into this. The stolen jewelry. Holly said she dropped the hair-comb when she was attacked in the flat. Maybe it's still there.

Crossing the river, he drives east through streets that are dotted with "For Sale" and "To Let" signs. People selling up, selling out, downsizing, belt-tightening, admitting defeat. The atmosphere in London has changed in the past two years. People are postponing retirement, driving older cars, eating out less; they're less conspicuous in their spending, less confident in the future. The city is circumspect rather than diminished.

Ruiz parks the Merc and squints through the windscreen at the Hogarth Estate. It looks different in daylight. Dirtier. Poorer. Some balconies are being used to dry clothes, others to store broken furniture.

Ruiz crosses the road and climbs the stairs to Holly's flat. Blue-and-white crime-scene tape is threaded in a zigzag pattern across a makeshift wooden door, bolted shut. Rocking back six inches, he shoulders it open.

Crossing the threshold, he eases the door shut and steps further into the flat. The broken furniture, shredded pillows and emptied drawers are just as before, although now there is fingerprint powder on every smooth surface. SOCO have dusted, hoovered, scraped and swabbed.

The place has a haunted quality that comes after death. It's like seeing the twisted shell of a car being hauled on to a tow-truck and wondering if anyone survived or was badly injured.

Ruiz goes into the bedroom, opens a wardrobe and collects some of Holly's clothes. Jeans. Blouses. Knickers. What else might she need? In the bathroom he fills a make-up bag with small jars, lipsticks, eyeliner and a toothbrush. Everything fits in two plastic shopping bags. He sets them down near the splintered front door and goes through the flat again, searching systematically, looking for letters, bills, bank statements, photographs, anything that might give him a sense of Holly and Zac.

There is a postcard from Ireland and a bundle of letters from Afghanistan in military-issued envelopes. The only picture of them is a shot taken on a ferry during a wild crossing to somewhere. They're laughing and holding each other as the swell pitches them backwards and forwards across the deck.

Standing in the living room, Ruiz tries to recreate the confrontation as Holly had described it. He pictures bodies in motion. She hit the wall. Scrambled up. Used the saucepan. Dropped it.

Beneath a side table he spies the shoulder bag that Holly was carrying when she left the audition and visited the jewelers in Hatton Garden. The contents have spilled. The hair-comb is half hidden by lipstick tubes, tissues and a half packet of mints. He lifts it carefully.

Scared it might break. Then he wraps it in tissue paper and places it inside a small wooden box, which he puts in his pocket.

Picking up the plastic bags, he steps outside and pulls the door shut, pushing the bolt across and reattaching the police tape. Then he knocks on neighboring flats. After a long wait a door opens.

"I'm not buying anything," says a pale man with red hair and doleful eyes.

"That's good," replies Ruiz. "Were you home the night before last?"

"I already told the police everything."

"What did you tell them?"

The neighbor looks at him nervously. "Nothing!"

Ruiz stands motionless, letting the silence work its magic. The neighbor fidgets. Scratches. Shuffles his feet.

"I did see this one guy run down the stairs. He almost knocked me over."

"What did he look like?"

"I only saw him for a second."

"What color?"

"I don't know. Muddy."

"What's that mean?"

"Foreign looking. I think maybe you should leave this guy alone."

"Why's that?"

The neighbor hesitates, still scratching his crotch. "He had a look, you know, like he came into the world with nothing except a name."

"Dangerous?"

"Hungry for something."

23

BAGHDAD

Daniela laces her fingers and stretches her arms above her head. She's tired—her own fault—too much sex and too little sleep. She has laid out dozens of documents on her desk, placing a shoe or a lamp or a glass on them because the ceiling fan is stirring the air.

Alfred Nilsen has come back to her. The Pentagon won't approve her request for information regarding Bellwether Construction. Instead she has been given a brief corporate profile in which Bellwether claims to employ 25,000 Iraqis on 315 different construction projects.

The work on Jawad Stadium was subcontracted to a dozen different Iraqi companies, each linked to a Syrian-based corporation called Alain al Jaria, which in Arabic means "Ever-Flowing Spring."

Ironic, thinks Daniela, as she looks for an office address in Baghdad but can't find one.

Glover appears at her door. He's wearing a baseball cap with a picture of a camel riding a surfboard.

"Can you tell Shaun to stop humming?"

"Humming?"

"He hums this one song. It's driving me crazy."

"What are you—six years old?"

Glover looks aggrieved. Pouts. Tilts his head. "You look different today."

"In what way?"

"Happier."

Daniela can feel blood warming her cheeks. She changes the subject. "What did you want?"

"I found something you might want to see."

As she follows him down the corridor, Glover keeps looking over his shoulder, uncomfortable about letting a woman walk behind him. The IT room has a bank of computers and shelves stacked with software manuals and ring binders.

Shaun is outside the door listening to an iPod and humming loudly. Daniela pulls an earphone from his ear. "Stop teasing the puppy."

He grins at her and then at Glover, who flips him the bird, having to hold down some of his fingers.

Glover speaks. "You wanted to know about Jawad Stadium. During the invasion it became a shelter for Iraqi families and then a compound for the US Army Motor Pool.

"It's one of the bigger football venues in the city. The Iraq Football Federation applied for the rebuild. The contract was awarded in 2005 to Bellwether."

"Did you get a copy of the contract?"

"Take a look."

She glances at the screen. Someone has scanned the paperwork but not before meticulously using a thick-tipped marker to black out details including names, dates, addresses, phone numbers and the signees. The file had been stamped "classified" with a Pentagon seal.

"So this is it?" asks Daniela.

"I managed to pull up a company address. It's a post office box in the Bahamas."

Glover adds, "There is a separate interim report from 2007. There were delays with some of the work. The wrong seats were delivered. The turf was coming from Sweden and got stuck at the border for three weeks. Died."

Daniela looks again at the anomalies. These problems could explain some of the duplicate payments. Each amount is under $200,000. This meant that a PRT commander could approve the payments without going to the next stage of review.

"Bellwether subcontracted the work to Alain al Jaria, a shelf company based in Syria. There must be local paperwork."

"It's probably in Arabic," says Glover.

"Get it translated."

Daniela knows she is overstepping her remit. Nilsen had been very clear that she should not go further back than May 2006, but this isn't natural wastage or an oversight. Most of all she's annoyed by the blacked-out sentences. She can picture an entire department of faceless public servants in the bowels of the Pentagon, hunched over desks, wielding black marker pens. Too lazy to actually read documents and make informed decisions, they label everything as "classified" and "top secret," blanking out every name, address and number.

She runs her finger over the hidden text before turning away.

"I'm going out for a little while."

"Where?"

"An excursion."

Jawad Stadium is in a safer area of the city, but Shaun and Edge still aren't happy. The journey will take them through Baathist strongholds, including al-Haifa Street, once known as "sniper alley."

They spend twenty minutes plotting a route and then briefing a security team. Edge will be in charge. Two vehicles. Four bodyguards. Shaun will stay behind with Glover and the rest of the security team.

Daniela follows the instructions without complaint. She'd prefer to be with Shaun, but holds her tongue. The cars arrive. Two Ford Explorers. Armored. Fully armed. She's escorted down the steps by Edge and Klosters, his second in command.

The doors shut and the cars are moving, weaving between barricades and joining the main road heading east along the river. The vehicles rarely pause, taking detours rather than risk getting stuck at bottlenecks or at checkpoints. Some of the side roads are dusty tracks between houses and apartment blocks.

The stadium is visible from half a mile away. First the lighting towers, then the covered stands that look like a series of arches, giving the impression of a sporting cathedral. Built in the 1960s, the stadium was a gift to the Iraqi government from a rich oil family. In the 1980s Saddam told architects he wanted it redesigned as a possible Olympic venue.

They reach the main gate. A grizzled Iraqi with a woolen hat and yellowing teeth emerges from a prefabricated hut. Behind him, the parking lot is littered with debris, broken concrete, discarded tires, drums and plastic bags. Weeds are growing through cracks in the tarmac and a broken water pipe has created a lake of oily black water.

Edge offers the caretaker a dinar note. He pockets the money like a conjurer and leans on the counterbalance, raising the boom gate. As the cars roll past he salutes Daniela, lifting his right arm and revealing a stump where his fingers used to be.

They park in the shade of the southern stand and climb a filthy stairwell to the top tier. Emerging on to a concrete ramp, there are banks of seats on each side and tiers that spread around the stadium. The playing surface is a muddy field, churned up by tank tracks and truck tires. The bleachers are pockmarked by bullet holes and riddled with cavities where the seats have been torn out, burned or broken. One of the light towers has crumpled over the players' entrances.

Edge looks at Daniela.

"Is this what you expected?"

"No."

She takes a small digital camera from her shoulder bag and begins taking photographs. Edge lights up a cigarette and watches her move between seats to get better angles.

"Why are you so interested?" he calls out from behind her.

"Does this stadium look rebuilt to you?"

Edge blows out a stream of smoke. "Iraqis don't go in so much for finishing things."

"It was an American company."

He shrugs. "Maybe they're running behind schedule."

"Work was supposed to have finished two years ago."

Edge spits into a puddle. "Well, I'm glad someone is making money."

Daniela glances at him with undisguised loathing.

"Hey, lady, don't go giving me that look. Let me tell you another story. An army buddy of mine got a bullet in his back, lodged in his spine. Paralyzed from the waist down. They flew him back on a C141 to Andrews, lying on a stretcher, surrounded by amputees and invalids and guys who were pissing, puking and dying. Even the healthy ones were fucked. Stateside they spent a week getting debriefed. Then their CO told them to go home, kiss their girl-friend and walk the dog. Walk the fucking dog—do you believe that?"

"They signed up to fight."

"Most of them couldn't piss straight with a hard-on. They were recruited straight out of school from Buttfuck, Idaho, where the only jobs were working in the local chicken factory. So these kids get to thinking, if they join the army, they get to go on this big adventure overseas and shoot at shit, which has got to be better than pulling chicken guts out of a carcass for the rest of their sorry fucking lives."

Edge spits again. Wipes his lips.

"I was one of them. I did more than a hundred patrols in this shithole country. I rode on tanks and flew in choppers and got rocked by roadside bombs. I lifted bodies on to trucks and built boxes to send them home. Now I'm here to make money. I'm here to kill or be killed, but I'm not going home poor. I'm going to suckle on the nipple until the milk runs dry."

Daniela lowers her gaze, still appalled by his uncouthness, but with a better understanding of his motives.

A distant explosion thumps the air, rattling the metal pipes and roofing iron. It's followed by an exchange of gunfire that lasts almost five minutes, punctuated by the wail of sirens. Ambulances. Fire engines.

They listen in silence, picturing the chaos.

Edge slings his weapon across his chest.

"Time to go."

24

LONDON

A note flutters beneath the wiper blades of the Mercedes. Not a parking ticket. The doors are unlocked. Ruiz glances inside and sees a large orange envelope on the passenger seat.

Walking slowly around the car, he crouches to peer beneath the chassis, checking the wheel arches and drive shaft. Four years in Northern Ireland taught him to be careful. Standing upright, he studies the street. Opposite there is a school with an asphalt playground. Boys kick a ball between painted posts on a brick wall and girls sit in groups on the benches. A dark blue Audi is parked on the corner. Engine running. Ruiz is no expert on cars. He doesn't watch *Top Gear* because Jeremy Clarkson is further right than Donald Rumsfeld and only half as funny.

The car is too bright and shiny and new. Out of place. Stepping on to the road, Ruiz walks towards it, but the Audi begins rolling further away from him. As he speeds up, so does the car. Cutting a corner, he tries to close the gap. Twenty feet away, the Audi accelerates. Gone.

He chastises himself. Dogs chase cars. His knees are hurting, a dull thudding pain, muscle memory from the rugby field, old injuries. Holly's clothes have spilled from the plastic bags he dropped. He gathers them together and tosses them on to the back seat. Then he pulls the note from beneath the wiper blade; a single page. Handwritten.

Dear Mr. Ruiz,
    We think this was stolen from you recently. You should have it back. This should pay for your daughter's wedding and make up for any losses. It's an intelligent alternative to

poking your nose into somebody else's business. We think you have something of ours. If you return it promptly you can double your reward.

The envelope contains two neat bundles of banknotes: four, maybe five thousand pounds. It's not the money that worries him. It's the fact that these people know about Claire and the wedding. It's less a bribe than a warning.

Flipping open his mobile, he dials the number at the bottom of the note.

"Nice of you to call," says a voice. American. Educated.

"Have we met?"

"I know you by reputation."

"You left me a package."

"Money owed."

"I don't think so."

"It can be a down-payment for services rendered."

Ruiz turns full circle, surveying the street. Something tells him he's still being watched.

"Pardon me for saying this, but you're making as much sense as a kosher pork chop."

The American chuckles. The guy won't be laughing when he gets bounced off a few walls, thinks Ruiz. He has memorized the number plate of the Audi. He's going to find him and they'll talk properly, face to fist.

"The girl has the key."

"What key?"

"I would like to talk to her personally."

"My person will call your person. We'll do lunch."

"You're not taking me seriously, Mr. Ruiz."

"Did you kill Zac Osborne?"

The question warrants a pause. "We're not animals, Mr. Ruiz. Your young lady friend is in danger. I can protect her."

"That's very gallant of you. The price is twenty-five thousand."

"That's more expensive than I expected."

"Inflation."

"I'm sure we can agree on a price when we meet. I'll give you an address. You can bring the girl."

Ruiz can hear a barge horn sounding in the background. He's heard it before on the river, closer to home. The American is keeping Ruiz on the phone. Trying to drag out the conversation. The question is why?

"Call me when you have the money," says Ruiz, hanging up.

Holly is watching television, *Wife Swap USA*. It's about a woman who raises pigs in Arkansas swapping with a belly-dancing Bohemian who has the fashion sense of Tinkerbell.

The phone rings. She presses the TV mute button and waits for the answering machine to pick it up. Ruiz's voice: "... *leave a message after the tone*..."

The beep.

"Get out now, Holly! Not the front door. The back. Over the fence. Mrs. McAllister lives in the house behind. Tell her you know me. Don't frighten her. Go now. They're coming for you."

Holly doesn't ask questions. She's up, grabbing the leather satchel, her shoes, she can't find her coat... it must be upstairs. She turns to the front door. A shadow darkens the frosted glass. Another at the window, crouching but not crouching low enough.

She runs to the kitchen and flings open the back door, jumps down the low stairs and sprints across the garden. Behind her comes the sound of glass breaking.

Hurry, says her inner voice, fearful and strangled. Throwing the satchel over the fence, she scrambles up and over. Her jeans catch on a climbing rose. She falls backwards, bracing herself. Soft earth. A dog barking. They'll know where she's gone.

On her feet, she turns and glimpses a figure in the second-floor window. Looking at her. Dressed in black. The dog is still barking. Small and white, it bounces behind the patio doors. Holly hammers on the glass. An old lady appears with blue-rinsed hair. Overweight. Shuffling on a walking frame.

"I'm a friend of Vincent's," she calls. "Somebody has broken into his house. Help me!"

Mrs. McAllister has to find the key. She's flustered. Forgetful. Her dog won't shut up. The man has gone from the window.

Key found, the glass slides open. Mrs. McAllister doesn't step back quickly enough and Holly almost knocks her over. She apologizes and runs through the house to the front door.

Mrs. McAllister is a hoarder. The house is full of boxes, crates and excess furniture. Holly had a grandmother who was like that. Kept every margarine container, every empty jar, every magazine and brochure.

"Call the police. Don't open the door."

"Where are you going?"

"I can't stay."

Holly pauses in the shelter of the doorway. Looks out. Left or right? The inner voice tells her to get her bearings, but there isn't time. A car swings into the street, dark blue, heavily tinted windows, travelling at speed. Decision made. She turns and runs, her bag bouncing against her spine. A footpath appears, too narrow for a car. It leads to the river.

Putting her head down, she pushes hard, hoping that nobody appears at the far end. Car doors slam behind her. Who are these people? Not the police. No warnings. Unmarked cars. She doesn't want to go through this again. Too many bad things already, the bloody mess of her childhood, Albie, her mother, her father, now Zac—why can't they leave her alone?

Emerging from the path, she crosses Rainville Road, ignoring a "don't walk" sign. A car brakes hard. Sounds the horn. Holly slips and falls. Grazes her knee. Scrambles up.

Turns right into Crabtree Lane, then left, her breath rasping in her throat. Adam Walk is ahead of her, leading to the river. She swings on one of the metal poles to change direction.

In front of her, two women pushing prams, a toddler on a

tricycle, a man reading a newspaper on a long bench; so normal. Something moves from behind the screen of foliage to her left, dressed in black, an object in his hand.

She kicks harder, dodging through the prams, hearing a cry of alarm from one of the mothers. The man on the bench seat has dropped his paper and found his feet, set himself to catch her. Confident. She has nowhere to go.

Holly swings her bag. It's heavy. A half brick will do that. Zac's idea. Always have a weapon. She has all the momentum. The bag hits him in the side of the head and he goes down, the newspaper fluttering across the concrete like an injured swan.

It's low tide, the muddy bank exposed, gulls fighting over scraps. Holly is growing tired. Lactic acid building in her muscles, slowing her down. Ahead she sees a small wooden boat moving slowly. Two fishermen.

The jetty is ten feet below the path, supported by pylons buried deep in the mud. She doesn't wait. Slinging the satchel around her neck, she goes over the side, face to the wall, holding on to the edge and then dropping, falling, landing hard. Her knees buckle. Bones jar. She's up, running along the pier, waving her arms at the fishermen.

One of them nudges the other. Points. A brief discussion and he pulls on the tiller. The boat swings towards her, bouncing on the swell. Holly turns. She sees the silhouettes of three men on the path above the jetty. One of them scrambles over. The others grip his arms and let him down.

The boat is coming in straight, spinning at the last moment, the engine in neutral. The man at the tiller has a battered cloth cap and a khaki vest. He's about to speak. Holly jumps, clattering into the wooden shell, landing amid tackle boxes and fishing rods. The boat lurches. The propeller leaves the water and whines.

The other fisherman catches Holly before she goes over the side, pulls her back, and she collapses between his knees. Her satchel swings loose. She tries to catch it but it lands in the water; floats for a moment before the brick takes it under.

The man on the jetty is twenty yards away. His forearm bent. A gun held upright.

Holly pleads, "Help me, please!"

So many questions, too little time. The first fisherman opens the throttle. It responds with a high-pitched roar, slow at first, picking up speed. The bow rises. The jetty sways in the wake.

Fifty yards...seventy...ninety...

Away.

Safe.

25

BAGHDAD

Daniela can tell something is wrong long before they arrive. Black smoke rises above the rooftops like a genie being released from a bottle. Five hundred yards from the Finance Ministry and the traffic is at a standstill. Sirens are competing to destroy the silence. Police. Fire engines. Ambulances.

The first blast destroyed the concrete safety barrier to the right of the outer checkpoint. A second vehicle tried to drive through the hole but crashed into the crater. It didn't reach the Ministry, but the blast has shattered some of the windows on the northern side. Curtains are flapping from the gaping holes and torn scraps of paper swirl across the ground.

Edge is out of the car and running. Daniela can't keep up. She can only watch him.

Avoiding the first security cordon, he uses a fire engine as cover and follows two paramedics who are carrying a stretcher. There are bodies in the foyer. One of the security guards is lying across the counter with a bullet hole in his forehead. Another is beside the X-ray machine, having dragged his body across the marble floor leaving a red smear like a snail trail. The cleaner is face down beside his polishing machine, a pool of blood beneath his chest.

Edge leaps the metal barrier, ignoring the shouts of two policemen, who draw their guns. He shoulders them aside and reaches the stairwell, taking the stairs two at a time. Already he can see what happened. The scene is played out in his mind like moving pictures behind his eyelids: a film with a soundtrack of gunfire and screaming.

The car bombs were a decoy. The gunmen were already inside the cordon, men in Iraqi military uniforms. Two of them are lying dead in the basement corridor. Shaun's body is ahead of them. He had lunged for the door, but was a fraction of a second too late. The muzzle of the weapon came through the opening. The first bullets hit his Kevlar vest, rocking him backwards. They expected him to be dead, but Shaun shot both of them. As one of them fell he kept firing, spraying the wall with bullets and Shaun's brain matter.

The rest of the security team had barricaded the door to the IT room. That same door is now hanging off its hinges. The Hispanic girl—Edge can't recall her name—is lying with one leg twisted beneath her. A shard of wood is sticking from her left eye. Ventura...he remembers her name.

They must have had heavy weaponry—a mortar or maybe an RPG. The shell came through the door and exploded against the opposite wall, where it blew a gaping hole and took Anderson through it. His body is lying in the next room.

Otis is sitting against the desk, the last to die. The legs of the chair next to him have been sheared off. They shot high and low, the vest-free zones, aiming for the groin and neck. He double-killed before he went. He also had time to get a morphine shot from the medical kit and find a vein. No pain.

Otis was first Gulf War, big and black, from somewhere down south. Edge had never asked where. The south was a different America. Otis was a different American.

Glover is missing. He was the target. Daniela Garner was meant to be with him.

Shaun. Vanessa. Anderson. Otis. Weigh it, dice it, julienne it—

makes no difference—they were carved up and cooked. Outnumbered. Outgunned. How many of the shifty cocksuckers did it take?

Edge should feel like crying. Instead he feels like getting even. He wants to tear down the world until he finds them. Then he'll bury them under the rubble of whatever's left.

As the taxi turns into his street, Luca senses something is wrong. The checkpoint is deserted. Normally the guards would be playing cards or tossing coins against the wall.

He tells the driver to stop. Pays. Walks forward, crouching behind a blast barrier. There are three police cars parked in front of his apartment block. Two officers stand outside the vehicles in green uniforms with berets and sunglasses. They light cigarettes and lean on the Land Cruiser, heavy boots resting on the tarmac.

Police are often not police. Not real. Imposters in stolen uniforms. He glances to his right and left, considering his options.

Cutting through a pathway between buildings and then along an alley, he tries to get closer without being seen. The pistol pressed against his spine feels as though it's wrapped in barbed wire.

Creeping along the backs of houses, he cuts the distance. Faces become clearer. He recognizes one of them—the flunky who was with General al-Uzri at the burnt-out bank.

Decision time. Fight, flee or stay.

A policeman steps on to Luca's balcony. He glances over the railing and takes a moment to realize that the journalist is below him. He yells to his colleagues and guns are drawn. Luca steps from his hiding place. His eyes go to the open car door, darkness inside.

"You must come with us," says the senior officer.

"Why?"

"The Commander of Police wishes to speak with you."

"Did General al-Uzri give a reason?"

"He gives orders, not reasons."

Luca is listening to an internal dialogue. He should run. Let them shoot. Better to fight than surrender. Better to die on the street than in some stage-managed execution. He glances up at his apartment. The barrel of an Uzi is pointed at him, the hole gaping blackly.

"I have an American passport. I want to call the US Embassy."

The policeman gives a rumbling chuckle.

"Why do people like you criticize America until you're in trouble and then all of a sudden you become patriots?"

BOOK TWO

A lie which is half a truth is ever the blackest of lies.
ALFRED LORD TENNYSON

1

LONDON

For the past five days Elizabeth North has woken early and reached across the sheets to the space where her husband used to be. Each time her fingers have relayed the message and her eyes have stayed closed. Missing. Lost. Misplaced. She won't go any darker in her thoughts than this. Instead she picks up her mobile phone from the bedside table and checks it again.

North has never been away this long—not since Rowan was born, not since they married. Five days. No calls or notes or text messages. No warning.

He should be waking up next to her in his Jermyn Street pajamas with his messed up hair and his morning breath. The selfish bastard! Why isn't he here with his family?

Elizabeth swings her feet to the floor and pauses, perched on the edge of the mattress, caught between getting out of bed or curling up and crying. She cups her pregnancy in both hands. She has to pee. Claudia is pressing on her bladder.

It's a girl, according to the ultrasound. Both she and North had said they didn't care, but secretly they did. Elizabeth's grandmother was called Claudia, which was one of six possible names they considered until they began using Claudia all the time and it just sort of stuck.

Rowan had complained, of course. Four-year-old boys want baby brothers and don't understand why swaps aren't possible; a change of order just like when they get Friday night takeaway from the Bombay Palace on The Green and want extra poppadoms.

Now he's getting used to the idea. Yesterday morning he brought his trains into Elizabeth's bed because he wanted to show them to Claudia. He pushed them up and over Elizabeth's stomach, through the mountain pass of her breasts, making the sound effects.

"Don't move, Mummy."

"But it tickles."

Then he frowned. "I'm worried, Mummy."

"Why's that?"

"What if Claudia doesn't like me?"

"She's going to love you."

The baby's room is only half done. Elizabeth is supposed to be making new curtains but has only finished measuring the windows and buying the fabric. She started with great plans for creating the perfect little girl's room—an echo of her own childhood—but nothing ever turns out quite like she imagines. She's not a finisher, that's her problem.

Making her way to the bathroom, she sits on the toilet and stares at herself in the mirror, frowning. She hasn't gained much weight in her face and her extremities, but God has seen fit to give her a huge arse, balancing out her belly.

Downstairs she can hear Polina unloading the dishwasher and filling the kettle. Polina is the nanny and she comes from one of those "istan" countries that Elizabeth can never remember because they all sound so similar.

Rowan is downstairs too. He and Polina tend to have very earnest, grown-up discussions about trains and superheroes and aspects of the world that puzzle him. Why do his fingers go wrinkly in the bath? How does he know when to wake up? Why can't he remember being born? Who would win out of Batman and Spiderman? Important questions when you're four years old.

One day in the park he asked Elizabeth if he could go and kick a ball with some of the older boys. "Those boys look a bit rough," she told him and Rowan said, "If I can find a smooth one, can I play with him?"

She should write these things down. One day she'll forget them and she'll have lost a precious memory like a first word or a first smile.

Back in the bedroom she opens the curtains and watches the sun struggle up beyond the rooftops. It's a view that normally soothes Elizabeth—the grass, the trees, the slice of moon suspended above the spire of St. Mary's Church—but today she feels nothing but irritation and foreboding. What if something terrible has happened? North might be hurt. He could be lying in a ditch or unconscious in a hospital. He could have lost his memory or be in a coma.

Squeezing into her maternity trousers, Elizabeth brushes her hair, puts on lip balm and goes downstairs to confront another day. Polina has made Rowan a boiled egg and put it in a ceramic eggcup shaped like a train. His buttered toast soldiers are lined up on either side of the cup. He marches them along the spoon, dunking them in the soft yolk. When Elizabeth boils eggs they are either too runny or too hard. Polina has told her the timings but Elizabeth can never seem to get them right.

Kissing Rowan's head, she lingers with her nose in his hair, which smells of apple shampoo.

"Did Daddy come home?"

"Not yet."

"You said today."

"Maybe."

"Where is he?"

"Working."

"At the bank?"

"Yes."

Through the window she can see Polina hanging washing on the line. She's wearing tight jeans and a blouse that looks too small for her. Her straight short black hair in a pixie cut and narrow neck make her look like a Russian gymnast or a child who has run away to the circus.

Elizabeth inherited her from her sister-in-law, although she could never understand why Inga had been so insistent. Yes, she'd been looking for a new nanny, but wouldn't normally have chosen someone as pretty as Polina. It was something her mother had always told her—never hire pretty cleaners or nannies. Why put temptation in your husband's way?

There were plenty of women, including some of Elizabeth's own girlfriends, who would happily have slipped into North's bed if she let the sheets grow cold. These were the same women who complained about their own husband's sexual demands or their inattentiveness—getting either too much sex or not enough. That's why Elizabeth made a conscious effort in that department, even during her pregnancy when she was "fugly," as she called it. It was a maintenance thing: 1) Change batteries in the smoke alarms. 2) Check the air in the tires. 3) Have sex with North...

"Can I watch TV, Mummy?" asks Rowan.

"Have you finished your egg?"

"I only like the runny stuff."

"That's called the yolk."

Elizabeth lifts him down from the chair and turns on the TV in the lounge. Polina has come inside, her cheeks pink with the cold.

"Good morning," she says, "did you sleep well?" Her English sounds as if she is reading it from a phrase book.

"Yes, thank you."

"Can I get you breakfast?"

"I can sort myself out."

Polina begins clearing up Rowan's crumbs. Composting the eggshell. Wiping the table. Elizabeth puts two crumpets in the toaster and feels Claudia moving again. What sort of husband leaves his wife a month before their baby is due? That's not something North would do. He's a sticker, a keeper, one of the good guys.

For weeks he's been out-of-sorts, working late, leaving home early, stressed, secretive. She thought he might be having an affair. Then she discounted the possibility. Then she convinced herself. That was in the space of a few days. She hired a private detective. What a terrible wife! Faithless. Suspicious.

Twice she canceled her appointment, the guilt gnawing away inside her like a rat in a wicker cage. I'm being paranoid, she told herself. It's the pregnancy. The hormones. Then she changed her mind and called him again.

Elizabeth smothers the crumpets with honey. Polina has gone to make the beds. She's been spring-cleaning these past few days, clearing out the cupboards and drawers, airing old clothes and moving junk to the attic. Routines are important for everyone when a husband disappears.

Rowan has to be dressed. Polina will walk him across the park to his nursery school. Elizabeth has a doctor's appointment: her thirty-six-week check-up. Her life is about numbers. Eight months pregnant. Seven years married. Five days alone. She can picture the last time she saw North. He went to work at the normal time. Kissed her goodbye. She lingered with her lips pressed against his. She and Rowan were going up to the Lake District to spend the weekend with her best friend from university. They didn't come back until Sunday afternoon. She had tried to call North all day, but he wasn't answering. She caught a cab from Euston Station and found the house in darkness. Inside it looked like it had undergone a subtle alteration, as if someone had cleaned up after a party but hadn't managed to put things back precisely where they'd been. Her jewelry was missing. Her passport. Her spare credit card, the ugly gold watch she inherited from her Aunt Catherine...

Elizabeth kept trying to call North, sending him text messages and emails. Finally she phoned her father. Sitting on the edge of the bed, cupping her hand over the mouthpiece, she spoke in whispers so that Rowan wouldn't hear her.

The family swung into action, calling hospitals, clinics, homeless shelters and finally the police. Two young constables came the next day and took a statement about the robbery.

"You'll need this for insurance purposes," said the constable.

"What about my husband?"

"I don't think your policy covers him."

The officers laughed. It was a joke. Elizabeth stared numbly at them. By then her mind was full of terrible scenarios: North disturbing burglars or being abducted, or worse.

A large drop of honey has dripped on her blouse. Elizabeth looks at the stain and wants to cry. Hormones.

Rowan is standing at the kitchen door watching her.

"Is you all right, Mummy?"

"I'm fine."

"Why is you crying?"

"I'm having a sad day."

"When Daddy comes home you'll be happy."

"Yes, I will."

2

LONDON

Standing outside the police station in London Road, Elizabeth gazes at the three-storey red-brick building squeezed between a hairdressing salon and the head office of the *Richmond & Twickenham Times*. Be polite but firm, she tells herself. Don't be fobbed off.

Rowan is dressed in a Spiderman T-shirt and mask. The eyeholes are slightly too wide for his head, which means that only one eye is visible at any given time. He flicks his "web finger" at passing pedestrians who are either arch-villains or super-villains. Elizabeth isn't an expert on comic book bad guys.

The uniformed officer at the front desk is a woman and she's not carrying a gun. Rowan is a little disappointed. He was expecting a fellow crime-fighter who could compare weaponry with him and swap tales of saving the world. After waiting forty-five minutes they are taken upstairs through a cluttered open-plan office that looks reassuringly productive.

The detective constable is called Carter and he's wearing a jacket and tie. He's quite handsome except for a buzz-cut that makes his ears look like jug handles.

"Please sit down, Mrs. North. Tea? Coffee? Water?"

"No, thank you."

DC Carter glances at her pregnancy and then smiles hesitantly at Rowan, who has crawled onto Elizabeth's lap and is staring at him with the intensity that only young children can produce.

"Have you heard from your husband?"

"I wouldn't be here if I'd heard from my husband."

There is an awkward pause and DC Carter uses the moment to open the file on his desk.

"It has only been forty-eight hours," he says.

"It has been five days."

"Yes, but technically we don't class a person as missing until a certain amount of time has elapsed."

"How long?"

"That depends upon the circumstances."

Rowan slips out of her arms and is now sitting on the floor linking paperclips together into a chain.

Elizabeth looks back at the detective. "What are you doing to try to find him?"

"Your husband is also over the age of eighteen and not considered vulnerable, Mrs. North."

"What does that mean?"

"He's not at risk of suicide or self-harm."

The words sound too harsh. He tries to make amends. "Your husband may have decided to spend a few days away, getting his head together. It happens sometimes."

"He wouldn't do that without telling me."

The detective looks at her tiredly. She's not going to make it easy for him. Consulting her statement, he goes over the details again.

"Your husband works for a bank."

"He's a compliance officer at Mersey Fidelity."

"Was he having any problems?"

"He was very busy."

"There is evidence that he used his ATM card at a machine in Regent Street early on Saturday morning. He also bought clothes in Oxford Street on Sunday."

"North never buys clothes—he hates shopping."

"Somebody used his cards."

"I told you we were robbed. It's in my statement. My jewelry is missing...our passports."

"Perhaps your husband was planning a trip."

"We were planning a baby."

DC Carter smiles at her as though she's being feeble and irrational. It's the same look her father used to give Elizabeth when they argued during her childhood.

"Is there anyone your husband could be staying with?"

"No."

"What about the other woman?"

"What other woman?"

"You hired a private detective because you thought your husband might be having an affair."

Elizabeth looks at Rowan, who is playing with a stapler and a piece of paper.

"I was worried about North. I knew something was bothering him."

"So you hired someone to follow him?"

"Yes."

"Why didn't you just ask him?"

Elizabeth can feel her features becoming squashed and color rising in her cheeks.

"Don't patronize me, Detective. Of course I asked him, but he wouldn't tell me. We argued. I got upset. Nothing changed."

"Something made you suspicious."

"I didn't know what he was doing. I didn't have any evidence. North said he loved me. I had a friend who recommended an agency. She'd been through a divorce."

"Were you considering divorcing your husband?"

"No, not at all! Never."

There is a cry of pain. Rowan has punched a staple through the webbing of his hand. One tooth of the staple is sticking from his skin. Elizabeth holds him tightly and pulls the barb free, kissing away his pain and his tears.

3

LONDON

Ruiz walks the surrounding streets, interviewing neighbors and passers-by, asking questions the police should have asked. Did anyone see a young woman? She was running. Which way did she go? What sort of boat? Two fishermen. Where did they take her? Upriver.

The men who came looking for Holly were professionals. They drove all-wheel-drive vehicles with heavily tinted windows. They wore dark clothing. Soft shoes. They were trained for this. How does someone train for this? Drowning kittens? Torturing animals?

She managed to get away, but where would she go? Out of London, if she has any sense. Somewhere safe. She needs a friend with a spare room or a sofa bed, someone who doesn't appear on her phone records or in her address book. How long can she stay hidden? If she doesn't use her mobile, if she doesn't call family or friends, if she doesn't break the law and get caught, if she doesn't visit a doctor, or withdraw money, or apply for a job...

She's not going to call him. She probably blames him for what happened.

Ruiz thinks of his own children and how he abandoned them after Laura died. Fled the memories. Replaced one horror with another. He lost himself in Bosnia, Sarajevo under siege, where snipers gunned down people as they queued for bread and collected water. He can remember flowers in the flower boxes, climbing roses that clung to the whitewashed walls like living tapestries.

He was gone for so long that he lost touch with Claire and Michael. One night, as he lay in bed, listening to distant gunfire, he tried to picture the twins but could only see holes in his mind, blank spaces. He had forgotten what they looked like. That's when he realized that he had to get out of that terrible place where blood ran in the gutters and bullets tore through children. If he didn't escape he'd be swallowed by the blank spaces, the black holes.

That was nearly twenty years ago. Water under the bridge. Blood. Washed away.

Sitting on a bench, Ruiz makes a phone call. He leaves a voicemail message for Vorland asking him to trace the number plate on the dark blue Audi and the mobile phone number left beneath his windscreen. He hangs up and notices a rowing eight skim past him with oars dripping, facing backwards but going forwards. His life feels like that—as though he's looking into the past, seeking answers to old questions, but getting further and further from them.

Back at the house, the locks have been changed and the broken glass replaced with plywood sheets. The uniformed police have been and gone, taking statements but showing little interest. Campbell Smith arrives unexpectedly to survey the damage, walking through the house like a bailiff deciding what furniture is worth seizing.

Ruiz tells him about the envelope of cash and his conversation with the mysterious American who said that Holly Knight had the key.

"Could be a key of heroin," says Campbell.

"I don't think he was talking about drugs. He offered me twenty-five grand if I gave her up."

"What did you tell him?"

"I told him I'd think about it."

Campbell smirks. "Maybe that's why you wouldn't press charges and invited her home."

Ruiz doesn't react. He knows Campbell is trying to wind him up. The commander fills the silence. "Money, narcotics and violence—ticks all the boxes for me. Holly Knight was a junkie's girlfriend."

"She's a victim."

"She's a *liar*."

"She needs protection."

"We *tried* to protect her, remember? But you got her released. Now if she wants our help, she can come and ask for it. She can start by telling us the truth about Zac Osborne. You tell her that."

Campbell tears a kitchen towel from a roll and wipes his hands, folding the paper into a neat square before placing it on the sink. He leaves without shaking Ruiz's hand, pausing at the makeshift front door to examine the damage.

One parting comment: "Enjoy your retirement."

Ruiz sits at the kitchen table, staring at the twisted grain in the wood. His stepfather made the table after the 1987 storms brought down dozens of oak trees on the farm. Sturdy, heavy, solid, it reminds him of the man.

He kneels in front of the sink and opens a cupboard, pushing aside bottles of floor cleaner, brass polish and old rags. There is a loose brick at the very back, with worn edges. Wedging his fingers at the corners he pulls out a stained rag with something heavy wrapped inside. A Glock 17, oiled, gleaming. Unused since he last took it to the range three, no four, years ago.

Setting it on the table he goes to the freezer and has to move ice trays and a leg of lamb to reach the frozen peas. Opening the packet, he takes out a zip-loc plastic bag with two boxes of ammunition.

He weighs the Glock in his hand, enjoying the way it fits into his palm. It's his old service pistol. He thought about getting rid of it when he retired, but there were too many skeletons rattling in his cupboards to feel completely safe. He doesn't like guns, but they serve a purpose. They speed things up and spell things out and they win arguments without words.

Carefully loading the ammunition clip, he snaps it into place and slides the pistol into a leather holster that fits over his shoulder. He tries it on. Adjusting the straps.

Picking up his car keys, he puts in another call to Vorland. He's gone for the day. Ruiz knows where to find him.

South of the river, opposite Battersea Park, a fitness center full of mirrors and narcissists; men with no necks and bulging forearms, women with hard bodies and little left that is feminine.

Vorland steps off a running machine. Ever since his heart attack he's been exercising as though death were only one step behind him, walking in his shadow. He slides along a weight bench, legs apart, arms braced beneath a bar carrying close to his body weight. Blowing out his cheeks, he starts his next set, sucking in air, grunting. Eight…nine…ten. Slowing down. The veins on the back of his neck are poking out, blue and hard.

"You want me to spot you?" asks Ruiz.

"I'm good."

"Suit yourself."

Vorland does another four reps and drops the weight bar into the cradle.

"You didn't return my call."

"So you came looking."

"I couldn't wait."

Vorland wipes sweat from his eyes. "How did you find me?"

"You're a creature of habit."

"Maybe I didn't *want* to get back to you."

"Care to elaborate?"

"That number you wanted me to run—the dark blue Audi—drew a blank."

"It's unregistered?"

"No."

"I don't understand."

"There's a lock on the information. I don't have the security clearance."

"There's hardly anyone above you."

"There's *always* someone with a higher clearance."

Vorland drapes the towel around his neck. "So I rang a mate of mine who works for Special Branch. I asked him if they were running an op in Hammersmith this morning."

"What did he say?"

"He told me he couldn't talk. Then he told me not to call him again. About an hour later I had a visit from a grey suit. Said he was from the police complaints commission. He wanted to know why I was accessing the DVLA computer. I said I was following up a tip-off. He wanted to know the details."

"What did you tell him?"

"The truth. I told him your house got broken into and you wanted to know if it was a special ops—MI5 or MI6."

"Did he react?"

"No."

"So what do you think?"

"I think you should tread softly on this one."

"I'm very light on my feet."

"I'm being serious, Vincent. Don't cross these people. I've seen how they operate. In South Africa, during the independence struggle, they simply made people disappear—and I'm not talking about the blacks. They were targeting the white journalists, sympathetic judges, social workers, doctors... You don't just lose a career if you cross these guys."

"That was South Africa."

"You remember Nick Maher?"

"Yeah."

"He worked undercover for SOCA investigating people-smuggling. He arrested one of the ringleaders, had him bang to rights, but MI5 came in and said the guy was one of their informants, so this guy walked. Maher decided to leak the story. Big spread in the *Sunday Times,* an Insight Team investigation."

"What happened?"

"A month later someone found a kilo of heroin in Maher's garden shed and sixty grand in his wife's bank account. Nick denied any knowledge. Two weeks later he jumped in front of a train at Clapham Junction."

Ruiz and Vorland look at each other, something knowing and sad in both their eyes.

"Don't contact me again," says Vorland. "Not for a long while..."

4

LONDON

From an office overlooking Tower Bridge, above the grey, grey river, the only signs of vegetation are smudges of green between the buildings. Brendan Sobel looks at his wristwatch and then at the row of whisky glasses gleaming on the shelf above the drinks cabinet.

It's too late for lunch, too early for sundowners. In Washington it is mid-morning. They'll have finished their egg white omelets and skinny lattes, ready to make decisions about current wars and future conflicts, discussing "ops," "intel" and "assets."

They must be drinking somewhere in the world, thinks Sobel. What time is it in Australia? Aussies like a drink. He pours two fingers of bourbon and drops in a handful of melting ice. Why can't the Brits make a decent ice-cube? How difficult is it to freeze water? Their pipes freeze all the time.

His secretary appears in the doorway, head to the side, noticing the glass in his hand. Sobel feels a pulse of embarrassment. Anita is twenty-four, fresh out of training, too young for him, but keen to learn the ropes.

"Mr. Chalcott is on line two."

"Thank you, Anita."

Sobel watches her calves as she leaves, wondering if she's wearing tights. Women don't wear stockings any more—not unless they're hookers or getting married.

"Artie."

"How's Blighty?"

"Small and soggy."

Arthur Chalcott chuckles with all the sincerity of a salesman. "Andy tells me we're close."

"There have been a few small complications."

"Complications?"

"We tried to pick up the girl, but we missed her."

"That sounds like a fuck-up, not a complication."

"We're searching for her."

"You've lost contact."

"For the moment."

Chalcott grinds his teeth. "Who did you send to get her?"

"A freelance team."

"Limeys."

"They've done the job before."

Sobel takes a sip of bourbon and pictures Chalcott in the bunker, sitting on his inflatable ball. The two of them were interns together. Old buddies. One was promoted faster than the other. Understood the politics.

Chalcott was a desk jockey who talked like a veteran despite serving only six months in the field — South America; a summer in La Paz, sipping sangrias and sleeping with cheap whores. Agents like him prefer to refashion their own history, making it sound like they served in Iraq or Afghanistan.

"OK, so let's be clear on this — you've lost Richard North and now you've lost the girl. Does she know anything?"

"Ibrahim believes so."

"How are you playing it?"

"I need clearance to pay twenty-five thousand."

"Dollars or pounds?"

"Pounds."

"Recoverable?"

"That's the plan."

Chalcott is silent for a time. Sobel thinks the line has gone dead.

"You there, Artie?"

"I'm here."

"We might have to involve MI6 on this one. You want me to liaise?"

"Say nothing about the main game."

"What do I tell them?"

"Tell them the girl has compromised one of our people—a married man. Stolen something of value. We're trying to be discreet."

Sobel thinks about the three men who stormed the house in Hammersmith. It was hardly discreet.

The call ends and he pours himself another drink, thinking about Kansas. Home has never seemed further away or felt less like home. He has been away too long, moving from one conflict to the next. The true America has become harder to identify.

He remembers a rendition prison in Afghanistan. A Taliban leader he interrogated for three days—sensory deprivation, waterboarding, stress positions—until he broke. Cried. Scratched at his face in shame.

"I weep for my land," he said, "but mostly I weep for yours."

5

LONDON

Rowan has stopped crying. His injured finger, wrapped in a sticking plaster, is held aloft so that everyone at the bus stop can see how brave he is. Then he imagines that his bandage is a new top secret Spiderman weapon. He aims it at an elderly gentleman who is crossing the road.

"Pchoong!"

Then he mows down a group of pre-school children who are walking in single file along the pavement.

"Perhaps you shouldn't shoot any more people," says Elizabeth. "It's not very polite."

"What should I do?"

"Say hello."

Rowan looks at his bandaged finger and back to his mother.

Then he turns to different people at the bus stop and says hello. They smile at him, wondering about the odd little boy dressed as Spiderman.

Elizabeth has a dozen messages on her mobile, none of them from her husband. Family and friends have rallied around her since North disappeared, which is why the fridge is full of casseroles and cakes. Why do people assume she wants to eat?

The bus pulls up. Elizabeth makes no attempt to get on. Rowan tugs at her hand. "Come on, Mummy."

"We're going somewhere else."

"Where?"

"On an adventure."

"I like 'ventures."

Elizabeth hails a black cab and checks her purse to make sure she has enough money. It drops her in Old Brompton Road. Rowan wants to look at the holiday posters in the Thomas Cook window. Beautiful young people cavorting in impossibly blue water.

Phoenix Investigations is on the third floor. They take the old-fashioned lift, which rattles and bangs as it rises through the floors. Along the corridor, there is light behind the frosted glass door. The receptionist has red-rimmed eyes and a rash under her nose. The tissues in the wastepaper bin look like melting snowballs.

"I don't have an appointment," explains Elizabeth. "I was hoping Mr. Hackett might see me."

The receptionist blows her nose.

"He just stepped out. Won't be long."

Elizabeth sits on the lone plastic chair. Rowan climbs on to her lap. There is a license in a wooden frame hanging on the wall, some sort of diploma. Elizabeth wonders what a private detective has to study. How to rifle through rubbish bins? How to peer through windows? The whole idea of seeing a private detective embarrasses her. She's not that sort of person. She trusts her husband.

There is a photograph next to the diploma—a young soldier in battle fatigues, war paint on his cheeks; a half-forgotten conflict.

There are footsteps outside. Colin Hackett nudges the door with his hip. He's carrying a tray of coffees and something sweet and sticky in a bag. Heavy-set with broad shoulders, he reminds her of Bob Hoskins with a full head of hair.

He hesitates for a moment, unsure if he's missed an appointment.

"Is everything all right, Mrs. North?"

Elizabeth shakes her head, unable to speak. Hackett motions her into his office, telling his secretary to look after Rowan.

"Just don't touch him. You're like a bloody plague ship." And then as the door closes, "She's my wife's niece, completely unemployable. I don't think it's contagious."

"I should have called."

"That's OK."

"Did you get my message on Saturday?"

"Yes."

"Did you do as I asked?"

"Of course."

"It just didn't seem right. He's a good man."

Elizabeth lowers her gaze, pressing her hands in her lap.

"Now I've changed my mind. I want you to keep working."

"Following your husband?"

"Finding him."

"I don't understand."

"He's missing. I came home on Sunday and he wasn't there. Nobody has seen him."

Hackett presses his fingertips together to form a pyramid, the apex of which touches his lower lip.

"Perhaps you should see my final report before you spend any more money."

Opening the drawer of a filing cabinet, he pulls out a blue manila folder. The name "Richard North" is on the label. Resuming his seat, he takes a pair of half-moon spectacles from his top pocket and perches them on the tip of his nose. Running a finger down the page, he begins detailing North's movements. What time he left home. When he returned. Meetings. Lunches. Commutes. Jogging routes. Elizabeth is mentioned once or twice, along with Mersey Fidelity.

"I followed your husband for seven days. He's a creature of habit. Leaves the house at just after seven, walks to Barnes Station, takes the same train to work, buys his coffee and a pastry, wears the same overcoat, carries the same briefcase.

"The only change to his routine was on the Thursday." He points to the date on the page. "He left home at his usual time, but instead of going to the office, he drove out of London, north along the M1 to Luton. I thought maybe he had a meeting, but he didn't visit an office. He found a parking space in Bury Park Road, about a mile to the west of Luton town center. He bought himself a coffee, a bottle of water and he just waited."

"Waited for what?"

"I don't know. He was parked outside a company that provides private mailboxes and offers a private mail forwarding service. People either collect post personally or have it forwarded in a plain brown envelope to an address they nominate. They might have a hobby they don't want their wives or girlfriends finding out about—know what I'm saying?"

Elizabeth doesn't. The private detective tries again. "Some people have got a thing for latex, or ladies' underwear, or bondage gear, or sex toys, and they don't want this stuff delivered to their homes. So they take out a private mailbox, which guarantees them a degree of privacy. Then again, it could be a company that doesn't have a registered office address so uses a private one."

Hackett looks back at his notes.

"At 1518 hours a Pakistani kid arrived and picked up a package from a postbox. Your husband followed him on foot for about a quarter of a mile until the kid went into a charity shop near the big Central Mosque.

"Mr. North waited outside the shop for about twenty minutes and then went back to his car. He drove back to London. I got details of the mileage if you want them."

Elizabeth shakes her head. Hackett turns the page.

"On Friday your husband went to work at the normal time, but came home again at 1046 hours."

This is news to Elizabeth. She and Rowan had already left for the Lake District. Why would North have come home mid-morning? Perhaps he forgot something.

"He stayed at the house until 1430 hours," says Hackett, "and then caught a cab to an address in Mount Street, just off Park Lane. The house is leased to a private company called May First Limited. A woman answered the door. In her fifties. Well preserved. Hardly the mistress type. Your husband seemed agitated. She wouldn't let him inside.

"He kept ringing the doorbell until she gave him a piece of paper. Maybe it was an address. He left and caught a cab to a restaurant in Maida Vale: The Warrington. Gordon Ramsay's pub."

The detective slides several photographs across his desk. Time coded. Shot from a distance. Grainy. Three men are sitting at an outside table beneath the plane trees. North is the clearest figure. A second man is sitting beside him, his face partially obscured by North's body. A third man is seated opposite. Overweight with a heavy beard, he looks Mediterranean or perhaps Middle-Eastern.

Elizabeth studies the photographs. She wants them to be clearer. She wants to see North's eyes.

"They talked for about twenty minutes," says Hackett. "I recorded some of their conversation with a directional microphone, which is illegal, of course, and cannot be used in any court of law. It doesn't make a great deal of sense because of the gaps and background noise, but I have provided you with a copy.

"Your husband left the restaurant and I followed him to a phone box in Clifton Gardens. He made a two-minute phone call."

Hackett shows her another photograph. The old-fashioned red phone box has clear glass panels decorated with escort agency flyers and the business cards of sex workers. North is just visible through the door, resting his head against the metal casing of the phone as though exhausted or upset.

Elizabeth wants to reach into the photograph and comfort him at the same time as she's asking herself questions. What is he doing? Why use a public phone box and not a mobile? Who were those men at the restaurant?

The private detective has paused. He has reached a point where the message is harder to deliver. He places another photograph in front of Elizabeth.

"Your husband then caught a cab to Kensington High Street. He went to a basement bar called The Chess Club."

Although poorly lit, the photograph shows North sitting with a woman. Young, attractive, well groomed, she looks barely old enough to be drinking legally.

The next image is clearer. They're outside on the street, getting into a cab. A third photograph shows the cab arriving at the house in Barnes. The woman is wearing North's leather jacket around her shoulders.

Something soft breaks inside Elizabeth, a single thread no thicker than a spider's web that has been holding her self-respect and her dignity in place.

"How long did she stay?"

"It's in the report."

"How long?"

Hackett takes a deep breath. "I left at two a.m. She was still there."

Elizabeth is willing herself not to cry. Forbidding it.

"I'm sorry to be giving you this news, Mrs. North. In my experience a wife's intuition is her most valuable instinct. You considered something untoward was happening, which is why you hired me. Your instincts proved correct."

Elizabeth is barely listening.

"Mrs. North?"

She whispers. "I need to know who she is."

The private detective scratches his jaw and grimaces. "I don't think that's a good idea."

"Please?"

Hackett pushes the manila envelope across his desk. "It's all in the report, Mrs. North."

"But I want you to find him."

"Did you bin-bag him?"

"Sorry?"

"Kick him out. You suspected he had a girlfriend and you told him to leave."

"It wasn't like that. I didn't know about the girl until now."

"But you suspected."

"Maybe if you find her, you'll find my husband."

Colin Hackett sighs. "Listen, Mrs. North, take the file home. Read it or burn it. Have a good night's sleep. If you still think this guy is worth finding, give me a call."

"I don't need to sleep on it. I'm having a baby any day now. I want you to find him."

Hackett nods. He wants to tell her not to waste her money and warn her that some rocks should never be turned over, but he can see a steely resolve in her gaze.

Elizabeth's feet manage to take her outside, where she sits at a café next to Rowan. An ice-cream seller is pushing a barrow along the pavement. Elizabeth searches for spare change. A tear springs from her right eye and runs down her cheek. The ice-cream seller gives her an extra napkin so she can blow her nose.

A small explosion has detonated within her. She is no longer solid, no longer pristine. Everything that she knows about her life now carries a question mark. This sort of thing doesn't happen to people like her. *Her* husband doesn't have affairs or sleep with prostitutes or keep secrets from her. Her entire life has been one of money, privilege and being envied rather than pitied. All that has changed in the click of a camera shutter.

"Why is you crying, Mummy?"

"I'm just having a sad day."

"Because of Daddy."

"Yes."

"Is he coming home?"

"I hope so."

Colin Hackett waits until Elizabeth North has gone before he emerges from his office. He tells Janice to print off an invoice and

post it immediately. Sometimes they change their mind about paying when you give them bad news.

Hackett set up his agency ten years ago when his own marriage
had disappeared in front of his eyes. He was angry at his wife's
infidelity, but later came to blame himself because he saw how
many husbands had emotionally left their wives years before they
bothered to clear their sock drawers.

For the most part, detective work had proven to be depressing
and dull rather than glamorous or dangerous. Missing children,
lost cats, dodgy tradesmen, background checks, insurance claims,
paternity tests, proving or disproving fidelity…he had seen almost
the full range of human failings and tribulations.

He first met Elizabeth North in a café just off Sloane Square.
She had crossed the café as though on a catwalk and Hackett was
sure he recognized her from somewhere. It was only afterwards
when he typed her name into a search engine that he discovered
her former career as a daytime TV presenter on one of those lifestyle programs watched by retired people, housewives and the
unemployed.

She was nervous about hiring him. A newbie. Some get cold
feet. Others have feet of clay. They want someone to peek behind
the curtains, but they're frightened of what they might find. Ignorance is often a happier state.

She had used the phrase "seeing someone else," which sounded
politely courteous coming from her lips. Most spouses tended to
voice their mistrust in cruder terms.

It hadn't taken him long to get the goods on Richard North. It
was a straight tail and surveillance job. The guy went running
every morning in a worn tracksuit and polar fleece, through the
maze of streets around where he lived. Then he left for the office at
the same time, on the same train, wearing the same suit. He probably had sex to schedule.

The only difference came on the last few days of surveillance
when North started acting erratically, coming home at strange
hours and taking unexpected trips like the one to Luton. Hackett
hadn't minded the drive. Mileage was a billable expense.

Now he has to find him, which shouldn't be a problem. The tracking device he placed on North's car will do that for him. Hackett hadn't mentioned this to Elizabeth — why make his job seem too easy? In a few days he'll give her a call and tell her that he's found her wandering husband. She seems desperate enough and pregnant enough to take him back.

That's the problem with marriage — the raised expectations. A man starts off being faithful because he wants a wife who appeals to his nobler instincts and higher nature, then after a while he wants another woman to help him forget them.

6

LONDON

Seagulls wheel and scream above Holly's head, bickering like siblings. The Thames is at full tide. Dusk gathering. The wooden boat is pulled on to a narrow beach. Fuel lines uncoupled. The outboard engine lifted from its mounts. The younger fisherman has been dropped off at a jetty. The remaining one is covering the boat with a tarpaulin, pegging down the faded fabric.

Thin and wiry with acne-divots in his cheeks, his name is Pete and he's dressed in overalls and heavy work boots. Holly follows him along a narrow, winding path between blackberry bushes until they reach a weathered caravan.

A skinny dog with a large square head emerges from beneath the axle, wagging its entire body. The dog sniffs at her crotch and she pushes it away.

"What is this place?"

"It's called Platt's Eyot."

"It's an island?"

"Used to be an old boat yard. Hasn't been used since the sixties."

"And you live here?"

"This is my weekender."

"It's not the weekend."

"Yeah, well, sometimes I stay here during the week."

Pete stores his fishing gear beneath the wheel arch and retrieves a key on a piece of string that is hanging from a secret hiding place. He opens the door of the caravan and pulls out two canvas stools, placing them beneath the awning.

Holly looks around the caravan. It has a bunk bed with a sleeping bag, a small TV, a gas stove and sink. Beyond the awning, just visible in the fading light, an abandoned building seems to crumble under the weight of vines and weeds. Rusting metal stanchions rise into the darkening sky to where the roof has partially collapsed and tin sheets hang from the frame. Oily water laps against a slipway and a sign strung across the entrance says, HAZARDOUS AREA: KEEP OUT.

"Are we allowed to be here?"

"I sort of look after the place...unofficially."

"What about the other guy?" she asks.

"Marty is a mate of mine. He lives in Sunbury. I take him fishing sometimes."

Pete sits on a stool and smokes a roll-up cigarette out of the corner of his mouth. Next to the caravan are empty fuel drums, gas cylinders and a hammock slung beneath the branches.

Holly's jeans are torn and a small patch of blood stains the left knee. Wrapping her arms around her chest, she watches him pour boiling water into cups.

"Are you cold?" he asks.

"No."

Pete rummages through a cupboard. Then he searches a duffel bag. Finally he hands her an old stained sweater that is so long in the arms Holly has to fold up the sleeves and push them up to her elbows.

Pete opens a can of beans and puts it in a metal saucepan, firing up a gas ring.

"What do you do?"

"I used to be a printer. Lost my job. Wife left me."

"When was that?"

"Ninety-six."

"So what do you do for money?"

"I got a disability pension. I catch fish. I salvage stuff."

The beans are bubbling. He spoons them into his mouth straight from the saucepan. Blowing on each one.

He hands Holly an extra spoon.

"I'm not hungry."

"You should eat."

Her stomach is rumbling. The beans are warm and good.

"Don't you have any plates?"

"This saves on washing up."

Pete's dog whimpers, looking at them expectantly.

"What's his name?"

"Dog."

"That's original."

"Somebody dumped him on the island when he was just a puppy. Stupid animal can't swim."

"What breed is he?"

"The non-swimming kind."

Pete opens a can of dog food and bangs the base, up-ending a turd-colored log into a plastic bowl and breaking it with the sharp edge of the can. Dog eats noisily and licks the bowl clean with a slavering tongue.

Pete hasn't asked her why the men were chasing her. He seems to accept that she'll tell him when she's ready or she won't. Privacy is something he understands. Holly has been going backwards and forwards over the details of the day. Ruiz had called to warn her. He told her to get out. Does that mean she can trust him? Maybe it's best if she stays on her own. People tend to die when they get too close to her.

A rim of storm clouds has swallowed the stars and the air is thick with the smell of rain. They sit for a long time in the dying firelight, until fat drops sizzle as they hit the coals.

Holly wants a bath. The most Pete can offer is to boil a kettle and she can mix it with a bucket of water from the river. He collects the water before the rain gets any heavier and carries it to a wooden block beneath the awning. Once the kettle has boiled, he turns away, tidying the caravan.

Holly takes off her blouse and washes her upper body with a warm cloth, feeling how quickly her skin grows cold. Pete might be watching her through the window. She doesn't care. A lone kerosene lantern hangs from the branch of a tree above her, attracting insects that bounce off the globe and come back again.

Buttoning her blouse, she lifts the bucket to the ground and washes her feet before pulling on her jeans.

"You can stay here tonight," he says, pointing to the bed.

"Where will you sleep?"

"I got a hammock."

She's in no position to argue. Pete takes a sleeping bag from a cupboard and lights a second kerosene lantern. He passes her window, throwing shadows on the ground as he walks. Dog looks at Holly and then at Pete before following him into the night.

7

LONDON

The Courier carries his breakfast in a brown paper bag with paper handles. It contains a sweet pastry, cheese, fresh dates and a boiled egg. He orders a double espresso laced with sugar and takes it to a table outside, sitting with his back to the wall so he can feel the weak sunshine on his face.

He has a wedge-shaped body, narrow at the hips, broad across his shoulders. Wide eyes. Oddly sensual lips. His lips embarrass him. They are not manly enough. Taking out a napkin, he places it on the table, setting out his breakfast as though making an offering.

Three women pushing oversized prams are watching him. He ignores them and taps the boiled egg against the table, peeling it slowly, prying off the shell in big pieces so as not to tear the albumen. Taking a pinch of sea salt, he dusts the crown of the egg and bites it in half.

Eggs had been a luxury when he was growing up. Food had been a luxury, to be queued for, haggled over and eaten with reverence. Every day had been a struggle for his mother, who raised six children on the West Bank, earning a few shekels by sewing for neighbors. His father was a man in a photograph; a stranger who spent eighteen years in an Israeli prison before dying of a heart attack at fifty-two. The Israelis wouldn't return his body to be buried in Ramallah.

The Courier finishes eating and brushes the crumbs from the table. He folds the paper bag, putting it into his pocket. Then he crosses the street, pausing to put on his gloves, tugging at the cuffs and smoothing the soft leather on his fingers.

Taking the stairs he climbs three floors and knocks on the door.

"Come in."

A voice summons him inside. The receptionist is a lank-haired blonde, barely twenty. Her hips and thighs are pushing against her skirt and her breath reeks of mentholated cough drops.

"I'm looking for Mr. Hackett," he says in a perfect London accent.

"Do you have an appointment?"

"We're old friends."

The receptionist sneezes into a tissue. Blows her nose.

"That's a nasty cold. You should be home in bed."

"Uncle Colin doesn't believe in sick days."

"Mr. Hackett is your uncle."

The Courier sits on the edge of her desk, toying with her pencil holder. His nearness makes her feel uncomfortable.

"What's your name?" he asks.

"Janice."

He repeats the name out loud. She doesn't like how it sounds coming from his mouth.

"Perhaps you should come back later."

"No, I'll wait."

His eyes slowly drop down to her chest, then to the hem of her skirt and her crossed legs. She checks the top button of her blouse self-consciously.

"Where do you live, Janice?"

"What's that got to do with anything?"

"You should go home. Crawl into bed. Stay warm."

"Someone has to look after the office."

"I can do that."

"I don't know you."

"Like I said, I'm an old friend."

The Courier has opened his wallet. He pulls out a handful of banknotes and begins placing them one by one on the desk blotter.

"How much do you earn?"

"Why?"

"Ten pounds an hour...twenty?"

"It's not really any of your business."

"What if I offered to cover your missed wages?"

A hundred pounds is sitting on the blotter. Janice looks at the money and trembles, a pool of heat burning on her forehead as though her hairdryer has been left on the same spot for too long.

She stands, picks up her coat, not making eye contact.

"Wait!" he says.

Janice stops. Trembling. She can feel the contents of her stomach liquefying and rushing through her colon. The visitor picks up the banknotes and pushes them into the pocket of her coat.

"Take yourself off to bed," he says. "I'll tell Mr. Hackett you went home."

He touches her shoulder. Opens the door. She wants to run but can't move quickly in her heels.

Outside on the street, not stopping, she calls Colin Hackett on his mobile.

"Where are you?" she asks.

"In Luton."

"There's a man in your office. He sent me home."

"What do you mean he sent you home?"

"He told me to leave."

"What's his name?"

"I don't know, but he says he knows you."

"What's he look like?"

She swallows. "I don't think he's a nice man, Uncle Colin. I don't think he's your friend."

8

BAGHDAD

Even in the muddy half-light, Luca can see the dark liquid stains running down the brick walls and smell the ageing feces and sweat. The damp eight-foot-by-ten-foot cell has no window or furniture, just a soiled pillow and blanket on the floor.

There are six cells side by side in the basement of the al-Amariyah police station. Luca knows this building. He came here once to investigate the deaths of six prisoners who were handcuffed and blindfolded before being lined up against a wall in a courtyard and shot. Witnesses claimed the man who pulled the trigger was a senior Iraqi politician in the interim government. One described it as an unintended act of mercy because the men had been beaten for so long they simply wanted to die.

The corpses were removed by the Prime Minister's bodyguards and driven off in a Nissan utility. Another witness said they were buried west of Baghdad, in open desert country near Abu Ghraib.

Luca imagines these men, naked and still, garlanded with bruises, lying in unmarked graves.

He dreams. He wakes. Reality is such a hazy, shallow state and his nightmares, the recurring ones, are full of the speaking dead and bones bursting out of the ground. How many days have passed since his arrest? They took away his watch, along with his belt and shoelaces. They took away his gun. They had laughed at the size of it. A woman's gun, they said. One bullet.

For the first few hours he had bellowed through the meal hatch, demanding to contact the American Embassy. When his voice grew hoarse he saved his strength, concentrating on small details like the chain hanging from the ceiling and the discarded length of hosepipe in the corner. He didn't want to imagine what they were for.

They came for him eventually. He was handcuffed and dragged along an unventilated corridor. A guard slapped the heel of his hand three times against the steel door, which creaked partway open, revealing the apprehensive face of a young soldier. Shoved forward, hard against a wall, Luca felt a stabbing sensation in his forearm. A man in white. A needle in his hand. The room began to dip and sway, rolling like the deck of a ship in a storm. Someone was speaking to him, but he couldn't focus on the face. What big eyes . . . such a big mouth . . . so many questions.

At some point he had fallen asleep or lost consciousness and woken back in the cell. He can hear people outside now . . . a key rattling in the lock . . . the hinges groan. The same guards pull him upright, pushing him along the passageway. He needs to pee. The desire borders on torment.

Another room. A table. Two chairs. A single light bulb. A window. A familiar figure. General al-Uzri takes off his jacket. His forearms bulge below the short sleeves of a cotton shirt. His jacket is folded and placed neatly on a spare chair.

"I am sorry to have kept you waiting," he says. "I trust you have been treated well."

"No."

"Perhaps our prisons aren't quite up to American standards."

He uses the word "American" like it belongs to a lesser life form.

"Why am I here?"

"You have been accused of killing two unarmed civilians in a village near Mosul."

"We were fired upon by insurgents."

"Not according to our witnesses."

"What witnesses?"

"The men you murdered had wives and families."

"They were insurgents."

"You targeted the pickup. You shot out the nearside tires causing the vehicle to roll. Then you stopped and poured petrol over the occupants and set them alight."

"That's bullshit! We were fired upon. I can show you the bullet holes."

"Your driver has given us a statement."

Luca struggles to breathe. He's talking about Jamal.

"I don't have a driver."

The general laughs. "Such loyalty is commendable, but you have left it rather late to be so protective of your accomplices."

Luca half rises from his seat, but strong hands shove him down.

Al-Uzri takes a matchstick from a box on the table and chews the end to a fibrous tail, painting spit across his teeth.

"What were you doing in the village?"

"Researching a story."

"What story?"

"The murder of four bank guards."

"A falling out among thieves."

"No, it was more than that."

Al-Uzri touches his chin with his index finger.

"Vigilante justice. Innocent people dying. Nobody ever held to account. Do you think that Iraqi law doesn't apply to you because you carry a foreign passport?"

"No."

"Do you think you're better than we are?"

Luca shakes his head. The general has taken a knife from the scabbard on his belt. It has one serrated edge and the other one smooth, sharp, tapering to a point. He splays one hand on the table and places the tip of the blade between his thumb and forefinger, holding the knife vertically.

"This country is old. My ancestors created writing and philosophy and religion when yours were painting drawings on rock walls. This was the cradle of civilization, but still you treat us like savages and barbarians."

In a blur of speed, the knife rises and falls, spearing the table between each of his fingers, back and forth, tracing his hand. He stops and raises his fingers. Not a scratch.

He signals a young officer to come closer. "Would you die for me?"

"Yes, General."

"Put your hand on the table. Spread your fingers. Would you lose a finger for me?"

He hesitates. Al-Uzri laughs.

"What is the more realistic fear—dying or losing a finger, eh? Perhaps you would like to try it, Mr. Terracini?"

"I'm not a fan of party tricks."

"No? I saw the result of your party near Mosul. Your visa has been canceled. You have two days to leave Iraq."

"On what grounds?"

"Undesirable activities."

"Bogus grounds."

The general chuckles wetly. "Complain to your embassy. See if anyone listens. You are not the most popular journalist in Iraq, Mr. Terracini. Messengers are not valued when they bring nothing but bad news."

Al-Uzri has a thin trickle of blood dripping from the end of his index finger. A nick. He slides the knife into a scabbard and adjusts his beret. Luca is dragged to his feet and pushed against the wall. Handcuffed and hooded, he is taken up the stairs, into the daylight. A gust of wind brings the familiar stink of the city beneath the fabric.

The car journey has none of the menace and uncertainty as when he was arrested. The police officers are talking about football and their favorite pastry shops. Anger replaces the fear. He's alive. Resentful. Worried about Jamal.

The hood is lifted. Brightness stabs at his eyes. They're moving through a checkpoint into the International Zone. A policeman leans across the seat and gives him a plastic bag containing his mobile phone, his wallet, but not his pistol.

He is handed over to a military attaché at the US Embassy. Two uniformed guards escort him along marbled corridors, past triumphant arches and iron busts of Saddam Hussein. He is taken to a waiting room with a view across the sluggish brown river. Downstream, two bridges, bombed and rebuilt, are bowing under the weight of traffic. Beyond them, flat-bottomed skiffs ferry passengers between the banks.

On a table there are copies of the *Wall Street Journal* and *Newsweek,* fanned in a perfect circle. A TV monitor is playing Bloomberg, with market quotes streaming under a woman who is speaking from half a world away.

Moments later an inner door opens and a man in his mid-forties ushers Luca inside, pointing to a chair. His eyes seem to radiate earnestness and goodwill.

His name is Jennings. He doesn't give a first one. The State Department seems to have dispensed with given names. He looks like a former college football star or a future politician, with one of those preppy hair partings that have been fashionable since John Kennedy was in the White House. Dressed in casual trousers, a shirt and tie, he has ink smudges on his fingers. He opens a briefcase and takes out a file, a stapler and a selection of pens. Props.

In a cracked-sounding voice, like he's hoarse from shouting, he begins listing charges.

"The Iraqis have withdrawn your visa. You have forty-eight hours in which to leave the country."

"I want to appeal."

"There is no process of appeal."

"You can make a request — government to government."

Jennings laughs. "This country doesn't *have* a government."

"I was drugged by the Iraqi police."

"So you say."

"I'm a journalist."

Jennings shrugs dismissively. "What do you think that means? Special privileges? The law doesn't apply? You think you understand this place, Mr. Terracini, just because you speak the language, but you're no different to the other hacks and glory hounds who turn up here wanting to put gloss on a new career or resurrect a fading one. You look at this country and think you're going to sum it up in a thousand crisp words, but you wind up in the bar of the al-Hamra trying to make sense of the horror. Nobody understands this place."

"They can't just kick me out."

"Yes they can."

Jennings forces himself to relax, pulling his neck from side to side until the vertebrae pop.

"What if I take my chances?" asks Luca.

"We won't allow that. Should you be arrested, or imprisoned or kidnapped, the American government would be expected to negotiate your release. We would prefer not to have that situation arise."

Jennings repacks his briefcase, putting each pen in the allotted place. It closes and he spins the combination lock.

"If you'll excuse me, I have five bodies to repatriate."

"American soldiers?"

"Civilians. Four Americans. One German. The attack on the Finance Ministry."

"What attack?"

Jennings straightens his jacket and opens the door. "Oh, that's right, you were in custody. There was an attack on the Finance Ministry. Four security contractors died and a UN auditor was abducted."

Luca croaks, "Who?"

"Their names haven't been released."

"The auditor?"

"They found his body this morning in the river. Tortured. Executed. I had to call his parents in Hamburg."

"There was a woman...?"

"Safe. The United Nations is pulling out all non-essential staff. You should get yourself on the same flight, Luca. Nobody spends any longer in Iraq than necessary. Your time is up."

9

LONDON

Elizabeth North sleeps on her side with one knee exposed and an arm dangling over the side of the bed. She dreams that she's naked in a dark tunnel, breathless and blind.

The phone is ringing. She rolls over too quickly and almost topples out of bed. Her fingers find the receiver.

"Hello?"

Silence.

"North? Is that you?"

Someone is breathing.

"What's going on? Who is this?"

She waits.

"I'm going to hang up now...Hello?...If you're not going to answer you can...can...you can get lost!"

Slamming down the receiver, she traps her finger between the handset and the cradle. The pain makes her eyes water. Sucking her finger, she sits on the edge of the bed. Once she owned a lap. Now she's full of baby. She can't see her pubic hair unless she looks in the mirror and she hasn't bothered waxing since they took their summer holiday to Jordan.

It was a strange choice, but North had business in Amman and Damascus. Afterwards they went to a resort on the Red Sea with bungalows and swimming pools and a kids' club. Elizabeth and North had fought because he spent so much time on his Black-

Berry answering emails instead of playing with Rowan. They had make-up sex afterwards. Angry. Passionate.

Standing at the bedroom window, she watches a jet pass overhead on its way to Heathrow, flashing silver. The noise penetrates the double-glazing. Pressing her fingertips to the glass, she can feel it vibrating and the sensation seems to reach into her chest and shake something inside her like a wine glass resonating at the perfect frequency of sound. Her marriage used to be like that — resonating with a perfect frequency. Now it has the discordant ring of a dropped sword.

She and North had met at Cambridge when she was studying politics and he was doing his masters in economics and sleeping with every impressionable undergraduate he could charm out of her knickers. His car had broken down — an old Citroën C5 — and he was standing by the road with his collar pulled up and a sodden newspaper over his head. Elizabeth had pulled over in her Peugeot.

"Want any help?"

"How are you with engines?"

"Terrible."

"Can you stop the rain?"

"Afraid not."

His hair was plastered to his forehead and he looked like a little boy.

"Get in."

"I'm all wet."

"It's only water."

North seemed too big for her car. His knees touched the dashboard and his head brushed the roof. She took him to his digs and he asked her out for a drink.

"I don't go out with strangers."

"You just picked me up."

"I saved you from drowning."

"Then let me say thank you."

"You have."

A week later North called her. He had tracked her down, found her number and done a little research. A bunch of flowers arrived five minutes before his phone call.

"About that drink?"

"I'm busy."

"Did you get my flowers?"

"They're very nice. Thank you."

"One drink."

"I'm seeing someone else."

A few weeks later Elizabeth bumped into North in the university library. He smiled and said hello, but didn't hassle her. She felt slightly disappointed. The following Saturday she went out with her girlfriends and they kicked on to a karaoke club in Cambridge Street. North arrived with six of his mates, none of them too drunk to be charming. Again North ignored her. One of Elizabeth's girlfriends began flirting with him and Elizabeth felt herself getting jealous. On the spur of the moment, she pulled North on to the stage for a duet and whispered in his ear, "I don't know what I hate most—you following me or you ignoring me."

"You're seeing someone."

"That was a lie."

That Mother's Day, Elizabeth went home to London for the weekend and found North sitting in the kitchen of the house in Hampstead, eating her mother's fruitcake and regaling her with stories of Cambridge.

"Oh, hello, dear," her mother said. "Look who's here! Richard has been telling me all about himself. Why didn't you tell us you had a new boyfriend? Look at the lovely flowers he brought. My favorite. Isn't that sweet?"

Elizabeth should have been annoyed. Instead she was amused. She didn't even mind when North laughed uproariously through the home videos—including the one of her naked in the bath and the ballet recital that she brought to a halt by tumbling off the stage.

Later that night, her mother showed North to his room and whispered, "I've put you next door to Lizzie in case you get lonely." She actually winked.

And so that's how it happened. North knocked. Elizabeth let

him in. They made love more than once. In the morning she could barely sit down without wincing.

After they finished college they lived together in London before they married. Elizabeth got a job as a researcher at ITV and later was offered a presenting role on a health and lifestyle show called *What's Good For You*. The first summer after they married they took a holiday to her father's hunting lodge outside of Aberdeen. North arranged it. It might have been quite romantic except that her father came too, along with his new girlfriend Jacinta.

North and Alistair Bach spent every day stalking deer together in the Highlands and their evenings discussing the merits of the international exchange rate mechanism and deregulation of the banking system. Elizabeth felt like a banking widow even though her new husband didn't work for a bank.

When North was offered a job at Mersey Fidelity, she fought against it. She didn't care about the salary package or the bonuses. She had married to escape her family and now she was being dragged back into the vortex.

Since then she'd come to accept that she would have to share North with Mersey Fidelity and her family, particularly her father.

There is a knock on the door. Rowan appears. His pajamas are stuck to his thighs.

"Someone wet the bed."

"Who?"

"The monster."

"But there are no such things as monsters."

"I think I saw him climbing out the window."

"So he's gone now?"

"Yes."

The kitchen has a high ceiling and a scrubbed pine table and matching chairs. Rowan is drawing with crayons, a study of concentration. Polina is loading the dryer in the laundry. She's wearing shorts, sandals and a pretty blouse.

"You are well this morning," she says, making a question sound like a statement.

"I'm fine."

"You will have something to eat. Orange juice? We have lots of juice."

That's because North isn't here to drink it, thinks Elizabeth.

"Did you see him on Friday?" she asks.

"I beg your pardon?"

"North. Did you see him on Friday? He came home from work. He must have forgotten something."

Polina chews on the soft inside of her cheek as if she's trying to remember.

"I must have gone to the shops."

"He was home for more than three hours."

"How do you know?"

Elizabeth doesn't want to explain about the private detective.

"He mentioned it," she lies.

Polina's eyes seem to glitter. "I must have been in and out. Perhaps he was working upstairs."

She makes it sound so obvious. Problem sorted.

Mid-morning, late summer hazing the air, Elizabeth drives east along the river until the glass and chrome towers of Canary Wharf come into view, gleaming in the sunlight. This view of London could grace the cover of a science fiction novel, but it's also a reminder of the 1980s, the decade that was brash, assertive and not very British at all. Margaret Thatcher. The Miners' Strike. Heysel. Hillsborough. The IRA. Elizabeth had been a young girl but she remembers these events because her perfect childhood had seemed so often under threat.

The foyer of Mersey Fidelity is tiled in black Italian marble and has matching leather sofas. Rupert and Frank are behind the security desk. Elizabeth has known them for years—ever since she'd visit her father after school, trying to get money for chips or chocolate.

The receptionist is a new face, immune to her smile.

"I was hoping to see Mitchell Bach."

"Do you have an appointment?"

"I'm his sister."

She rings upstairs. Cups the phone.

"I'm afraid Mr. Bach is busy."

"How long will he be?"

"Perhaps you could come back later or make an appointment."

"I'll wait."

The receptionist punches the number again. Whispers. "No... yes... that's right... she wants to wait... I see... OK."

Addressing Elizabeth, "Someone is coming down to collect you."

Felicity Stone, the head of public relations, is in her forties with blonde cropped hair and very white teeth, which are too large for her mouth. She is masculine looking. Businesslike. She presses Elizabeth's right hand in both of hers for a fraction of a second before leaving it suspended in mid-air.

"We haven't been introduced. I'm Felicity. What a terrible way to meet. How are you holding up? We're all so concerned about North. I'm sure everything is going to be fine. I once had an uncle who went missing for a week and we found him in a homeless shelter in Manchester. Transient Global Amnesia, they called it—short-term memory loss. You're so pregnant. You must want to sit down."

A lift carries them to the upper floors. Miss Stone continues talking, as though worried about losing her turn. They cross a large open-plan office dotted with computer screens. The European Desk. Global Equities. Forex. Futures. The traders are cradling phones beneath their chins and staring at charts and numbers.

They arrive at Mitchell's office. Miss Stone takes a seat and logs on to a computer screen.

"How long will Mitchell be?" asks Elizabeth.

"He's a very busy man. He's asked me to co-ordinate things. We're liaising with the police, calling hospitals, checking passenger manifests...We're most concerned about your welfare. I've arranged for you to have a full check-up. Dr. Shadrick is a Harley Street OB..."

"I have my *own* doctor."

"Yes, but Dr. Shadrick is the best. I've made a provisional appointment for tomorrow at eleven, but change it if you need to." Miss Stone taps at the keyboard again. "Where are you going to stay?"

"At the house."

"By yourself?"

"I have Rowan and the nanny."

"Mitchell has suggested you move in with your father."

"I want to stay in Barnes."

"Oh!"

"He *is* coming home, you know."

"Who?"

"My husband."

"Of course, I didn't mean to suggest otherwise." Miss Stone smiles apologetically. Her mobile is ringing. The sound is coming from a leather pouch clipped to her belt. Drawing it out like a gunslinger, she flips the phone open.

"Yes...No...I didn't approve that...Nothing goes out unless I read it first...Tell them to wait...I don't care what that arsehole wants, we're not releasing a statement until we're good and ready."

Elizabeth tries not to look surprised by the language. Miss Stone closes the phone.

"Must dash. You'll be all right on your own? Mitchell shouldn't be long. Don't answer the phone. The switchboard will pick it up."

Alone now, Elizabeth gazes out the window looking west along the Thames to the Houses of Parliament just visible through the haze. Her feet hurt. The sofa is too low. Instead she sits in Mitchell's desk chair. Two lights are blinking on his phone. Behind her on a bookcase is a leather-bound copy of the company history: the anniversary edition. A hundred years of Mersey Fidelity—the humble building society transformed into a global bank. Elizabeth knows the story. The history of the bank is almost her own family's history.

Her father, Alistair Bach, had started working as a trainee bank teller in 1960 when Mersey Fidelity was a Liverpool-based building society giving respectable working-class folk the chance to buy their own homes. In the mid-eighties when "demutualization" became the buzzword and Thatcher's Big Bang revolution set free the finance markets, Alistair Bach took advantage of the changes and turned the building society into a bank which could earn profits and pay dividends to shareholders, making the directors rich in the process. Bach became the youngest chief financial officer in the history of the FTSE 100 list of companies and Mersey Fidelity grew to become the fifth biggest retail and investment bank in the UK. He only stepped down as chairman in early 2007. By then Mitchell had been groomed for a senior position—a younger version of his father, cloned from the same stem cells—with a first-class mind and degrees from Cambridge and Harvard.

Elizabeth can feel Claudia stomping on her cervix. Up until a few days ago she was kicking up near her belly button, but now she's lower down, pressing on her pelvis. Picking up the phone, Elizabeth punches North's extension, knowing that his secretary will most likely pick up.

"Richard North's office."

"Hello, Bridget, it's Elizabeth." There is a pause. "I know you're busy, but I'm in the building. Can we get a coffee?"

Another pause. "I've been told not to talk to anyone."

"Why?"

"I don't know."

Bridget Lindop hesitates again, torn between self-preservation and common decency.

"This is me, Bridget. Elizabeth. I just want to talk."

Silence echoes through the handset. Then comes a whispered reply. "I'll meet you in the cafeteria."

Opening Mitchell's door, Elizabeth looks along the corridor.

Then she walks quickly to the lift, crossing the open-plan office, keeping her head down. None of the traders take any notice of her.

The cafeteria is on the tenth floor. They order tea in mugs and take a table near the window. On the far side of fifty, Bridget Lindop is tall and straight-backed with polished silver hair bound in a tight bun. A religious woman, who goes to Mass every day, she has a small silver cross on a chain around her neck.

"How was North when you saw him last? Was he worried about anything?"

The older woman hesitates and filters her words as if straining tea leaves. "Mr. North didn't really confide in me."

"But you saw him every day. Did he seem preoccupied? Why was he working late so many nights?"

"We were very busy."

Elizabeth feels a lump forming in her throat.

"I think he was having an affair."

Miss Lindop doesn't react. She sits with her back straight, her knees together and her hands folded in her lap.

"I'm sure you're mistaken. Richard talked only of you and Rowan."

"He took a woman home while I was away."

"Are you certain?"

"Yes."

"Did you ask him?"

"I would if I could."

The statement vibrates in her throat. Miss Lindop reaches across the space between them and squeezes Elizabeth's hand. Her voice drops to a whisper.

"He's a good man, you know that."

Elizabeth feels the skin on her face tighten. "What's wrong?"

"He told me something a few weeks ago. He said a terrible thing had happened and it was his fault."

"What?"

"I don't know, but he said I wouldn't respect him if I knew. It was about two weeks ago. He took the day off. He said he was trying to find the owner of an account. It was some sort of unlisted charity receiving money from one of our accounts. I shouldn't be talking to you about any of this."

"Why?"

"I've been told not to say anything."

Miss Lindop looks up and her whole body stiffens. Her lips draw back from her teeth in a pained smile. She pulls her hand away from Elizabeth, breaking physical contact. Felicity Stone has appeared in the cafeteria, flanked by two security guards. Scanning the tables, her eyes come to rest on Elizabeth. She flips open her mobile and makes a call, moving between tables, closing the gap.

Miss Lindop stands and mumbles an apology.

"I'm praying for him, Lizzie."

"Should I be praying?"

"I find it helps."

She leaves without saying goodbye, her sensible shoes click-clacking on the tiles.

Felicity Stone is no longer full of smiles. "I told you to wait in your brother's office."

"The baby was kicking. I had to move around. I think she's going to be a dancer."

"How nice for you."

Mitchell has finished his meeting. Elizabeth struggles up from her chair. He kisses both her cheeks then holds her at arm's length, a hand on each shoulder.

"Where the fuck is he, Lizzie?"

His anger shocks her. It triggers a memory from her childhood; Mitchell holding one of her dolls just out of her reach. Older. Faster. Stronger. He put the doll on a makeshift raft and launched it into the center of the pond where he bombarded it with rocks, clods and sticks until the raft tipped over and the doll bobbed face down in the water.

Her brother had always been a bully. Now he was doing it again.

"He can't just have disappeared. He must have said something. Called. Emailed."

Elizabeth knocks his arms away.

"No."

"Why didn't he go with you last weekend?"

"He said he had too much work to do."

"You must know something, Lizzie. This is a very inopportune time for him to go missing. We have an audit..."

Elizabeth looks at him incredulously. "Is that all you care about? He's *my* husband. He's *your* brother-in-law. I don't give a fuck about your audit. I want to know why everyone is being so secretive. And why was North so scared?"

"You think he was upset?"

"No, he was *scared*. There's a difference."

A secretary knocks. Mitchell has another meeting. Elizabeth doesn't want to let him go.

"Why has Bridget Lindop been told not to talk to me? What are you trying to hide?"

Mitchell is gathering files from his desk. Elizabeth blocks the doorway. "I'm not leaving until you talk to me."

Her brother sighs, angry but accepting. He glances at his watch.

"We're rather concerned that North took materials with him — internal memos and sensitive documents."

"Why would he do that?"

"Someone has been feeding information to outside parties."

"What outside parties?"

"A journalist." Mitchell raises his hands. "I'm not making accusations, Lizzie. We just want to talk to him. I'm sure there's an explanation. Right now I have auditors waiting in the boardroom. I can't stay."

Elizabeth wants to follow him, to argue, but Felicity Stone materializes in the corridor, blocking her way. Chaperoned to the foyer and through the security barriers, Elizabeth hands over her visitor's pass and finds herself in Cabot Square. People have to step around her to reach the revolving door.

Almost without thinking, she begins walking with no destination in mind, feeling her certainty run down inside her like a wind-up toy. Reaching the river, she watches a group of teenagers, black and white, boys and girls, hanging out on benches. One couple is French kissing with all the desperation of those too young to share a bed yet.

Elizabeth can feel objects grow bigger in her imagination, magnified by the silence of the river and the din of voices in her head. Up until six days ago, if asked, she could have taken North apart and put him back together again blindfolded, just like some people can put guns together in the dark. Now she's not so sure. Now he seems like a stranger. An imposter. Someone who tricked his way into her heart.

10

LONDON

Colin Hackett pauses on the landing, slightly out of breath. He should lose weight. Cut down on the carbs. In his army days he could tab eight clicks with a sixty-pound Bergan on his back, barely breaking a sweat.

He's sweating now. Jangling.

Standing outside his office door, he listens for a noise that shouldn't be there. Who has he upset this time? What cheating husband or insurance fraudster or child support defaulter?

Reaching for the handle, he pushes it open.

The outer office is empty. Nothing has been disturbed. Moving to the next room, he checks the office safe and the drawers of his desk. All as it should be. For the next twenty minutes he searches, running his fingers beneath the desk and windowsills, checking the electric sockets, light fittings, looking for bugs or hidden cameras.

The place is clean.

At the top of the stationery cupboard is a sports bag with his camera equipment, including a tripod and telephoto lenses. He lifts it down to his desk. Holding the smooth black camera body, he checks the battery and settings. The memory card slot is empty. Someone wanted his photographs.

Sitting in his chair, he leafs through his diary, working out which case might have triggered the robbery. Most of them were background checks, missing persons and debt recovery. He printed out photographs for Elizabeth North showing her husband with the woman he brought home. She looked more like a shopgirl than a callgirl. Pretty. Young. Dirty looking. That's often the way with men and affairs. They can have prime beef fillet at home but they go for the cheaper cuts. When you've been eating steak for a long long time, brisket tastes fine.

Hackett had spent the morning searching for Richard North—tracking the transmitter he planted behind the bumper of the banker's car. He was lucky the battery had lasted this long. He had traced North's car to an industrial estate in Bury Park, Luton, full of factories, marshalling yards, warehouses, workshops, and sur-rounded by run-down housing estates, second-hand clothes shops and Asian clothing emporiums.

The BMW was parked in the forecourt of a derelict motel. Most of the rooms were padlocked but one or two were being used for storage. Charity collections. Donated clothes and blankets.

Hackett waited five hours for North to show up. Figured he was with a girl. Maybe hookers were using the rooms. Just when he was contemplating a wasted morning, a Pakistani youth dressed in baggy jeans and a hooded sweatshirt emerged from one of the rooms. He walked to the BMW. Unlocked the doors. Checked the glove box, opened the boot, lay down a plastic sheet and then went back inside.

That's when Janice had phoned to say he had a visitor in the office—someone who gave her the creeps.

The mystery man has gone now. Hackett's bladder has been clenched for too long. He needs a leak. The toilet is along the corridor. Unzipping his trousers, he rocks on his heels and relaxes, closing his eyes.

The door opens behind him. Hackett looks over his shoulder. The bathroom is small and the man is standing by the sink, arms by his sides. He's wearing a leather jacket. Dark jeans.

"Are you Colin Hackett?"

"Who's asking?"

"People call me the Courier."

"Is that because you deliver messages?"

"I also collect things from people."

The detective estimates the threat posed. Height. Weight. Speed.

"You finished?" asks the Courier.

"Unless you're here to help me shake this thing, you can wait outside."

"I'm good here."

Hackett is trying to think. What's he not seeing or remembering? The banker can't have sent this guy.

"What can I do for you?"

"I want to talk to you about some photographs you took."

Hackett glances at his shoes. A drop of urine has settled on the polished leather. He pumps soap on to his hands, turns on the tap, washes them carefully and then triggers the dryer, rubbing his hands beneath the warm stream of air.

"They don't provide paper towels anymore," he says. "Got to save the trees. Instead we burn fossil fuels to run these things."

The Courier doesn't add anything to the observation. He's not a talker. Hackett considers his options. His mobile is in his coat pocket. His Smith & Wesson Airweight .38 is locked in the office safe.

The dryer falls silent.

Hackett tugs at his cuffs. Straightens his tie. Smoothes down his hair. He's waiting for someone else to come into the gents.

"You followed a banker," says the Courier.

"Did he send you?"

"You took photographs. Who has copies of them?"

"You took the memory card from my camera. There are no more copies."

"The banker had a notebook."

"I never met the man. I just followed him."

"What about the girl he was with?"

"I don't know who she is. How about we go back to my office? We can talk about it."

Hackett moves towards the door. If he can reach the hallway, he can turn right and run towards the stairs. The Courier is behind him. Stepping closer, something in his hand, a gun maybe, pressed hard between his shoulder blades.

Hackett pivots, aiming an elbow at his face. The Courier ducks it easily and delivers a short sharp jab to the kidneys. Hackett's knees buckle. Pain breaks over his face. The next punch sends him to the floor, half in the room and half out. The Courier grabs the door and slams it closed across the detective's head. He slams it again.

A forearm closes around Hackett's throat, hinged with the opposite elbow, adding to the pressure, sealing off his windpipe. Hackett's fingers claw at the arm. Kicking. Jerking. He can see a pinpoint of brightness in front of him and feels his mind drifting to a distant battlefield, a rocky island in the Atlantic, where pissing rain has turned to sleet and artillery shells are shaking the ground with a deafening roar.

Squashed flat against the frozen earth, he crawls forward and swings himself into an Argentine trench. Then he sees a soldier wearing a grey poncho, a teenager, sitting in the mud, mouth open in a scream.

The soldier has taken a direct hit from a phosphorous grenade. His head rocks back and forth. Blood pumps from his stomach. Still he screams, the same word, over and over. "*Madre! Madre! Madre!*"

The Company Commander yells, "Will you shut that fucker up!" He's talking to Hackett, who tries to make the boy be quiet, holding a finger to his lips. Covering his mouth. Making shushing sounds. Still the kid screams for his mother until Hackett puts a hand over his mouth and nose, squeezing them shut, telling him to be quiet, holding him until he falls silent.

The kid's eyes are open. Watching. Welcoming the darkness.

11

LONDON

Elizabeth is late picking up Rowan from nursery. The center manager has heard all the excuses before. Polina is never late. Polina doesn't leave Rowan's raincoat behind, or forget to pack his painting smock, or leave his fruit salad in the fridge. Polina has wet wipes to clean his face after an ice cream. Elizabeth has to spit on a tissue.

Strapping Rowan into his car seat, she heads north to Hampstead to see her father. The gates are open and she parks opposite a garage that holds matching silver Mercedes side by side.

She follows the crushed marble path around the side of the house. The lawns are mown into green strips and the garden beds turned and composted. Rowan runs ahead to the rear terrace. Shielding her eyes from the sun, Elizabeth spies her father kneeling on the turf, turning the soil with a hand fork.

Alistair Bach looks up. As brown as a medicine bottle, with a tangle of grey hair poking out from an old hat, he dresses like a younger version of David Attenborough in chinos and a heavy cotton shirt rolled up to below his elbows. Soft spoken. Gentle. Conservative. Someone from another age. This is his life now—gardening. Planting. Watering. Trimming the topiary into geometric patterns that seem to float above the flowerbeds.

Bach takes a moment to rise from his knees. Rowan runs to him and is hoisted aloft, spun around until his legs are horizontal with the ground.

"Careful, he's just had an ice cream."

"The lucky sod!" He kisses Rowan's cheek. "Let me guess. Chocolate?"

"Is you a magician, Granddad?"

"How do you think I made this garden grow?"

Elizabeth wants to smile but can't make her face move. Hugging her father, she clutches him a little too tightly. Bach untangles himself.

"You haven't heard from him?"

"No."

She averts her eyes, determined not to cry. "The garden is looking good."

Bach knows that she's changing the subject. "My trailing violas are being eaten. Your stepmother won't let me use insecticide. Everything has to be organic. You should see what she makes me eat."

"You'll live longer."

"It feels like it."

He's doing this for Elizabeth's benefit; pretending to be henpecked and harried. It's a little boy's plea for reassurance. She won't give him the satisfaction.

Alistair Bach acts like an everyman but belongs to the truly wealthy. He has a beach house in Florida, a chalet in St. Moritz and a hunting lodge near Aberdeen as well as the house in Hampstead. It's a far cry from his childhood when he grew up in a two-up-two-down in Liverpool, the son of a boilermaker and a seamstress, one of eight children, Catholics. He joined Mersey Fidelity straight out of school and in spite of having no banking qualifications rose to become chairman. One of his first decisions was to move the bank's headquarters from Merseyside to the City of London. Since then he's only been back to Liverpool a handful of times. Some working-class people are proud of their humble roots. Bach is proud of the climb.

"I'll defend Scousers," he once told Elizabeth. "I'll support their football teams and I'll give money to their charities, but don't ask mc to live with them."

Elizabeth turns to gaze at the house. She can see her old bedroom on the second floor, the window surrounded by ivy. This is where she grew up, surrounded by bankers, financiers and money people.

Bach pulls off his gloves, flexing his hands as though fighting arthritis.

"Come inside. Let's have a cup of tea."

They leave Rowan running around the garden, chasing an overweight Labrador called Sally, who is the latest in a long line of "Sallys"—each one related to the one before. The Bachs keep everything in the family.

Elizabeth's stepmother is in the kitchen talking to a tradesman on the phone. Wearing gym leggings and a tracksuit top, Jacinta is thirty years younger than Elizabeth's father, with well-cut white blonde hair and breasts that cost as much as a small car. She gives Elizabeth a little wave but nothing shows in her eyes. It's different when she smiles at Bach, who she treats like a sex god. All praise to the properties of Viagra.

Bach begins opening cupboards and drawers looking for the teabags. "You really don't have to bother, Daddy."

"Nonsense. I could use a cup."

He calls out to Jacinta. "Have you seen the teabags?"

She goes straight to the correct cupboard without interrupting her conversation. Then she smiles at him with such total and unprompted love that it's like a fourth person has walked into the room.

Bach continues talking to Elizabeth. "What do the police say?"

"They think he's run off."

"Who's handling the case?"

"A Detective Constable Carter."

"A constable! Sounds as if they're not taking this seriously. I'll make a few calls. Get them to re-prioritize."

That's how her father talks. It can be like listening to a management seminar.

"Have you talked to Mitchell?"

"He says North was leaking information to a journalist."

Bach blows out his cheeks. "I don't believe it for a minute."

Elizabeth runs her finger along the curve of the sink.

"He's more worried about the bank than about North."

"I'm sure that's not true."

"I was escorted from the building."

"I'll talk to him."

Elizabeth turns away. On the opposite side of the lawn, past the pond, over the sandstone wall that surrounds the gardens, she can see the treetops of Hampstead Heath, an ocean of greenery in a broken landscape of rooftops, chimney pots, TV aerials and satellite dishes.

"You should come and stay with us—just until North shows up," says Bach.

Elizabeth turns and sneaks a glance through to the sunroom where Jacinta is still on the phone.

Bach follows her gaze. "She's not the wicked witch of the East."

"Just Hampstead."

Her father smiles wryly. "She cares about me."

"I know."

Elizabeth's mother died of a brain aneurism ten years ago. Bach waited seven years before he remarried. Said he needed someone to grow old beside. Fine, thought Elizabeth, but did she have to be so young?

He's pouring the tea, clutching the teapot in both hands to stop the lid from falling off. Elizabeth looks at her cup. He's given her too much milk. She doubts if her father has made tea more than a handful of times in his life. Other people do it for him. Maids. Secretaries. Wives.

Elizabeth picks at her chipped nail polish.

"I think North was having an affair."

The statement feels like it might scald her esophagus.

"You're sure?"

She nods.

"How?"

Opening her bag, she takes out the photographs and places them on the kitchen table, not looking at them. Unable to.

"Who took these?"

"A private detective."

"You were having him followed!"

"I know, I know, I felt guilty for not trusting him. I thought I was being paranoid, but now I'm glad."

Bach has taken the photographs to the window where the light is better. He arranges them in some sort of sequence.

"Do you know who she is?"

"No."

"Are there any more?"

Elizabeth retrieves the rest of the photographs. Bach pauses when he sees the images of the outdoor meeting in Maida Vale.

"Do you recognize anyone?" asks Elizabeth.

Bach doesn't answer.

"I thought it might have something to do with the bank."

"I don't think so. I could be wrong. Ex-chairmen are like former prime ministers—we retire gracefully, never comment on company business and enjoy the benefits of a generous pension scheme."

"I don't know how you can be so flippant."

Bach looks hurt. "I'm sorry if I gave that impression."

He goes back to the photograph of the girl. "Are you sure you don't know her?"

"I'm sure." Elizabeth sighs. "I should be angry. I should want to kick his sorry arse out the door, but I just want to find him."

"Men do foolish things sometimes."

"Were you ever unfaithful?"

"That's not a fair question."

"Does that mean yes?"

"It means I'm not going to answer you."

Elizabeth apologizes. She has no right to ask. And she has no right to blame her father for the sins of her husband.

Her mobile is ringing. She looks at the screen but doesn't recognize the number.

"Hello? . . . Is anyone there? . . . Hello?"

There is no sound at all except for a faint pulse that might be the blood in her ears. She exhales and squeezes her eyes shut, ending the call.

12

WASHINGTON

Artie Chalcott sits in his home office, feeling his skin prickle and sweat on his forehead. His ulcer is also acting up and his bowel movements are all over the place. Stress-related. Shit-related. Things are also going south in London. First the banker gets robbed, then he goes missing and now they can't find the girl who robbed him.

During the afternoon he'd tried to take out his frustration on the driving range, hitting balls. Smacking them with a club head the size of a Christmas ham. Made no difference to his mood.

Now he's home and the kids are asleep upstairs and his wife is outside on a pool lounger, wrapped in a silk kimono, smoking a cigarette and getting drunk. She smokes in the same hungry way that she has sex. Not with him. He doesn't know what gym instructor or pool boy or realtor she's screwing now.

Chalcott can't punch a turd, but he can punch a number. He calls Sobel in London. Apologizes for the hour.

"Don't worry about it, Artie, sleep was so last century."

Chalcott feels a flash of annoyance. Sobel sounds too cheerful and he should be calling him "sir."

"What news on our banker?"

"He'll turn up."

"That's the issue, isn't it, Brendan? Where will he turn up? You should have pulled him in before he went AWOL. The list would be safe by now."

"The robbery was a coincidence."

"I don't believe in coincidences. Someone killed the boyfriend."

"Maybe it was North?"

"You don't believe that."

"Who then?"

"Ibrahim."

"Ibrahim doesn't do his own dirty work."

"Maybe he hired someone. North was getting nervous and making threats. He made a phone call on Friday from a call box to a journalist."

"Who?"

"Keith Gooding on the *Financial Herald*. He left a message."

"Had they ever met?"

"We're going back over his phone records."

Chalcott has the television muted. Pictures of a building in Baghdad with shattered windows and curtains flapping through the holes. The Finance Ministry. A crowd outside being kept back by soldiers. A rolling banner on the screen: *Missing UN auditor found dead in Iraq.*

"What about the wife?"

"North hasn't been in touch with her."

"And the girl?"

"MI6 are looking."

"Six couldn't find their ass-cheeks with both hands." Chalcott belches. "While we're on the subject of Ibrahim?"

"He's dropped out of sight."

"Christ almighty! This is a clusterfuck, Brendan. You know how much time and money have gone into this. Remember Afghanistan? Khost? We lost seven agents in one day. They trusted al-Balawi—they made him a fucking birthday cake—and the prick was playing them all along. He walked right into a secure base wearing a suicide vest and blew them all to pieces."

"The Jordanians vouched for al-Balawi."

"Yeah, well, I don't trust any of these cunts. We control that list and we're two years ahead of the game. We'll nail every last one of the murdering scumbags."

13

LONDON

Joe O'Loughlin is slowly crossing the concourse at Paddington Station. Ruiz recognizes the professor's distinctive stoop and stiff-legged gait. He looks like a scientist or a doctor, more Einstein than Freud, with unkempt hair and a tweed jacket. Some weeks he forgets to shave and a salt-and-pepper stubble covers his chin and cheeks.

Ruiz takes his suitcase. Judges the weight. "You bought me a present?"

"It's a bottle of something."

"If I were a religious man I'd bless you."

"If *you* were a religious man the bells would be ringing at Westminster Abbey."

The two men weave through the crowds. Ruiz has to wait for the professor to catch up.

"Can you move any slower?"

"We're all slow in the West Country."

Through the automatic doors, they reach the cab rank where Ruiz has double-parked and displayed a disabled sign in his windscreen.

"Does that still work?"

"I got shot in the leg—there have to be some perks."

Joe looks around. "So where is the young lady?"

"Now that's a good question."

Ruiz drives and talks—telling him about Zac Osborne's death, the bribe and Holly running away. The professor interrupts occasionally to ask a question, focusing on the murder scene and the injuries inflicted.

"It had to be personal," he says. "Very few people can torture someone so directly, hands-on, inflicting injuries over a long period, ignoring their pain…you're dealing with a sadist who was very comfortable in a strange environment. He wasn't panicked. He didn't rush. He took his time, looking for information or waiting for the girl. What do the police say?"

"They're calling it a drug turf war."

"You don't agree?"

"They found no drug paraphernalia in the flat."

"Which doesn't prove anything."

"I talked to the pathologist this morning. Osborne had no drugs in his system. The tox screen came back negative."

Joe leans over the seat and unzips a pocket on his suitcase.

"I had to call in some favors at Social Services. It's not easy getting someone's juvenile files."

"What did you find?"

"Both of Holly Knight's parents are dead. A murder suicide."

"Domestic?"

"Her father strangled her mother and then hung himself. Holly's brother died the same year. Brain aneurism. Holly must have been seven, maybe eight. She was made a ward of the court and fostered to six different families before she was fifteen. That's when she ran away. She was found living with a man twice her age and was sent to another foster home, which she burnt down."

"Did she give a reason?"

"Wouldn't talk about it."

Ruiz has seen how Holly reacts to authority figures. Her resentment borders on hatred.

"At seventeen she spent a year as a kitchen hand. Then she took a job waitressing. She was arrested in April 2009 during a G20 protest in London and a couple of months later she made a rape allegation that wasn't pursued by the CPS."

Joe continues to précis the file, aware of how brutally casual he sounds, giving a banal rendering of a terrible life. What does it do to someone, an upbringing like that? They grow up scared of the dark, scared of being alone, scared of their own dreams.

Ruiz rubs his thumb over his lips. They're nearing the house. He makes a point of parking three blocks away.

"Forgotten where you live?"

"I like the walk."

The professor senses another reason.

"Are you being followed?"

"Not sure."

They go through a break in the buildings, past an upholstery shop, a plumbing store and a new childcare centre. Ruiz is watching the cross-streets, noting the cars.

Joe has a question. "You mentioned that Holly Knight could tell when you were lying."

"Yeah. Is that possible?"

"You're a former detective. You were pretty good at telling when you were being fed bullshit."

"Not like she can. Some people sweat too much, or look to the left or start shaking, or mumbling their answers. This girl just knows."

"Highly unlikely."

"But not impossible?"

Joe falls silent, unwilling to make such a leap of the imagination.

"What is it?" asks Ruiz.

"Nothing."

"Tell me."

"I remember once reading about a police officer in Los Angeles who pulled over a sports car late one night in a rough area of the city. As he walked towards the vehicle with his gun drawn, a teenager jumped from the passenger seat and pointed a semi-automatic directly at him. They were yards apart. The officer held fire. For some reason, in that instant, he knew the teenager wasn't a threat. He called it a hunch. The teenager surrendered."

"So the guy got lucky?"

"A while later, a team of psychologists tested the officer; showed him a series of videotapes of people who were either lying or telling the truth. One tape showed people talking about their views on the death penalty or smoking in public. The same test had been given to hundreds of judges, lawyers, psychotherapists, police sharpshooters and Customs officers. On average they scored fifty per cent."

"Which means they could have been guessing?"

"Exactly, but this police officer—the same one who had the gun pulled on him—he had a success rate of over ninety per cent."

"So you're saying some people are good at spotting liars."

"Not just good, he was a virtuoso."

"How did he do it?"

"Nobody knows for certain. I mean, there are studies on face-reading. Some people train themselves to look for micro-expressions, tiny telltale indicators of stress or deceit. There is a university professor in America, Paul Ekman, who has spent his whole career studying face-reading."

"But you're not convinced?"

Joe doesn't respond. There are things about the human brain that he can't explain: freakish feats of memory, or people with the ability to calculate prime numbers into the trillions. Autistic savants. Geniuses. Brain-injured patients with unique abilities... Neuropsychology is one of the last great frontiers of science.

Inside the house, Ruiz dumps Joe's suitcase and pulls a tray of ice-cubes from the freezer.

"You going to join me?"

"No."

The professor's thumb and forefinger are rubbing together as if rolling a pill between them. He threads his fingers together as if in prayer and the twitching stops. He's not embarrassed or disappointed. He long ago made his peace with the "other" that inhabits his body. Mr. Parkinson.

"So what do we do now?" he asks.

"We wait."

"You think she'll call?"

"Somebody will."

14

BAGHDAD

Luca steps gingerly over the debris in his apartment, trying not to break the unbroken. Bottles and plates are shattered on the floor, amid the contents of his pantry. His furniture lies in pieces and water leaks from a toilet cistern, torn from the wall.

On the floor of the bedroom he finds the photograph of Nicola. He picks it up and brushes the broken glass away. Removing it from the frame, he folds the photo and slips it into his shirt pocket.

In the kitchen, he picks up a chair and sits down. Dirty, unshaven and two days without sleep, he drinks bottled water and takes a moment to feel sorry for himself.

Where to now? America seems like a foreign country he visited a long time ago, like a childhood book he remembers reading. Over the years, moving from war to war, from coups to independence struggles, he has come to realize the arbitrary nature of nationality. There are places in Europe where four or five different countries are separated by just a few miles. One man's country is another man's prison. One man's coup is another man's dispossession. The dead always look the same.

He unhooks a gas cylinder beneath the stove; the lower half twists off to reveal a hidden compartment. A satellite phone is tucked inside. He calls the news desk of the *Financial Herald* in London and asks for Keith Gooding, the chief reporter.

The two men met in Afghanistan in 2002, which seems like a lifetime ago. They both traveled to Kabul via the Khyber Pass, escorted by forty Afghan fighters, men and boys, crowded into pickup trucks, clutching grenade launchers and belts of ammunition.

Four years later Luca was best man at Gooding's wedding in Surrey when he married his childhood sweetheart Lucy, whose father worked in the Foreign Office.

Gooding answers the phone abruptly.

"How's Lucy?"

"She's still beautiful."

"Tell me something—how did a man like you get a woman like that to touch your dick?"

"She grabbed it with both hands."

Luca laughs. His chest hurts. He's out of practice.

"So tell me, Mr. Terracini, how are things with you?"

"Been better."

"What have you done this time?"

"I upset the chief of police."

"Other people fish for minnows, you harpoon whales."

Luca can hear phones ringing in the background and can picture Gooding at his desk, spinning in his chair, feet off the ground like a child on a roundabout. Luca has never been comfortable in an office environment. Never lingered. Gooding is different, a political animal with eyes on the editorship.

"They're kicking me out of the country, revoking my visa."

"Maybe it's not a bad thing."

"I'm getting close to something."

"Care to elaborate?"

"Stolen cash smuggled out of Iraq into Syria and possibly Jordan."

"How much?"

"Tens, maybe hundreds of millions."

"Reconstruction funds?"

"And banking assets. Mostly US dollars."

"What can I do?"

"Find out who monitors international currency transfers. There must be some international body that investigates big movements of cash."

Luca is about to go on, but stops. Someone is at the door. He glances at the intercom. Bare wires hang from a hole in the wall.

"I have to go."

"Stay in touch."

Walking to the window, he peers through a crack in the curtains.

An SUV is parked out front along with the Skoda, which is now a muddy green color. One of Jimmy Dessai's mechanics is leaning on the hood.

Jimmy is sweating from the stairs. He's wearing a cut-off Levi's jacket, showing off his tattoos. "I got your wheels."

"I saw. What's with the color?"

"I had a job lot of green paint. Bought it from a company that paints oil pipelines."

"I'm not paying extra."

"I know."

Jimmy looks at the state of the apartment.

"Some housewarming."

"I wasn't even here."

"Shame."

Jimmy lifts his stubbly chin. The light from the window shines through the jug-ears, turning them pale pink.

"Hey, that thing you wanted to know about truck driving, I might have found someone. His name is Hamada al-Hayak. He's been smuggling petrol over the border since the end of the Iraq–Iran war in the late eighties. A few months back he got shot up on a run to Jordan. Lost his arm. Now he works as a cook at a trucking camp outside of Baghdad. He'll want payment…talking of which, you owe me five grand."

"You'll get your money."

"Sooner rather than later."

"What's the rush?"

"That bull's-eye painted on your back."

Luca returns to the gas cylinder and pulls out a wad of US dollars, counting out five grand. Jimmy pockets the money without recounting.

He looks around the apartment again. "So who did this?"

"The Iraqi police."

"Was it something you said?"

"I looked at them the wrong way."

Jimmy chuckles and cracks his knuckles. At the door, he turns. "Are you leaving town?"

"Looks like it."

"People are gonna miss you."

"You trying to tell me something?"

"I just did."

A pine-scented air freshener shaped like a Christmas tree swings from the rear-vision mirror of the Skoda but it still reeks of fresh paint. Luca drives to the al-Hamra Hotel and gives the keys to the concierge. He tries to call Daniela's room from downstairs. She doesn't pick up. She hasn't checked out. One of the housekeepers opens the door for him.

Daniela is lying in darkness, curled up on the bed. Luca reaches for the light switch but she tells him to go away, anguish in her voice, a soft wet sound.

The housekeeper leaves quickly, pocketing a banknote. Luca moves into the room. Sits on the edge of the bed. Catches a glimpse of her face.

"I'm sorry to hear about your German friend."

"He wasn't my friend."

She rolls on to her back, pulling the sheet up to her stomach. Her hair is matted into greasy clumps, her eyes dull and listless. Luca takes her hand and pulls her up. Groaning softly in protest, she's like a refugee being told what to do and following automatically. He leads her to the bathroom where he turns on the shower, letting steam billow and the air grow humid.

Button by button he undresses her until her blouse falls open and slips from her shoulders; her drawstring pants are pushed down, one foot raised and then the other.

Standing before him in quivering stillness, she waits while he undresses. Then he leads her beneath the stream of water where he soaps a flannel and gently washes her arms and legs, her feet and hands, her shoulders and breasts. He shampoos her hair, massaging his fingers into her scalp, letting the soap stream down his forearms and over his penis.

Only when he's finished does she open her eyes and gaze into his. Her lips move slightly apart. She wants to be kissed, but he holds her at arm's length and begins drying her. Wrapping a robe around her shoulders, he takes her back to the bedroom and pours her a drink from the mini-bar.

"Shaun is dead," she whispers.

"I know."

"So are the others."

"What happened?"

"They were dressed like soldiers. They came into the Ministry and started shooting."

"Where were you?"

"Away..." She sucks in a breath. "I had to identify Glover's body. They tortured him with an electric drill and then cut his throat. He was covered in flies..."

Her voice has a mechanical quality, devoid of emotion, like a person who has spent a lifetime tethered to the banks of a river, only to wake one morning and discover that someone has severed the mooring lines overnight and she's drifted into a dark new place.

"The attack was premeditated. We were the targets. They went straight to the basement."

"Why would they do that?"

"To stop the audit."

"Had you discovered something?"

"The software had only been running for forty-eight hours. There were some double payments and overpayments..." The statement tails off.

"Except?"

"Do you know of Jawad Stadium?"

"It's south of here."

"According to the financial records it has been completely refurbished. Work began in 2005 and was finished two years ago. But the work was never done. I've seen the stadium. That's where I was when they launched the attack."

"How big was the contract?"

"Ninety million dollars."

"And the duplicate payments?"

"Forty-two million." She pulls her knees up and takes another sip, unused to the harshness of the vodka.

"Who knew you were looking at the contracts?"

"Glover called the Iraqi Reconstruction Management Office and asked what team approved the project."

"Did they tell him?"

"No."

"Did you talk to anyone else?"

"I sent an email request to New York asking for information about the main contractor, Bellwether Construction. They sent a file, but most of the important details had been blacked out."

They lapse into silence.

Swinging her legs out of bed, Daniela moves barefoot across the floor. She opens her satchel on the luggage rack and retrieves a single sheet of paper.

"You asked me about cash deliveries to banks. I did a search of the Central Bank database."

Luca leans forward expectantly, his knees touching the edge of her robe.

"And?"

"I've probably broken a dozen laws." She hands the page to Luca and begins explaining the figures. "The first column is a code used to identify each bank branch. Next there is a date and then the amount of cash requested in the nominated currency. I concentrated on US deliveries."

Luca looks at the first three transfers.

BI (74-312)	092609	US$5.3m
RB (74-212)	020610	US$15.6m
ITB (74-466)	021110	US$1.8m

Even without checking, he knows these cash deliveries correspond with the robberies — preceding them by twenty-four hours.

Somebody must have leaked the information to the armed robbers. How many people had access to the information? It could be an insider at the Treasury, or the Iraqi Central Bank, or the delivery company.

Daniela curls up next to him, reaching between the lapels of his robe and running her fingers down his chest, loosening the knot at his waist. She flattens herself against him, pressing her loins tightly to his and he feels a desire stirring that he tries to ignore.

"Don't you want me?" she asks.

"I don't want you mistaking my motives."

"I'm leaving tomorrow."

"I know."

"I might not see you again."

"You will. There's someone I want you to meet."

Daniela crosses the foyer, moving from memory on marble tiles that are polished and cool. Her cheeks have color now. Her hair is drying and her clothes are clean. Outside the air is hot and harshly bright, thick with the smell of wood fires and paraffin stoves.

They drive east along busy roads. As they approach each checkpoint, Luca tells Daniela to lower her eyes and cover her face with a scarf. Once they pass through, Luca continues his story, telling her about his arrest and interrogation — as much as he can remember. The account seems so strange, so pulled out of shape and littered with broken and jagged pieces.

"So you don't have a visa?"

"No."

"What will you do?"

"Leave."

Sadr City is an immense suburb in eastern Baghdad full of ramshackle one-storey buildings covered in dust and patched together with scavenged building materials. The city has many neighborhoods like this one — sectarian strongholds, full of widows, orphans and the dispossessed; Sunni or Shiite, bombed back to the Stone Age. Amid the poverty, children play football using oil drums as goal posts. Their mothers, in full chadors, look like shadows in the darkened windows. The only splash of color comes from billboards advertising mobile phones and flat-screen TVs.

Jamal and Nadia have two rooms behind a shop that sells water barrels and tools. Luca parks beside a mound of broken bricks and discarded planks. He fixes a lock to the steering wheel and another to the gearstick.

A woman opens the door just a crack, one eye visible, suspicion in it, then fear, then anger. This is Jamal's wife, Nadia. Two young boys are clutching her legs, peering from the folds of her dress.

She covers her mouth and nose. "You should not have come."

"I need to talk to Jamal," says Luca.

"You have caused enough trouble."

Her gaze switches to Daniela and her anger evaporates. She opens the door wider. "You take too many risks and put other people in danger."

The boys run away and hide in the second room, peeking out through a curtain, one head below the other. Electrical wires sprout from the walls and a kerosene lantern hangs from a beam, revealing woven rugs and bedding rolled in the corner.

Jamal emerges from the second room, his handsome face transformed. Rearranged by fists or clubs, his almond eyes, his white smile, his youth. Gone. Beaten from him. His lips are blown up to twice their size and his right eye is full of blood, while the left has almost closed completely. Daniela can't hide her shock.

Jamal opens his mouth to speak. No sound emerges. He tries again, his voice altered by his swollen lips and broken teeth.

"Please leave. It's not safe for you to be here."

His voice is loud in the tiny room.

"What happened?" asks Luca. "Why did they do this?"

"I work with Americans—this is the reason."

"Abu?"

"He is safe, but they're looking for him."

Jamal wipes the spit dribbling down his chin. Luca reaches out and touches his friend's shoulder.

"I'm sorry."

"It is not your fault. We both knew this could happen."

Nadia is making coffee. From the plastic container she carries from the pump each day she pours just enough water into a saucepan. Daniela introduces herself and crouches down, talking to the boys, who are losing their shyness.

Jamal pulls cushions from the corner and asks Luca to sit down. His modesty and politeness are a study in respect passed on by his parents. He glances at his wife. Speaks softly.

"I met Nadia at university. I remember thinking I could never marry someone so beautiful, so I didn't talk to her . . . I was too nervous. Then one day I found her crying. Her father had been taken by Saddam's secret police for something he'd done or said or not done or not said. I told Nadia I would find him. It took me two weeks. It cost four thousand dollars to buy his freedom. Nadia married me out of gratitude, but it has become love."

He wipes his mouth on his sleeve.

"None of my five sisters are married. My father says he won't find them husbands until the militias stop killing each other. He prefers to keep them safe at home."

"What does your father do?"

"He runs a market stall. I did have a brother, but he's dead."

They are silent for a moment and Luca tries to apologize again.

"You are not to blame. There is too much blame in Iraq. The Sunnis blame the Shiites, who blame the Baathists, who once poisoned the Kurds, and they all blame the Americans. We've become a country of nasty, pissed-off people with guns and third-grade educations. My generation has been at war ever since I was born. We are so familiar with it we have coffin makers on every corner, moving bodies like melons.

"The new Iraq was never going to be perfect, but we hope, we dream, we survive. The Americans will leave one day. And what will be left behind? All things light and all things dark."

Jamal's eyes find the floor. "They tried to drown me. Now each time I fall asleep, I dream of swallowing water. I can taste it, smell it coming out of my mouth and nose. I wanted to die in the end. I didn't care anymore. I made a statement. I wrote what they told me."

"I know."

He blinks back tears, looking like a man whose life has undergone a violent decompression, a diver returning to the surface too quickly.

Jamal taps his chest. "They could not change who I am. They could not touch me inside."

Daniela joins them, bringing a jug of rose-scented water and a tray of sweet pastries. Luca takes one and feels the sugar melting on his tongue. They speak in English for her benefit.

Jamal remembers something else. "There was an American... when they were interrogating me. I saw him just once, but I remember his voice. He was feeding them the questions."

Daniela interrupts. "What did he look like?"

"Like an American," says Jamal. "He asked me if I was scared. I told him no. He laughed and said I was too stupid to be scared."

Daniela: "Did he have a side-parting?"

"Yes."

"What about his voice?" Luca asks. "Did it sound cracked or broken?"

Jamal nods and all three of them are staring at each other, wondering how they could know the same man.

"His name is Jennings," explains Daniela. "He was assigned to us by the US Embassy as our local liaison officer."

"I was told he works for the State Department," says Luca. "I met him this morning."

Luca takes a moment to consider the ramifications. US involvement in the arrest and torture of an Iraqi civilian doesn't come as a complete surprise to him, but normally such operations don't feature personnel from the State Department or the CIA as eyewitnesses. The US government prefers to remain in the background, promoting the culture of deniability.

"When did you last talk to Jennings?" he asks Daniela.

"After the attack on the Finance Ministry. He wanted to know what files had been taken. He also wanted my laptop and whatever results we'd obtained. I told him the program had only been running forty-eight hours, but he still wanted the records."

"Did you tell him about the double payments?"

"Yes."

"What about the cash deliveries to the banks that were robbed?"

"He knew that too."

They fall silent and watch Jamal's two boys drawing pictures on butcher's paper, sharing colored pencils between them. What sort of future awaits them, wonders Luca. Jamal has been identified and labeled as a collaborator. He and Abu will be targets from now on. Friendless. Never safe.

Reaching into his pocket, Luca places the keys to the Skoda on the tea tray.

"These are yours now."

Jamal looks at him. "Why?"

"You can be a taxi driver—until you become a doctor."

"You do not owe me anything."

"I owe you more than I can ever repay."

Jamal drives them to the al-Hamra Hotel and drops them inside the security perimeter. They say goodbye with the engine running.

"I will come back one day," says Luca.

Jamal shakes his head. "Iraq is a place to leave, not to live."

"What will you do?"

"I have family in the south."

Daniela turns away as the two men embrace wordlessly. She takes Luca's hand as they watch the Skoda leave, waving one last time before going upstairs to their room where they undress each other.

Luca can't find the clasp of her bra.

"Try the other side."

"I never say no to the other side."

Unhooking the clasp, he reaches for her breasts. "These are nice."

"So I've been told."

"Firm."

"They hold my bra up."

She turns, expecting a kiss, but Luca avoids her lips.

"I thought you were going to kiss me."

"Not yet."

He wants to change the rhythm of her breathing. He wants to make her skin flush and her toes curl. He wants to see her self-control dissolve and for Daniela to exist on the same plane he does.

Afterwards, they lie together. She takes his hand and can feel it beating softly as if it contains its own tiny heart.

"Who's Nicola?" she asks. "Nadia mentioned her."

"A woman I knew."

"You were close?"

"Yes."

"What happened?"

"I lost her."

Daniela looks at him steadily and for a moment the intelligence in her eyes seems to be absolute and unshakable.

"Why did you take me to meet Jamal and his family?"

"To show you why I do this."

15

LONDON

Elizabeth is leaning out of the top-floor window, puffing on a cigarette but not inhaling. The last time she remembers doing something like this she was fourteen. It was a Pall Mall and she was hiding from her parents. Now she's thirty-two and hiding from her son's nanny. Age doesn't make us any wiser or less prone to guilt.

She found an old packet of cigarettes when she was searching

North's study, looking for clues, trying to piece together his last days, checking his credit card statements, mobile phone bills and emails; lipstick on his shirt collars; or another woman's scent on his clothes.

Suddenly nauseous, she breaks the cigarette in half, wrapping the butt in a tissue before flushing it down the loo. The tissue dissolves but the dog-end is still there, bobbing in the bowl, mocking her.

She brushes her teeth and goes back to the study, sitting at North's desk, feeling the contours in the old leather chair, worn shiny in places. She found the chair in a second-hand shop in Camden just after they bought the house in Barnes. North had wanted a new chair, but she told him this one was a classic. It reminded her of something you see in old movies about newspaper offices where reporters hammer on manual typewriters and yell at copy-boys to run their words to the subs desk.

Her personal dreams of journalism had made this image seem romantic. At university she imagined herself as a famous columnist— the next Julie Burchill or Zoë Heller or Lynn Barber. Instead she'd presented a "lifestyle" program, as forgettable as a phone number.

Elizabeth opens the report from the private detective. Her husband's days are broken down into hours and minutes: times, dates and places. Tucked into the front sleeve of the folder is a USB stick. Using a directional microphone, Colin Hackett had recorded some of the conversation between North and the two men he met at The Warrington in Maida Vale.

Plugging the stick into her laptop, Elizabeth opens the audio file and presses "play." There are background voices, car sounds, wind rustling the leaves. Three voices, one of them North's, another speaks a guttural-sounding English, his words like gravel rolling in a drum. The other accent is almost too perfect, like listening to someone mimicking Roger Moore.

Voice 1: ...you should stop saying these things and calm
   down...

North: Don't tell me to calm down...I approved the
   transfers. I signed off on the details...

Voice 1: You did your job...due diligence...nobody is
    suggesting otherwise...

North: ...it's a bad sign...the money came from
    somewhere...it's going somewhere...tell me.

Voice 1: These are not questions you need to ask. Worry
    about life, worry about your wife and family...

North: Leave my family out of this.

Voice 1: These things will pass...

Voice 2: We have a proverb where I come from, Mr. North.
    If you have done nothing wrong, don't worry about the
    devil knocking at your door...

North: But I am doing something wrong...

Voice 1: You're exaggerating...nothing has changed.

There is a garbled section of the recording. North appears to have
walked away from the table, but the men are still talking.

Voice 2: ...he's rattled...

Voice 1: ...I will call our friend. Tell him we're
    concerned...

Voice 2: The time for talking is over...this is what happens
    when you deal with amateurs...

The recording ends. Elizabeth plays it back and listens for
names, but there are too many gaps and unintelligible words. She
concentrates on North's voice, feeling something snag in his chest
when he mentions the word family.

This wasn't a normal business meeting. These weren't normal
business contacts. North told Bridget Lindop that he'd done something terrible and on the tape he talked about wanting to know
where money had come from and gone. Perhaps Mitchell was right
to be concerned.

Elizabeth looks at the daily log written by Colin Hackett. Before
North went to The Warrington, he visited a house in Mount Street,
just off Park Lane. She glances at her watch. Rowan won't be
home from nursery for another few hours. Polina can pick him up.

Grabbing her car keys and her bag, she gets in the car and programs the satnav for Mayfair. The journey takes her across Hammersmith Bridge and along Hammersmith Road past Olympia and through Kensington to Hyde Park Corner.

Late summer and there are still plenty of tourists in London, eating sandwiches on the grass and taking photographs from open-top buses. London has never seemed like a destination to Elizabeth, but for others it is a postcard, a photograph or the backdrop to their holiday videos.

Mount Street is lined with Edwardian mansion blocks and rows of Italianate houses, every corner has a CCTV camera bolted to the brickwork. Curtains don't twitch anymore and neighbors no longer study neighbors. Instead cameras record every dropped piece of litter and unscooped dog turd.

Walking up the front steps, Elizabeth presses a large bronze bell. The blue-painted front door is heavy and old. It opens after a moment. A woman in a black smock dress peers from inside. Elegant. Her hair is silver tipped and her features as delicate as a porcelain figurine.

Elizabeth realizes that she should have thought of a story.

"I've lost my dog," she blurts. "I live around the corner. I'm asking everyone."

The woman shakes her head. "What does your dog look like?"

"Umm, he's white, ah, he's a sort of terrier like a Jack Russell."

"I haven't seen any stray dogs."

"Is there anyone else at home? Perhaps you could ask your husband."

A man's voice comes from the top of the stairs: "Who is it, Maria?"

"Someone has lost her dog."

The door opens a little wider. Elizabeth takes the opportunity. She steps into the hallway, glancing up the stairs.

"It's been two days and my little boy is heartbroken. I thought I'd knock on some doors."

The man has gone. She didn't see his face. The woman ushers her into a large front room with dormer windows and a fireplace. Every piece of furniture seems to fit perfectly. Antique or expensive copies, they match the artifacts — Byzantine mosaics, swords, pottery and statues displayed around the room. The beauty of the items seems to distract Elizabeth, who doesn't realize she's being spoken to.

"I beg your pardon?"

"What is the dog's name?"

"Ummm, ah, well, his name is Fred, short for Frederick."

The woman is almost ageless with a casual elegance that makes Elizabeth feel clumsy and shabbily dressed. She could be Middle Eastern. She could just be wealthy.

"Where do you live?"

"Around the corner."

"What road?"

Elizabeth can't think of a neighboring street. She mumbles something and Claudia kicks her as though punishing her stupidity.

"Do you have a photograph?" asks the woman.

"Pardon?"

"A picture of the dog. You could put it on lampposts."

"Yes, what a good idea."

Elizabeth wants to ask her about North and why he came to the house. She has the photographs in her handbag. What would the woman say if she just came straight out and showed them to her? She raises her eyes to the ceiling, hearing something upstairs. "Maybe your husband has seen Fred."

"He's busy."

"What does he do?"

The woman ignores the question and stares at Elizabeth for a long time. "Why are you really here?"

Elizabeth's skin prickles with embarrassment and Claudia squirms wetly in her belly.

"I feel so bloody silly. I didn't work out what I was going to say."

"I don't understand."

"My name is Elizabeth North. My husband came here about a week ago. It was a Friday afternoon. Now he's missing. I'm trying to find him."

The woman is watching her with her almond-shaped eyes,

giving nothing away. Elizabeth takes the photographs from her handbag. They are curling now at the edges and stained with something sticky that Rowan put in her handbag.

"Who took these?"

"A private detective."

Suspicion flares in the woman's eyes. "Watching this house?"

"No. He was following my husband. I was concerned about him. I knew something was wrong. He came here. Is one of these men your husband?"

The woman stands and straightens her dress, brushing it down her thighs. "I don't know who you are—or what you're doing, but I want you to leave."

"I'm telling you the truth. His name is Richard North. Can you just ask your husband?"

The woman walks to the entrance hall telephone. "Do I have to call the police?"

"I'm leaving," says Elizabeth.

As she tries to step past the woman, a hand shoots out and grips her wrist. "Tell me why you're following us."

"I don't even know who you are. I'm trying to find my husband."

Elizabeth feels a sudden sharp cramp in her abdomen that takes her breath away. She has to lean on the edge of the table, breathing in and out against the pain.

The woman lets go and her voice softens. "You should go home."

"I know he came here."

"I will ask my husband—but you must leave."

A voice from above: "Is everything all right, Maria?"

It's one of the men from the photograph—the one with the clipped English accent. Taking off his glasses, he studies Elizabeth, his eyes neither hostile nor interested.

"I'm looking for my husband, Richard North. He met with you."

"And what makes you say that?"

"I have photographs."

"What photographs?"

"You were sitting at a table outside The Warrington. There was another man with you."

"I'm afraid you're mistaken."

Elizabeth can feel the skin on her forehead itching. She fumbles through the photographs, looking for the right one. Pulls it free. Holds it up. The man doesn't want to look at her pictures. He hasn't moved from the stairs.

"The other man in the picture—do you know his name?"

Nothing alters in his face, which has all the emotion and depth of a pie plate. Elizabeth presses on. "I just want to find him. Do you know where he is?"

"Show her to the door, Maria."

Elizabeth wants to make him listen. "I know about the transfers," she blurts, making things up as she goes along.

The man scratches at the corner of his mouth with a fingernail. "I don't know what you're talking about. Please leave my home."

He turns away, pulling a mobile phone from the sagging pocket of his sweatshirt.

Elizabeth finds herself on the front steps where dead leaves are chasing each other in a circle of wind. The man was lying to her. Hiding something. Had she made a mistake coming here? Claudia has stopped kicking, but her heart still races, beating like the wings of a bird against the bars of a cage.

16

LONDON

Colorful saris, black chadors, minarets and Halal butchers— it could be Bangladesh or Mogadishu or Hackney or Lambeth. Extended families. Illegal immigrants. Sweatshop workers. Flotsam washed up on British shores.

It took the Courier longer than expected to find Bernie Levinson. Following him had bordered on the banal—tracking him between his various businesses and his very ugly mock Tudor house in Ilford with its swimming pool and revolving sunroom.

A bell tinkles above his head. He spins a CLOSED sign on the back of the door. The shelves of the pawnshop are lined with DVD players, iPods, satnavs and TV sets.

"I won't keep you," says a voice in the back room. The Courier walks behind the counter and through the door.

"Hey, I told you to wait!" says Bernie, who is trying to repackage a CD player. "You got to stay out there—the other side of the counter."

"How long will you be?"

"When I'm ready, I'm ready."

The Courier walks back to the service counter, sure now that Bernie is alone. The pawnbroker appears, wiping his hands on his thighs.

"What can I do for you?"

"I'm looking for a girl called Holly Knight."

"Never heard of her."

"That's a shame."

The Courier has taken a golf club from a two-toned Slazenger bag in the corner. He holds it in his fists, more like an axe than a seven-iron.

"They're a fine set of clubs," says Bernie. "Belonged to a pro golfer who retired."

"Is that right?"

"You like golf?"

"Not even a little bit."

The Courier waggles the club.

"Hey, if you're not into golf, have a look at these." Bernie opens a drawer full of DVDs. "I got something for every taste in here. Fat Girls. Big tits. Nurses. Maybe you like them young. This isn't your typical East European shit. It's American—better production values. No dubbing. They moan in English."

The visitor doesn't take his eyes off Bernie. This is weird, thinks the pawnbroker; even the whacked-out crackheads and ice-addicts like porn, but not this guy. Instead he keeps grinning like he's got dancing monkeys in his head.

Still talking, Bernie edges along the counter towards the cash register where he keeps a sawn-off shotgun on a shelf.

"Buy one and you get the second one free," he says, "and if you don't have a DVD player I can fix you up with one." His right hand drops below the level of the counter and his fingers touch the stock of the shotgun. All he has to do is pick it up but for some reason he can't do it. He's staring at the smiling man, unable to focus.

"What do you want, mister?"

"You're going to show me what Holly Knight sold to you. Then you're going to tell me where to find her."

"I told you—I don't know anyone by that name. Why are you grinning at me like that?"

The golf club shatters the counter and Bernie leaps backwards, knocking over a rack of second-hand CDs. His mouth flaps wordlessly.

"Where is Holly Knight?" asks the Courier.

"She lives on the Hogarth Estate."

"Not anymore."

"Then I don't know where she is."

"What did she sell you?"

"Bits and pieces," says Bernie. "Some of it I already sold."

The Courier puts the seven-iron back in the bag and selects another.

"I mean, you're welcome to the rest of it," says Bernie. "I'll show you. It's in my office. Upstairs." Bernie lifts his chin to the ceiling.

The Courier waits for him to lock up the shop and follows him around the side of the building and up the staircase.

"Why are you so fat?" he asks.

"I eat too much."

"You don't exercise? Walk every day. Twenty minutes."

"That's what my wife says."

"You should listen to her."

Once inside the office, Bernie fusses over opening cupboards, clumsy with nerves. He hands over the briefcase, a laptop, digital camera and a mobile phone.

"What about the notebook?"

"Why would I want a fucking notebook?" Bernie opens his palms, trying to sound reasonable. "That laptop won't be much good to you. When I booted it up I got an email. I opened it up and a window popped open, then another one. It was a virus chewing through the files—emails, the calendar, contacts, spreadsheets...I held down the power button and then rebooted but it was too late. I got the black screen of death. All gone."

The Courier glances around the office. Something bothers him. Maybe it's Bernie's wheedling voice. No, that's not it. Then he notices the CCTV camera in a corner of the ceiling. Careless. He follows the wire to a DVD recorder below the pawnbroker's desk and smashes it with his boot heel.

"It wasn't on," says Bernie, one hand trembling on his temple. "I got no beef with you, sir. I gave you what you asked for."

The Courier turns towards the window where raindrops have left a pattern of dust on the pane.

"I got to figure out what to do with you," he says. "Nothing personal, but you irritate me."

"A lot of people say that," says Bernie. "Even my wife says I'm irritating."

"She's a very perceptive woman. Do you think she'd mind if you were dead?"

"I hope she would."

The Courier takes the keys from Bernie and pushes him into the storeroom, hooking the padlock through the latch. He puts his mouth near the door.

"What are you going to do if Holly Knight contacts you again?"

"I want nothing to do with her."

"That's the wrong answer, Bernie. You see, I know where you work and where you live."

"I'm going to call you."

"Now we're communicating."

17

BAGHDAD

Luca finds Edge at a bar in the International Zone holding a shot glass of bourbon up to the light as if looking at a rare jewel. His right hand is wrapped in a discolored bandage and a Filipino woman is sitting on the stool next to him. Dressed in a halter top and denim shorts, she's wearing spiked heels that don't reach the floor.

"You look like you slept in the restroom," says Luca.

"Not true. I slept with this little lady," says Edge, almost inhaling the shot, before sipping a beer more slowly. "Say hello to Marcella. She's a hooker."

Marcella doesn't appreciate the description. She swings her handbag at Edge's head and calls him an ape before tottering away on her heels, which make her legs look longer and her head smaller.

"Can I join you?"

"It's a free country. Operation Iraqi Freedom—name says it all."

The barman has left the bottle of bourbon so Edge can free pour. That's one of the things the contractor hates about foreign countries—the measuring cups and penny-pinching.

Flexing his damaged hand, Edge picks up a cigarette. He has six of them lined up on the bar. Lighting up, he sucks on it like oxygen.

Luca narrows his eyes against the smoke. "What are you doing?"

"I'm getting drunk and then I'm gonna pick a fight."

"In that order?"

"Yep. Which bit are you here for?"

Luca points at Edge's bandaged hand. "Is that from your last fight?"

"I hit a wall."

"Who won?"

"We both suffered superficial damage."

Edge sips his beer.

"I heard about Shaun," says Luca. "You want to talk about it?"

"Nope."

"Might help."

"That's what the counselor said. I told him I wanted to turn this shithole country to rubble."

"What did he say?"

"He suggested I take anti-depressants. I said I wasn't fucking depressed. Depressed is when you can't get out of bed and you can't taste your food and you can't laugh or cry. Depressed is when you feel nothing at all. Right now I'd love to feel nothing."

"You shouldn't blame yourself."

"I should have been there."

"Then you'd be dead too."

"Yeah, well, I could have lived with that."

Luca orders a beer. They sit in silence for a while. The bar is empty, except for a young man reading a newspaper near the window. Every so often he turns a page and glances at them. Taller than average, with a short haircut and an expensive leather jacket, he looks American. It's the teeth. An orthodontist winters in Florida thanks to those teeth.

Luca motions to Edge's hand. "Is it broken?"

"Maybe."

Edge gingerly unwraps the bandage as though expecting to see something green and gangrenous. Instead it's bruised and swollen.

"Can you still drive?"

"Yeah."

"Can you hold a gun?"

His eyes brighten.

"Sure."

"I need security."

"Will I get to shoot anyone?"

"I'd prefer it if you didn't."

Edge seems to teeter on the edge of a direct response, his eyes charged with a strange energy.

"What's the job?"

"I'm trying to find out why Shaun and the others died."

"How you gonna do that?"

"You remember Watergate?"

"Nixon and stuff."

"An informant was feeding information to Woodward and Bernstein—they were the journalists who linked the break-in to the White House."

"Deep Throat. Right? The guy in the underground car park."

"You saw the movie—that's good. Deep Throat kept telling them one thing, over and over."

"What was that?"

"Follow the money."

"That's *my* sort of message."

"I thought it might be."

"When do we leave?"

"First light."

The trucking camp is a makeshift township of tents, shipping containers and clapboard buildings five miles south-west of Baghdad on the main highway to Jordan. It's a strange atavistic and tribal world, set amid a wasteland of stony desert, sand dunes, rocky islands and dried up riverbeds.

More than fifty trucks are parked in bays, some with canvas awnings strung from the cabs and pegged to the ground. Other rigs are jacked up on cinder blocks undergoing repairs. Most of the vehicles are stained with rust or scarred by bullets and shrapnel.

The gatekeeper is small and brown with a frayed coat and woolen hat the same color as his beard. Pressing his palms together, Luca talks in Arabic, wishing him good morning.

Springsteen is playing on a beatbox from within a nearby tent.

"That's what I'll never understand about this place," mutters Edge to Daniela. "These bastards hate us, but they watch our movies and listen to our music."

"Maybe music doesn't belong to anyone," replies Daniela.

"Yeah, well Springsteen doesn't belong to these fuckers."

Luca comes back to the Land Cruiser.

"Two hundred yards straight ahead, building on the right."

The drivers are waking, emerging from their tents, stiffness in their bodies, shirts unbuttoned and belts undone, scratching navels or testicles. Most of them are foreigners, uneducated and poor, hapless and a long way from home. One of them urinates loudly on the side of an empty drum.

Edge parks near the largest of the buildings and watches Luca and Daniela walk across the dusty street and push through a doorway slung with a hessian curtain. Inside the air smells of pea soup, eggs, rice and noodles. Large metal pots are propped on cinder blocks above glowing charcoal.

Four cooks turn in unison. Only one keeps his back to them, continuing to stir a pot. Luca bows and asks for Hamada al-Hayak.

Al-Hayak turns and wipes his left hand on a dirty cloth tucked in the rope that serves him as a belt. Instead of a right arm he has an empty sleeve, knotted above the elbow.

The cooks and dishwashers are focused on Daniela, whose headscarf has slipped back from her forehead. Self-consciously, she tugs it back in place. One of them is huge, in a checked shirt and overalls that are two sizes too small and ride up over his ankles.

"Can we talk?" asks Luca.

Al-Hayak motions to the rear door. Stepping past a makeshift pyramid of gas cylinders, he leads them into a small courtyard and storage area fenced in by shipping containers. A diesel generator chugs noisily, producing power for the fridges and the lights. Goats are tethered to wooden stakes, their eyes luminous and curious.

The cook turns on Luca.

"What sort of dumb shit are you? Coming here. Bringing a

woman like that." He motions to Daniela without making eye contact with her. "Some of these men will look at you and see nothing but a reward." He pinches one nostril and blows out the other. "Who gave you my name?"

"Jimmy Dessai."

"You're lying."

Luca takes a fifty-dollar bill from his pocket. "I need some information."

Al-Hayak ignores the request and puts a cigarette between his lips, hunting in his shirt pocket for a match. Finding a light, he holds the smoke deep in his lungs like he's trying to digest it. "So now you're going to bribe me. How much is my life worth? What about my arm? What will you pay me for my good arm?"

"What happened to your arm?" asks Daniela.

"What do you care? You will go home one day soon and you'll call this a victory and say you did your best."

"You used to be a truck driver," says Luca.

"When I had two of these." He holds up his hand.

"What happened?"

"I lost my truck. They blew up the lead vehicle in the convoy, blocking the road and opened fire on the rest of us."

"What were you hauling?"

"Diesel."

"Ever take anything else?"

He shrugs. "Cigarettes, paraffin, wheat, cooking oil..."

"What about cash?"

Al-Hayak shakes his head, his mouth a tight line. The odor of cooking fat and wet nicotine rises from his clothes.

"I earn two dollars a day serving food. With two arms I could earn five times that much. I'm a cook, not a criminal."

Luca pulls out another banknote, holding it between his index and forefinger. The gesture seems to reveal something in the cook's eyes, a small dull yellow light burning in the corners like a parasite feeding. Taking the money quickly, he pushes it deep into the front pocket of his apron.

"I have no stake in this."

"I understand."

"I delivered a container. I didn't know what was inside."

Al-Hayak stares at the burning end of his cigarette. "Seven months ago a man came to my brother-in-law and asked him about doing a run into Syria. He wanted two trucks, so my brother-in-law called me. He told me we were hauling oil, but I could tell by the weight it was something else."

"You didn't see the trailer being loaded?" asks Daniela.

"No."

"What about a manifest?"

"The paperwork says what they want it to say."

"What did you think you were carrying?"

Al-Hayak scratches his face. His fingernails are edged with dirt. "Drugs. People. I didn't ask. We had an escort. Guards. Usually only the military convoys get protection, but we had two Land Cruisers with us all the way to the border."

"Where did you cross?"

"Husaiba."

"Into Syria."

"Yes. The Land Cruisers didn't cross with us. I was given a number to call once we had cleared immigration and Customs. I had to ask for a man who would give me orders. The man was angry because we had come a day earlier than he expected. He told us to wait and he would send an escort.

"Mazen, my brother-in-law, wanted to find shade, but I told him we couldn't move. We waited all day in the heat. I thought if there were people inside they would be dying of heatstroke and dehydration. I put my head against the side, listening, but I couldn't hear anything."

The cook's cheeks are dented as he sucks the saliva out of his mouth and spits.

"The man didn't come until past midnight. There were two more vehicles. He ordered us to drive, but I said it wasn't safe at night. He laughed at me and waved a gun. That stretch of road from Ash Sholah to Palmyra is treacherous even during the daylight. The edges are soft and the escarpment has switchbacks and blind corners.

"My brother-in-law was ahead. He missed a turn. Maybe he fell asleep. Maybe his brakes failed. I saw the truck go over the edge and roll down the mountain. It opened like a giant tin of peaches. I expected to see bodies being flung into the air, but there weren't any people inside."

Al-Hayak motions for Luca to give him another banknote. "This is what I saw," he says, holding the note in front of Luca and Daniela's eyes. "Fluttering like butterflies in the moonlight, caught in the updraft. I knew Mazen was dead. The truck had fallen two hundred feet. A guard pointed a gun at my head and told me to keep driving. He asked me if I saw anything. I said no. They would have killed me then. No question."

"What happened to the money?"

"The mountainside was covered in shale and loose rocks. It was too dangerous to climb down. They made me drive to a warehouse on the outskirts of Damascus, near the airport."

"Can you remember the address?"

"There was a sign on the gate: Alain al Jaria."

"Ever-flowing spring," says Daniela.

"You speak Arabic?"

She shakes her head. Luca looks at her, puzzled, and al-Hayak grows nervous at how much he's said. More drivers are waking and wandering past, peering at the strangers, eyes hooded, shoulders hunched.

"Did you hear any names?" asks Luca.

Al-Hayak scratches his chin. "I was told to forget."

Luca gives him another twenty.

"The man who came to the border to meet us—I heard one of the guards use his name. Mohammed Ibrahim."

Daniela's eyes widen. She tries to recover, but the cook has seen her reaction.

"Enough! No more questions!"

He turns away, pushing through the flapping hessian curtain.

Daniela follows him. "Did you ever see this man? What did he look like? Was he a big man? Overweight?"

The cook lifts the lid from a dirty steel pot, dropping it loudly. Steam billows into his face.

"Did he have another name?" says Daniela. "What did they call him?"

Al-Hayak spins like an animal trapped in a box. This time he has a heavy steel lid in his fist.

The rest of the kitchen is suddenly silent. The big cook dressed in overalls is beside him, the muscles swelling across his shoulders like cords of wood on a woodpile.

Luca steps in front of Daniela. He avoids the first blow, but someone punches him from behind, finding his kidneys. He goes down, mouthing the air like a fish feeding on the surface of a lake. Strong hands pick him up and carry him outside on to the street where drivers are queuing for breakfast. Al-Hayak is breathing hard. White flecks cling to the corners of his mouth.

Edge is running, the semi-automatic in his damaged hand. All hell is going to break loose. His good fist snaps out three professional punches, sending the big cook to the ground. He swings the gun in a wide arc, almost daring the others to give him an excuse.

Lifting Luca to his feet, he pushes him into Daniela's arms.

"We're leaving."

Backing away from the crowd, swinging the semi-automatic from side to side, he waits for them to reach the car. Then he slides behind the wheel, the engine running, finding reverse where it should be, accelerating backwards down the narrow street, spinning the wheel, sending the Land Cruiser into a 180-degree turn. First gear. Stamping on the accelerator. Gravel spitting from the tires and rattling against a pyramid of fuel drums.

Edge doesn't look back until they reach the smooth tarmac of the highway. Tossing his weapon on to the passenger seat he lights a cigarette and opens the windows. Pushed back by the rushing wind, nobody speaks for a dozen miles.

"Who is Mohammed Ibrahim?" asks Luca.

Daniela brushes hair from her eyes. "Remember I told you how I used to work for Paul Volcker?"

"The former head of the Fed Reserve."

"We were investigating the Oil for Food program. Saddam skimmed nineteen billion dollars in bribes and kickbacks. That's how he built his palaces and paid rewards to the families of Palestinian suicide bombers."

"And Ibrahim?"

"One of the mysteries we had to solve was how Saddam got this illegal revenue into Iraq. It took a while but eventually we found dozens of bank accounts set up in the name of front companies in Jordan, Syria and Lebanon. The bribes and pay-offs were channeled through these into accounts in Iraq's state-owned banks. One name kept coming up: Mohammed Ibrahim Omar al-Muslit. The Iraqis called him the Fat Man, but we had another name for him."

"What was that?"

"Saddam's banker."

18

LONDON

Elizabeth isn't ready for this baby. It's not the unfinished projects that concern her — the nursery curtains and the baby clothes still in boxes in the attic — her mind is in the wrong place. She's supposed to be eating properly, taking vitamins and conserving her energy, but her body won't allow her to pause. In the meantime, Claudia is like a parasite feeding from a host, carelessly taking what she needs.

The phone is ringing. The answering machine picks it up.

Elizabeth is in the shower, rinsing shampoo from her hair. Drying herself, she puts on something feminine to make her feel less frumpy.

This time her mobile is ringing. Her father's voice: "Have you seen the TV?"

"What is it? Is it North?"

"I'm so sorry, Lizzie."

Her throat closes. She fights against the panic.

"What? Tell me."

"It's absolutely foul. So fucking unfair."

Sinking to her knees in front of the television, Elizabeth holds the remote control in both hands. She flicks through the channels. Stops. BBC News. There are images of Mersey Fidelity's head office, footage of a trading room, dealers waving their arms and shouting. The banner says: MILLIONS MISSING IN HUNT FOR ROGUE BANKER.

She turns up the volume.

"A fugitive banker is being hunted today following the discovery of a 'black hole' in the bank's accounts. Mersey Fidelity, one of Britain's biggest investment banks, says it is investigating a series of suspicious trades and transfers following an official audit. Fiona Gallagher reports."

The camera switches to a reporter standing on the steps of Mersey Fidelity, a skinny woman with big hair who Elizabeth is sure has never been eight months pregnant.

"Authorities have spent the morning retrieving hundreds of documents and computer disks from the banker's office. Forensic accountants have also been brought in to trace transactions.

"Today's revelations follow in the wake of Mersey Fidelity announcing record profits and being praised by the government and the Bank of England for having weathered the global financial crisis. Chancellor of the Exchequer George Osborne told Parliament last week that Mersey Fidelity would provide the blueprint for new banking laws in the UK, which he would take to the G20 summit in South Korea in November..."

As she watches the coverage and commentary, the ache of uncertainty inside Elizabeth is replaced by a dull thudding like clods of earth rattling on a coffin lid. Her father is still talking. "It must be a mistake. The wrong end of the stick."

"Are they talking about North?" she asks.

"We'll get to the bottom of this..."

"Why would they say such things?"

She doesn't hear what he says next. Her mind has gone to Rowan. She has to go shopping. She promised him pasta shapes for dinner. He likes the spirals or the tubes but not the shells.

"Did you hear me, Lizzie?"

"Sorry."

"The police will want to talk to you. They'll want to search the house."

"Why?"

"In case he left something."

"Left what?"

"It's a mistake, I know, but we have to co-operate."

Polina is standing in the open doorway, listening to her conversation. She's carrying a box of Rowan's toys and his favorite bath towel.

"I'll send Jacinta over," says Alistair Bach.

"No."

"You shouldn't be alone. Come and stay with us."

Elizabeth doesn't want to see her stepmother. She wants to talk to Mitchell. She wants to know why he hasn't called to explain. Why didn't he warn her?

The landline is ringing. "I have to go."

She picks up the new call. It's an unfamiliar voice.

"Mrs. North?"

"Yes."

"I'm from the *Daily Mail*. Can you confirm that your husband is being sought by the police?"

"I have nothing to say."

"Do you know where your husband is?"

"Please don't call this number again."

She drops the handset as though scalded.

"Is everything all right?" asks Polina.

"Fine. I'm going to pick up Rowan."

"It's not even midday."

"He had a sore throat this morning. I should have kept him at home."

"Do you want me to fetch him?"

"No, I'll go."

Elizabeth grabs her coat and her keys. She needs to be outside. Moving. Thinking.

It takes her fifteen minutes to reach the nursery. The carers don't seem surprised to see her. Rowan is playing in the sandpit. She collects his things. Forgets his lunchbox. One of his shoelaces is undone, but she doesn't stop.

"Slow down, Mummy, you're hurting."

His coat sleeve has been pulled off one of his arms.

"I'm sorry, sweetheart."

"Is Daddy home?"

"Not yet."

As they turn the final corner she spies the police cars parked in front of the house.

"It must be Daddy," Rowan cries, pulling free from her hand.

Elizabeth tries to stop him. Calls out. He's running and she can't keep up because she risks giving birth to Claudia on Barnes Green. Rowan runs with his head down and a loping stride like a puppy let off a leash.

Polina is standing outside the open front door. She catches Rowan before he can get inside. A detective emerges from the house. He hands Elizabeth a search warrant and delivers a speech warning her not to interfere.

"There has been some mistake," Elizabeth tells him.

"Please step aside, Mrs. North."

"We've done nothing wrong."

Four officers move past them, each dressed in light blue cotton overalls carrying aluminum cases. They're not just searching the house, they are vacuuming and scraping and dusting for evidence.

"Do you know the whereabouts of your husband?"

"No."

"Has he been in contact with you?"

"No."

Rowan is tugging at her hand, wanting to ask a question. "Not now, sweetheart."

The detective has moved her into the garden. She can feel the neighbors' eyes upon her from across the road, their fingers creasing the venetians. Rushing to judgment.

"I need you to come to the station with me," the detective says. "We'll need a statement."

"I've given you one."

"That was before."

Elizabeth glances at Rowan and then looks to Polina. "Can you stay? Just until I get back."

The nanny nods.

Elizabeth follows the detective to a waiting police car. She's told to mind her head. At the last moment she looks up at the sound of an approaching car. A black Lexus parks across the driveway, blocking the unmarked police car. Felicity Stone emerges; her only wrinkle in the lap of her tight skirt. The young detective watches her approach, his eyes on her hips and her calves. Miss Stone gives him her widest smile.

"You'll have to move your car."

"Of course, whatever you say. I'm here with Mrs. North's lawyer. Nobody is to speak to her unless he's present."

A large man struggles with his seat belt as he emerges from the Lexus. He has a fringe of brown hair combed over his head. He reaches up to pat his scalp, checking that everything is still in place.

"You don't have to say anything," says Marcus Weil. "You don't have to comment at all."

"I don't need a lawyer. I've done nothing wrong."

"Of course not, but Mitchell wants to be reassured," says Miss Stone.

"Where is he?"

"Busy. But he's on your side."

Elizabeth looks at her and wonders why there are "sides."

Hustled through a side door and up a set of internal stairs, Elizabeth follows a new police officer, a florid, beefy man, who carries his weight like a weapon. Uniformed. More senior. A commander. How different this is from her last visit to the police station. Now everybody wants to talk to her.

"Sorry about the stairs," says Campbell Smith. "We thought it best to bring you in the back . . . away from the cameras."

The lawyer is puffing behind them, dabbing his forehead with a handkerchief, which he tucks into his breast pocket. When they reach the interview suites he demands a private consultation with Elizabeth. Campbell Smith grudgingly agrees and clears the room.

"The police make this sort of thing seem so dramatic," says Mr. Weil. "The sirens and flashing lights—they do it to intimidate people."

"I'm not intimidated."

"Good."

He takes a legal pad from his briefcase. "You cannot be compelled to give evidence against your husband, Mrs. North. You do not have to say anything, but you may get in trouble if you fail to mention something that comes up later in a court case."

"I have nothing to hide."

A pen clicks beneath his thumb. "You haven't seen or spoken to your husband?"

"No."

"Did he show you anything?"

"Like what?"

"Documents. Papers."

"No."

"Did you share or otherwise have access to your husband's laptop?"

"No."

"Are there any documents or computer disks in your possession either at your home or in some other location that are the property of Mersey Fidelity? This relates also to copies of documents or disks as well as your husband's notes."

"I don't understand."

"Did he take notes?"

"Pardon?"

"Some people use notebooks. Seems very old-fashioned, I know."

"Why is this important?"

"I'm just saying that if you become aware of anything or if you discover any sensitive materials they would be better off in the bank's hands than any third party."

"By 'third party' you mean the police?"

Mr. Weil puts down his pen and leans back, lacing his fingers together on his stomach like a man about to pontificate on the state of the world.

"People don't like banks, Mrs. North. They'll happily rake up muck or blow things out of proportion. Do you understand what I'm saying? If you have confidential information—either written or passed on orally—it remains the intellectual and commercial property of the bank. If your husband whispered any secrets in the bedroom, or made any remarks about Mersey Fidelity, you should be wary of repeating them."

Elizabeth hesitates. The lawyer wets his lips with the tip of his tongue. It's a nervous, almost reptilian mannerism.

"Who do you work for, Mr. Weil?"

"I beg your pardon?"

"Who is paying you?"

"I don't understand."

"Are you here to represent Mersey Fidelity or me?"

The lawyer pauses with the pen resting on the page. "I have been retained by Mersey Fidelity."

"I see."

Rising slowly from the table, unsteady at first, Elizabeth moves to the door. "Thank you for your advice, Mr. Weil, I won't be needing your services anymore."

What she wants to say is thank you for the lesson in sophistry and doublespeak. Thank you for riding roughshod over my marriage and my husband's reputation. Thank you for showing me what I'm up against.

Mr. Weil tries to argue, but Elizabeth stops him.

"Leave now or I'll tell the police exactly what you've asked me to do."

The overweight lawyer is no longer smiling. He packs his briefcase and departs, moving along the corridor without swinging his arms.

Moments later Campbell Smith takes his place in the interview room and begins asking Elizabeth questions. There is a pattern to them. Politely put, but aimed at picking apart her marriage like a cheap sweater. Her phone calls, her emails, her friendships... They have copies of her bank statements. They want to know about North's parents in Spain, his friends, properties he might own or places he liked to visit. Did he gamble? Did he have any secret accounts? Where did they holiday?

"Does your husband have a share portfolio?"

"A small one."

"What about offshore bank accounts?"

"No."

"Have you ever visited the Middle East?"

She mentions the holiday in Lebanon and Jordan. This triggers another line of questioning.

"What do you think has happened to your husband, Mrs. North?"

"I have no idea."

"You must have a theory."

"No."

A figure is mentioned: fifty-four million pounds. Elizabeth has no idea where it comes from. The TV report had referred to a black hole. Missing money. More numbers. North had been worried about something. He told Bridget Lindop that he'd done something terrible.

Campbell continues to question Elizabeth about the family finances.

"Do you really think my husband would steal £54 million and then bother taking my jewelry? He didn't pack a suitcase. He didn't take any clothes."

"He took his passport," says Campbell.

"All our passports were taken."

"Maybe you were *all* going to run away."

Elizabeth wants to laugh, but can't clear the ball of anger that is lodged in her throat.

"You seem to be missing the obvious. I'm pregnant. I can't fly anywhere."

Campbell isn't going to back off.

"You made a statement to police in which you described your husband as acting strangely. You hired a private detective. Perhaps you overheard him on the phone or read his emails..."

"No."

"Oh, come on, Mrs. North. You thought he was scratching some other woman's itch, yet you never once spied on him or asked him what he was up to or looked in his diary or checked his receipts."

Elizabeth feels her face flush. Tears close. "I hired a private detective—I thought that would be enough."

"Enough for what?"

"My husband did not steal that money," she says, wiping her eyes, but she doesn't know if she says it aloud because the words are being drowned out by a thousand other voices in her head that are asking, *What if you're wrong?*

19

LONDON

Ruiz can't find his shoes. A man can't go to his daughter's wedding without a decent pair of shoes. He should have looked earlier. He should have polished them. The polish is somewhere under the stairs with dozens of other things he won't be able to put his hands on when he needs them.

"When did you last wear them?" asks Joe O'Loughlin.

"I can't remember."

"Try."

"A funeral maybe…"

"When?"

"In March."

Ruiz looks at his full-length profile in the mirror, sucking in his stomach, his chin up, not too shabby, he thinks. He's been working out for the past few days, curling sixty-pound barbells and doing push-ups. His trousers are too loose and he needs a haircut.

Claire has been on the phone twice already and it's only ten o'clock. She and the bridesmaids are getting ready at Phillip's house. The groom has been banished to a hotel in Hampstead so he doesn't see the bride in her dress.

"It's supposed to be the biggest day of her life," the professor reminds him.

Ruiz grunts. "One day she'll get pregnant, she'll have a child, *then* she'll know a big day."

"A wedding is still in the top three."

"None of mine were top three."

"What about the first?"

"Yeah, well, maybe the first."

"You're such a romantic."

Ruiz hooks a finger inside his collar, trying to make it stretch, feeling as comfortable as a penguin in a microwave.

"Let me tell you about romance in this day and age, Professor. You might appreciate the lesson since your Charlie is going to be dating some time soon. My daughter's fiancé has been putting his Ukrainian Kovbasa into my Claire's vagina for the past two years — which is a sentence I wish I had never uttered out loud or in my head. Where is the romance in that? Whatever she had to give away, she's given away . . . pretty frequently."

"Kovbasa?"

"It's a sausage."

"Oh. You didn't sleep with Laura before you married?"

"Nope."

Joe stares at him in disbelief.

"Why are you looking at me like that?"

"No reason."

Ruiz gets annoyed. "I mean, I wasn't a virgin, but Laura had this thing about waiting."

Joe has found Ruiz's shoes beneath the laundry sink. He wets a dishcloth and wipes the dust from the leather. Ruiz breaks a lace and curses. He steals one from another pair of shoes and checks the street before they leave. In a house on the far side of the road he sees a figure silhouetted in a window. He wants to believe it is an ordinary person, a good one: a mother putting a baby down for a nap or a shift worker going to bed after a long night.

That's the thing about trying to protect someone — or failing to — you start to think that danger lurks around every corner and that shadows hold secrets. Holly Knight needed his protection but he let her down. Now he has no way of finding her unless she contacts him.

The wedding is at a church in Primrose Hill, opposite Regent's Park. Ruiz has to pick up his mother from the retirement home in Streatham and then go to Claire's house.

Daj could be a problem. Some days her dementia is so profound that she refuses to believe Ruiz is her son. Either that or she mistakes him for Luke, the brother he lost as a child. At other times she remembers every single detail of her past, which is almost as tragic.

Somewhere in her rambling mind is the riddle of Ruiz's existence. Daj fell pregnant in a concentration camp. She was a teenage gypsy girl used as "recreation" by the SS officers and guards. One of the officers took her out of the camp brothel and had her cleaning his house and warming his bed. Ruiz had never discovered the officer's name. Daj claimed to have forgotten. Instead she talked about an attempted abortion and how the "bastard child" had "clung to my insides, not wanting to leave, wanting so much to live."

She was three months pregnant when the war ended and the camps were liberated. She spent another two months looking for her family but they were all gone—her twin brother, her parents, aunts, uncles, cousins…No countries were accepting gypsies as refugees. Daj lied on her application form at the displaced persons' camp. She took the identity of a young Jewish seamstress who was nineteen, instead of sixteen.

Ruiz was born in a county hospital in Hertfordshire that still had blackout curtains and tape across the windows. They bulldozed it in the seventies—did what the Luftwaffe couldn't do. Progress marches in jackboots.

Parking the Mercedes outside the retirement home, Ruiz and the professor go through the reception and find Daj in her room. She is watching a daytime chat show where people seem to be shouting at each other and throwing chairs.

"Hello, Daj, do you remember Joe?"

"Are you a doctor?" she asks suspiciously.

"No, I'm a friend of Vincent's."

"I have a son called Vincent."

"That's me, Daj," says Ruiz.

She looks at him suspiciously. The skin of her face seems to be covered in finely lined tissue paper and her hands are bony branches. She's wearing a floral dress and a short jacket. The nurses have helped her put on lipstick.

"Are you ready, Daj?"

"Where are we going?"

"To the church."

"I don't like churches."

"It's the Catholics you don't like," says Ruiz, and then to Joe, "A priest comes round once a week and Daj tries to convert him to atheism." He looks back at his mother. "Claire is getting married."

"Claire?"

"Your granddaughter."

"She's too young."

"She's thirty-two."

"Nonsense. I want to talk to Michael."

"Michael's not here."

"Is he coming to the wedding?"

"We're not sure."

Ruiz feels a pang of guilt. He hasn't seen his son in nearly four years. They talk every three or four months, snatched conversations from whatever port Michael has washed up into after a month at sea. Duty phone calls, he calls them, but every time Ruiz feels aggrieved, he remembers his own youth, working as a young police officer in London, rarely phoning home, visiting even less often.

"Bring a cardigan—it gets cool of an evening."

"Where are we going?"

"The church."

"I hate churches."

"I know that, Daj, but Claire is getting married."

This is how the conversation doubles back on itself and loops into elaborate knots that confuse Daj even more as they drive across the Thames, heading north to Primrose Hill.

Claire and Phillip have a large terraced house with glimpses of the park. It's only a short walk to the church. One of Claire's girlfriends opens the door. A bridesmaid. Gina. She's an old school friend, now married. Ruiz can picture her being eight years old, dancing around Claire's bedroom to Madonna songs.

The other bridesmaids are in various stages of dress, being fawned over by a hairdresser, a beautician and a stylist. There are yards of lace and flashes of bare shoulder.

Women in groups have always intimidated Ruiz. Their mystery increases exponentially when they're together, laughing and exchanging news. Champagne can also be a factor. Perhaps his anxiety dates back to his youth when girls would congregate in groups on the far side of the dance floor and necessitate the "longest walk" and a mumbled request to dance. Success meant a few minutes of touching a female waist and hand. Failure meant public humiliation.

"Can I see Claire?" he asks.

"She's still getting ready."

Gina knocks on the bedroom door. "It's your dad."

"Is he drunk?" comes a voice from inside.

Gina addresses Ruiz. "You're not drunk, are you?"

"No."

"I don't think he's drunk," she yells back.

The door opens. A breath catches in Ruiz's throat. For a split second his mind flashes back and he sees Laura standing in their hotel room, breathless and giggling, having been carried across the threshold.

"Well?" asks Claire. She completes a twirl. "It's Mummy's wedding dress. I had them copy the design."

"You look beautiful," he says, struggling to find words.

"And you're very handsome."

She kisses his cheek. Behind her in the room is another vision from his past. Miranda Louise Mills. Ex-wife number three. Dressed all in black.

Miranda straightens his tie and Ruiz glances at her delicate hands and past them to her cleavage. Ex-wives should be fat and frumpy. Not like this.

"Have you heard from Michael?" she asks.

Ruiz shakes his head.

"Maybe he'll surprise us."

Claire gives him a pained smile that says, I'm not a child any more, Daddy, you don't have to lie to me.

Ruiz reaches into his pocket and pulls out a creased envelope and a small wooden box with a hinged lid.

"I have something for you," he says. "It was given to me a long while ago with very specific instructions that I was to give it to you on your wedding day."

Claire can hear the slight tremor in his voice. "It was your mother who gave it to me. It belonged to her mother and her grandmother, so it goes a long way back, and now it's yours." He opens the box. Claire's hand flutters to her mouth.

Ruiz continues, "I think she thought maybe you might wear it today...as the something old, you know, but maybe you have the dress now, so you don't need anything else."

Claire shakes her head and holds the envelope in trembling hands. She looks at Miranda and back to her father and then at the envelope. Opening it nervously, she unfolds the handwritten page and turns away as she reads the letter.

When she finishes, she folds it again, holding it against her heart.

"Now look what you've done," she says. "I'm going to cry and my make-up is going to run. I'll look like a panda."

"Pandas are very cute," says Ruiz.

Miranda takes the hair-comb and slides it in Claire's hair, tucking it beneath the veil. Then she ushers Ruiz into the hallway and gives him a kiss on the lips, before rubbing the lipstick away with her thumb.

"You haven't returned any of my calls."

"Were they urgent?"

"It's called being polite."

"I took you to dinner a fortnight ago."

"To that tacky fish restaurant—the meal left me faster than a fire drill."

"I thought you'd lost weight."

"Flattery will get you nowhere." She punches his shoulder. "Go outside. We're not ready."

Ruiz doesn't need a second invitation. Retreating to the front steps, he takes a boiled sweet from a round metal tin in his pocket and sucks on it thoughtfully. Michael should be at his sister's wedding. What excuse will he give this time? Bad weather. Missed flights. Forgotten dates. Michael is his father's son. Ruiz wishes that he could warn him that one day he'll regret spending so much time away from his family. Maybe that's wishful thinking.

There are no bridal cars. They're going to walk to St. Mark's, which is just around the corner; a true wedding procession through the streets of Primrose Hill.

Joe takes the step next to him and they sit comfortably in silence, listening to the champagne corks being popped inside. Ruiz notices a car parked on the corner. It's the same dark blue Audi that was outside Holly's flat in South London. Two figures are visible behind the dark-tinted windows. Ruiz feels a pain in his chest like someone has placed a fist against his breastbone and is twisting knuckles into the cartilage. This is his daughter's wedding day.

Without a word, he stands, walks down the steps and crosses the road. He taps on the driver's window. After a long pause it glides down. The man behind the wheel has close-cropped hair and a three-day growth. His shirt is rolled up revealing a long pink scar running down the inside of his forearm.

Ruiz can smell the new leather of the seats. "Can I help you?" he asks.

"No, sirree."

He's American. A southerner.

"Are you waiting for me?"

"We're just waiting."

His passenger is younger, also unshaven, with blond highlights. His sunglasses are hinged on the frames and flipped upwards like wiper blades. His left hand is tucked out of sight below the level of his thigh.

The driver motions to the house.

"Fine day for a wedding," he drawls. "Who's getting married?"

"The bride and groom."

"Well, you make sure you pass on our good wishes."

"I'll do that," says Ruiz, who can feel his molars grinding saliva.

He tucks his hands into his pockets. "Maybe we can come to an arrangement."

"What would that be?"

"How about we agree to meet up tomorrow? I can make myself available all day. I'll even come to the office...meet your boss. That way you guys can go home and gel each other's hair and my daughter can get married."

The skin tightens around the driver's eyes. "You're a funny guy. Is that what you Brits call irony?"

"You want me to explain irony?"

The driver closes his fingers, all except the longest, and pushes his sunglasses up his nose. That's his answer.

Ruiz walks away. Twenty yards down the street he pauses at a builder's skip full of debris and broken bricks. The red-black color is rising from his chest to his face and he can hear a tearing sound behind his eyes like fabric shredding. Picking up a half brick, he weighs it in his hand.

The driver and passenger of the Audi are laughing about something. The side window shatters with the sound and fury of a shotgun. Ruiz reaches through the window and bounces the passenger's head off the dashboard, making his nose bloom. He's a bleeder.

The driver reaches below the seat, but Ruiz has already taken a gun from his partner's hand. Now he's aiming it across his crumpled body with one eye closed, the other looking along the barrel, his hand steady as a barber with a cutthroat razor.

A thought passes across the driver's face. Ruiz has always referred to it as the Dirty Harry moment—that fleeting instant when a person wonders: Am I fast enough or lucky enough?

Something tells him no.

Ruiz takes out his mobile and punches the number that was left beneath the wiper blades of the Merc, along with the envelope of cash. It's ringing...being answered. There are five seconds of dead air.

"Mr. Ruiz?"

"You still want the girl?"

"That was our deal."

"Don't talk to me about deals. You kicked in my front door."

"A mistake, I admit."

Another long pause, a low rumble in the background—aircraft noise.

"The price has doubled."

"Why?"

"Because I'm pissed off."

The American mulls this over. "How can I be sure that you've got her?"

"You can't."

"Where do we meet?"

"I choose the location, but it won't be today. In the meantime, call off your dogs. One of them might need a vet."

Ruiz hangs up and turns the phone to silent. Blood is pouring from the passenger's nose and across his lips and chin, staining his shirtfront. Tiny cubes of glass decorate his lap like diamonds on a jeweler's cloth.

"You hear that, ladies? You get off early today."

He leans through the window and presses the release on the ammunition clip, letting it drop into the lap of the passenger, who has his hand cupped under his nose.

As the pistol falls to the floor, Ruiz simultaneously drops his mobile behind the bucket seat. Then he turns away, joining the professor on the footpath. The entire wedding party is standing on the steps of the house—Claire, her bridesmaids, Miranda and Daj. Claire looks ready to throw the first punch, but Miranda has a dangerous left hook.

"Very smooth," says Joe.

"I was being diplomatic."

"I'd hate to see you go to war."

Ruiz gives him a smile that means nothing.

"Can I borrow your mobile?"

"What happened to yours?"

"I must have left it somewhere."

20

LONDON

The TV lights leave white spots swimming behind Elizabeth's eyelids. She tries to blink them away, but the cameras are recording every twitch and grimace. She reaches for a glass of water. A few droplets spill, beading like mercury on the smooth table. She wipes up the water with her sleeve, worried it might leave a mark.

Campbell Smith whispers in her ear. "I'll give you the signal. Then you just read the statement."

All the seats are taken. It's standing room only in the briefing room at New Scotland Yard. The TV cameras are at the back; press photographers at the front. Radio microphones hooked up to the feed.

The police have talked Elizabeth into this — an emotional plea from a pregnant wife to her husband. Not running. Missing. She said no at first, afraid of the publicity. The shame. The thought of people recognizing her in the street, whispering, pointing; not just her neighbors and friends, but the mothers at Rowan's nursery and in her Pilates class or complete strangers passing her in supermarket aisles. Then she realized that she couldn't care less about what people thought.

Speaking with deliberate slowness, Campbell Smith calls for order. Waits. Elizabeth seems to be growing smaller beside him.

"As of 1200 hours today a warrant was issued for the arrest of Richard North. Interpol has also been advised and we're monitoring departure points. Mrs. Elizabeth North is now going to make a statement. She won't be taking questions and I would ask you to respect her privacy."

He signals to Elizabeth. She stares at the page, trying to focus on the words.

"If you're watching this, Richard, if you can hear me...if you're able to call…" A barrage of flashguns are firing, recording every pause. "I just want to know you're OK. I know you can explain. I know you're a good man…"

She doesn't finish the sentence. Raising her eyes, she concentrates on a point at the back of the room, above their heads.

"Rowan misses you. We all do…Whatever has happened, whatever you think you've done, nothing could be as bad as not knowing…worrying…"

The words dry up, evaporating in her mouth. Her mind becomes lost in the flashguns. Questions are being shouted from the floor. A field of hands are raised. Campbell takes Elizabeth by the forearm and leads her through a side door to a long corridor. Polished. Brightly lit. Felicity Stone is bustling towards her with a wide smile, air kissing her cheeks.

"You were marvelous, grace under pressure and all that. Is there anyone I can call? Do you have a rabbi or a priest?"

"No."

"I can find you a counselor—a woman, perhaps. There are some very good trauma specialists. Caring. Discreet."

"I'm fine."

Miss Stone is tapping on the screen of her mobile. "We've found a quiet house, somewhere away from London and all the attention. You can be anonymous, recover your balance."

"I'm going home."

"Right. OK. Of course you should avoid commenting. No press interviews. You're perfectly entitled to say nothing at all. Don't even say, 'No comment.'"

They have reached the lift.

"I just want to reassure you that, whatever happens, Mersey Fidelity will look after you. You don't have to go through this alone. Mitchell will make sure—"

"Where is Mitchell?"

"He's talking to the police."

Elizabeth turns away from her and walks back down the corridor. Banging on the doors, she starts yelling. "Mitchell? Are you here? I want to talk."

Faces emerge. A female officer tries to stop her, but she pushes past her.

"I want to see my brother. Mitchell? Where are you?"

Turning a corner she sees him. He's talking to a man in a suit. Heads together. Whispering.

"You should have warned me," she shouts, storming towards him.

Mitchell raises his hands submissively. "I'm sorry, Lizzie. I wanted to call you but the lawyers told me not to interfere. I have a duty to shareholders and investors…"

Before he can finish the statement Elizabeth strikes him across the face with an open hand. She can't remember ever hitting him before—not even as a child when he teased her or tortured her dolls or let her pet rabbit escape and get eaten by a fox on Hampstead Heath.

Mitchell's eyes go out of focus for a moment, swimming in pain.

"I'm your sister, Mitchell. Doesn't that mean anything?"

"Of course it does."

"You're hanging him out to dry. He didn't steal any money."

"Calm down, Lizzie."

"I won't calm down. I know what you're doing. You're covering something up."

The other man speaks. "We're handling this, Mrs. North."

Elizabeth takes a moment to recognize him; his grey hair is brushed back in an elegant bouffant and he's wearing a Paul Smith suit instead of a tracksuit. It's the man from the house in Mayfair who lied about meeting North.

Elizabeth turns on him. "Who are you?"

Mitchell answers. "This is Yahya Maluk. He's on the board of Mersey Fidelity."

Elizabeth is still focused on Maluk. "Why did you lie to me about meeting my husband? I have the photographs. You were there."

Mitchell looks from face to face. The older banker raises his hand. "Be careful what you say, Mrs. North. Unfounded allegations can be very dangerous." There is a veiled threat behind the softness of his voice.

"You really should listen, Lizzie," says Mitchell, nursing his cheek.

"I'm not going to shut up. I'm not going to stay quiet. And I'm not going to hide myself away."

21

LONDON

Low tide. A long thin shingle beach has appeared during the night, exposed by the tide. Holly has slept all morning and into the early afternoon, the water and the birds entering her dreams. Now she can hear Pete moving outside the caravan, laboring with a heavy object and running the outboard engine to clear the water intake pipe.

Rising from the narrow bed, she runs barefoot to a drop toilet surrounded by hessian curtains. She squats, urinating, wishing she'd worn shoes. Dog is watching her. She tries to shoo him away, but he cocks his head and wags his body.

After washing her hands in the river, she walks back to the camp.

Pete is cooking over a gas burner. He's dressed in a rugby jumper that's too big for him — more Ruiz's size. The mental comparison makes Holly angry because she feels betrayed by the former detective. One more act of betrayal in a life littered with them.

Sitting on a stool beneath the awning, she watches Pete cook her scrambled eggs for breakfast. She eats hungrily, avoiding his gaze, feeling the heat of the Tabasco sauce on her lips.

Pete takes the saucepan to the river, crouching on the edge of the shingle spit. When he's out of sight, Holly opens the drawers and cupboards in the van, searching the pockets of Pete's clothes. She finds ten quid and coins. Staring at the crumpled bill, she contemplates what to do.

She has two pounds and fifty-three pence. She needs money and somewhere to stay. What would Zac do? He'd scam someone. Pete would be an easy mark—innocent as a puppy—but it doesn't seem fair after what he's done for her.

She puts the money back where she found it and steps out of the caravan. Pete is wiping his hands on his trousers.

"Do you want to know why those men were chasing me?"

"I figure you'll tell me or you won't."

"Do you think I'm a criminal?"

Pete scratches his cheek. "You are what you are."

"They weren't the cops . . . at least I don't think so."

"I'm not so fond of coppers."

Pete packs away the frying pan and lets the knives and forks dry by resting upright in a can. A boat putters past them, invisible behind the willow trees.

"You can stay here for a while . . . I mean, if you want to . . . until you decide."

"I don't have any money."

"I got enough."

Holly eyes him carefully. She can smell the dampness of the river and the sweat on his clothes.

"You wouldn't take advantage of me, would you, Pete? I mean . . . you wouldn't . . . you know."

Pete adamantly shakes his head. Then he packs a satchel with envelopes and a pen.

"I have to post some letters and pick up supplies."

"Where?"

"I usually go to Richmond."

"Can I come?"

"Sure."

They take the fishing boat downriver. Holly isn't sure of the direction because the sun has disappeared behind a high layer of cloud. They pass lovely houses on the river's edge, with manicured lawns and small jetties jutting out into the water. Pete waves to a woman hanging her washing and a man mowing his lawn. There are people cycling along the river paths and waterfowl that flap from the reeds, clumsy until airborne.

They moor in the shadow of Richmond Bridge near the floating restaurant and the "boats for hire." Holly steps ashore. Pete has some shopping bags and a list.

"Is there anything you don't eat?"

"I'm not very fond of baked beans."

"I'll get something else."

They walk up the worn granite steps.

"Pete?"

"Yeah."

"I need to pick up a few things, women's stuff, you know, and I don't have any money."

"I can get them."

"Women's products?"

"Oh. Right." He fumbles in his pockets and gives her a ten-pound note.

"I don't know how much...if you need more..."

"Maybe just a little."

He gives her another tenner. She unfurls the crumpled notes and folds them neatly.

"How long will you be?"

"An hour."

"I'll meet you back here."

Holly goes into Boots and buys a toothbrush, toothpaste, tampons and deodorant, along with a cheap pair of sunglasses and two pairs of knickers. She walks outside and transfers her purchases into an old plastic bag, which she hides in a rubbish bin. Then she goes back into the Boots and picks up exactly the same items—same brands, same amounts—putting them into the original bag.

She goes to the checkout.

"I'm really sorry. I just bought all this stuff not realizing my boyfriend had already picked it up. We both had the same shopping list. Great minds, you know..."

"Do you have the receipt?" asks the checkout girl.

"Of course, it's here somewhere." Holly makes a show of searching her pockets. She finds the receipt. The girl checks off the items and opens the cash register. She gives Holly nineteen pounds and seventy-five pence.

"It's nice that your boyfriend goes shopping for you," she says.

"Yeah, he's a real sweetheart."

Outside Holly retrieves the stuff she hid in the bin. She can smell the coffee and muffins at Starbucks across the road. She now has money, clean underwear and toiletries... why not give herself a treat? She's walking past the front window of Dixons and notices a bank of TV screens all showing the same images, a news report.

A photograph flashes across the multiple screens. Holly pauses, trying to remember how she knows the face. Where? When? The scrolling banner says something about a missing banker. The shot changes to a press conference. A woman is reading a statement into a microphone. Holly pushes through the glass door and stands in front of the screens.

"If you're watching this, Richard, if you can hear me... if you're able to call... I just want to know you're OK. I know you can explain. I know you're a good man..."

Holly stares at the row of TVs. She finds herself looking from one to the other, expecting the story to change. She remembers the missing banker and his house. There were toys in his living room. He said his wife was away for the weekend. They met at a bar in the City. He was drunk. Horny. Worried about something. He took her home.

The rolling banner gives his name: Richard North. Missing millions, it reads. Is this why Zac died? Is this why people are chasing her?

A shop assistant is standing next to her in a pressed white shirt and narrow tie. Indian. Early twenties.

"Can I help with something?"

"Do you have a phone?"

"Our phone section is over there?"

"I don't want to buy one — I want to borrow one."

The sales assistant takes out his own mobile. Emptying her pockets, Holly finds a worn square of white cardboard: Ruiz's name and his home phone number. She punches the keys, tucking the phone between her shoulder and ear. There's no answer. She starts to leave a message, but pauses, turning to the assistant.

"What day is it today?"

"August twenty-eighth."

Holly looks at her watch and remembers the wedding.

22

WASHINGTON

Chalcott is on the sideline, watching his teenage son play football. His phone is ringing: Sobel from London.

"I tried you in the office."

"It's my day off."

"You're outside."

"My boy has a game."

"Who's winning?"

"Forty minutes and no score—foreplay shouldn't last that long."

A whistle blows. Chalcott shouts at the referee, "The kid dived—are you blind?"

"What position does your boy play?"

"There are positions?" Chalcott finishes his takeaway coffee and crushes the paper mug. "What news?"

"According to the bank Richard North ran off with fifty-four million."

"Dollars?"

"Pounds. All sorts of theories are being bandied about."

" 'Bandied'? You've been in Blighty too long. You're starting to sound like a Limey shirt-lifter."

Sobel laughs hollowly. "We've intercepted a phone call from Holly Knight to the ex-detective. She left half a message on his answering machine. The call was traced to a shopping mall in Richmond."

"Did you pick her up?"

"She was gone by the time we arrived, but we've managed to get CCTV footage of her talking to some guy. The Brits may have an ID. He's a tramp. No fixed address."

"What about the ex-detective?"

"Ruiz says he'll do a deal for the girl if we back off."

"Do you believe him?"

"No."

"How much do the Brits know?"

"Green shoots."

Chalcott is walking along the sideline, ignoring the crowd noises. He pauses. "We may have a problem from another quarter."

"What's that?"

"Someone is asking about Ibrahim."

"Who?"

"A journalist called Luca Terracini, based in Baghdad. He's like Osama's Lord Haw Haw."

"Didn't he win a Pulitzer?"

"That's him. Sometimes I wish we were still in the fifties. We could haul guys like Terracini up before the Anti-American Committee and get them labeled communists and traitors. Instead we give the cunts prizes. If it weren't for us, Terracini would be picking through the rubble of the next Ground Zero."

"How did he trace Ibrahim?"

"He hasn't, but he's sniffing around. He's with a woman—a UN auditor. She likely made the connection."

"How are we playing it?"

"I don't want Ibrahim spooked. The Iraqis are kicking Terracini out of the country."

"That should solve our immediate problem."

"You just worry about the girl."

23

LONDON

The wedding is over, the rice has been thrown and photographs are being posed until the smiles look painted on. Ruiz slips away from the guests and well-wishers, taking a gravel path around the side of the church. He walks to the edge of the Grand Central Canal where brightly painted canal boats look like children's toys left behind after a summer picnic. A group of eager ducks navigates within range, expecting bread to be thrown, bored with the daily grind of paddling.

Ruiz takes out the tin of sweets and puts one in his mouth, rolling it over his tongue. There is something quite melancholy about seeing a daughter married, walking her down the aisle and handing her on to another man. Claire has not been *his* little girl for twenty-five years, but for a brief instant in the church the past and present had collapsed into a single moment and he saw her as a child, turning to him, saying, "Look at me, Daddy. Look at me."

Ruiz glances over his shoulder. The photographer is waving his arms, trying to marshal everyone on to the front steps, the bride and groom at the centre. He might be directing aircraft or sending semaphore messages. Phillip's family are standing together — charming sociopaths with top-drawer accents and expensive clothes. His mother, Patricia, is wearing a fur coat that is totally out of season and cost the lives of countless small mammals.

Ruiz takes out the mobile he borrowed from the professor and punches a number. He listens to the call being redirected electronically... once... twice... Finally, he hears it ringing.

"Hello, Capable."

"Mr. Ruiz."

"You should call me Vincent."

"I'll remember that, Mr. Ruiz. How's your mother?"

"Still complaining."

"Mine too."

Henry Jones, otherwise known as "Capable," is one of those individuals that people sometimes call unlucky but really believe are somehow jinxed. Awkward and anxious, things break when he's around. Vases topple. Light bulbs pop. Motors burn out. Fuses short. Doors lock with keys inside. The only exception is with computers, which seem to respond to Capable like a violin in the hands of a virtuoso.

In his callow and foolish youth, Capable had been an expert hacker—famous for penetrating one of the biggest UK banks and giving Gordon Brown, then Chancellor of the Exchequer, a zero account balance. He didn't steal the money, he simply transferred it to the Inland Revenue with a note from Brown saying, "Merry Christmas, have a drink on me."

Ruiz came across Capable a few years later, when the poacher had turned gamekeeper, advising banks on cyber security. He had been arrested after a misunderstanding with an undercover copper in a public toilet in Green Park that had resulted in a broken jaw and a public indecency charge. Ruiz gave Capable a character reference and saved him from being passed around by the cell-block sisters at Wormwood Scrubs like a party bong.

"What can I do for you, Mr. Ruiz?"

"I need you to trace a mobile phone."

"Stolen?"

"Mislaid."

"What was the last location?"

"I dropped it on the back seat of a dark blue Audi in Primrose Hill."

"Turned on."

"Of course."

Capable is already tapping on a keyboard, listening to some techno beat on his sound system. Ruiz can picture him in his pokey flat in Hounslow, surrounded by computer screens and hard drives; dressed in jogging gear and sporting one of those droopy Mexican bandit moustaches that nobody—not even Mexican bandits—sport any more.

Most of his "security" work is done on the wrong side of midnight when internet speeds are faster and less people are monitoring their machines. He can piggyback off other systems, working through proxy computers, leaving no electronic trace.

Ruiz has a limited understanding of the technology, but he knows that mobile phones can be tracked because they constantly send out a signal looking for the nearest phone towers. Signal strength and direction can be triangulated to pinpoint the location of a handset down to as little as fifty yards.

"I need one more favor," says Ruiz. "I want you to reroute my calls."

"What number?"

"Use this one."

Ruiz hangs up and wanders back towards the wedding party. Claire and Phillip are being photographed beneath a fig tree with the canal in the background. Miranda drags him into the next picture: The bride and her father. Smiling stiffly, Ruiz looks past the camera to the main doors of the church. That's when he sees her in the shadows, her arms wrapped around herself and her feet splayed slightly inwards.

He wants to raise his hand. He wants to call out. The photographer demands that he smile. Just one more . . . look this way . . .

Ruiz slips his hand around Claire's waist and gives her a squeeze. "This is not my sort of gig. Do you mind?"

"Away you go," she says, not surprised.

As Ruiz gets nearer, Holly glances over her shoulder, as though ready to run. Something makes her stay.

"Did you send those men?" she asks.

"No."

"Who were they?"

"I don't know."

"What did they want?"

"They think you stole something."

Silence. Holly looks over her shoulder again.

"I tried to call you," he says.

"I lost my phone in the river."

"How did you get away?"

"A boat. I slept on an island. Did you know there were islands on the Thames?"

"Yes."

She nods and glances at the wedding party. Claire and Phillip are being posed beneath the arch. The photographer has set up reflectors to soften the light.

"She looks beautiful," says Holly, wistfully.

"Yes."

Another silence.

"There's something you should know. I saw a story on the TV about a banker who stole lots of money."

"What about him?"

"That's one of the guys we robbed, Zac and me. You asked me who they were. He was one of them."

"You're sure?"

"Yeah."

"When was it?"

"About a week ago, maybe longer."

"Where?"

"He had a place in Barnes."

"Could you find the house again?"

"I don't know. Maybe."

Ruiz takes a pen from his pocket. He doesn't have any paper. He takes her hand, turning her wrist so he can write on the pale skin of her inner arm. The name of a hotel. An address.

"Call yourself Florence. Take a room at the back on the first floor. There's a fire escape. Don't make any phone calls. Don't talk to anyone."

"What about money?"

Ruiz gives her sixty pounds.

"I'll send someone to see you tomorrow. He'll ask for Florence. Don't open the door for anyone else."

"How will I know him?"

"You'll know if he's lying."

24

LONDON

It is after dark by the time Elizabeth is allowed to leave the police station. Campbell Smith says a car will drop her home, but she chooses a cab instead, sinking into the vinyl seat, smelling the sneaked cigarette the driver has just stubbed out.

Halfway home she glances at the meter and checks her purse. She doesn't have enough money to pay the fare.

"Do you take debit cards?" she asks.

The driver has a big head and a short neck, making it hard for him to turn. He uses the mirror.

"No, love."

"Could you find me an ATM, please?"

He sighs and pulls over in Knightsbridge, blocking one lane. Elizabeth crosses the pavement to a cash machine, where she inserts her card and follows the instructions.

Nothing happens.

The card emerges from the slot. She tries again, slowly retyping her PIN. The result is the same. Choosing a credit card, she requests a cash advance. The screen freezes for a moment and then says, "Transaction Canceled." This time her card doesn't reappear.

Each card. Every account. How is that possible?

Elizabeth glances over her shoulder at the cab driver. She can feel his impatience growing just like the cold creeping into her toes. There is a helpline number on the ATM screen. Elizabeth opens her mobile and follows the automated instructions. In the meantime, she searches the pockets of her coat and the compartments of her purse, hoping to find cash.

A voice answers, an Indian accent, half a world away. Elizabeth tries to explain. The operator wants her password. The cab driver toots his horn. Elizabeth holds up two fingers and shouts, "Two minutes."

"Your accounts have been frozen, Mrs. North."

"But we have sufficient funds."

"It has nothing to do with the account balances."

Elizabeth can hear her voice growing shrill. "What about my credit cards?"

"Suspended."

"Who did this? Let me talk to your manager?"

"I'm afraid you'll have to visit your branch."

"But I need money now."

"Talk to your branch."

"It's nearly ten o'clock at night. I have a cab fare to pay."

The call center operator apologizes for the inconvenience. Elizabeth argues, demands, yells down the phone, but the line is dead.

The cab driver is standing on the pavement now, hands on hips, tattoos on his forearms.

"The machine just ate my cards," she explains. "I only have fifteen pounds and thirty-five pence, but I'll find some money at home. Polina will have some."

"Polina?"

"It doesn't matter. Just take me home."

The driver gets back in the cab, not bothering to open the door for her. They travel in silence along King's Road, which is still busy on a Wednesday night. Elizabeth once worked in a boutique here during a summer holiday. One jacket cost more than a week's wages. She wishes she had that money now.

They cross Putney Bridge and turn along Lower Richmond Road. A group of young men spill from a pub. One of them jumps into the road, waving his arms. The driver swerves. Misses. Takes his hand from the wheel.

"Morons!" he yells, and then to Elizabeth, "Idiots!"

Familiar streets now, turning left and right. There are more vehicles than usual parked in Elizabeth's street. The cab pulls up, engine running. A dozen car doors open in unison. Reporters, cameramen and photographers close around the black cab like baying hounds on the scent of a fox. The cab driver is shouting at them to "watch the motor" and "give the lady some room." He opens the passenger door for Elizabeth and shields her, shouldering people aside as she makes her way along the front path.

Someone grabs at her arm. She pulls away. A tape recorder is thrust in her face.

"Has your husband contacted you?"

"Do you think he took the money?"

"Why has he run?"

Elizabeth reaches the front door. Pushes it closed. There are two suitcases in the hallway. Polina is sitting on the stairs, texting on her mobile.

Elizabeth asks breathlessly, "Do you have any cash? I need twenty pounds."

Polina pulls a bundle of loose bills from the pocket of her jeans, a twenty among them. Elizabeth notices the suitcases.

"Is everything all right?"

"I'm leaving."

"What?"

"Rowan is asleep. The ironing is done. I have made his lunch for tomorrow. I cannot stay."

"Why?"

Polina motions outside. "They have been ringing the doorbell. Phoning. Yelling through the letterbox."

"I'm sorry."

The nanny shakes her bobbed hair. "I cannot stay here. I cannot."

Elizabeth follows her gaze. She notices a dustpan and brush. Broken glass. The bay window has been smashed. A broken paver sits on the phone table, along with a single-page note. Three words.

Bankers are scum!

Polina squeezes past her, struggling with her suitcases. The cab driver gives her a hand. The reporters and photographers step aside.

"Please don't go," says Elizabeth. "What about your money?"

"You can owe me."

25

LUTON

The old motel is boarded up with plywood on the barred windows and padlocks on the doors. The Courier waits for the young men to arrive, watching from a distance. One of them will be late—Taj. He's older and more level-headed than the others, but he lacks conviction.

The one called Rafiq has shown promise. He killed when he was asked. Held his nerve. Pulled the trigger. He has been quiet since then, looking at himself in the mirror as though expecting to see some visible change in himself like the notch between his eyes grown deeper.

Two of the young men have arrived. They are arguing and joking, throwing fake punches and kicking at a soft-drink can in the gutter. How many others are there like them—white, black, Asian, rich, poor, educated, uneducated—praying in Madrasahs, surfing the internet, dreaming of Jihad?

Syd is the youngest. He runs his fingers over the contours of the dark-colored BMW parked at the rear of the motel screened by an overgrown hedge.

"This would be such a sweet ride, you know. I reckon Jenny Cruikshank would go out with me if I had a ride like this."

"Jenny Cruikshank still won't do the business," laughs Rafiq, "not even in a BMW. She's a prick-tease, man."

"Don't talk about her like that."

Rafiq laughs even harder, his cheeks etched with tiny acne scars like needle marks. "Don't let the Courier catch you leaving your prints on that thing."

Syd bunches his sleeve in his fist and begins wiping the car.

Built on either side of a tarmac courtyard, the red-brick motel has two stories with an open walkway along the upper floor. The Courier lets himself into the dining room, which is stripped of furnishings except for a dozen chairs and a tea-urn. There are boxes of donated clothes and blankets—some for disposal, some for sale.

Rafiq and Syd are in Room 12, setting up a digital camera. Folding a magazine, Rafiq jams the pages under one leg of the tripod, which is shorter than the others. Syd sits cross-legged on the floor wearing cargo pants, trainers and an Arsenal strip.

"Should the light be blinking?" he asks.

"It's still charging."

"You got the lens cap on."

Rafiq checks, then glares at Syd.

"You're a funny prick."

Syd giggles and adjusts the *shemagh* on his forehead. His round face is made rounder by an attempted beard that sprouts from his cheeks like alfalfa in wet cotton wool. His father calls it bum fluff. Says it out loud to embarrass Syd when girls come into the shop. He hates his father then. Hates his braying laugh. Hates how everything is a competition.

"We should have crossed swords in the background."

"We don't have any swords."

"Well, I should be holding a gun. We're supposed to look like soldiers."

"You got khaki trousers."

"Can you see them? Maybe I should stand up."

"You're fine."

"It still looks kind of lame."

Rafiq seems to make a decision. He goes to his rucksack and removes a cloth-covered object, placing it carefully on the table. Unwrapping it with great ceremony, he steps back. The pistol has a black rubber grip and snub-nosed barrel that soaks up the light.

Syd whistles through his teeth and reaches for it. Rafiq slaps his hand away.

"I just want to touch it."

"Be careful."

Syd's fingers close around the grip. He picks it up and feels the weight, marveling at how balanced it feels. Swinging it left, he aims it at a blank TV screen.

"Is it loaded?"

"You got to treat every gun like it's loaded, that's what the Courier says."

"Where did you get it?"

"The Courier gave it to me."

"Am I going to get one?"

"You don't ask him shit like that."

Syd closes one eye and looks down the barrel. "Why we need guns for, anyway? We're just gonna blow shit up."

"Insurance."

"Against what?"

"Problems."

Syd glances at the camera. "Can I hold it—just while we're filming?"

Rafiq takes his time deciding and nods. Syd sits on the floor, crossing his arms with the pistol braced against his chest.

"Do I look like a soldier?"

"You look good."

"One day of fighting..."

"...is worth eighty of praying."

He looks into the camera.

"Oh, glorious prophet and vanquisher of the infidels, bless me now as I prepare for holy Jihad against the unbelievers..."

"What's wrong?"

"I forgot what I was going to say next."

Syd pulls a slip of paper from his pocket and begins memorizing.

"Just read it."

"I don't want to read it. I want to know it off by heart."

"We're wasting memory."

"I got it now. Was I speaking too fast? Sometimes when I get excited I speak too fast."

"You were fine."

"Could you hear the words?"

"Yeah."

"So it was OK?"

"You should say something about being a martyr."

"But we're not going to be martyrs. That's what the Courier said. I'm not going to even pretend. I'm not interested in virgins in Heaven. I'll be happy if Jenny Cruikshank lets me feel her tits."

"Don't let the Courier hear you say shit like that."

"I'm not scared of him."

"Bollocks!"

"I'm not."

Syd looks up and his bowels seem to liquefy. The Courier is standing in the doorway as if he has suddenly materialized from thin air. Syd scrambles to his feet. Bows his head. Palms together. Salaam.

"Where is Taj?" asks the visitor.

"He's running late," says Rafiq. "His wife wanted him to mind their baby."

"I can go look for him," suggests Syd, who likes being around Aisha, Taj's wife, even though she makes him nervous. Pretty girls do that to him and Aisha is so beautiful he finds her painful to look at. How did Taj manage to get a wife like that? Honey-colored eyes. Perfect skin. Glo-white teeth. When Syd's time comes, his parents are likely to choose some fat cow with a stutter.

The Courier has moved into the room and taken a seat on a plastic chair. He motions them to sit down. He has a job for them.

"We have to dump the banker's car."

"What about his body?" asks Rafiq.

"That too."

26

BAGHDAD

Daniela's bags are packed and waiting on a luggage trolley by the door. Her flight leaves in four hours, the first leg to Istanbul and then on to New York. By this time tomorrow she'll be back in her one-bedroom apartment with its dodgy plumbing and her weird neighbor who works all night in a basement under strange flickering lights.

"Have you decided?" she asks Luca.

"Decided?"

"Are you coming with me?"

"New York in the fall."

"It's lovely. Not too hot. Not too cold."

"You sound like Goldilocks."

Forty-eight hours. That's how long Jennings gave Luca to leave Iraq. He can picture his visa smoking and then self-destructing like a Mission Impossible tape.

"I have three questions," asks Daniela. "Do you know what you're doing?"

"Not exactly."

She purses her lips. "What if I begged you to leave?"

"Don't."

"Do you think Glover was killed because of this?"

"Yes."

She sighs and leans back on the bed. The motion tightens her sweater, molding it against her body. It hurts Luca to look at her. It hurts him to think of her leaving. He should go with her to New York and shag her into next year. It would mean admitting defeat—the leaving, not the shagging—but what's one more humiliation after being arrested, drugged and interrogated by the Iraqi police?

The satellite phone interrupts. Keith Gooding on the line from London:

"You wanted to know about Ibrahim? I found someone at the Foreign Office who pulled his file. Nothing new. This stuff dates back to the invasion."

"What stuff?"

"I'll tell you the story the way it was told to me."

Gooding talks in a type of journalistic shorthand, full of half sentences and abbreviations.

"Twenty-first March 2003, Shock and Awe. Forty Tomahawk missiles began the assault, launched by navy vessels in the Persian Gulf and the Red Sea. Then came the precision-guided bombs dropped on Baghdad from stealth jets. Three hours after the raids began Saddam Hussein appeared on state television calling on Iraqis to defend their country. By then Baghdad was burning.

"Saddam knew the attack was coming, so three days before the air assault he sent his son Qusay to the al-Rafidain Bank in central Baghdad. He had a handwritten note from the President, written in Arabic, authorizing the withdrawal of nine hundred and twenty million US dollars.

"It took them two hours to load the cash on to three tractor-trailers. The bills were sealed in aluminum boxes, each containing four million dollars."

"Whose money was it?"

"Semantics," says Gooding. "What belonged to Iraq belonged to Saddam."

"Four weeks later, twentieth April, US ground forces had captured Baghdad and Saddam was in hiding. The second brigade of the Third Infantry Division had taken up residence in Saddam's new presidential palace on the west side of the Tigris. Two US Army sergeants went searching for a chainsaw to clear branches. Staff Sergeant Kenneth Buff and Sergeant First Class Daniel Van Ess noticed a windowless cottage. They broke it open and discovered forty galvanized aluminum boxes, riveted shut, with lead seals and plastic strapping. Another forty cases were found next door. Six of them were selected at random and opened. Each contained four million US dollars in neatly stacked hundred-dollar bills. Third Infantry organized a wider search. By nightfall they'd found one hundred and sixty-four boxes. That's a haul of six hundred and fifty-six million dollars."

"What's this got to do with Mohammed Ibrahim?"

"I'm getting to that. Like I said — the cases were sealed, signed and dated. The signature was that of Mohammed Ibrahim, Saddam's paternal cousin and a lieutenant colonel in the Republican Guard.

"Two days later, reservists from the 354th Civil Affairs Brigade found another stash in a wooded neighborhood where top Baath Party officials lived. Twenty-eight cases were hidden in dog kennels that had been bricked up with cinder blocks and cement. The seals bore the same signature."

"And this came from the original bank robbery?"

"They recovered all but one hundred and fifty million US."

Luca glances at Daniela, who is sitting near the window. With the light behind her, he can't see the look on her face.

"What about Ibrahim?" he asks.

Gooding answers. "After the invasion, most of the leading Baathists scattered, mainly to Syria and Jordan. Mohammed Ibrahim stayed under the radar because nobody considered him to be very important. He was a junior public servant. It was only later they discovered he was Saddam's bagman."

"Where is he now?"

"The US military stumbled upon him almost by accident. They were searching for Saddam and rounded up dozens of his former drivers and bodyguards in December 2003. Ibrahim was among them, but he wouldn't talk. Over the next thirteen days they arrested forty of his relatives and closest friends. They had the names of another twenty. Ibrahim did a deal. He gave up Saddam and his family were released.

"The task force flew to a farmhouse near Tikrit. It still took them three hours to find Saddam. Ibrahim had to show them the entrance to the rat hole. You know the rest. Saddam was put on trial. Executed. Ibrahim was sent to Camp Bucca and later transferred to Abu Ghraib. Classified as high security."

"So he should be in prison, awaiting trial?"

"I assume so. Why?"

"No reason."

"Tell me."

"I met someone who claimed to have seen him on the border between Iraq and Syria seven months ago."

"A credible witness?"

"A paid informant."

Luca needs another favor — the name of a stringer working out of Damascus; someone who can ask questions and check out an address. Gooding gives him the number of Tony Castro.

"What's he like?"

"Can't write, can't spell, but he has the instincts of a ferret."

"Ferrets are much-maligned creatures."

"You'd know more about that than me."

Gooding wants first refusal on the story and they negotiate expenses, but the price will have to wait. Luca has spent most of his cash reserves buying a new engine for the Skoda. Hanging up, he calls the stringer in Damascus.

Tony Castro has a booming voice and an Italian accent that makes him sound as though he's yelling out orders for takeaway pizzas. The introductions are brief. He's heard of Luca, remembers the Pulitzer Prize, but doesn't seem impressed.

Luca tells him about the warehouse near the airport in Damascus. The sign: Alain al Jaria — Ever-Flowing Spring.

"I need to know who owns it and what it's used for."

"Anything else?"

"Look out for the name Ibrahim."

"No shortage of Ibrahims here."

"This one is an Iraqi. His full name is Mohammed Ibrahim Omar al-Muslit, also known as the Fat Man."

"I'll get back to you."

Luca hangs up and continues making calls. For the next two hours he runs an obstacle course of transfers, denials or being put on hold. He is passed between four different sections at the Interior Ministry before getting a "no comment" regarding Mohammed Ibrahim. Jenkins at the US Embassy is "in a meeting" and then "gone for the day." The US military command wants the request in writing and approved by the Iraqis.

Out of ideas, he calls Jamal. "I know I said I wouldn't ask you for any more favors…"

"What do you need?"

"Information. The prisoner's name is Mohammed Ibrahim Omar al-Muslit. Arrested December 2003. Interned at Abu Ghraib awaiting trial." Luca doesn't mention the link to Saddam or the smuggled cash. "Don't push it too hard," he says. "Make a call and then leave it alone."

At two p.m. the phone rings in Daniela's room. Edge is twenty minutes away. He's ready for the run to the airport.

Daniela leans forward and takes Luca's hands in hers, pressing down hard with her thumbs. Her eyes fasten on his. "Give this up. You're fixated on something that can only bring trouble."

"Don't you want answers?"

"I can live without them."

The last woman Luca cared about had accused him of sitting on the sidelines, unwilling to get involved, a spectator not a player. This one wants him benched and out of the game.

Opening the flap of his shirt pocket, Luca touches the folded photograph of Nicola. He opens it on his lap, smoothing the crease with his fingers.

"I owe you a story."

"You don't have to," says Daniela.

"I want to."

He begins at the beginning. Nicola had worked for the National

Library of Iraq, tracing and restoring the priceless manuscripts and books that had been looted or damaged during the invasion. It shouldn't have been a dangerous job, but the library had been bombed twice and attacked by snipers who had shot out several windows.

Luca had gone to do a story on the restoration and Nicola took him on a guided tour of the library, explaining the importance of the collection and how much was still missing. Passionate and beautiful, she'd been educated in Geneva where her father had worked as a diplomat before falling out with Saddam. Later she studied bookbinding and restoration in Venice.

It took Luca six weeks to convince her to have a coffee with him. Her sister acted as chaperone. "I'm not going to fall in love with you," Nicola told him, "because you will leave me one day."

They were together for nearly two years, "not in love" she insisted, but that was just playing with words. One Friday afternoon the wages didn't arrive at the library. Nicola offered to collect them from the bank because it was a long weekend and people needed money for food and fuel. She took a taxi as far as al-Mutanabi Street, which was only five hundred yards from the library. The street is named after one of the greatest Arab poets, who lived in Iraq in the Middle Ages. Famous for its bookstores, it is a favorite place for writers and impoverished intellectuals.

An explosion shook the windows of the National Library. Amid the grey smoke, there were tens of thousands of papers, flying high, as if the clouds were raining books. Some of the pages were burning.

Nicola was blown off her feet and showered with glass, but recovered. She saw two children crouching next to their dead mother. She picked them up and carried them to the side of the road, away from the fire trucks and police cars. An ambulance arrived. She ran towards it and called to the driver, but the man just looked at her. He was praying, rocking back and forth.

She must have realized he wasn't a paramedic. She pushed the children away as the second bomb exploded. Fifteen killed. Forty injured. They found her broken body amid the rubble.

Daniela takes the photograph from Luca's hands and examines

the image of a serious-looking young woman with dark eyebrows and large eyes.

"Were you in love with her?"

"Yes."

Flinching almost imperceptibly, she studies Luca's face as though she's seeing the details for the first time; his brown eyes, his long lashes, the dark beard trimmed tight to his jaw. She wants to ask him if *she* means that much to him, but she won't. Instead they sit in silence, listening to the distant sirens and the steady hum of the air conditioner.

Luca slides his back down the wall and perches on his heels. It's a universal posture of men who can't find any more words and are too exhausted to search for them.

Edge accelerates on the divided highway, crossing the wind-ruffled river and passing suburbs of yellow and brown buildings, dotted with trees and rusting water tanks. No hint of rainclouds on the horizon. No hint of relief from the scorching white orb.

Route Irish was once the most dangerous road in the world. Now the military patrols have reduced the roadside bombings and hijackings. The wrecks have been cleared away and the hiding places bulldozed.

There are four checkpoints on the journey—two of them are run by the US military—mirrors sweep the chassis and suitcases have to be unlocked and searched.

Daniela rests her head on Luca's shoulder, exhausted and pleased to be going home, but mostly sad. There have been very few men in her life since her husband. None of them like Luca. There was the German diplomat with a wheat allergy; a French activist, who wanted her to stop shaving under her arms; a Dutch translator with a kink in his penis—none of them had Luca's passion for life or streak of self-loathing.

People had warned her about him. They said he was crazy living outside the wire, a maverick with a death wish, hunting his own headlines. Every line of reasoning told her to walk away, to not get involved, to wish him luck and leave him behind. This is stupid, she thinks. We hardly know each other. He doesn't know my middle name, or my favorite book, or movie, or what flowers I like, or how I used to work on my uncle's farm every summer until I broke my leg falling off a horse.

The Land Cruiser has stopped outside the terminal building. A passenger jet passes overhead, complaining noisily as it climbs.

Edge is out of the vehicle, unloading suitcases. Through the doors there are X-ray machines and body scanners. Daniela waits in line at the check-in.

Luca has taken a phone call. It's Jamal.

"Where are you?"

"At the airport."

"Are you leaving?"

"Not yet."

"I found someone at the prison. A cleaner. He asked the office staff about Ibrahim. He's no longer at Abu Ghraib."

"Transferred?"

"According to the records, Mohammed Ibrahim died in custody four years ago."

"Cause of death?"

"Not given."

"What about a death certificate?"

"Could take months. You could ask the Commission of Public Integrity. Judge Kuther is supposed to investigate deaths in custody."

Luca checks his watch. Daniela's flight is due to board any minute. He puts in a call to Ahmed Kuther. Waits. Thinks. Stares at the red-and-white control tower, the coppered glass, the minarets like sharp pencils jammed into the sky. The events of the past few days have left him with a dangerous sense of incompletion. Secrets still buried. A job half done. He never supposed this search would have a good end, but what sort of ending is this?

The judge finally picks up. "I hear you're leaving."

"Good news travels fast."

"I will be sorry to see you go."

"You could do me one last favor. There was a prisoner, Moham-med Ibrahim Omar al-Muslit. He's a former lieutenant colonel in the Republican Guard. Arrested December 2003. Last known address, Abu Ghraib, where he died four years ago."

"What do you need from me?"

"Confirmation."

Daniela has her boarding pass. She has to stand on her toes to kiss Edge on the cheek. He bends and picks her up. Her heels are off the ground.

Luca has to say goodbye to her now. He doesn't want to lose this woman. He wants to go to bed with her an infinite number of times. He wants to take her somewhere with white sandy beaches, palm trees and blue water; taste the salt drying on her skin and between her thighs.

His phone is ringing again. Daniela wants him to leave it. He looks at the screen. It's Tony Castro from Damascus.

"Bad time?"

"Could be better."

"That warehouse you asked me about: Alain al Jaria is registered in Syria as an import/export company. It has a postal address in Damascus and a couple of local directors who don't appear to exist. The only listed shareholder is a company called May First Limited, with a registered address in the Bahamas. And the only name associated with both companies is an Egyptian national with a British passport — Yahya Maluk."

"Never heard of him."

"He's a big player. Connected. He's a friend of President al-Assad in Syria and Mubarak in Egypt. Made his money smuggling oil for Saddam, according to the rumors. Nobody could ever prove it."

"Where is he now?"

"Apart from his place in Damascus, there's a house in the South of France, another in London. According to his housekeeper, he's in London."

"For how long?"

"She didn't know."

"What about Ibrahim?"

"I mentioned the name but the housekeeper didn't react. She was nervous. I didn't hang around."

A boarding announcement echoes through the terminal. Daniela's flight is being called: Turkish Airways to Istanbul. She's waiting at the security barrier.

Luca closes the gap, standing a foot away. Silent. Daniela looks past him at the security station. Beyond is the boarding gate. The last of the passengers are joining the end of the queue.

"My husband wants me to go back to him," she says. "That was the phone call I had on the night we met at the al-Hamra."

"What did you tell him?"

"I told him no."

She gazes at him, willing him to say something more. The slightest signal might tilt their lives towards each other, maybe for a long time. Luca's phone is ringing again. He glances at the screen. It's Ahmed Kuther.

"Can you wait for just one second?"

"No, I can't, Luca."

The phone is against his ear. Daniela turns away and puts her bag on to the conveyor belt before stepping through the body scanner.

"Who told you Ibrahim was dead?" asks Kuther.

"It came from a contact at the prison."

"The information was incorrect."

"So he's still in Abu Ghraib?"

Daniela has picked up her bag. She's walking across the concourse.

"Mohammed Ibrahim was accidentally released from prison four years ago. He was mistaken for another prisoner."

Luca glances at the departure board. Feels for his passport. There is a Royal Jordanian flight to Istanbul via Amman leaving in two hours.

He yells to Daniela, who turns at the last minute.

"Wait for me in Istanbul."

She can't hear him. He tries to get closer, but a guard stops him. He shouts again. "Istanbul. Wait for me!"

"Why?" she mouths.

Luca doesn't answer. If she can't find a reason, she won't be there.

27

LONDON

The wedding reception is at a Georgian villa on the northern edge of Hampstead Heath. Heritage-listed, whiter than a wedding cake, it looks like a film set from a BBC period drama, minus the bonnets and the horses.

"Do you remember *Notting Hill*?" asks Miranda, hooking her hand through the crook of Ruiz's arm. She's walking on tiptoes so her heels won't bruise the turf. "Julia Roberts was the American movie star and Hugh Grant had a travel bookshop on Portobello Road. They filmed one of the final scenes at Kenwood House."

"I've never really seen the point of Hugh Grant," says Ruiz. "He's like a male version of Meg Ryan—always playing wishy-washy romantic losers."

"I thought you fancied Meg Ryan."

"When she stops whining."

The Orangery is swathed in white linen with splashes of yellow from the sunflowers on each table display. A string quartet is playing in the corner. Daj, seated like a queen at her own table, is complaining loudly about her inconsiderate son, who never visits or calls. Her voice has a Lady Bracknell quality, slicing through the chatter like a well-honed cleaver.

Claire and Phillip had wanted a child-friendly wedding because most of their friends have started families. Now there are children running between the tables or imprisoned between their parents, going crazy with self-pity. One young boy slides a toy train along the seat so his sister will sit on it when she retakes her place. She lets out a cry. The toy is confiscated. More tears.

Ruiz does the rounds, visiting each table, trying to avoid the trays of champagne. Wedding receptions are strange rituals full of melancholy and a sense of time passing. Unmarried women of a certain age looking slightly forlorn, while those with long-term boyfriends are extra-attentive, hoping the day and the free bar might prompt them to pop the question.

His stepfather's relatives consist of an ageing aunt and uncle who have flown from Florida, their skin like petrified wood. He was some sort of biologist, but Ruiz can barely remember him apart from the smell of formaldehyde that clings to him like cigarette smoke.

Most of the men have taken off their jackets, loosened ties and rolled up their sleeves. As the night wears on, young people cavort on the dance floor and children are taken home to bed. Miranda asks him to dance. She puts her arms around his waist and hooks her thumbs into his belt. Pressing against him, she tilts her face so her mouth is inches from his.

"I thought you didn't dance," she says.

"I like this kind of dancing."

"Mmmm, I can tell you're rather pleased. Are you thinking about kissing me?"

"No, I'm thinking about going down on you."

"Would you think less of me in the morning?"

"Five per cent at most."

The festivities are paused while the wedding cake is cut. Ruiz finds himself standing next to Phillip's mother, who reeks of perfume and the sweet smell of rotting fruit.

"Don't they make a wonderful couple," she says, showing lipstick smudges on her teeth. "You must be very proud of your Claire."

"Yes."

"She does have a lovely complexion. Phillip once brought home an Asian girl from university. I think she was from Hong Kong. Pretty, in a Chinese sort of way. I think her father was involved in horse racing. They're very big gamblers, the Chinese, and they have those terrible Triads. I have nothing against foreigners, of course. I love a good Chinese…"

"But *not* in the family?"

The woman's mouth opens but the message has finally reached her brain. Ruiz is already retreating outside where he looks at the lights of London and goes over the events of the day. The confrontation in the street seems like a memory plucked from a past life. Public displays of violence are not his style, but he doesn't have the patience or the reflexes of his youth. Cat-and-mouse games annoy him. He's an intelligent man but not a complicated one.

At the top of the slope where the road cuts across the lawns towards the car park, Ruiz notices a dark car pull up. A figure emerges, silhouetted by the streetlights, tugging at the cuffs of a suit. Not police, but official.

The man says something to his driver and walks down the gravel path. He's about to pass by when he turns.

"Mr. Ruiz?"

"Yes."

"Douglas Evans from the Home Office."

"Have we met?"

"I don't believe so."

The man has the kind of English voice Ruiz dislikes. Upper class. Privately educated. Eton and the Guards most likely. He also has that telltale military bearing, as though always on the verge of snapping to attention and saluting.

"How was the wedding?"

"Beautiful. You should have been there."

"I wasn't invited."

"Exactly."

Mr. Evans taps the top of his wrist as though he's forgotten his watch.

"I understand that you know the whereabouts of a young woman called Holly Knight, who is wanted by the Metropolitan Police for further questioning. You guaranteed to make her available."

"She ran away from some of your men in black."

"Men in black?"

"Spooks. Dark suits. You know the sort. Fake identities. Cover stories. Everything hush hush."

Mr. Evans shakes his head. He taps his wrist again.

"Tell me something, Mr. Evans: why are you so interested in Holly Knight?"

"She's a suspect in a murder investigation."

"It's more than that."

Mr. Evans taps again. "We've had a request from our American counterparts to assist in finding Miss Knight."

"Why do they want her?"

"We're not entirely certain, Mr. Ruiz. That's one of the reasons I'm here. The spirit of co-operation between America and Britain has always been healthy, of course, but occasionally information is overlooked or left out of communiqués."

"They didn't tell you?"

"I'm trying to fill in the blank spaces." Mr. Evans attempts a smile. "We're on the same side, Mr. Ruiz. We both want to know what this is all about. If Miss Knight does break cover, I could guarantee her safety."

"If she speaks to *you* first?"

"She's a British citizen on British soil."

"I'll bear that in mind."

Ruiz turns to leave. He feels a firm grip on his forearm.

"I am trying to help her."

"Then tell me what this is about."

"That's above my pay grade."

Ruiz shakes his arm loose. Mr. Evans hands him a business card. "My numbers...should you change your mind. Give it some thought." He looks Ruiz up and down. "Nice suit."

The reception is winding down. Claire and Phillip have made their public escape, chauffeured away in a white limousine trailing tin cans, streamers, and covered in a year's supply of shaving foam.

Ruiz finds the professor and the two men share a moment on the patio while the waiters are clearing tables and stacking chairs. The wind has picked up — a storm is coming.

"You see that over there?" asks Ruiz, pointing at a pattern of lights. "That's Camden. I remember investigating a hit-and-run. She was knocked off her bicycle. Nine years old. And just off to the right — see that tower block? A four-year-old fell from a window on the sixth floor. His mother and father were junkies and had gone out to get a fix. Oakshot Avenue, Highgate: the wife of an alcoholic ex-sergeant blew his brains out when she found out he was having an affair.

"St. George's Catholic School, Maida Vale: Philip Lawrence, the head teacher, was stabbed to death while protecting a pupil. Cobbold Road, Shepherd's Bush: an elderly woman died of exposure because her landlord turned off the heating. Horn Lane, Acton: a hooker had her throat cut when she shopped her pimp for trading in underage girls..."

"Why are you telling me this?"

"Most people look at a city and they see people or buildings. All I see are the dead."

"Maybe you should get some help about that."

"I gave up being a detective because I got tired of dealing with all the rules and regulations, the red tape. I could handle the psychopaths and scumbags, until they started turning up in uniform and carrying badges."

"What's this about?" asks Joe.

Ruiz hesitates, draining the last of his Guinness. "Those men in the car this afternoon... I lost control. I'm sorry."

"You don't have to apologize."

"I've spent most of my life trying to keep a lid on my temper, but I've always known it's there. Sometimes it frightens me."

"You're scared of what you might do."

"I used to wonder what motivates people to do great harm — terrorists and the like. What makes them want to blow up buildings and bring down airliners, but when I feel that red-and-black mist rising up in me, I reckon I could lay waste to the world."

"I don't think that's likely to happen."

"I'm losing my sense of balance. My moral compass."

"Your compass is just fine."

Ruiz hesitates. "I'm going to tell you something now—and you're probably going to question my judgment."

"Go on."

"Holly Knight came to the church."

"Where is she now?"

"Somewhere safe."

"Did you call the police?"

"No."

"They can keep her safe."

"They'll hand her over."

"Maybe that's not a bad thing."

Ruiz's eyes are flat, his hands motionless. "First these people offered me a bribe, then they kicked down my front door and terrorized my neighbors, then they turned up at my daughter's wedding. You don't *work* with people like that. If you're lucky they'll yell 'watch out' before the freight train runs you down."

Ruiz pauses and contemplates a long career when he submitted himself to playing by the rules, upholding the law, protecting the weak, prosecuting the wicked. There was a time when he believed that it was his duty. He would pause outside New Scotland Yard at night and stare at the lighted windows, telling himself, "I did good work today. I served the people."

At the same time he had accepted the fact that, as a police officer, in all probability, he would become an instrument that delivered irreparable harm to a variety of individuals; some who designed their own destinies; others who were simply bystanders. He could even argue that occasionally innocent people are expedient and might have to die or go to prison for the benefit of many.

What had changed? Why is he now so determined to protect Holly Knight against forces he can never hope to identify, let alone defeat? Maybe there is a bit of Don Quixote in all men his age. They tilt at windmills because they don't want to grow old.

Joe is still waiting for an explanation.

"Holly saw a TV report—the one about the missing banker," says Ruiz. "She and Zac robbed him a week ago."

Joe holds his drink to his lips, but it doesn't go any further. The information warrants a pause.

"You think the disappearance is related to Zac's murder?"

"I'm working on that theory."

"I can't imagine a banker being the sort who would torture someone. It takes a very special individual to rip off pieces of flesh with a set of pliers."

"I take it you mean 'special' in a negative way."

"A psychopath or someone wired to the eyeballs."

"Maybe the guy had a meltdown."

"Over what?"

"Embezzling funds. Laundering money. Something illegal."

"That still doesn't explain why everyone is so interested in finding Holly Knight. What did they steal?"

"Good question."

"She must have some idea."

"Maybe it's not obvious. Maybe she doesn't know."

The two men drink in silence, contemplating the path ahead. Ruiz raises his glass and works his throat, wipes his lips, belches quietly.

"I want you to look after her."

"Me?"

"My phones are being tapped and they're following me, so you might have to keep her safe."

"Where is she?"

"A tourist hotel in Bayswater." Ruiz scratches at his jaw, making a sandpaper sound. "You should talk to her. Do that thing you do."

"What thing?"

"The mental picturing."

"A cognitive interview?"

"That's it. Find out what she can't remember. If she's hiding something." Ruiz glances at a kissing couple. One of the bridesmaids is giving mouth-to-mouth to her boyfriend. "You can't go home to Rainville Road. Stay at the hotel with Holly. Do you have any cash?"

"A little."

"Find a hole in the wall and get cashed up. After that don't use credit or debit cards. Cabs rather than public transport. No Oyster cards."

"Is all that really necessary?"

"They're trying to get to Holly through me and they'll know about you soon enough."

Ruiz still has the professor's mobile. He removes the SIM card and hands it back.

"How do I contact you?"

Ruiz scrawls a phone number on the back of a business card. "You call and leave a message with Capable Jones. Use a public call box well away from the hotel. Don't use my name on an open connection or the computers will kick in. Don't stay too long on the line."

"Now you're starting to scare me."

"It's going to be fine. I'm just thinking ahead."

"I hear that great chess players can think five moves ahead."

"I'm not a great chess player."

"How many moves ahead are you?"

"One."

"That doesn't seem like enough."

"It is when it's the right one."

28

LONDON

Late evening, the weather has turned. Wind thrashes branches against the sides of houses and rattles rain against the windows. Keeping to the shadows, he approaches the house from the darkest end of the street, using the trees to shield himself. Rain sluices off the brim of his baseball cap as he studies the rear façade, noticing the downpipes and windows. There is a light on in the upstairs bathroom, a woman moving behind the frosted glass. Steam rolling across the light, fogging the mirror, condensing on the tiles.

Leaves cling to his wet shoulders, making him look like an extension of the hedge, more plant than animal, more animal than human. He doesn't like the set-up. He prefers long-range targets viewed through the scope of a rifle.

She has read her little boy a story. Put him to bed. Brought him a glass of water.

Peering through a downstairs window, he looks for the security panel on the wall. It's not armed. The broken window did its job.

Gloves on. The key. Upstairs.

───────

Elizabeth soaks in the bath, her eyes closed, her head resting on a towel. She hears something outside and holds herself, listening. The wind and rain are like watery insects in her ears. A car engine starts then disappears down the street.

When the water begins to cool she pushes herself up, wrapping a robe around her body. She pauses at the fogged mirror, rubbing a hole to examine her face. There are lines she hasn't noticed before. Delicate cracks like soft pencil marks.

Pulling on a nightdress, she crawls into bed, asleep almost

immediately, dreaming she can feel North's warm body next to her. In the early years of their marriage, before Rowan was born, North would sometimes wake her in the middle of the night, kissing her nipples and stroking her stomach and thighs. She would moan and smile with drowsy expectation, her legs opening almost instinctively.

At some point she wakes. The wind seems to breathe through the upper windows, locked open a few inches to create a cross draught. Rowan is snuffling on the monitor. He snores like his father, only softer.

"Hello, Elizabeth," rasps a voice.

Her eyes are wide open now. She looks around the room.

"Can you hear me?"

It's coming from the monitor; from lips pressed against the plastic microphone.

"Such a fine-looking boy, he sleeps so peacefully."

Out of bed she crosses the floor, running along the corridor. Rowan's bedroom door is open. The nightlight casts a soft yellow halo. Her eyes search for him. They open to someone else.

A gloved hand covers her mouth and nose, warm and hard against her lips and teeth. He wrenches her head back into his own, drawing her body into his loins, a belt buckle hard-edged against the small of her back, his unshaved jaw scraping like emery paper across her cheek.

He drags her along the corridor into the darkness of her bedroom, throwing her on to the mattress, where he presses the gun to her temple.

Elizabeth pulls the bedclothes around her.

"Please don't hurt us. Take whatever you want. My purse is over there, but I don't have any money."

"You utter another sound and you die here and now."

She nods. The cold ring of steel is pressed above her left eye. His face is covered in a handkerchief like a cowboy. His sodden black shirt is molded to his chest.

He twists the gun into her temple. "Who else is in the house?"

"Nobody."

He presses the barrel to her mouth, forcing it between her lips, into her throat, making her gag.

"Who else is in the house?"

Her lips move around the barrel. She shakes her head, pleading with her eyes.

Pulling the gun free, he wipes the barrel on the bedding.

"Are you afraid?" he asks.

"Yes."

"Of what?"

"Of you."

Elizabeth can see into his eyes. Empty. Bottomless. They remind her of something from her childhood—an old abandoned well in the garden, covered up and sealed with a metal grate. She would lie upon the cover and peer into the blackness, feeling the updraft as if the hole was breathing like the nostrils of a sleeping giant.

"You have some photographs."

She shakes her head.

"You know the ones I mean."

"In my handbag...on the dresser. Take them."

Tucking the gun in the waistband of his jeans, he searches the bag. Finding the photographs, he folds them roughly and stuffs them inside his shirt.

"Where are the rest of them?"

"That's all."

"You're lying to me."

"No."

"Do I have to bring your boy in here?"

"No. Please."

"Your husband had a notebook—where is it?"

"I don't know what you're talking about."

"What about the girl he brought home?"

"I don't know who she is."

The Courier sits on the bed. The sheets are knotted in Elizabeth's hands and drawn up beneath her chin. He traces the barrel of the gun down her cheek across her lips, over her chin to her neck. Lower still…between her breasts…brushing against her pregnancy.

He reacts as though scalded, rearing backwards and pointing the gun at her stomach. Elizabeth lowers the bedclothes. Her nightdress is bunched between her closed thighs. He's staring at her pregnancy as though witnessing a miracle.

"Turn around. Face down. Hands above your head."

"Do you know where my husband is?"

"Count to a thousand."

"Please tell me where he is."

"Louder! I want to hear the numbers. If you call the police, if you tell anyone, I will come back and cut your baby out of your womb. It will be the last thing you see before you die."

Elizabeth begins counting slowly, her mouth almost too dry to make the words. The room is quiet. She stops. Listens. Rain gurgles in the downpipes. Wind shakes the trees.

Crawling out of bed, she goes to Rowan's room, placing her hand upon his chest, feeling for his heartbeat. Then she slips into bed next to him, placing her arms around his sleeping form, protecting him from the monsters.

BOOK THREE

We are not descended from fearful men. Not from men who feared to write, to speak, to associate, and to defend causes that were for the moment unpopular.

Edward R. Murrow

1

LONDON

Holly opens the curtains, dividing the room with angled light. The overnight storm has passed and the sky is the color of tarnished silverware. The bruise on her cheek has faded but if she presses it hard enough she can still feel it beneath her skin. Zac's bruise: the last one he inflicted upon her. A souvenir. No, that's not the word she wants. A reminder.

She should call his parents. Help make arrangements for the funeral. She only met them once. Zac told them that she was a legal secretary and was helping him sue the army for compensation. Can you sue the army for war injuries, she wondered. Maybe the government doesn't allow it.

There is a knock on the door. Her heart leaps. She checks the window. The fire escape is her escape route.

"Who is it?"

"I'm looking for Florence."

"Just a minute."

Holly pulls on a pair of jeans and picks up a lamp from a table between the beds. Unlocking the door, she steps behind it, holding the lamp above her head.

The door opens. Nobody enters.

"You don't need that," says the voice.

Holly looks across the room and sees her reflection in the mirror. The man in the hallway can see her.

"I'm a friend of Vincent's. You can call me Joe."

She studies him for a moment, looking for the lie, then lowers the lamp on to the table. Joe steps into the room.

"I brought you something to eat," he says, handing her a paper bag with handles. "I didn't know if you were a vegetarian so I brought you both."

Holly rips open the wrapping and bends into a sandwich greedily, forcing the corner of the bread into her mouth.

"How do you know Vincent?" she asks between mouthfuls.

"We've worked together."

"Are you a copper?"

"A psychologist."

Holly searches his face. He's telling the truth. She starts on the second sandwich.

"Can I sit down?" he asks.

"Do what you like."

The hotel room is just big enough for two single beds, a wardrobe and an armchair worn smooth by many buttocks. It smells of ancient lacquer and cheap perfume and, somehow faintly, of wet tobacco trodden into the carpets.

"So?"

"So what?"

"How did you sleep?"

She laughs. "This conversation sounds like a real winner."

Joe is studying her. "Do I make you nervous?"

"No."

She opens the soft drink and gulps it noisily, wiping her mouth with the back of her hand. She's sitting cross-legged on the bed, barefoot, shoulders hunched. Pausing for a moment, she looks at Joe again, examining him like a strange animal that has crossed her path. Mid-forties, slightly stooped, he has a tangle of hair and baggy clothes. He has kind eyes and a bumbling sort of air, like a man who's forgotten something.

"Where are you from, Holly?"

"Why?"

"I'm interested."

"Why are you interested?"

"I've read your Social Services file."

"Isn't that illegal?"

"I called in a favor."

"What about my privacy?"

"Have you talked to someone like me before?"

"Yes."

"When was that?"

"You want dates?"

Joe gives her a pained smile. "Vincent thinks you can tell when someone is lying."

"He's wrong. I tricked him."

"How did you do that?"

"It doesn't matter."

Holly tilts the soft-drink can, draining the remainder. She toys with the can, running her finger around the rim.

"What's the difference between a psychologist and a psychiatrist?"

"Psychiatrists can medicate."

"Just my luck."

"Why wouldn't you talk to the police?"

"Same reason I don't want to talk to you."

"But you *are* talking to me. You don't trust them, do you? You've spent time in custody. Did something happen to you?"

She's not looking at him now. Her lips are thin lines.

"Can you really tell when someone is lying?" he asks.

"You don't believe it."

"I keep an open mind."

"Things get polluted if you leave them open. They collect rainwater. Litter. Leaves."

Joe has had people like Holly in his consulting room. Patients unwilling to trust or frightened of what their thoughts and words might reveal about them. Sometimes Holly acts as though she has all the self-awareness of a hairdryer, but she's picking up on every detail of their conversation, his unspoken signals, mannerisms and micro-expressions.

Holly asks him what time it is.

"Does it matter?" he asks.

"Is everything with you a question?" She bounces off the bed and walks to the window, her bare feet making the floor creak. "I need to get out of here."

"Vincent said you should stay put."

"Nobody knows I'm here. Just for half an hour. A walk."

He agrees. They stop at a café on Edgware Road with metal tables and chairs on the pavement. Holly is hungry again. She orders a muffin and a cappuccino. Joe pays. He's still trying to fathom this girl, whose piercings seem to multiply in her ears, three in her left ear, four in her right; another in her navel, which he glimpses when she yawns and stretches her arms above her head.

"Get a good look?" she says. She flips up her T-shirt, showing her bra. Her breasts. He looks away. Wrongly accused. Within moments, Holly acts as though the entire incident never happened. She flicks through magazines on a wooden rack. A newspaper lies open on a table. The headline: ROGUE BANKER FLIGHT RISK. Holly turns to the full story and reads about Richard North, her lips forming the words.

"How does somebody spend that much money?" she asks. "He could buy an island or his own plane. If I had fifty-four million quid I'd go to Jamaica and spend the rest of my life on a beach."

"Do you remember him?"

"I guess."

"What do you remember?"

"He was married. His wife was away for the weekend. They had a small boy." Holly breaks her muffin into pieces, picking at the crumbs with her fingertips. "He asked me if I had ever done something wrong. He meant illegal. I thought maybe he knew we were going to rob him."

"Where did you meet him?"

"He picked me up."

"Just like that?"

Holly fixes him with a pitying look. "That's what married men do—they look at someone like me and they want to know what I'm like in bed, what I look like naked, what I'll do with my pretty little mouth. You're doing it now."

"No I'm not."

"Yes you are. All men are the same. They either hit me or hit on me or do both."

"That's a very sad view of life."

"It's the truth."

Joe doesn't want to argue with her. He sticks to his questions, asking what she stole.

"The usual stuff—phones, laptops, cameras, jewelry—things we could carry in the saddle bags of Zac's bike."

"What did you do then?"

"We fenced it."

"Where?"

Holly rolls her eyes. "There's a guy I know in the East End. Bernie Levinson. He owns a pawnshop. Bernie bought the stuff from me. He's tighter than a duck's arse but sometimes he lends me money when I'm short of the rent."

Holly brushes the crumbs from her lap and looks around for something else to do. She's sick of answering questions. "Now it's my turn," she says. "Are you married?"

"Technically."

What does that mean?"

"I'm not divorced."

"Separated?"

"Presently."

"Why is your hand shaking?"

"I have Parkinson's."

She remains silent.

"Is that it?"

Holly shrugs. "It's no fun unless you lie to me."

2

ISTANBUL

The hotel in Istanbul is in a filthy side street between a Chinese wholesalers and a factory where African workers make knock-offs of European labels for Russian tourists. Globalization in a microcosm; profit as god.

Inside the arched gateway, along a narrow passage, there is a courtyard filled with apricot and orange trees around a rectangular pool with water the color of green moss.

Daniela emerges from the bathroom, dressed in a robe, her hair dripping and the ragged curls falling around her neck. Luca is still toweling off.

"I'm probably going to regret this," she says.

"What happened to the post-coital glow?"

"I'm not talking about the sex."

Luca holds out his arms and she comes to him, tucking her head beneath his chin, her breasts against his ribs. He can feel the warmth of her breath against his neck.

"Are you really going to London?" she asks.

"Yes."

"What are you going to do?"

"I'm going to ask Yahya Maluk why one of his companies is smuggling stolen money from Iraq. I'm also going to ask him if he knows Mohammed Ibrahim—a man who helped Saddam steal billions of dollars from his own people."

"Just like that?"

"Yep."

"And I suppose he's going to throw up his hands and confess everything."

"That would be nice."

"You have the word of a one-armed former truck driver and a series of coincidences."

"They're more than just coincidences."

"Yahya Maluk has unlimited funds and an army of lawyers. He'll get injunctions to stop any story. He'll sue you for defamation."

"I know that."

"Why then?"

"Sometimes the only way to rattle someone like Maluk is to shake his gilded cage."

"That's a dangerous game."

"I'm just following the money."

"You could stop."

"What if it's funding the insurgency?"

"Nobody is going to be surprised."

Luca feels like a mediocre gambler trying to bluff an expert. Daniela has slipped away and gone to the latticed window. It has grown dark outside. The courtyard is strung with fairy lights that follow the contours of tree trunks and branches. Over the rooftops, the dome of Santa Sophia is bathed in gold.

"Come to London with me," he says.

"Why?"

"I don't want you lose you."

"We're different people, Luca. I deal in numbers and balance sheets. You deal in hunches and hearsay."

"I search for the facts."

"But you never have them all. You gather just enough, write a story and move on."

"You make me sound like a gigolo."

"No, you're not *that* good."

Luca can see what she's like—her father's daughter, practical to the point of impracticality. He leans forward, brushing his lips against hers, holding the kiss.

Later, lying naked in the air-conditioned room, his heartbeat returning to normal, Luca wonders what it's like for a woman, that moment when pleasure overcomes self-control and the wave breaks inside her.

"Do you still want me to come to London?" she asks.

"Yes."

"Then I'll come to London."

3

LONDON

Rowan has to shake Elizabeth awake. She is twisted in the sheets, lying on a bed shaped like a racing car with a Green Goblin toy wedged under her hip.

"Why did you sleep here, Mummy?"

"I had a nightmare."

"What about?"

"It doesn't matter."

There is a faint pervasive scent in the room that transports her back to last night and she feels her stomach cramp and the vomit rising. A man had wanted to kill her. Her life meant nothing to him until he saw that she was pregnant. Maybe he drew the line at murdering an unborn child.

Why hadn't she called the police? She had lain awake thinking about it, ashamed of how he had touched her; embarrassed by how her hands had hung stiff and useless at her sides. This time the vomit reaches her mouth and she has to swallow hard.

She picks up the phone and starts to dial. Stops, uncertain what number she's calling. She puts the receiver back in the cradle. What would she say? What would *they* say? They'd want to know why she waited. It would all come back to North's guilt, just like the needle of a compass.

Elizabeth goes to the bathroom and scoops water into her

mouth. Rinsing. Then she turns on the shower, keeping her head under the hot water for a long time, scrubbing at her skin. Dressing in her elasticized denim skirt and a cotton shirt, she strips the beds and washes the sheets. She shouldn't be doing any of these things. There might be DNA. Fibers. Evidence. She doesn't care.

As she takes the mattress protector from Rowan's bed, she notices a large white envelope sticking out from between the base of the bed and the mattress. Pulling it free, she recognizes North's handwriting on the cover. A message is written in thick black capitals, half an inch high:

KEEP THIS SAFE LIZZIE

Tearing open the flap, she pulls out a folder containing a dozen sheets of paper, written in North's hand. A list. Deposits and withdrawals. Accounts that have numbers instead of names. Some of them are circled or underlined. Grouped. He was hiding it from someone. Leaving it for her to find.

There is a name and phone number scrawled on the inside cover of the folder. North's handwriting is messy at the best of times. She spells out the letters: G.O.O.D.I.N.G.

Instead of being intrigued, she's annoyed. Why the secrecy and the cryptic message? This is North acting like a criminal. She hurls the file in disgust, sending pages into the air where they rock and turn and settle like falling leaves.

Claudia chooses that moment to kick Elizabeth in the cervix and she doubles over. Punishment delivered from her unborn child. Breathing through the pain, she goes downstairs and pulls back the curtains. The reporters have returned, fewer than yesterday.

An early model Mercedes pulls up beneath the branches. The driver gets out and walks towards the house. He's dressed in a shabby raincoat with stretched pockets. Unkempt. Bear-like. He rings the doorbell.

Elizabeth shouts from within. "Please leave me alone."

"I need to talk to you."

"I don't talk to reporters."

"I'm not a reporter. I may have information about your husband."

A tremor passes through Elizabeth, a hopeful surge. "Do you know where he is?"

"No."

"Then I have nothing to say."

Ruiz tries again. "You were robbed a week ago. You lost a jewelry box, a camera, a laptop...and they took a small crystal swan from your dressing table, which held some of your rings."

There is a pause. Elizabeth opens the door.

"I didn't tell the police about the crystal swan."

"I know."

"Who are you?"

"I'm just trying to help someone."

Ruiz waits in the lounge while Elizabeth makes tea. He notices the broken window, sealed with a sheet of plywood. The sound of a children's TV show drifts from another room. It's a nice place with polished floors and oriental rugs. Tasteful. Homely. The bookcase is full of holiday reads by Marian Keyes and Michael Connelly. On the mantelpiece there are several framed photographs. A wedding shot of a bride sitting on her husband's lap. He's tipping her back and she's laughing.

Elizabeth North is haughty and beautiful in a cultured way, like a woman captured in a painting. She sits upright, hands on her lap, nervously appraising him.

"When are you due?"

"Three weeks. How do you know what was stolen?"

"I've met the person who took it."

Ruiz tells her the story of meeting Holly and Zac. Seeing them argue. Stopping their fight. Consoling Holly. Letting her use his phone. Taking her home.

Elizabeth grows impatient. "Why are you telling me this?"

"I was drugged and robbed. I believe the same thing happened to your husband."

Elizabeth is staring straight through him. "What does she look like — this woman?"

"Blue eyes, black hair..."

"Cut short?"

"Yes." Ruiz knows something is wrong.

"She met him at a bar in the City."

"How did you know?"

Rising unsteadily, Elizabeth crosses the room and stands for a moment at the broken bay window, wrestling with a thought. Anguish in her voice.

"A private detective took photographs of North leaving a bar with a girl and bringing her home."

"Here?"

"Yes."

"You were having him followed?"

"I thought he was having an affair." Her eyes meet his, looking for understanding. "But you're saying that he tried to help her. And she stole from us?"

"She did."

Elizabeth sharpens her tone. "Did she do something to North? Does she know where he is?"

"No."

"Did she sleep with my husband?"

"No."

"Is that what she told you?"

"Yes."

"I want to meet her."

"I don't know if that's a good idea."

"I want to meet her."

Ruiz isn't an expert on human behavior like the professor, but Elizabeth is a woman on the edge of reason. Humiliated. Betrayed. Abandoned. He makes her sit, waits for the tension to leave her shoulders.

"What did your husband do for the bank?"

"He was a compliance officer."

"Did he ever bring files home, documents, sensitive material?"

"I don't know. Maybe. Why?"

He speaks softly. "The boyfriend I mentioned—he was tortured and murdered five days after the robbery."

Elizabeth's eyes are like black marbles. "My husband isn't a killer."

"I'm not suggesting—"

"What are you suggesting?"

"I think the people who killed Zac Osborne were looking for something that your husband had with him."

"A notebook."

Ruiz stops and studies her almost scientifically. Elizabeth crosses the room and picks up the phone. "You have to tell the police. You have to tell them."

Ruiz takes the receiver from her hand. "First tell me about the notebook."

Elizabeth shakes her head, caught between wanting to unburden herself and remembering the intruder's last words. In the same breath she rediscovers her doubts. Why should she trust this man? How does he know about the notebook?

Elizabeth backs away. "Did he send you? Did he tell you about the notebook?"

"Who are you talking about?"

"Why are you here?"

"I'm trying to help someone."

"That girl!"

"Not just her."

"Get out! Get out or I'll call the police!"

Elizabeth is screaming at him, fighting at his arms. Ruiz takes her punches on his chest, waiting until she runs down like the spring of an alarm clock. He sits her on the sofa where she grows smaller and more distant, hiding behind a fringe of hair. For a long time nothing is said. Breathless and a little dazed, Elizabeth feels embarrassed by her outburst. Exhausted.

Ruiz continues. "How long had the private detective been following your husband?"

"About a week. He made notes and took photographs."

"Can I see them?"

Elizabeth wraps her arms around her chest as if holding someone. "I don't have the photographs anymore."

"Where are they?"

She rocks back and forth, her voice flat. "A man broke into the house last night. He had a gun. He took them."

"Did you call the police?"

"No."

Still she rocks, empty inside. Disconnected. Once the world had seemed so rich to her, a colorful place. Now all she sees is the poverty of things. She can still taste the metal of the gun in her mouth and feel his hands on her skin.

Ruiz speaks to her calmly, getting her to repeat the story again. Each sentence takes time to form, as if she's dictating a letter. She tells him about hiring Colin Hackett—first to follow her husband and then to find him.

"Tell me about these photographs."

"They were of North and the woman."

"Holly Knight."

"Is that her name? I didn't know. She looked very young...and pretty. Why did she choose North? She could have had anyone. Why didn't she choose someone else?"

"I don't know."

Elizabeth tells him about North's meeting in Maida Vale with Yahya Maluk and a second man. She describes going to the house in Mayfair, where Maluk denied having met North at The Warrington.

Rowan appears in the doorway. He's peering through the dark holes of his Spiderman mask.

"Is you a policeman?" he asks.

"I used to be."

"Why did you stop?"

"I retired."

"Why did you get tired?"

Ruiz smiles. "I decided to give someone else a turn at being detective."

"You were sharing?"

"That's right."

Rowan sticks his finger through an eyehole, scratching an itch.

"Are you getting a rash again?" asks Elizabeth. "You should take off that mask for a while."

Rowan shakes his head. "Spiderman never shows his face."

"Can't you be Peter Parker today?"

His head shakes again.

"Come on, my little Spider hero—I have some cream upstairs."

"Superpower cream?"

"Good for defeating rashes."

Ruiz watches them go and can hear their echoing conversations from a bathroom at the top of the stairs. Moving through the house, he examines the door and window locks, noticing the movement sensors blinking from an upper corner of each ceiling. The alarm was turned off last night. The shattered window had broken the connection. The intruder planned this carefully, watching the house, waiting for Elizabeth and Rowan to be alone. No sign of forced entry. Elizabeth would have locked the doors. Whoever broke into the house could well have had a key.

Ruiz walks into the back garden where the sun shines in a glitter of green. He passes the rose bushes and an old rain barrel beneath a downpipe. In a soggy patch of ground near the paling fence he notices a set of footprints. They are deeper where someone jumped and then paused to stamp them down, smearing mud with his soft shoes. There is also mud on top of the fence. On the far side, beyond a thicket of shrubs and trees, he notices a flash of silver from the railway line.

Returning to the house, he finds Elizabeth upstairs. Rowan is playing with Lego blocks, building cities for Spiderman to protect. She cups her pregnancy in both hands.

"Who has keys to the house?" he asks.

"North. Polina. Me."

"Polina?"

"Our nanny, but she resigned yesterday." Elizabeth's mind starts to wander. "I don't know what I'm going to do now. She used to look after my brother's children and Mitchell passed her on to me."

"Where is Polina's key?"

"She left it on the mantelpiece."

Ruiz ponders the timeline. If Elizabeth is right, the only key not in the house belongs to Richard North.

"I found something else this morning," she says, leading him across the landing.

The folder and sheets of paper are still scattered on the floor of Rowan's room where she threw them. Crouching clumsily, she tries to collect the pages.

"There was an envelope under Rowan's mattress. My name was on the front."

"It was hidden?"

"He must have known I'd find it — either me or Polina."

Ruiz is reading the handwritten pages. Numbers but no account names. The right-hand column must be amounts, thousands or tens of thousands, unless there are zeroes missing.

"Why would he leave this for you?"

Elizabeth shakes her head.

"I was going to call Bridget Lindop, North's secretary at the bank. I talked to her last week. She was anxious. Secretive. North told her a terrible thing had happened and it was his fault. He thought the auditors would find out."

"Have you mentioned this to anyone else?"

"Only my brother."

Ruiz notices the name and phone number written inside the folder. He goes to the study to use the phone, punching the digits. Speakerphone.

Hello, you've reached Keith Gooding at the *Financial Herald*. I'm not available at present, but leave a name, number and short message and I'll get back to you.

Ruiz replaces the receiver in the cradle.

"That's the man who left a message," says Elizabeth.

"When?"

"It was on the answering machine after North went missing. He said something about rearranging their meeting."

"You didn't call him back."

"I was told not to talk to journalists." She's gnawing at her bottom lip, leaving a crimson mark. "We have to call the police. We have to tell them about the girl and the notebook."

"OK, but first I want to talk to the private detective."

4

WASHINGTON

Chalcott is walking uphill on a treadmill with sweat dripping from his nose. He can see an aerobics class through the glass windows of the gym, a young blonde wearing a black leotard and loose vest. She pauses and drinks from a water bottle, her throat moving rhythmically. If only he were twenty years younger, he thinks. Ten would do.

Upping the speed, he begins running, his waistline shifting beneath his T-shirt, bouncing with each stride. He's concerned about London. Years of planning and millions of dollars are in jeopardy. It was supposed to be a career-defining operation. Pull it off and Arthur Chalcott would be talked about in the same breath as legendary spymasters like Allen Dulles, Miles Copeland and even Markus Wolf. Not household names, but what spies ever are?

September 11 had caught them bare-assed, pants around their ankles. The Cold War had been fought and won, but they didn't see the next one coming. First they were blamed for supplying bad information; then for not finding Osama bin Laden or predicting the insurgencies. Of course we fucking predicted them, he thinks. Stevie fucking Wonder could have predicted it, but Cheney and the hawks weren't listening.

For almost a decade the Agency had been scrambling to catch

up, while the government prosecuted two wars and spent billions on homeland security. Every success had been short-lived. It was like playing a game of Whac-a-Mole with the "mole" being a skinny, ragged man living in the caves of Tora Bora—the world's most famous phantom, holed up in a mountain complex built with CIA money back when America was fighting the communists instead of the terrorists.

Chalcott's phone is buzzing. Slowing the treadmill, he hooks a wireless earpiece over the pink shell of his ear. Recognizes Sobel's number.

"The police have issued a warrant for Richard North. They think he might have left the country. They're checking airport car parks and passenger manifests."

"What about the girl?"

"We're doing everything we can."

"That's *so* reassuring."

Sobel doesn't let the sarcasm distract him. "We think she's with a psychologist—a friend of the ex-cop."

"Where is Ruiz now?"

"He's talking to the banker's wife."

"You're following him?"

"Of course."

Sobel has another piece of news. Hesitates in the telling.

"We may have an ID for the guy who killed Holly Knight's boyfriend. MI6 identified a suspect coming through Heathrow a fortnight ago. He was travelling on a Moroccan passport. Facial recognition software has linked him to the suicide of a Lebanese politician in Athens six years ago. He's also been tied to the death of the Egyptian industrialist Ashraf Marwan in London in 2007. Marwan was suspected of being an Israeli spy. Fell off his balcony. Fifth floor. Ground broke his fall."

"This guy got a name?"

"Four or five of them. Calls himself the Courier."

"Droll. What have we got on him?"

"A grainy CCTV picture from Athens six years ago."

"Last known location?"

"Mombasa in April."

"Don't you love the fucking Africans? We give them an extra twenty-five billion in aid and they repay us by harboring every low-life scumbag terrorist they can fit through the door."

Chalcott presses the cool down button. The incline on the treadmill begins to flatten out. His calves are burning and sweat has stretched the collar of his T-shirt. Toweling down, he keeps talking.

"Listen to me, Brendan, things want to start getting better real soon. I just heard from Jennings. Luca Terracini didn't catch a flight to New York. He's in Istanbul and he's just used his credit card to buy two tickets to London."

"Two tickets?"

"He's with the woman from the UN."

"Why is he coming here?"

"Yesterday he briefed a freelance journalist in Damascus, who has since been knocking on doors, asking questions about Yahya Maluk and Ibrahim."

"What do you want me to do?"

"Put Terracini on a plane to the US."

"This is England. I can't just extradite people."

"I don't give a fuck how you do it, Brendan. Plant drugs on him or kiddie porn or whatever other dirty little tricks they taught you in spy school. If this guy gets close to Ibrahim he'll blow this operation." Chalcott sits in the locker room, splaying his legs. "I got people here shitting themselves about this. And it costs a lot of money to get people to shit themselves these days."

"I'll take care of Terracini. He can be my problem."

"Your *other* problem," says Chalcott. "One solitary fucking girl—you had her on a plate and missed her. Now she's hiding somewhere and running rings around you. I cannot fucking believe..."

"Can I just say...we've had some—"

"Don't say bad luck, Brendan. You're starting to whine like a Limey. Make this right. No loose ends."

5

LONDON

Luca and Daniela have a long walk to Heathrow immigration and a longer queue. They go to the counter together. A Sikh man wearing a bright blue turban flicks through Luca's passport, looking at the many stamps.

"Where have you come from today?"

"Istanbul."

"And before that?"

"Iraq."

"What was in Iraq?"

"Oil. Sand. Terrorists."

"Are you making a joke about terrorism, sir?"

"I never joke about terrorism."

The immigration officer holds the information page over a scanner then waits. He picks up a phone and presses a button before placing it down again. Then he tucks Luca's passport under his keyboard and begins processing Daniela. He stamps her passport and hands it back to her.

"Enjoy your stay in the United Kingdom." Then he turns to Luca. "Please step to one side, Mr. Terracini."

"What's wrong?"

"The computer has flagged your name. I'm sure it's nothing."

Luca glances at Daniela. Over her shoulder he can see three armed airport police officers making their way quickly along the rows of immigration desks.

"Pick up the bags. I shouldn't be long."

"I want to stay with you."

"I need someone on the other side. Call Keith Gooding."

As he embraces her, he slips his notebook into her shoulder bag. The police officers have arrived and Luca is escorted past the queues of hollow-eyed travelers to an interview room furnished with a table and three plastic chairs. The white walls seem to blur the corners and the only sound is the hum of the air conditioning.

An hour passes. Luca takes a copy of the *Herald Tribune* from the front pocket of his small rucksack. More suicide bombings in Iraq. Fifty-nine dead in Baghdad. More than a hundred injured. Most of them young men lining up to enlist outside an army recruiting centre. Luca keeps turning the pages. Another ship captured by Somali pirates; the Lockerbie bomber still alive after a year; Robert Pattinson the world's sexiest man; a missing banker in London...

The door opens. A head comes into view. He's in the right place. The tall thin man is dressed in a pinstriped suit and trousers that are fractionally too short for his legs. His name is Douglas Evans and he reeks of public service.

He has brought Luca a sandwich and a bottle of water.

"Sorry about the delay," he says, businesslike. "I suppose you're wondering why you're here."

"Yes."

"Is that your only luggage?"

"I travel light."

"I will need to search your bag."

"Is that necessary?"

"A routine requirement of anyone coming through UK Customs."

"I thought you were immigration."

"Two hats."

"You'll have some form of identification then?"

Evans smiles with less enthusiasm and produces a Home Office ID card.

"You sound quite paranoid, Mr. Terracini."

"I'm just very careful."

Evans unzips Luca's bag and searches through the underwear and clean shirts that Luca purchased in Istanbul. Daniela helped choose them.

"Are you going to tell me what this is about?"

"We've had a complaint from the caretaker government in Iraq, via the US ambassador, that you fled their jurisdiction while still the subject of a criminal investigation."

"My visa was revoked two days ago. I was told to leave the country. Check with the American Embassy in Baghdad. Mr. Jennings."

"Why was your visa revoked?"

"The Iraqi government doesn't always see the point of a free press."

Evans touches his chin with a long index finger. He has feminine hands, which remind Luca of a girlfriend he once had. Penny, that was her name. They shared a bedsit in Paris for six months. When she orgasmed she used to call out her own name, which either made her completely narcissistic or so unsure of herself that she needed reassurance.

"I've been asked to review your status here, Mr. Terracini."

"My status?"

"Why have you come to England?"

"I'm here to see my commissioning editor at the *Financial Herald*."

"You're working on a story?"

"Yes."

Evans taps at his wrist as though checking that his watch is working.

"You left Iraq in a hurry."

"I left Iraq as instructed by the Iraqi police and the US Embassy."

Evans taps again. "It seems the Iraqis may want you back."

Luca smiles wryly. "You and I both know that the British government is not going to extradite an American journalist back to Baghdad."

"You can be denied entry to the UK."

"On what grounds?"

"Undesirable activities."

There is a knock on the door. A uniformed Customs officer whispers a message to Evans. The door closes on a heavy spring. Luca is alone again.

Opening the water, he sips it thoughtfully. The English are so polite yet Hollywood is always portraying them as fiendish villains. Christopher Lee, Alan Rickman, Charles Dance. Jeremy Irons. The lip-curling sneer, the cut-glass accent — it is just another cartoonish stereotype, of course, like the amusing Indian, the arrogant Frenchman and the inscrutable Asian.

Luca's father loved the English poets. Donne and Blake were his favorites, but he didn't like Wordsworth, who he said was a rock star poet, famous in his own lifetime, as if that were his worst crime.

More time passes. Luca closes his eyes and tries to doze. Daniela will be through the airport by now. She'll call Gooding. He'll pull strings.

The door opens. It's not Douglas Evans this time. Two airport police officers escort Luca along stark corridors and through swinging doors until he emerges into the arrivals hall. Daniela and Keith Gooding are waiting. Gooding gives him a bear hug. Their bodies don't fit well together.

"You didn't tell me you were bringing someone," Gooding says. "Daniela wanted me to call out the Queen's Guard."

"I inspire loyalty."

Daniela shakes her head. "You attract trouble."

6

LUTON

The café has three computer screens at the rear of the far wall, squeezed between shelves of canned goods, breakfast cereal and soap powder. Internet access is four pounds an hour. The Bangladeshi owner, Mr. Rahman, has three unmarried daughters and has already quizzed the Courier about whether he needs a wife.

Ibrahim is twenty minutes late, sweating profusely. Big pores, he explains. A bad diet, thinks the Courier.

Coffee is ordered, double espressos with the consistency of tar.

"Why haven't you found the notebook?" Ibrahim asks.

"Maybe it doesn't exist or the ex-soldier threw it away. He died slowly. I gave him every opportunity to tell me."

Ibrahim grunts and spoons four sugars into his coffee. Across the road, through a first-floor window, he notices a girl making a bed. She's wearing a black skirt and a blue apron. Something about maids, he thinks. He once offered a hotel housekeeper three hundred pounds to sleep with him. A Filipino girl. She got offended. It was more than she earned in a week. Foolish pride.

"Are they ready?"

"They're boy soldiers."

"They can still be ready. Soldiers or dogs, they all obey."

Ibrahim studies him for a while. He expected more of the Courier. Average height, average looks—only his eyes are predatory. Normally, they communicate via internet cafés, logging into an email account. Instructions are left as a draft message in the draft folder: a message that is never sent. Untraceable.

The Courier returns his gaze and Ibrahim looks down, touching the collar of his shirt. Outside a long-legged woman, dressed in black, is buying fruit from a stall. She steps around a couple sitting on the curb sharing a bottle, a beggar on one corner, a drunk on the next, invisible to her.

Ibrahim can feel his heartbeat increase as the caffeine and sugar fire up synapses in his brain.

"The operation is brought forward."

"I don't have the materials."

"They'll be provided."

"The payment is double."

Ibrahim mumbles in agreement.

"And the notebook?"

"If it falls into the wrong hands, we clear the accounts."

"How long will that take?"

"A keystroke."

7

LONDON

Rowan likes the old Mercedes. The smooth leather bench-seat in the back is perfect for sliding across when they turn corners. Elizabeth keeps telling him to sit still and buckle his seat belt.

"This is the way to Granddad's house," he says, recognizing his surroundings. "You said you were going on a venture."

"An *ad*venture," she corrects him.

As they near the house, Ruiz pauses at a set of lights.

"There's Polina," says Rowan, pointing out of the window. Elizabeth catches a glimpse of the nanny in a smart VW Golf that crosses the junction and disappears from view.

"Maybe she's visiting Granddad," says Rowan.

"I don't think she knows Granddad."

The electronic gates glide open and stutter to a stop, revealing a long, sweeping driveway and verdant lawns that slope down to a pond. Ruiz notices the security cameras and broken glass embedded in the perimeter wall. How the other half lives: the rich and the anxious.

As the Merc pulls up in front of the main house, Alistair Bach emerges from inside and jogs down the steps. Fit for his age, with teak-colored forearms and a full head of hair, he hoists Rowan aloft and holds him giggling and kicking above his head.

Elizabeth touches Ruiz's shoulder. "Don't tell him about what happened. Not until we've talked to the police."

"Someone broke our window," Rowan announces breathlessly. "And Mummy slept in my room because of the monsters."

Bach glances at Elizabeth looking for confirmation and then back at his grandson, who has spotted the Labrador and is squirming to be put down. Soon he's running across the grass calling Sally's name.

"Does he ever take off that costume?" asks Bach.

"When he has a bath," replies Elizabeth.

"I don't know if it's a healthy obsession."

"He doesn't want to save the world…just his daddy."

Bach notices Ruiz for the first time.

"This is Vincent Ruiz," explains Elizabeth. "He's a former detective."

Bach shakes hands. He has the sort of handshake and "look-'em-in-the-eyes" attitude that has been practiced in a thousand business meetings.

"What's this about a broken window?"

"A glazier is coming today," says Elizabeth, pulling an overnight bag from the boot of the Merc. "I just saw Polina. Was she visiting?"

"She came to see Mitchell."

"Is he here?"

"Upstairs. He wants to talk to you."

Elizabeth doesn't show any emotion. "I thought Rowan and I might stay for a few days," she says. "If that's all right."

"Of course it is."

He pries Elizabeth's fingers from the handle of her luggage and carries it inside. She goes through to the sunroom where she can watch Rowan from the French windows and wait for Mitchell to finish his phone call.

Ruiz feels he shouldn't be here. This is a family matter. He wanders on to the terrace, overlooking the garden where Rowan is throwing a ball for Sally to fetch. Elizabeth and her father are arguing inside. Loud whispers. Pleadings. Recriminations. A door slams and the dog looks up towards the house.

Alistair Bach joins Ruiz on the terrace. He's carrying two long-necked beer bottles. Imported lager. Cold.

"Thank you for bringing Lizzie."

"That's OK."

Bach's nostrils swell with air and he looks genuinely unsure of what to do. Like a lot of powerful men, every word he's ever spoken and every action he's ever taken has been an attempt to control his environment, but now he's frustrated by his inability to comfort his daughter.

"Lovely place," says Ruiz.

"I bought at the right time."

"When was the right time?"

"The eighties."

"Early 1800s I might have had a chance."

Bach chuckles hollowly. "It's not rocket science."

"What isn't?"

"Being a banker."

Ruiz doesn't respond.

"You don't like bankers, do you?" says Bach.

"I don't know any," says Ruiz, which is a diplomatic answer. Even before the recession he had never given much thought to whether bankers were the architects of global prosperity or the sackers of civilizations. He had always been more worried about gangbangers dealing crack to black teenagers and bikers selling crystal meth into school playgrounds.

"You don't like what we represent," says Bach. "What you perceive we've done. You think we've caused nothing but grief."

"I try not to judge people."

"You're a lousy liar, Vincent. Once upon a time we were the good guys. People admired us. They wanted to be like us. When Gordon Gekko said, 'Greed is good,' people lapped it up. They wanted our Italian silk suits, our Porsches and our penthouse flats. The tabloids wrote stories about East End barrow boys without an O-level who were pulling in six-figure salaries and seven-figure bonuses. We made money. We created jobs. We paid most of your taxes. We turned the City of London into the second biggest financial capital in the world."

Bach pauses and points to Ruiz's chest with the neck of his beer bottle. The skin along his hairline is shiny with perspiration.

"Do you own a house, Vincent?"

"Yes."

"Has it doubled in value? Trebled?"

"I've done OK."

"More than OK, I'd say. You should thank bankers for that. All that wealth we created had a knock-on effect on property prices.

Ordinary guys like you, living in suburbia, became millionaires because of what we did. You bought houses and sat back and watched the values rise. You thought you were geniuses. You thought it was down to *you*."

Bach looks at the recently hoed garden. He did the work himself, churning the soil until his shirt was soaked in sweat, working through the heat of the day as though avenging himself. He sucks air through his nose and spits into the garden.

"Then it all fell apart," he says, "the meltdown, the credit crunch, the global financial crisis. People panicked. They wanted out. They cashed in their investments, withdrew their money, and it all came crashing down. They squealed when governments bailed out the banks with taxpayer funds. Hated us even more. But none of them realized how those funds were also propping up their property prices and their jobs and the glorious consumer bubble they had grown to know and love.

"They blamed the bankers. They wanted us put in jail. They wanted to curb our bonuses and tax our salaries. But the only way America and Britain and Europe are getting out of this mess is if the banks recapitalize. And the only way taxpayers are getting their money back is if banks do what they do best. Trade. Hedge. Lend. Make profits.

"People might hate us, Vincent, but you *need* us. And when things turn around, when things pick up, when wealth returns, they'll want to be just like us again. They'll want what we have."

His face flexes in an idle thought, as though an annoying insect has buzzed across his field of vision. Then he looks back towards the house, thinking of Elizabeth.

"Why are you doing this?" he asks.

"I'm trying to help."

"In my experience, Vincent, most people don't do anything unless they see something in it for themselves." He looks at Ruiz for a long moment. "Why don't you leave this alone and let my daughter get some rest? She's about to have a baby."

Never blinking, he raises the bottle to his lips and drinks it dry.

Inside the house Mitchell Bach has finished his phone call and comes sweeping into the sunroom, calling for "Lizzie." Kissing both her cheeks. Keeping his hands on her shoulders. "I'm so sorry," he says. "I should have called you. It was stupid. Thoughtless." He leads her to a chair, insisting she sit down. He kneels, not wanting to break physical contact.

"I hear the reporters have been giving you a tough time. They're all shits. I wish someone would doorstep them for a change. We should rent a mob and send them around to the editors' houses. I bet they've all got mistresses or rent boys in the closet."

Mitchell looks for agreement, but Elizabeth isn't about to let him change the subject.

"Why was North so worried about some of the transactions?"

"Isn't it obvious?"

"Not to me."

Mitchell contemplates the question, as though wrestling with bad news.

"I hate to say this, Lizzie, but the last time I spoke to North he was quite hostile to me. He was spouting conspiracy theories and making all sorts of wild claims about secret transfers and hidden accounts. I told him to put together a report, but he said he didn't trust anyone at the bank."

"When was this?"

"About a week before he went missing. He drank almost two bottles of wine at lunch. He was a mess. Making ridiculous statements. Sounding paranoid."

Elizabeth knows these descriptions aren't fabrications. They are carefully chosen statements that are distorted through the lens of self-interest until facts become slurs but still look like facts. North's reputation is being artfully dismantled, taken apart piece by piece.

A wave of nausea seizes her. She wants to argue. Defend him. A wife's belief should be enough. Bracing her hands on each side of the armchair, she raises herself up. One hand automatically cups her pregnancy, as though reassuring Claudia that she's in control.

"You're a shit, you know that? You've always been a shit."

Mitchell lets her go.

Ruiz and Alistair are still in the garden when Elizabeth emerges from the house. She has fixed her make-up and brushed her hair, pulling it back from her face with a hairband. She has also changed her clothes and is dressed in a high-necked white blouse that makes her look like a pregnant choirgirl. The angel waif. With all the detachment of someone who has witnessed a car wreck, she tells her father she needs him to look after Rowan for a few hours.

"Where are you going?"

"To see Mr. Hackett."

Bach presses his thumbs against his closed lids, his hands holding his forehead. "I don't think you should get involved, Lizzie."

"I *am* involved, Daddy."

8

LONDON

Bernie Levinson isn't at the pawnshop. One of the machinists from the factory downstairs says Bernie lunches at his club every day—an all-hours drinking hole in the shadows of Spitalfields Market. "Hole" being the optimum word. Darker than a cave, the only light comes from a neon advertising sign above the bar and the copper lamps on the tables. No windows. No clocks. Time doesn't matter in a place like this. Life is put in abeyance, chemically or alcoholically.

The barman is young, good-looking, dressed in a black T-shirt and Levi's. Eyes only for Holly. "What can I get you?"

"Mineral water."

"That's not a real drink."

"Alcohol goes straight to my head. Makes me do dangerous things."

She's flirting. He's hooked.

"Is Bernie about?"

"Why do you want Bernie?"

"He promised to look after me."

"I could do that."

"Maybe later."

The barman points across the warped wooden floor that is dotted with old cigarette burns. Up a handful of stairs there is a raised restaurant area with private booths. Only one of them is occupied. Bernie Levinson is sitting by himself, a serviette tucked into his collar, dipping bread into a broken piecrust.

Holly takes her glass of water to a table near the fire doors where Joe O'Loughlin is waiting.

"He's here. Maybe I should talk to him first," she says. "You might make him nervous."

"You're mistaking me for Ruiz."

"OK then."

They cross the floor and climb the stairs, slipping into the bench seat opposite Bernie. The pawnbroker grimaces at the sight of Holly as though something has given him heartburn or blocked his colon. Then he looks at the professor. "Who the fuck are you?"

"Joe O'Loughlin. I'm a friend of Holly."

Bernie ignores his outstretched hand and goes back to eating, keeping both elbows on the table.

"That stuff I brought you, Bernie. I need it back," says Holly.

"I don't know what you're talking about."

"The nice leather briefcase and the laptop."

"Huh?"

"This isn't a set-up, Bernie. I'm not wearing a wire. See?" Holly lifts her top, showing her pale stomach and light blue bra. She turns left and right, showing her back. Bernie waves his hand dismissively.

"How do I know you're not wearing a wire down there?" He points to her jeans.

"You'll have to take my word for it."

"*Your* word!" He laughs.

"I just want the stuff. I know you haven't sold it."

Bernie covers his ears. "I'm not listening."

Joe notices the enlarged tips of his fingers and nail clubbing, which suggest low oxygen levels in his blood and congenital heart disease. Mid-fifties, overweight, a signet ring on the little finger of his right hand, a plain wedding band on his left; married, children most likely. Bernie puts down his knife and fork and pats the breast pocket of his coat. There's something important inside. Not a weapon. Not a mobile phone. Medication.

"Someone killed Zac," says Holly.

Bernie searches her face, looking for a lie. He shakes his head, wobbling his chins. "Oh, no, no, no, I'm not involved in this shit. I'm just a businessman. I buy things. I sell things." He's addressing Joe now, trying to convince him. "I run a family business. My grandfather. My father..."

Bernie has taken a phone from his pocket and placed it on the seat beside him. The screen is lit up. He's calling someone... sending a message.

"We just want the stuff back," says Holly. "We'll pay you the money."

Bernie's lips peel away from his teeth. "Let me get this straight. You came to me with certain items—which, by the way, I had no idea were stolen—and you sold me these items in good faith, but now you want them back?"

Holly nods.

"That suggests to me that someone has made you a better offer. Maybe I should negotiate with them directly."

"It's not a question of money."

"In my experience, it's *always* a question of money. What's this item that's so valuable?"

"We're not sure," says Joe.

"You're not sure?"

"Holly is hoping she'll know it when she sees it."

Bernie laughs but it turns into a coughing fit. Tugging his

serviette from his collar, he tosses it on his plate and calls for the bill. Beneath the table, Holly's hand touches Joe's thigh. She leans closer, cupping his ear.

"Something isn't right," she whispers.

"What do you mean?"

"He's lying."

Joe glances at Bernie, who is peeling off two ten-pound notes. Holly confronts him outright. "You're lying."

Bernie looks offended. "What are you talking about?"

"I don't think you have the gear anymore."

"Maybe we should give him the benefit of the doubt," says Joe.

Holly looks at him angrily. "Why doesn't anyone believe me?"

She needs the bathroom. She makes her way across the dance floor to the ladies. Joe follows Bernie outside into the whiteness of the afternoon. The pawnbroker holds open the heavy door.

Two paces into the alley, Joe is shoved from behind, driven hard into the wall. Bouncing back, he meets a man who delivers a short sharp punch to his stomach, enough to deny him air and double him over.

Bernie puts his face close. His breath smells of steak-and-kidney pie.

"This is my employee, Mr. Tommy Boyle. He used to box. Now he breaks things for a living. He works in a wrecker's yard. Bones break easier."

Bernie takes Joe's wallet from his coat pocket and checks his driver's license.

"So tell me, Professor Joseph O'Loughlin of Station Road, Wellow, near Bath, what are you doing with that moist little bint and why is someone so interested in what she stole?"

"What do you mean?"

"Other parties are looking for her—one man in particular. You're going to tell me why."

The door opens. Holly emerges, holding something behind her back. She doesn't seem particularly surprised to see Tommy Boyle.

"Ah, here she is, my little princess," says Bernie.

Holly raises a short crowbar above her head and brings it down on Tommy's shoulder, raking down his arm. In a blur of movement, she swings it again, this time connecting just below his right knee. Tommy goes down like a felled tree, groaning and clutching his leg.

"Get up and fight," says Bernie.

Holly raises it again, aiming at the pawnbroker, but he reels away with his hands in the air like a mime artist in a glass room.

"OK, OK, settle down."

"She broke my fucking leg," moans Tommy.

Holly looks at Joe. "Did I hit him too hard?"

"It's not your fault."

"Of course it's *her* fault!" says Bernie.

"You started it," says Holly, sounding like a petulant child. "You shouldn't have lied."

"You're a freak!" Bernie spits the words. "I haven't got your stuff, OK? A guy came and took it. Cleaned me out."

"What guy?"

"A total nutjob—he didn't like Jews or women or porn or golf."

"Golf?"

"That's not the point. This complete psycho came to see me last Friday; grinning at me like every sentence was a punchline. He wanted to see everything I'd bought from that evil bint." He points his chin at Holly. "I was six hours locked in a storeroom. I'm lucky the guy didn't kill me."

"What was he looking for?" asks Joe.

"Some notebook."

"Did you report the robbery?"

Bernie hoots sarcastically. "Rozzers would have laughed me out of the station."

Joe looks at Holly for confirmation.

"He's telling the truth."

Bernie lowers his hands and jabs a finger at her, spitting the words. "What have you got me mixed up in?"

<hr />

Adjusting the side mirror, the Courier keeps Holly Knight in view, marveling at how much anger and energy are contained in her small frame. How brittle she seems, yet strong. How fragile, yet unbreakable. He wants to take this girl in his arms, to feel her ribs against his chest, to cup her delicate throat in his palm and taste the salty ichor of her fear.

Screwing up his eyes to see her better, he congratulates himself. He knew if he waited long enough she'd visit Bernie.

"You shouldn't park there," says a voice. An office worker has stepped outside for a cigarette. "The weasels will get you."

"Weasels?"

"Wardens."

Short and rather plump, she touches the corners of her mouth as though checking to see that she's smiling.

"I won't be staying, but thanks for the tip."

The woman continues puffing and talking, telling him how many times the wardens have given her parking tickets. Maybe she's flirting with him. Is she batting her eyelids or blinking away smoke?

"Do you know what you tell a woman with two black eyes?" he asks.

"What?"

"Nothing. She's already been told twice."

9

LONDON

She's lower today."

"Lower?"

"Her head is engaged. It means she's upside down, ready to come out."

"Does that mean..."

"She's just ready. It doesn't mean she's knocking."

Elizabeth gazes out of the window of the Merc, feeling Claudia moving inside her, fighting for room in a shrinking world. Her conversation with Mitchell has been replaying in her head. What he said. What she said. He had lied to her. In her overheated imagination it feels like something final, as though he's broken more than some bond of filial love.

Ruiz parks in a street of white Victorian terraces with iron railing fences and front doors that are set above street level up a dozen stone steps. Lower stairs lead to basement flats where leaves and rubbish have collected against the doors.

Even before they turn into Old Brompton Road, they see flashing lights reflecting from the windows. Police cars have blocked the traffic in both directions and a white, tunnel-like tent covers a doorway.

Gerard Noonan emerges, holding a mobile phone six inches from his mouth and shouting because he's unwilling to risk brain cancer. Anyone who cuts open dead people must fear myriad ways of dying.

Ruiz tells Elizabeth to go back to the Merc. She doesn't respond. There is a particular light in her eyes as though she has come to a realization that isn't obvious to the rest of the world.

On the far side of the road, a constable in a reflective vest is controlling a small crowd behind fluttering police tape. Further along the street, a young woman is sitting in the back of a patrol car. Peroxide hair. Black mascara tears. Ruiz ducks under the tape and walks with purpose towards the crime scene. The constable stops him.

"I'm on the job," says Ruiz. Although six years retired, he still looks and sounds the part. The constable hesitates and Ruiz strides onwards, veering slightly to the left and disappearing behind the SOCO van. The door of the patrol car is open.

"Are they looking after you?" he asks.

The young woman blinks at him. She's wearing a crimson blouse, short skirt and angel earrings. There are pain lines in the corners of her mouth.

She nods.

"You work for Mr. Hackett?"

Another nod, even more rapid. Ruiz slides on to the seat next to her. She tugs at her skirt, covering more of her thighs.

"He's my uncle," she adds. "I told that other detective."

"What's your name?"

"Janice."

"That's a nasty cold, Janice."

A shiver runs through her shoulders. "That's what *he* said to me."

"Who?"

"The man who came to the office on Friday. He said he was an old friend of Mr. Hackett, but I didn't believe him. I rang Uncle Colin and I said, 'That man isn't your friend,' but I don't think he listened. Uncle Colin isn't frightened of anything. He used to be a soldier. He went to the Falklands."

She is speaking in a rush, words and sentences running together. Ruiz waits for her to pause for breath.

"This man—did he give his name?"

"He said he was a courier but he didn't have any packages and he didn't look like a messenger. He told me to go home for the day. It's this flu. Uncle Colin said I was spreading the plague."

Janice takes a ball of tissue from the sleeve of her cardigan. "Auntie Megan called me this morning and said he hadn't come home and wasn't answering his phone. I knew something was wrong."

She blows her nose and takes another big sniffle. "I found him in the loo. There's blood everywhere."

"When you talked to your uncle, where was he?"

"On a job."

"What job?"

"He was looking for that missing banker."

"Did he say where he was calling from?"

"Luton."

Campbell Smith emerges from the white canvas tunnel. He struggles to remove his blue plastic overalls and shoe covers. When he notices Ruiz he ignores him for a split second as though he's simply part of the familiar. Then the information registers and anger blooms in his cheeks.

"I want that man arrested! Get him out now!"

Ruiz is pulled from the car and pinned across the bonnet. His arms are wrenched back. Wrists handcuffed. Campbell is raging about interference with a murder investigation and impersonating a police officer.

"I'd be careful of your blood pressure," says Ruiz, his cheek pressed to the warm metal.

"What are you doing here?"

"I had business with Mr. Hackett."

"What business?"

Elizabeth North yells from behind the barricade. "I brought him here."

Campbell glances at a handful of reporters who are getting every word. He holds his tongue.

Ruiz speaks next. "Can I go now?"

"My office in an hour—be there."

The young constable jerks Ruiz back roughly, making the handcuffs bite into his wrists.

"Take those off," says Noonan, who's been listening to the confrontation. "And you treat him with respect. He's a former DI."

Campbell is already at his car. The door slams shut. A liver-spotted hand emerges from the window and places a flashing blue light on the roof. Moments later the siren sounds.

"That guy is going to be on my slab one day soon," says Noonan.

"Heart attack?"

"Either that or someone is going to punch him too hard."

The pathologist has work to do. Ruiz has questions.

"How did Hackett die?"

"A forty-five; small hole going in, big hole going out."

"Is that a medical opinion?"

"Observation is one of my gifts."

"Same caliber as killed Zac Osborne. It's going to be the same gun."

"What makes you so sure?"

"There's a link. Zac Osborne robbed Richard North a week ago Friday."

"Why wasn't it reported?"

"Elizabeth North made a statement but everybody concentrated on her missing husband."

Noonan's curiosity has been piqued. Ruiz tells him how the private detective had been hired to follow Richard North and had photographed him leaving a bar with Holly Knight.

"It was a scam. Holly and her boyfriend robbed him."

"Same sting they pulled on you."

"You know about that."

"The email has gone viral. So you were saying..."

"Zac Osborne is dead and so is Colin Hackett. Same weapon. Same killer."

Ruiz glances again at Elizabeth, who is still on the far side of the road. She's shifting from foot to foot, mouthing the words, "I need to pee."

"Is there a toilet she can use?"

Noonan addresses the constable. "Take her to the café over the road. Try not to lose her."

Ruiz watches them leave. "Was anything taken from Hackett's office?"

"Memory cards from his cameras and his computer hard drive."

Ruiz nods. "Somebody wanted the photographs of Richard North."

"Any idea why?"

"Not yet."

Sunlight shines through the branches above, making shifting patterns of shadow on Noonan's smooth, pale head. As they linger there, Ruiz senses that he's being watched. His eyes slowly scan the crowd until they rest on a dark-haired man whose face is lifted at an awkward angle, as though his eyes are not looking at him directly but are still studying him with peculiar interest. There is a strange air about him, sinister yet jaunty: an impression of hidden laughter. For a moment they scrutinize each other before the man turns away and slips into the crowd.

"You'd better go, Vincent," says Noonan. "Don't underestimate Campbell. You don't have any goodwill left."

10

LUTON

The flat is small, just three rooms, overlooking a run-down series of shops with broken neon signs and metal grates protecting the windows and doors. On warm evenings, Taj climbs out the upper window and sits on a narrow ledge smoking and drinking coffee while Aisha puts the baby to sleep.

He can hear the clatter of his Asian neighbors echoing up and down the stairwells and through the open windows: arguments, music, children and TV sets. Sometimes he can even convince himself that he is among the chosen people, the lucky ones.

But there are indignities to be suffered. Insults to be endured. Rejections. One particular woman, obese and choleric, always gives him a hard time when he collects his jobseeker's allowance and housing benefit. She scowls at him behind her desk, mispronouncing his name even after he corrects her; and she treats his payments like money meant for her kidney transplant.

Aisha is calling him inside. Taj puts out his cigarette and climbs off the ledge, swinging his legs through the window and arching his body like a gymnast. His wife looks pretty in tailored trousers and a smock with beading around the neck.

"Didn't you hear the phone?"

"No."

"Syd wants to see you."

"Did he say why?"

"Something about the courier coming." Aisha looks at the dishes piled in the sink. She's been working all day at Homebase. On her feet. The least Taj could have done was wash up after breakfast.

She's annoyed, but she won't say anything. Taj has been on edge for months, ever since he lost his job. Short-tempered. Angry. She won't risk starting an argument.

"Stay in tonight," she says, rubbing his shoulders.

"Syd and Rafiq are expecting me."

"You're not married to Syd and Rafiq."

"I missed the last meeting."

Aisha turns her back on him, trying not to show her feelings.

"Why don't you like them?" asks Taj. "They're my friends."

"I don't like the way Syd looks at me."

"He's just jealous."

Taj puts his finger on her lips. Aisha kisses it and giggles when Taj tries to pull her closer. Lithe as a fish, she twists past him and loops an apron over her head, letting Taj tie the bow. All thumbs.

"What do you do at these meetings?" she asks.

"We talk."

"What do you talk about?"

"The Koran. How we're treated. The problems we face."

"We're better off than our parents."

"This is our country too."

Aisha runs hot water, squeezing in dishwashing liquid, watching it foam. She can see Taj reflected in the curved chrome of the tap.

"You say Pakistan is our country and England is our country. Which is it?"

"Both."

"Can we belong in two places?"

"Only if we make them ours."

"What does that mean?"

"We have to tear this country down and rebuild it. Make it the way we want it to be."

"I don't think we should tear things down."

"Sometimes it's the only way."

Taj begins drying the dishes, his back pressed to the bench.

"Did you pay that bill I gave you?" she asks.

"I didn't have enough cash. I'll do it next week."

"I gave you the money."

"I spent it."

"What on? We barely have enough for food."

Taj throws the tea towel into the soapy water. "And that's my fault."

"That's not what I meant."

"Yes, it is!"

"Shhhh, you'll wake the baby."

"Don't tell me to be quiet in my own home."

"I'm sorry. I'll pay it tomorrow. I'll use the money we're saving for Ramadan."

They wash the dishes in silence. Taj slips his hand around her waist, trying to show that he's sorry. He won't use the word. She closes her eyes and shivers.

"I know you're worried," he whispers. "You must not be. We have money coming. Lots of it."

"Don't make up stories, Taj."

"I mean it. Next week. We'll have all the money we need."

She throws her arms around his neck, pressing her body against his.

"Did you get a job?"

He smells her hair and cups her buttocks in his palms as though judging their soft weight.

"Yes, a job."

LONDON

The Soho wine bar has black painted walls, black doors and black furniture. It's full of the kind of people who en masse intimidate Luca most: men in designer suits and women with ballerina bodies and little black dresses. Daniela doesn't look out of place — she's a New York girl — she probably has a wardrobe full of cocktail dresses and tailored suits.

Keith Gooding has been entertaining her with stories about Afghanistan; shared adventures with Luca, embarrassing moments. He's telling her the story about a grizzled old warlord in Jalalabad who promised to show them a former al-Qaeda training camp. Two days into their journey through the mountains the old warlord crept into their room and Luca woke with hands fondling his genitals. His scream brought the warlord's bodyguards bursting into the room, threatening to shoot them.

"What in God's name were you doing?" Gooding had hissed.

"The old pervert had his hands on me."

"Couldn't you give one up for the team?"

Daniela laughs and Luca tells her that she shouldn't believe everything Gooding tells her.

She kisses his knuckles. "I know."

He needs the bathroom. The doors are marked XX and XY — the language of chromosomes. As he exits he notices a tall man with craggy eyes sitting opposite a woman in a camisole and skirt. Holding hands. Lovers. His eyes aren't looking into hers. Instead they're focused on Luca.

"What's wrong?" asks Daniela.

"I've just seen someone I recognize, but I can't place him."

"In Baghdad?"

"Maybe. Go to the bathroom in a couple of minutes. He's sitting near the pillar." Luca looks at Gooding. "Did you book this table?"

"Yes."

"Who else knows we're here?"

"Oh, come on, Luca, relax, you've been living in a war zone for too long." He raises his glass. "This is supposed to be a celebration."

Luca smiles and apologizes, but the disquiet stays with him like an unpleasant aftertaste.

"So what did you find out about Yahya Maluk?"

Gooding takes out his iPhone and runs his finger across the screen.

"Egyptian billionaire. Educated at Charterhouse. Second eldest son of Salim Ahmed Maluk, who rose from being an illiterate moneychanger to found banks in Egypt, Syria and Lebanon. Married. Three grown-up children. Personal wealth estimated at three billion pounds. Family fortune twice that much. Dozens of companies and charitable trusts."

"Does he still have links with banks in the Middle East?"

"He's a former director of a Dubai-based private equity firm and non-executive director of the Bank of Syria."

"What about in the UK?"

"He's a non-executive director of Mersey Fidelity."

Luca repeats the name. He's heard it before.

"It's been in the news," explains Gooding, biting a wedge of lime between his teeth and sucking, letting the sourness hollow out his cheeks. "A missing banker."

Luca remembers the story that he read in the *Herald Tribune*.

"Richard North disappeared more than a week ago," explains Gooding. "The bank says fifty-four million pounds is missing."

"Tell me about Mersey Fidelity."

The journalist picks at the label of his beer bottle. "Now there's an interesting story. It's the only UK bank that rode out the global financial crisis without needing a taxpayer-funded bailout. Barclays, Lloyds, Bank of Scotland—they were all rescued from bankruptcy and effectively nationalized—but Mersey Fidelity weathered the storm."

"How come you know so much about it?" asks Luca.

Gooding looks at him sheepishly. "I've been working on a book."

"A book?"

"Don't look at me like that. Newspapers are dying. You make money where you can."

"What's the book about?" asks Daniela.

"The global financial crisis—why some banks survived and others didn't."

"So how did Mersey Fidelity survive?"

"There were whispers."

"What sort of whispers?" Luca asks.

Gooding leans a little closer. "OK, let me draw you a picture. First you have the credit crisis, the meltdown, major banks hemorrhaging. Lehman Brothers has filed for bankruptcy. Nobody is lending any more. You're on your knees. Facing ruin. What do you do?"

"You ask for a bailout?"

"Yes, but before that—before you know that central banks are going to ride to the rescue."

"I don't know."

"You take anybody's money. And I mean *anybody*. The Mafia, Triads, Colombian drug barons, corrupt regimes, criminal gangs—anybody."

"Is that what happened?"

"Two years ago the UN Office on Drugs and Crime released a report saying that drug money was the only thing keeping some major banks in business. The UN estimates that three hundred and fifty-two billion dollars of drug and Mafia money was laundered by major banks at the peak of the global financial crisis. That's a third of a trillion dollars."

"What about the regulators?"

"They turned a blind eye because it helped keep bank doors open."

"And you think Mersey Fidelity was involved?"

"It's a theory."

Luca glances at Daniela, wondering how much to tell Gooding. Scanning the bar, he notices the couple from earlier have gone. A fresh beer arrives. He centers it on a coaster and begins.

"Just over a week ago the Zewiya branch of the al-Rafidain Bank in Baghdad was robbed. Four bank guards helped engineer the break-in. We aren't sure how much they stole — perhaps as much as fifty million US dollars. Less than twenty-four hours later they were found executed outside of Mosul. This wasn't the first such robbery — Iraq has been averaging about one a week — but this was US dollars. Daniela checked with the Iraqi Central Bank and discovered that the money had been delivered only a few hours before the bank was raided."

"What does this have to do with Mersey Fidelity?" asks Gooding.

"Before we flew out of Baghdad we found a former truck driver who told us how he smuggled cash out of Iraq into Syria. US dollars. There were two truckloads, but one lorry went off the cliff and spilled the payload. The second lorry went to a warehouse on the outskirts of Damascus owned by an import/export company registered in Syria. Alain al Jaria. It doesn't have a physical office address, just a postbox. And no tax returns in ten years…"

Daniela adds, "The same company was subcontracted to rebuild a stadium in Baghdad in 2005 and paid forty-two million dollars. The work was never done."

Luca: "The controlling shareholder of Alain al Jaria is a company called May First Limited, with a registered address in the Bahamas. And the only name associated with both companies is Yahya Maluk."

Luca places his elbows on the table, lowering his voice to a whisper.

"I think stolen money is being smuggled out of Iraq using the same routes that Saddam Hussein set up to overcome the international sanctions and blockades of the nineties. Maybe that's how Mersey Fidelity avoided the credit crisis: it found a new source of funds."

"What evidence do you have?"

"Not enough."

Gooding is staring at him, his eyes slightly glazed by the alcohol, but there's something skulking behind his countenance—a tense energy or the shadow of a secret. Luca searches his eyes for a clue. Over Gooding's shoulder, he can see a miniature version of himself in a far-off mirror.

"There's something else," says Luca.

"I'm listening."

"The truck driver who delivered the cash to Damascus said he was met by a man called Mohammed Ibrahim."

Luca nods towards Daniela.

"His full name is Mohammed Ibrahim Omar al-Muslit," she says. "He was responsible for setting up dozens of bank accounts in the name of front companies in Jordan, Syria and Lebanon for Saddam Hussein. He was arrested in 2003 and gave up Saddam's hiding place."

"Why isn't Ibrahim in prison?"

"Four years ago he walked out of Abu Ghraib. Accidentally released, due to a case of mistaken identity. It was just before the US handed over control of the prison."

"Unfortunate."

"I would have chosen another word."

12

LONDON

Seated on a plastic chair with his hands outspread on a table, Ruiz looks like a pianist playing a final chord and listening to the music fade. Campbell Smith doesn't seem to appreciate the performance. His lips have disappeared and his face is as pale as poached chicken.

"Why didn't she call the police?"

"She was traumatized. He threatened to cut the baby from her womb."

"And he wanted some notebook?"

"Apparently."

Campbell wants to go over it again: Zac Osborne, Richard North, Colin Hackett—two dead, one missing—he can see how the dots are joined but can't make out any discernible picture.

There is a knock on the door. Dinner. Campbell is happier once he's eaten (pork ribs in black bean sauce, delivered from the local Chinese). Ruiz no longer feels hungry after watching him eat.

Licking sauce from his fingers, Campbell begins listing all the mistakes that Ruiz has made and how he should have done things differently. Hindsight is always twenty/twenty with Campbell, the ultimate I-told-you-so personality.

"Let me tell you a story," he says finally, as if he's only just decided to share it. "I'm telling tales out of school, which could get me suspended, but maybe you should be aware of the context."

"What context?"

"Not ten minutes after I got back to the Yard today, I had a request from the Deputy Commissioner. He wanted to see me in his office. There was someone with him. Said he was from the Home Office. I didn't catch his name."

"Douglas Evans?"

"That's him," says Campbell. "They had all your Met files. Every bit of paperwork—who you arrested, who you didn't, every complaint, every mistake. Suspended twice. Dismissed once. Reinstated. Cautioned at least a dozen times. You went AWOL when your first wife died."

"I don't need a history lesson."

"That guy wasn't Home Office, but somewhere closer to Vauxhall Bridge Road. The spooks are all over you—your phones, your house, your car, they've got surveillance teams tracking you 24/7, listening to you crunching your Bran Flakes and taking a crap. You're out on a limb, Vincent. Isolated. Even your best friends are ducking for cover. Maybe if you could give them this notebook..."

"I don't know where it is."

"What about Holly Knight?"

Ruiz doesn't answer. Campbell gets to his feet again, pacing. Reaching the far wall, he turns, paces again. It's like watching a duck in a shooting gallery.

"Do you know where she is?"

"You can't guarantee her safety."

"And I suppose you can?"

Campbell stares at Ruiz for a long time, but it's not a tactic or a psychological ploy. He moves across the room to his desk. Opens a drawer. Pulls out a plain white envelope.

"We found this at the back of a filing cabinet in Richard North's office. The London postmark is dated sixteenth June. No return address."

Inside the envelope are a dozen photographs of Richard North with a woman who isn't Elizabeth; a brunette with a model's cheekbones and a tight body, dressed in jeans and a fitted top. They're sitting in an outdoor café holding hands. Kissing. The trees in the background are bare. The photos were taken in winter with a telephoto lens.

"Who is she?" asks Ruiz.

"Polina Dulsanya."

"The nanny?"

"SOCO took samples from the house and found semen stains on her sheets. Got a positive match. Richard North was shagging the nanny."

"It says something about the man."

"It says he cheats on his wife."

The two men regard each other as if somehow all men have been diminished by this one act of betrayal.

"We're looking for the nanny now, but she gave the police a fake address."

"Does Elizabeth know?" asks Ruiz.

"I thought it could wait."

"Where is she?"

"I had someone drive her back to her father's place."

Ruiz looks at the images again. "Why does someone send photographs like this to Richard North?"

"To warn him off."

"Or to blackmail him."

A knock on the door. DI Thompson. He's wearing his undertaker face. He motions to the commander "Can I talk to you, guv?"

"What is it?"

"They just pulled Richard North's car out of the River Lea."

"Any sign of North?"

"Traces of blood."

Campbell glances at Ruiz, wanting to say so many things. Instead: "You're coming with me."

13

NEW YORK

Chalcott is sitting in a business-class seat on the tarmac at JFK, sipping a glass of complimentary champagne. He's not a happy flyer; hates the rigmarole of security screening, boarding queues and pre-flight safety demonstrations. The only benefit of flying long haul is being forty thousand feet above sea level and out of communication.

Not yet. His mobile is vibrating. London.

"Talk quickly," he tells Sobel.

"They found North's car."

"What about North?"

"Traces of blood but no body."

"You think he's dead?"

"We have to consider the possibility."

Chalcott scoops peanuts into his fist and inhales them between sentences. A stewardess leans over him.

"Excuse me, sir, but all electronic devices must be turned off for take-off."

Chalcott waves her away. "What about Terracini?"

"He's being monitored."

"Has anything else changed?"

"We're still looking for the girl."

"Are you a religious man, Brendan?"

"Yes, sir."

"Maybe you should say a prayer."

He hangs up. Turns off his phone. Closes his eyes. In seven hours he'll be in London and he can sort out this mess. So far he's given his superiors a minimalist rendering of the situation. Two lessons he's learned from twenty years with the Agency—refuse to recognize anything is amiss and keep your answers short.

Ibrahim is cleaning up. He's hired himself an assassin, but this hasn't changed the game. Every side has men who kill for a cause, but it's easier dealing with a hired gun than a teenager with a hard-on for heavenly virgins and a vest packed full of explosives.

Money or God—some motives are easier to understand.

14

LONDON

The *Financial Herald* has floor-to-ceiling glass doors and a marbled lobby fringed with indoor gardens. A lone security guard sits behind a brightly lit island counter. Gooding waves his ID card in front of a scanner and signs Luca into the register before handing him a visitor's pass.

A lift rises above the foyer until the security guard is only a bald spot five floors below. Gooding scans his ID again to enter the newsroom. Lights trigger as they weave between cluttered desks and colored partitions that are pinned with newspaper clippings, cartoons and calendars. At the far end of the newsroom a subs desk is pooled in light and half a dozen men sit behind oversized computer screens. Most have hunched shoulders, midnight tans and the tics and twitches of ex-smokers.

Nearby the night news editor is poring over copies of the first editions, seeing what stories their rivals are running. What did they miss? Who scooped whom? It's too late now to make any major changes. Only a big breaking event would warrant stopping the presses and dropping in a new front page.

Luca's father had been a sub-editor on a paper in Chicago back in the hot-metal days when the printing presses would shake the entire building like a distant earthquake. Every line of type was cast in molten metal — an alloy of lead, antimony and tin — before being wedged into metal galleys on stone tables.

Luca was seven years old when he was first taken down on to "the stone." The setters were rough-looking men in ink-stained overalls with paper hats folded from newsprint. His father would lean over the galleys, subbing the raised lead type, reading stories back to front and upside down faster than most people read normally. He cut paragraphs, trimmed sentences, added fillers and corrected mistakes.

New technology put paid to the setters and linotype machines. Now it is all done by computers in sterile, temperature-controlled rooms without the screaming machines and clanking metal.

Gooding's desk is protected by partitions that block everything except the view from his window across the rooftops. Luca had pressed him for access to the newspaper's archives and library. Initially, Gooding had hesitated, which puzzled Luca. Something about the journalist's lugubrious face had registered too little when they were talking about the missing banker. Daniela had been awake to the deficit, catching the subtle change in Gooding's tone.

"He's not telling you everything," she whispered to Luca as he hailed her a cab. "Be careful." Then she had peppered his face with kisses. "I think I'm in love with you."

"I wouldn't recommend that."

"Why?"

"I'm a fully paid-up pessimist."

"I thought journalists were supposed to be idealists."

"We start off as idealists and then we become pragmatists and finally pessimists. You can join the club. We have vacancies."

She had laughed and he closed the cab door, giving directions to the driver.

Sitting at the computer screen, Luca waits for Gooding to type in a password.

"So where did you and Daniela meet?"

"At a hotel in Baghdad."

"What were the first words you said to her?"

"Why?"

"I'm interested in first words. I collect them. If you remember the first words I figure you must think someone is special."

"What were the first words you said to Lucy?"

"Pass the salt."

Gooding laughs drunkenly, his eyes shining. Then he taps the keyboard lightly with his fingertips. A password. The archive opens. He steps back and lets Luca put in the parameters of the search, looking for links between Mersey Fidelity and Iraq. The screen refreshes. The first article is from *The Economist*: fifteen foreign banks had applied for a license to operate in Iraq since the relaxing of the banking laws in 2004. Five licenses had been granted—one of them to Mersey Fidelity—but none of the banks had opened local branches.

Next he searches for articles on Mohammed Ibrahim. There is a reference to his arrest in 2003, just prior to the capture of Saddam Hussein, but no mention of his accidental release from Abu Ghraib. Luca finds a black-and-white photograph taken at a military parade in Baghdad in the mid-nineties. There are three men in military uniform standing behind Saddam Hussein. The caption indicates the man on the far right is Ibrahim. He has a round face, the ubiquitous moustache and is wearing a beret at a jaunty angle.

The photo library has a dozen pictures of Yahya Maluk taken at society events: a polo tournament at Cowdray Park, a fundraiser for Great Ormond Street Hospital, the Opera at Covent Garden. Luca prints out one of the images and calls up information on Richard North, reading the various accounts of his disappearance and looking at a vodcast of a media statement made by his wife.

North's career trajectory had been a steep curve—from public school and a third-class degree, to marrying the chairman's daughter and heading the compliance department at Mersey Fidelity.

A new window opens on screen, headed, "News Alert." A breaking story from Associated Press:

The search for missing banker Richard North took a new twist last night when his car was discovered in the River Lea in Hackney, East London. Police were last night examining the BMW for clues to the banker's whereabouts. Police divers are expected to search the river at first light.

Luca looks up from the screen. Keith Gooding is dozing with his feet on the desk and his chair tilted back. Luca throws a balled-up piece of paper.

"What?"

"They just pulled Richard North's car out of the river."

A nerve twitches in Gooding's jaw and something passes across his eyes that Luca can't read. It's the same reaction he saw at the wine bar. Gooding leans back in his chair and stares vexedly at the ceiling.

"What aren't you telling me?"

Gooding contemplates a lie. Something sways him.

"About a month ago I called Richard North. I thought he might be a source for the book but he said he wasn't interested. Then out of the blue, nine days ago I got a call from him. It was a Friday afternoon. He was in North London. Upset. Rambling. Saying we had to meet. I was in the middle of the afternoon news conference. We were putting the pages together for Saturday's edition. I told him that I'd call him back, but he said it wasn't safe to use his mobile and he wouldn't come to the office.

"I gave him the name of a bar in Kensington High Street and told him that I'd try to meet him there by ten. I couldn't make any promises. We were doing a special report on the last US combat troops being pulled out of Iraq."

"Did you go to the bar?"

Gooding shakes his head. "I didn't get away from the office until midnight. I had no way of contacting him. I figured he'd call me back. I didn't think...you know. I phoned his office the following Monday, but he hadn't shown up. Then his wife reported him missing."

Gooding falls silent, glancing at Luca from the corner of his eye. Each time he blinks his eyelashes rest for an instant on his cheeks.

"Did you call the police?" asks Luca.

"What would I tell them?"

"What about his wife?"

"I left a message on her answering machine. She's the daughter of the former chairman, Alistair Bach. Nobody can get close to her."

"You didn't want to get involved?"

"That's unfair."

"You're right. I'm sorry."

Luca tries to think it through. Richard North's job was to investigate suspicious transactions and approve new accounts at Mersey Fidelity. If the bank was involved in laundering illegal funds, he should have known about it.

"We need someone at the bank who'll talk."

"Good luck with that."

"North must have had a secretary."

"Why would she speak to us?"

"Her boss is missing. His car has just been found. She'll be worried or scared or angry. It can go a lot of different ways."

"I'll get you a name and address."

15

LONDON

The only access to this stretch of the river is via a strip of waste ground behind a row of factories that are crumbling from neglect. The padlocked gates have been opened and two police cars block the entrance.

"Jesus wept," says Campbell Smith as TV cameras and photographers surround his car. Questions are shouted through the closed windows. Bodies are jostled aside. Bleached of color by the bright lights, Campbell's face looks like a white balloon bobbing on his shoulders, ready to drift loose and float into the night.

"Who leaked this?" he barks. "I want to know. And get someone down here from the media unit."

White spots float behind Ruiz's closed lids as he shields his face from the flashguns. The car pulls up next to an old railway line, the silver ribbons disappearing into the darkness.

Above the factories and warehouses, the Olympic stadium is a white exoskeleton rising in concentric circles like a giant spaceship descending from the night sky. The River Lea ripples in the breeze, black as ink in the shadows. Spotlights have been set up on gantries and a portable generator provides a droning soundtrack. The only other noise comes from a news chopper flying above them, aiming a spotlight on to a floating dredger moored in the center of the river.

"I want them out of here!" bellows Campbell. "This is a fucking crime scene, not a reality show."

A security guard is waiting on the edge of the light. Dressed in heavy boots, Levi's and a company shirt, he stands with his legs spread like a man who enjoys being the center of attention. A tattooed serpent curls along his forearm and around his wrist.

"Dredger came through today," he tells Campbell. "I thought

the car was going to be an old wreck, until they lifted it out of the water. Looks like a brand-new Beemer. Fucked now.

"You can see the tire tracks across the way," he motions to the far bank. "The fence is down. Tree fell on it. Council never bothered sending out a work crew."

"Jesus, what's that smell?" asks Campbell, wadding his handkerchief and holding it over his nose.

"The Deepham Sewage Works is north of here," says the security guard. "Pumps out a quarter of a million cubic meters of treated sewage every day."

"Is that why they're dredging?" asks Ruiz.

"That's the theory. This whole area is being done up for the Olympics. Dredging the river, re-vegetation, new towpaths...They don't want any of them IOC dignitaries coming here and having to smell London's shit."

Two police divers are standing on the deck of the dredger, peering into the water. Neither looks keen to get wet. They'll wait till morning when the sediment has settled.

Gerard Noonan is already at work lifting aluminum boxes from the van. "Whatever happened to Sunday being a day of rest?" he says.

"I didn't take you for a religious man," says Ruiz.

"Oh, yeah, I do my praying on my sofa watching *Match of the Day*."

"Who are you praying for?"

"Birmingham City."

"And you *still* think there's a God?"

The BMW is on the towpath. The roof crushed. Mud on the wheels and bumpers, a fine layer of silt covering the bodywork. Ruiz follows Noonan. Leaning through an open car door, he notices the keys in the ignition and the automatic shift in drive. The windows were left open so that it would sink more quickly.

Something moves near his knee. He leaps backwards and lets out an expletive. Noonan reaches into the car and pulls out an eel that twists and squirms in his hands, black as sump oil.

"Didn't you ever catch eels as a kid?"

"When I was a kid they came in jelly with mashed potato."

The eel splashes into the river, leaving no trace on the surface.

Campbell has finished talking to the security guard. "What have you got?" he asks Noonan.

"Traces of blood in the boot — enough to be worried."

Ruiz walks along the tracks until he reaches an overhead bridge. Crossing the river, he follows a cyclone fence separating a freight yard from the water. The muddy hinterland is littered with drums, broken palettes, dumped tires and a crippled shopping trolley. Bits of broken glass glint in the dirt.

A black woman is watching him from the doorway of a flat-fronted terrace, one of the few left in the street. This area of London was hit hard during the Blitz and bombed terraces were like broken teeth, filled with something concrete and ugly.

Ruiz wishes her good evening.

"When are they gonna turn off them generators?" she demands.

"I can't tell you that," he replies.

"I know what they found. I saw it go in there."

The woman is in her fifties, with a pink dressing gown cinched tight around her waist. Hair trapped in a net.

"What's your name, ma'am?"

"Mrs. Abigail Westin."

"What did you see, Mrs. Westin?"

"I saw them fellas push a car into the river."

"What did they look like?"

"Pakis or Indians — can't tell the difference, me."

"When was this?"

"Early hours. I don't sleep so good, me. I was in the bathroom. I heard them boys arguing. One of them was saying how it was such a waste, ditching a motor like that. Like he wanted to keep it."

"How many voices?"

"Two."

"Would you recognize them again?"

"Their voices maybe. I didn't get such a good look at their faces."

Ruiz tells Mrs. Westin that the police will want to interview her and wishes her good night.

"It'll be a good night when I can sleep till dawn," she says, switching off the outside light.

Ruiz turns back to the river where the BMW is a broken silhouette against the spotlights, like a sea monster dragged from the depths in a fisherman's net. A flat-bed truck has arrived to take it away to a police impound. The driver is slinging cables beneath the chassis.

Retracing his steps across the bridge, Ruiz passes on the information to Campbell and asks if he can go now.

"That thing we talked about earlier. Do you think they followed me out here?"

The commander glances at the gates. "They're like shit on your shoes."

The BMW has been winched on to the truck. The driver has grey mutton-chop sideburns and hair growing from his nostrils.

"I need a ride," says Ruiz.

"Do I know you?"

"I used to be on the job. Vincent Ruiz."

"Thought you looked familiar." He waves a clipboard. "Climb on board."

Minutes later, the truck is rocking over the railway lines, springs groaning. At the main gate Ruiz slides sideways on the seat, below the level of the dashboard.

"Who you trying to avoid?"

"I'm just camera shy."

They travel in silence for another mile.

"I remember you," says the driver.

"Have we met?"

"Name's Dave," he takes one hand off the wheel to shake. "My wife's younger brother used to be a boxer, beautiful to watch, fists like bricks. He detached a retina just before the Sydney Olympics. Crying shame. Got a job as a bouncer in Acton. One night he threw a drunk out. The guy came back with a gun and tried to shoot my brother-in-law but he shot a girl instead. Innocent bystander. Almost killed her. Remember the case?"

Ruiz nods.

"Anyway, this girl gets out of hospital and decides to sue the nightclub and sue my brother-in-law. You sorted that out for us. Made her see sense. I appreciate that."

"How is your wife?" asks Ruiz.

"She left me for a dog breeder."

"I'm sorry to hear that."

"I got a Pekingese in the divorce settlement."

Fifteen minutes later the truck drops him at West Ham Station and Ruiz catches a tube to Earls Court. He goes to a twenty-four-hour convenience store and buys a toothbrush, toothpaste and mouthwash. He passes a nightclub. A drunken girl dances on the pavement clutching a miniature bottle of champagne. She's wearing a tiny black dress and high heels, impervious to the cold or the hungry stares of passing men.

Sitting on the steps of a terrace house, Ruiz watches the Mercedes for half an hour, making sure that it's not under surveillance. Satisfied, he runs his fingers under the wheel arches and the bumpers, looking for tracking devices. Then he gets behind the wheel and drives away, heading east along Old Brompton Road, running the first red light just to make sure.

At Lancaster Gate he wakes the hotel night manager by leaning on the buzzer. Pays extra for a room. He slips a note under the professor's door, not wanting to wake him. Opening the window, he undresses and lies down on top of the sheets, with one arm across his eyes. The curtains, printed with small pink flowers, are lifting and settling in the breeze. He can hear cars and horns in the street. A party. People fighting on the pavement. Glass breaking.

Sleep never comes on its own terms. Insomnia is part of his metabolism, lying awake in the dark of the night, his breath loud in his chest. He used to rage against it, medicate, drink too much, exercise to exhaustion, but now he's learned to survive upon less, tasting the ash in his mouth each morning and feeling the grit in his eyes.

When he finally dozes, he remembers the American with his southern drawl, wishing Claire a happy wedding. He can still feel the weight of the gun in his hand, his finger on the trigger. He can picture putting a neat hole in the American's forehead, red mist on the window behind. He had contemplated pulling the trigger. Wished for an excuse. Not a good state of mind.

16

LONDON

The seven-hour flight ends with a bump on the runway and a delay getting to the gate. Chalcott rolls his carry-on bag through Customs.

"How was the flight?" asks Sobel.

"Terrible."

"London is lovely at this time of year."

"What are you, my fucking tour guide?"

Sobel tries to remain stoic as they weave through the crowd to a waiting car. Chalcott has several moods that range from bullying to wheedling self-pity, but bullying is his favorite. A boarding school background most likely, his parents in the diplomatic service, his holidays spent with relatives or in guarded compounds in Third World countries.

"Any sign of North?" asks Chalcott.

"They're searching the river."

"He's dead then?"

"Not confirmed."

"If we keep Terracini quiet, we should be back on track."

"In essence."

"What does that mean?"

Sobel adopts a passive-aggressive tone. "Luca Terracini accessed the newspaper archives last night. He downloaded photographs of Yahya Maluk and Ibrahim."

"You said you had Terracini under control."

"We have someone at the newspaper keeping watch. We're ready to intervene."

"If Ibrahim is spooked, he'll clear the accounts."

"We can follow the trail."

"You're stating the obvious, Brendan, but things that are solid can melt into air."

Chalcott goes to the wrong side of the car. Forgets about the left-hand drive. Curses. Gets in the passenger seat. The drive from Heathrow takes them over the A4 flyover, past buildings used as billboards and a neon sign flashing the temperature: 21 degrees. It is four years since Chalcott was last in London. Each year it gets more crowded, less charming and slightly shabbier. Changing by the week or by the day, leaving most people confused.

"There is one more thing," says Sobel. "The audit at Mersey Fidelity could show up some discrepancies."

"What sort of discrepancies?"

"Unexplained deposits and withdrawals. It could set off alarm bells."

"Who's conducting the audit?"

"Not one of ours."

"Can we change the personnel?"

"This is England, we can't just…"

"What? Change an auditor? Pardon my fucking ignorance, but aren't we supposed to be allies? We fought two fucking wars pulling their skinny white butts out of the European mud. Where's the quid pro quo, eh? Where's the 'you scratch my back and I'll scratch yours'?"

"Let me tell you something, Brendan, if this goes pear-shaped, our political friends in Washington are going to wash their hands of us. Remember the Iran-Contra Affair? Secret arms sales to fund that dirty little war in Nicaragua? This will make it look like a fucking accounting error."

17

LONDON

Ruiz wakes mid-morning. Joe O'Loughlin is sitting in a chair beside the window, his face tilted to the light, color in his hollowed cheeks.

"I knocked. You didn't answer. The chambermaid let me in."

"What time is it?"

"Ten. How did you sleep?"

"Lousy."

"You're not very clear on this sleep concept, are you?"

"It's overrated."

Ruiz rubs his jaw. He needs a shave. He should have bought a razor as well as a toothbrush. Sitting on the side of the bed in his underwear, he props his forearms on his thighs.

The two men recount their yesterdays. Ruiz tells him about Elizabeth North's photographs and Colin Hackett's murder; worlds within worlds, bleeding into each other. Joe has a way of listening that encourages people to add the small details, but doesn't judge the story or the way it's being told.

"How's Holly?" asks Ruiz.

"Demanding. Bored. Monosyllabic. It's like being at home with my own teenage daughter."

"Charlie is still a princess."

"To you maybe."

"Where is Holly now?"

"Watching DVDs in her room. She's very fond of you—she keeps asking me questions."

"What sort of questions?"

"She says you're the saddest person she's ever met."

The statement rattles something inside Ruiz, but he refuses to let it show. He opens the curtains. A wind sweeps wetly through the trees and a damp sunlight glistens from the leaves.

"You were supposed to be finding stuff out about her."

"I think I know why she doesn't trust the police."

Ruiz looks over his shoulder, waiting for the rest.

"Remember I told you about the rape allegation. It involved a twenty-year-old engineering student who she met at a party in Hounslow. The rape was supported by forensic evidence — semen and vaginal tearing — but the CPS didn't proceed."

"What happened?"

"Holly's alleged rapist was the son of a senior police officer. He claimed she consented and had begged for rough sex. He produced a dozen witnesses who said Holly had initiated the encounter. His lawyers dragged up Holly's juvenile record — the fire at her foster home. She was considered to be unstable. An unreliable witness."

"She was shafted."

"Poor choice of words."

Ruiz showers and puts on the same clothes. He rubs a bar of soap beneath the arms of his shirt, trying to neutralize the odor.

Ever since he met Holly Knight, he's been clinging to the belief that he would find someone who could answer her questions. Either that or the facts would be dragged to the surface until he had enough to form a picture. He was prepared to be patient, ignoring the background "noise," but the mystery had merely deepened.

Joe is still sitting by the window.

"I asked Holly about the notebook. She can't remember it."

"Maybe you should ask her again."

Ruiz picks up the bedside phone and punches a number.

"Capable."

"Mr. Ruiz."

"Don't use my name. What have you got for me?"

Capable begins explaining how he accessed the computer records, circumventing firewalls and piggybacking from one database to the next. Ruiz interrupts. "I don't care how you did it, Capable. That's like wanting to know what my butcher puts in his sausages."

"Huh?"

"I'm in a hurry. What about my mobile?"

"Oh. Right. I traced the blue Audi to a basement garage in an office block near Tower Bridge. Serviced offices. Ten floors. The parking space is reserved for a company that doesn't put its name on the board in the foyer. It has unlisted numbers and a high-speed broadband connection. Serious firewall protection."

"How many employees?

"No way of telling." Capable is tapping at a keyboard. "I managed to get into the garage. The Audi had a service sticker on the windscreen. A dealership in West London does the work.

"The Audi has false plates, but the chassis number was sold to a dealer in Watford in 2009. Then it was leased to a private company in London that quoted a non-existent VAT number. I've been through Companies House. It was a shelf company set up in the mid-nineties by a firm of accountants in Hampstead. The company was first registered in July 1997. Listed as an IT security operation. It's the affiliate of a Washington-based company called Holyrod Limited. The company director is listed as an Andrew Broderick who works for a law firm in Washington. Four identical Audis are listed at the same office address. The bills are paid on a company credit card owned by a Brendan Sobel."

"He got a private address?

"Not that I can find."

"OK," says Ruiz. "I need another favor. Get a list of restaurants in the area. See if they take bookings from a Brendan Sobel."

"You think he dines out?"

"The man has to eat."

Walking as far as the Edgware Road, Ruiz finds a florist near the tube station. The bunch of flowers costs him twenty-five quid with a card in plain white envelope. He pays cash and is very specific about the delivery instructions to an address in Hampstead. Mrs. Elizabeth North must sign for the flowers personally. Nobody else.

He takes a moment to compose a message.

> Elizabeth,
>   I need you to trust me. Find an excuse to leave the house. Be aware that you may be followed. There is a car wash on Archway Road in Haringey. Ask for a wash and wax. Go inside and order a coffee. After five minutes get up and go to the ladies. There is a fire door. I'll be waiting for you.
>   Ruiz
>   PS Don't tell anybody about this.

18

LONDON

Elizabeth can hear her father arguing with someone over the intercom. A van is parked at the gates, visible on the CCTV camera. The driver is holding a bunch of flowers.

"How do I know you're not a reporter?" asks Bach.

"Because I'm not," says the driver, who looks bemused rather than frustrated. "The flowers are for Mrs. Elizabeth North."

"Who sent them?"

"I don't know. I just deliver them. I don't grow them. I don't pick them. I just deliver them."

Elizabeth interrupts. "Let him in, Daddy. He's just doing his job."

She meets the driver at the front door with her father hovering. Then she puts the blooms in the kitchen sink. Reads the card.

"Who are they from?"

"Mitchell," she lies.

"Is he apologizing?"

"Yes."

Afterwards she borrows Jacinta's car, not the matching Mercedes, but a low-slung Japanese sporty number with sleek lines, minimal headroom and a surfeit of horsepower. If ever a car suited her stepmother... Squeezing behind the wheel, she has to adjust the seat to give Claudia some room. The indicators are on the opposite side and she hasn't driven a manual in years, but she makes the journey without destroying the clutch or the gearbox.

Heads turn as she pulls into the car wash. The young cleaners admire the car, wondering if the driver is equally sexy. They see her pregnancy and go back to their buckets and sponges.

Ordering a coffee, Elizabeth sits at a table by the window, pretending to browse through a magazine. After a few minutes she goes to the ladies and finds the fire door. Pushing it open, she steps outside, skirting rubbish bins and parked cars, wishing she'd worn more practical shoes.

Ruiz is waiting at the end of the alley.

"Do you have your mobile?" he asks.

"Yes."

"You should turn it off. People are following me. They might also be following you."

Elizabeth stops walking. "Did you talk to Holly Knight? Does she have the notebook?"

"We'll talk in the car."

"I want to meet her."

"That's not going to help."

"I want to know what they talked about; what North said to her. Did he talk about me? Did she know he was married?"

"Holly didn't start all this. She's not the cause of North's problems — you know that."

They're arguing on the street — a heavily pregnant woman and a man old enough to be her father. Ruiz puts his hands on the small of her back, steering her towards the door. Elizabeth stands her ground.

"Don't treat me like a child. You have no stake in this."

Ruiz stops. Holds up his hands. "You're right. I don't have to be here. It's not my problem. I should go home."

The harshness in his tone takes Elizabeth by surprise. She apologizes and gets in the car, letting Ruiz adjust her seat belt.

"They found North's car," she says, trying to explain. "They don't know if he's . . ." She can't finish the sentence. Instead she grimaces and her body folds forward over the seat belt. A cramp. A contraction. She takes short breaths until the pain eases.

"How often is it happening?"

"It's not a real contraction, only pressure pains."

"When was the last time you saw a doctor?"

"I'm fine."

They drive in silence across North London, taking the North Circular through Golders Green, past Brent Cross and down Hanger Lane and Gunnersbury Avenue into Chiswick.

"The photographs that Colin Hackett took — who did you show them to?"

"The police . . . my father . . . Yahya Maluk."

"Anyone else?"

"I don't think so."

Ruiz changes the subject. "Can I ask you something? Your nanny . . . Polina."

Elizabeth stops picking at her nail polish. "What about her?"

"Why did she leave?"

Elizabeth lifts one shoulder and drops it again. "It was all too chaotic . . . North had gone missing, the media were camped outside, the phone always ringing . . ."

"How did you come to hire her?"

"She was working for my brother and his wife. Mitchell and Inga's children had started school. My need was greater."

"When did she start?"

"Eight months ago." Elizabeth has turned to look directly at

Ruiz, whose eyes stay on the road. "Why are you so interested in Polina?"

He doesn't answer.

"What is it?" she asks again.

"Nothing."

"Tell me."

"It's not my place."

"What sort of answer is that? I'm sick of people keeping secrets or telling me lies or tiptoeing around me like I'm going to break if they make a loud noise. My husband lied to me. He kept secrets. Maybe he broke the law. If you're not going to tell me the truth, you can stop the car and let me out here."

They're in Chiswick, close to Bridget Lindop's house.

"How did your husband get on with Polina?" asks Ruiz.

Elizabeth narrows her eyes. Her mouth opens but no sound emerges. She is focused on something miles away that seems to be coming closer, getting larger, like a speeding freight train.

"The police found semen stains in Polina's bedroom," says Ruiz. "They matched the DNA to your husband. Maybe you accidentally swapped sheets."

"Polina's bed is a single," says Elizabeth.

For a moment Ruiz thinks she's missed the point, but Elizabeth knows exactly what she's being told. Brash, seductive, hungry Polina with her graceful body, textbook English and strangely beautiful, heavy-lidded eyes had been sleeping with North. She had ironed his shirts and folded his socks and serviced him in other ways.

Reaching back through her memories of the previous months, Elizabeth searches for evidence: North's hand brushing Polina's hip as he squeezed past the ironing board; another on her shoulder as he reached past her for a mug. He would tease Polina about her accent, or stay up late to watch a movie with her, or laugh at some private joke that Elizabeth could never quite understand.

Polina had denied seeing North that Friday when Colin Hackett followed him back to the house. They were three hours together. Alone.

For a moment Elizabeth's courage seems to fail and she coughs as though she's inhaled something toxic and has to clear out her lungs. Ruiz pulls over and opens the door. She leans out, her innards heaving. Gagging. Retching. He holds back her hair as she vomits into the gutter.

No words for her.

19

LONDON

The corner house is a two-storey terrace with parrot-green window frames and flower boxes full of summer annuals. Nobody answers the turtle doorknocker. Another turtle peeks from the garden bed and a third has a metal frame for scraping mud from boots.

Luca knocks again. He crouches and opens the letterbox, peering along a hallway.

"Miss Lindop," he calls. Listens. Nothing. She's not at work. He phoned her office.

"Maybe she's gone out for a while," says Daniela, glancing up at the first floor. Luca goes to the front window and presses his face to the glass, looking through a crack in the curtains. He can see a thin strip of polished floor and an oriental rug. More turtles are visible on a mantelpiece.

"You wait here," he tells Daniela.

"Where are you going?"

"To check out the back."

The terrace is on a corner with one boundary on a different street. There is a garage with a raised roller door and a small Fiat hatchback parked inside. Luca tries the internal door. Locked.

Retracing his steps, he stares at the garden wall, judging the height. He runs and jumps, gripping the top of the wall and scrambling up, scraping his shoes on the painted bricks as he tries to get purchase. On his elbows, peering into the small neat garden, he can see the back of the house. The rear sliding door is open; a newspaper is spread out on the kitchen table. Nearby the refrigerator door is open. A milk carton lies on its side and a large tortoiseshell cat licks at the edge of the puddle.

Luca scrambles higher and lowers himself down into the garden. He calls Bridget Lindop's name. The cat comes to him, weaving figure-of-eights between his legs. In the kitchen he calls out again. The newspaper is a day old. A full cup of tea has grown cold on the table, leaving a milky skin on the surface. *Woman's Hour* is playing on the radio.

Luca unlocks the front door. Leaves it open.

"What are you doing?" hisses Daniela. "You can't just break in."

"The back door was open. She might be hurt."

They move through the house going from room to room. The dining area has a display case with more turtles — figurines made of jade, amethyst, quartz and mother of pearl. An oversized couch faces a television in the living room. The coffee table is laden with books on interior design and gourmet food.

"You want to wait here," says Luca, climbing the stairs. On a landing there is a potted plant that has been knocked over. The damp dark earth has stained the carpet. The main bedroom smells of talcum powder and aromatherapy candles.

There are small signs of a search but none to indicate a struggle. Her jewelry is still on the dressing table along with her purse and her mobile phone. Not a robbery. Not a trip to the shops.

The second bedroom is a sewing room and office. The door is splintered. It was locked. Someone kicked it open from inside.

Luca looks over the banister. "You should come and see this."

Ruiz pulls into an empty parking space and checks the house numbers. Elizabeth is still pale and shaking beside him. He offered to take her home. She refused.

"Is that the place?"

She nods.

The front door is open. A woman living alone doesn't leave her door wide open. Ruiz scans the street, studying the cars parked on either side. Across the road is a playground with brightly colored climbing frames and swings. A British Gas van moves slowly past.

He approaches the house from the north side, pauses at the front door, listening. There are voices upstairs. Male and female. American.

Glancing along the hallway, he can see as far as the kitchen where a milk carton lies in a shiny puddle. His fingers slide inside his jacket, finding the butt of the Glock. Four paces. He's at the bottom of the stairs, looking up, listening.

He climbs, putting as little weight as possible on each step. Eyes up. He can no longer hear their voices, but can feel their presence. He reaches the landing. The main bedroom is on the left, second bedroom on the far right, a bathroom in between. There is a man squatting in the doorway, examining something. A woman is standing beside him, silhouetted against the haze of white light. Both of them turn in unison, looking down the barrel of the Glock.

"Stand up! Hands against the wall!"

"You got this all wrong," says Luca.

"Shut up!"

Ruiz kicks Luca's legs apart, using one hand to pat him down — shoulders, chest, back, right leg, left leg.

"Are you a policeman?" asks Daniela.

Ruiz ignores her. "Where's Bridget Lindop?"

"I don't know," says Luca.

"What are you doing in her house?"

"We were looking for her. I'm a journalist."

"What paper?"

"*Financial Herald.*"

Ruiz pushes Daniela hard against the wall.

"I didn't think British police officers carried guns," she says.

"That's an urban myth."

She lowers her arms. "I don't think you're a policeman at all."

"You want to test that theory?"

She's a ballbreaker, thinks Ruiz, either crazy-brave or stupid. Her off-sider is more diplomatic. He's explaining how he found the back door open and thought Miss Lindop might be hurt.

"She's been gone a while. Her cat hasn't been fed."

Elizabeth calls from below. "Is everything all right?"

"I told you to wait in the car," says Ruiz.

"I heard you talking."

Elizabeth has reached the landing. "Who are they?"

"They broke in."

"I didn't break in," says Luca. "I'm a reporter." He takes a moment to recognize Elizabeth — the missing banker's wife, heavily pregnant. He's seen her photograph and watched her media appeal. "We were looking for Bridget Lindop. If you call Keith Gooding at the paper he'll vouch for us."

That name again.

Ruiz and Elizabeth exchange a glance. At that moment her uterus contracts and she hollows out her cheeks in a whistling intake of breath. Eyes shut, she exhales in shallow puffs, trying to ease the pain.

Daniela glares at Ruiz like he's personally responsible for making a pregnant woman climb the stairs.

"When are you due?"

"A few weeks."

"You should sit down."

Luca points to the broken door. "Someone was locked inside and had to break out."

Ruiz runs his finger over the splintered frame. It was kicked open. Someone strong did this. A man. A prisoner.

20

LONDON

Are you going to hypnotize me?"

"No."

"Then why do I have to lie down?"

"I just want you to be comfortable."

Holly is dressed in a thin floral-print cotton dress, machine faded, which clings to her body like wet tissue paper. She looks at the bed, which is covered with an old lady bedspread.

"Lie down, close your eyes and relax," says Joe.

She shoots him a look. "You better not try anything."

"I'm going to sit over here by the window. I won't leave this chair."

Holly stares at the ceiling, which has water stains and a cracked plaster rosette.

"So what is this called if it's not hypnosis?"

"A cognitive interview."

"What does that mean?"

"I'm going to take you back to the night you met Richard North. I'm going to ask you lots of questions. Some things you won't remember. Some things will come back to you."

"I've already told Vincent..."

"We're going to do it again."

"I'm hungry."

"You've just eaten."

Joe O'Loughlin takes a seat. The window provides some breeze and he can hear birds in the trees. He begins as he always does, by setting the scene—the bar on that Friday night. Where was she sitting? What was she drinking? Who else was around her? He has a nice voice, thinks Holly. Kind eyes. But he asks too many questions.

Lady Gaga was playing on the sound system. Zac had never liked Lady Gaga. Said she was a wannabe Madonna. Then again, he didn't like Madonna, who he called "that ridiculous old bag." Lady Gaga had the better voice. Madonna was the better dancer.

"I didn't think he was going to notice me at first," says Holly. "He was sitting at a corner of the bar, going through vodka like he had Smirnoff shares. I thought he might be gay."

"Why choose him?"

"He looked rich . . . lonely. I like to watch them for a while — just to be sure."

"Sure of what?"

She shrugs. "Sure they're not rapists or psychos. I'm looking for the Good Samaritan, remember?"

"So you can rob him?"

Holly opens her eyes and looks at Joe scornfully. He marvels at how someone barely educated past fifteen can make him feel like he's just stepped off the bus from Stupidville.

"What was he doing?"

"He looked like he was waiting for someone."

"Did he have anything in his hands?"

"No . . . maybe." She chews on the inside of her cheek. "He was writing something."

"What was he writing on?"

"I didn't see."

"With a pen or a pencil?"

"A pen. He dropped it and I thought he was trying to look at my legs, but he just went back to writing. He only really noticed me when Zac and I kicked off."

"You started arguing?"

"That was our shtick, you know. Our grift. That's what Zac called it. We argued. He hit me. I cried."

"Someone else could have stepped in."

"We've been doing this for a while. I know how to position myself, so the mark is closest. I was just a few feet away when Zac hit me across the face. I went down, but this guy just didn't react. I mean, Zac was standing over me and this guy was just staring straight through me like he was watching it all on TV and any moment he was going to reach for the remote and change the channel."

"What happened then?"

"Zac calls me some names and storms out. I was sitting on the floor pretending to cry, thinking to myself, this guy must be really cold. What does a girl have to do to get his attention? Then he finally reacted."

"He came over."

"Yeah. He picked me up. Got some ice. Bought me a drink. He wanted to call the police, but I talked him out of it. Then I did the old, "My keys! My phone!" routine and started to cry again. He put his arm around me and I sort of leaned into him. That's when I knew I'd hooked him, you know. Physical contact. You melt into a guy's body and it triggers his protective instincts."

"Where were you sitting?"

"At his table."

"What did you talk about?"

Holly screws up her features. "It was odd."

"What was odd?"

"He didn't offer to let me use his phone. It was sitting on the table on top of a book."

"What sort of book?"

"It had a dark cover."

"He'd been reading it?"

She pauses, thinking. Then she opens her eyes and lifts her head, staring at Joe like he's just performed a magic trick. "He'd been writing in it."

"A notebook?"

"Yeah. Must have been."

Holly is annoyed at herself for not remembering earlier. Joe doesn't labor the point. He takes her through the encounter, minute by minute until she reaches a point in the story where they leave the bar.

"What did he do with the notebook?"

"How the fuck should I know?"

"Was it still on the table?"

"No..." She pauses. "He put it in his jacket pocket."

"Which pocket?"

"Inside. Just here."

She puts her hand on her left breast.

"I remember that jacket because Zac liked it so much."

"What do you mean?"

"When we were robbing his place, Zac was saying how much he liked the jacket. It was camel-colored, you know. Cashmere. Expensive. Zac had his share of problems, but he knew stuff about clothes. He had this dress uniform—he kept it after he left the army—and every button on that thing shone. It was kept like brand new, folded in tissue paper and stored in a special box."

Holly closes her eyes again and Joe takes her mind back to the house in Barnes. She has grown accustomed to describing scenes in detail, picturing them in her mind, not rushing the chronology of events, but slowing it down. Richard North had been quite drunk when they arrived at the house. He couldn't get his key in the lock. She did it for him.

"He still wanted to get into my pants. They're all like that. They start off telling me I can use their phone and then they offer me the spare room and then they try for the big prize."

"Is that what Ruiz did?"

Holly opens one eye. "Not exactly."

"What about Richard North?"

"He was Mr. Hopeful. He said he had condoms, but couldn't find them. I poured him a drink, which I spiked. He slobbered all over me and then passed out."

"Where?"

"On the sofa downstairs. That's when Zac arrived in a foul mood because it was raining and miserable on a bike. I searched upstairs. He took downstairs. Cash. Jewelry. Mobile phones. Nothing too big, because we had to carry it on the bike."

She describes the house, picking out colors and features, remembering the posters in the little boy's bedroom and his bed shaped like a racing car. Joe doesn't mention the coat again until Holly describes putting their possible haul on the floor of the hallway and deciding what to leave behind.

"What about the jacket?"

Holly purses her lips. "It was hanging over the banister."

"Did Zac take it?"

"I don't know. I don't remember seeing it again."

Something bothers her. She falls silent, going over the events.

"He went to the kitchen to get a plastic bag."

"Zac?"

"He must have wanted to protect the jacket from the rain." Holly opens her eyes. "He must have taken it with him, but I don't remember seeing it again."

"Relax. Go back there... to the house... you're in the hallway, deciding what to take..."

"We were loading the panniers. I put on my coat. A helmet... We found a nice briefcase in the study. I had to carry it on my lap. Zac drove carefully. No point in taking risks. Being picked up by the cops would be silly."

"Where did you go?"

"Back to the flat."

"Where did you park?"

"Zac has this lockup around the corner. That's where he leaves his bike."

"A lockup?"

"Yeah."

"Where is the bike now?"

Holly shrugs. "Still there, I guess."

Joe looks at the phone on the bedside table. First he'll leave a message for Ruiz.

"Come on," he tells Holly.

"Have we finished?"

"Yes."

"Where are we going?"

"To get a notebook."

21

LONDON

The Shelby Arms had been one of Ruiz's favorite watering holes when he was running the Serious Crime Squad in West London. Back then it had been a dive with decent beer and passable grub. Now it's a gastro-pub with a dozen different boutique beers on tap and cooling cabinets full of imported lagers. The menu has also been tarted up: a ham-and-cheese toasted sandwich is called a *croque-monsieur*. Potato and leek soup is *vichyssoise*.

Elizabeth and Daniela are sitting opposite each other, sipping soda waters. Ruiz has ordered a Guinness and Luca the same, sipping it somewhat curiously but trying hard to win respect.

Ruiz studies him, scratching an eyebrow, giving nothing away. The journalist is carrying scars, mental, not physical, but he's a tough son-of-a-bitch. Daniela is interesting. She has a chill, scientific detachment. Dynamite between the sheets, he suspects. The cool ones often are. Why does he bring everything back to sex? Hard-ons of the mind.

Through a picture window, he sees a line of schoolchildren wearing hats and holding hands. Two women teachers at either end, cajoling them to stay in line and "walk don't run." Advice for life.

Now Luca begins talking, starting in Iraq with the bank robberies and missing reconstruction funds. He mentions an attack on the Finance Ministry, people dying. Friends. Cash smuggled across borders. Mersey Fidelity. The name Yahya Maluk seems to electrify Elizabeth.

"I've met him," she says. "I've been to his house. He lives in Mayfair."

Everyone is looking at her. "North visited Yahya Maluk the day before he disappeared. I asked Maluk about the meeting, but he denied it ever happened."

"How do you know they met?" asks Luca.

"I saw the photographs."

Luca reaches into the pocket of his shirt and unfolds the photocopies that he made last night at the newspaper office. "Is that the man?"

Elizabeth nods. "He's on the board of Mersey Fidelity."

Luca puts another picture in front of Elizabeth.

"What about this man?"

Three men in uniform are standing behind Saddam Hussein. She places her fingers around the face of the man on the far right, framing his portrait.

"That's the other one."

"Are you absolutely sure?" asks Luca, glancing at Daniela.

"I'm sure," says Elizabeth.

"What is it? Who is this guy?" asks Ruiz.

Daniela answers, giving details of Mohammed Ibrahim Omar al-Muslit, the former Baath Party moneyman who helped Saddam Hussein steal billions from his own people.

"He should be in Abu Ghraib, but he escaped four years ago."

"What's he doing in London?"

"That's a very good question."

Ruiz silently places the details in context. A wanted war criminal, a terrorist—that could explain why the Americans are so interested.

Luca continues. "We've established a link between money stolen in Iraq and Yahya Maluk. Through him we have a connection with Mersey Fidelity and Richard North. That's why I wanted to talk to Bridget Lindop."

Sitting opposite, Elizabeth doesn't leap to her husband's defense by denying his involvement and arguing his innocence. Instead she remains quiet, gazing out the window at a sunlit afternoon that should be darker, stormier, less radiant. North was sleeping with the nanny. How prosaic of him, how clichéd. Men can be so bloody predictable.

"She's a devout Catholic," says Elizabeth, almost thinking out loud.

"Who?" asks Ruiz.

"Bridget Lindop—she goes to Mass every day."

Our Lady of Grace and St. Edward Church is a listed building with red-brick walls darkened by soot, exhaust fumes and the sins of the forgiven. An old woman is dusting the pews. Her skirt is tucked up in her apron revealing pale calves that are bulging with veins like a fleshy Rorschach test.

She's Polish. Ruiz speaks to her in German, asking after the priest. He's in the presbytery. She fetches him, complaining about the interruption. Some people will find their own grave too crowded.

"Where did you learn to speak German?" asks Luca.

"Where did you learn to speak Arabic?"

"My mother."

"We both have one of those."

Daniela has gone to meet Keith Gooding and get the latest news on the search for Richard North. Police divers entered the river at first light, using sonar equipment in the zero visibility.

A row of candles is burning beneath a statue, the wax almost glowing from within, creating flickering shadows on the skirts of the Virgin Mary.

Ruiz leans back in a pew, feeling his muscles let go. High above his head there are dust motes drifting in a shaft of sunlight and a strand of web clings to a beam, moving back and forth as though the entire building is inhaling and exhaling.

"Do you know any prayers?" asks Elizabeth, struggling to kneel.

"I've forgotten the only prayer I ever learned as a kid," says Ruiz. "That one about dying in your sleep."

"You're scared of dying."

"Better than being scared of living."

Elizabeth lowers her eyes and clasps her hands. "What makes a man who has a woman who loves him risk it all?"

"Are you asking me or Him?"

"You."

Ruiz rubs his forehead. "Sometimes when a man feels bad about himself, he doesn't want to be with a woman who looks at him with nothing but love. Instead he wants to lie on top of a woman who knows how nasty and shallow and faithless he can be...a woman who doesn't put him on a pedestal or expect him to be a knight in shining armor...a woman who's happy with the *worst* he can be."

The priest appears. Young. Frizzy-haired. Dressed in a multi-colored shirt with silver crosses on the collar, he looks like a Woodstock wannabe, forty years too late for the party.

"I'm Father Michael," he says, bowing slightly from the waist as though his spine is hinged on a spring. He notices Elizabeth's pregnancy and is trying to place Luca and Ruiz in the picture as either a husband or a father.

Elizabeth speaks. "I'm looking for Bridget Lindop. I know she comes here."

"What makes you sure she's here now?"

"Is she?"

"I'm not in a position to discuss—"

Elizabeth interrupts him. "I'm sorry, Father, but they found my husband's car in a river last night. Some people think he's dead. Some think he stole a lot of money. I have a little boy at home...a girl coming. Please don't lie to me or treat me like an idiot."

Father Michael passes his hand over his jaw. Before he can answer there is a movement from deeper in the church. Bridget Lindop emerges from the shadows where she's been kneeling in prayer.

The two women embrace. Elizabeth's shoulders are shaking, but there are no tears. This is an English middle-class grief. Reserved. Contained. They sit down, holding hands, their knees touching, as though drawing strength from each other. Miss Lindop's dress has a ruffled collar that has collapsed like a chain of wilting flowers around her neck.

Father Michael offers to make tea. He and Luca retreat to the sacristy.

"I come here every day," says Miss Lindop. "Father Michael gives me chores to do."

"We've been to your house," says Ruiz.

"Is Tinker all right? I've been worried about him. I didn't leave him any milk."

"He found some," says Ruiz.

"Did he open the fridge again? He's learned how to do that. He's very cheeky."

"He's very fat," adds Ruiz.

Miss Lindop stiffens, less than impressed. "He's *not* fat. He's big boned." She turns away from him and seems to be talking to the shadows. "A man came and said he was a detective. I asked to see his badge and he held something up in front of the peephole, but it was too quick for me to read. He knew about you being pregnant, Lizzie, and about your little boy, so I let him in."

"What did he look like?" asks Ruiz.

"Dark hair. Medium height. Foreign looking. I couldn't place his accent. There was something different about him. His eyes. Something cruel. It was like he *hated* being in his own skin."

Ruiz presses her again, wanting more detail, but she gives him a disapproving scowl. "I don't have a photographic memory, sir."

He apologizes. "What did this man want?"

"Mr. North had a small Moleskine notebook about this big. It was black with an elastic strap." She uses her fingers to show the dimensions.

"What was in it?"

"Lists of some kind."

"Lists?"

Miss Lindop cocks her head to one side. Her opinion of Ruiz isn't improving because he keeps repeating things that she's said.

Luca and Father Michael have returned with a tray of mugs. Miss Lindop delves into her bag and produces a small pillbox of saccharine tablets. She smiles at Luca, perhaps imagining having a son his age.

"North was always scribbling notes," she says, "but he stopped whenever I walked in."

"This man that came to your house—did he say anything else?"

Miss Lindop gazes sadly at Elizabeth. "He said Mr. North was sleeping with someone. He wanted to find her.

"I called him a liar and said Richard was a good husband and father, but the man just laughed."

"Did he mention a name?" asks Elizabeth.

Miss Lindop hesitates, not wanting to inflict more heartache.

"What name?"

"Polina."

Ruiz checks himself. How did this man know about North and the nanny? The police only made the connection in the past twenty-four hours. At some point during the winter, somebody photographed North and Polina together at a café. The images were sent to him as a warning or a threat.

"The man wanted an address for Polina," says Miss Lindop. "I told him that I might have one upstairs. I thought if I could distract him I could use the phone and call the police. But he followed me."

"How did you get away?" asks Luca.

"He was searching the spare bedroom when I locked him inside." She looks at her hands. "He was yelling terrible things and kicking at the door, but I ran...I have a bicycle; I know the cycle paths and shortcuts. I can pedal pretty fast for someone my age."

Behind them a door opens and an elderly man in a homburg dips his hand in the holy water, making a sign of the cross, before taking a seat in the shadows. Kneeling. Praying.

"Why didn't you call the police?" asks Luca.

Miss Lindop frowns. "Afterwards, I thought maybe he *was* a detective and I was going to be in trouble for locking him up. I didn't go to work today. It's the first day I've missed in eight years, but ever since Mr. North went missing I've had nothing to do. They took everything away."

"The police?"

"The lawyers. They went over his appointments book and diary, wanting to know who he spoke to and where he went..." She glances at Luca. "They asked me about a journalist: Keith Good-ing. Is that you?"

"A friend of mine."

"They wanted to know if Mr. North had ever spoken to him."

"What did you say?"

"I had no idea. I don't think so. Then they made me sign a confidentiality document. They said I'd go to prison if I talked to anyone. Am I going to get into trouble?"

"No," says Ruiz.

Elizabeth squeezes the older woman's hand, surprised at the shallowness of her own grief. Ruiz glances over his shoulder. The man praying in the rear pew has gone. The church is empty again.

Outside the sun is coming and going, giving little warmth. Ruiz pauses on the pavement. Ponders his next move. Every new detail comes back to the notebook. The murder of Zac Osborne. The break-in at Elizabeth's house. The search for Holly Knight. Richard North had been investigating certain accounts, according to his secretary. That was his job as a compliance officer, but these inquiries were private. Hidden.

Elizabeth lets out a cry of pain and muffles the sound with her fist. Another contraction, this one is real. It forces her to lean back, legs splayed slightly, trying to take pressure off her cervix.

"How often are they coming?" asks Ruiz.

"I don't know."

"Since the last one?"

"Ten minutes maybe."

Ruiz holds his hand to her forehead. "You're burning up."

"I'm fine. Claudia isn't due for three weeks."

"I don't think Claudia is going to wait."

Chelsea and Westminster Hospital is less than fifteen minutes away. Ruiz parks and waits as Elizabeth fills in a form and changes into a hospital gown. A midwife is summoned, bell-shaped with blue trousers and a white blouse. Ruiz feels clumsy and out of place.

"I can wait outside," he says, fidgeting with his car keys. "Is there someone I can call?"

"You can give me my phone back," says Elizabeth, who is sitting on the bed, her knees together and hands flat on the mattress. Ruiz puts the SIM card in her mobile.

"How long since you've been in a place like this?" she asks.

"Thirty-two years. My wife was having twins. They wouldn't let me stay. Not that I minded. I didn't really want to see the business end of things."

"The business end?"

"You know what I mean."

The midwife pulls the curtains around the bed and asks Elizabeth to lie back and part her knees.

"You can stay away from *my* business end," says Elizabeth, motioning him to the top of the bed.

Grimacing slightly at the intrusion, she stares at the ceiling, letting her left hand reach across the gap and take hold of Ruiz's fingers.

"You're six centimeters," announces the midwife. "Call who you have to call—this baby is coming today."

Fifteen minutes later Ruiz watches as they wheel Elizabeth along the corridor and into the lift. Her father and brother are on their way. They're going to welcome a new addition to the Bach family—another limb to the family tree, a dynasty in progress.

Ruiz uses a payphone in the visitor's lounge.

"Capable."

"Mr. Ruiz. Sorry. Shit! No names. Stupid of me."

"Relax."

"OK. Yeah."

"Any messages?"

"Your friend called. Is he really a professor? I've never met a proper professor."

"What did he want, Capable?"

"Ah, I wrote it down, he said, 'Holly remembers the notebook' and he gave me an address."

Ruiz jots it down on the back of his hand. "Another favor,

Capable, I want you to find someone for me. Polina Dulsanya. She might be working as a nanny. You could try the agencies."

"What do you need?"

"An address."

22

LONDON

As the last rays of token sunlight strike the towers of Canary Wharf, four divers tumble backwards from the Zodiacs. Slick as seals, they disappear beneath the surface leaving barely a trace save for the brown bubbles that fill and pop.

The officer in charge is short and barrel-chested, clad in a wetsuit that makes him look as if he's carved from ebony. He swings an air tank into a boat and uses a towel to wipe his face and neck before washing out his mouth with bottled water.

Campbell Smith is standing on a narrow strip of beach that bleeds back to a stand of willow trees.

"We found the body about eighty yards from here," says the senior diver. "You can see the orange marker buoy. They weighted the body with chains and breezeblocks."

Campbell glances at his shoes, which are sinking into the fetid ooze. Paul Smith brogues. Unsalvageable.

"How?"

"One bullet. Back of the head. Execution style."

"We likely to recover a shell?"

"Entry and exit wounds. We'll keep looking for the murder weapon but it's blacker than black down there. Visibility nil. We're working a circular search pattern from a single anchor chain, moving further and further out, working by touch."

Behind him, a white tent has been raised around a bloated and discolored torso, strung with weed and wrack. The body is curled in an embryonic position, with drying mud giving it the color and texture of desiccated leather.

"Where's Noonan?"

"On his way."

23

LONDON

The lockup is one of a dozen single garages in the laneway, each with double doors that are scrawled with graffiti signatures, crude diagrams and territorial markings. Streetlights barely shift the gloom and trains clatter past on the main line from Waterloo.

Joe watches the faces in the brightly lit carriages, passive and incurious about the world outside their windows.

There is a car parked at an angle halfway along the lane. The door opens, but no light comes on. Even in silhouette Joe can recognize Ruiz. He walks like a bear, rocking from side to side, the legacy of a bullet that tore through his thigh six years ago.

Holly lets out a squeak of excitement and runs to Ruiz, stopping suddenly when she seems certain to hug him. Instead Ruiz takes hold of her shoulders. It's strangely intimate, like watching a grandfather admonish his granddaughter for running in the house.

"Have you been avoiding me?" she asks.

"I've been busy."

"I've been crazy bored." She glances back at Joe. "I mean, no offence, but he's got this creepy way of looking inside your head."

"Yeah, I know, but you two are made for each other. You're a human lie detector and he's a professional mind reader."

"You're making fun of me."

"Quite the contrary."

He nods to Joe. "I got your message. Which one is it?"

Holly points. "Zac has the only key."

Ruiz goes to the boot of the car and pulls out bolt cutters along with a torch. Running his fingers over the padlock, he notices the gleam of scratched metal. Someone has tried to pick the lock.

The teeth of the cutters slice through the padlock. Lifting the floor bolt, Ruiz swings the doors open and runs his hand along the wall at chest height, feeling for a switch. A tube light blinks and blazes.

Holly's shoulders sag under another defeat.

The floor is swept clean except for a pile of rubbish that includes old clothes, oil bottles, paint tins, polish, leather protector and a sponge. An old bicycle frame hangs from one wall, along with the wheels of a pram.

"It's gone then," says Holly.

"Who knew about the lockup?" asks Joe.

"Locals. Kids mainly. They play football in the lane. They were always pleading with Zac to give them a ride of the bike. He used to pay them to keep an eye on the place."

Ruiz crouches and begins sorting through the large pile of rubbish on the floor. Pulling at a strap, he drags a scarred leather pannier across the oil-stained concrete, into the light. It belongs to a motorbike. Inside the pannier is a plastic bag. Inside the bag is a jacket. Inside the jacket is a notebook.

24

LUTON

The three men get off the bus at Dunstable Road and walk beneath the railway underpass and along Leagrave Road. Syd and Rafiq are kicking a squashed Coke can along the pavement while Taj listens to music on his headphones.

Syd is puffing hard, unfit and overweight. He's hungry. They stop at a chippy opposite the Britannia Estates and buy five quid's worth of chips with curry sauce, sharing a feast on butcher's paper. Afterwards they throw rocks at an abandoned bus propped on bricks and push a supermarket trolley into the stormwater drain, where it bounces end over end and settles in the mud.

When they reach the Traveller's Rest, they follow a side path along the chain-link fence, out of sight from the main road. The air smells of exhaust fumes and chemicals that blow across the industrial lots and freight yard. Syd goes first because he knows how to work the lights. As he puts the key in the lock he hears something behind him, beyond the fence in the freight yard. Maybe it's a dog scavenging for food, he thinks, peering through the fence. There are shipping containers stacked in neat rows and freight cars rusting on the sidings.

Stepping inside the room, he kicks aside a crumpled cardboard box and closes the curtains, before turning on the lights.

The others follow him. Taj sniffs the air. "What's that stink? Smells like somebody rubbed shit on the walls. Did you take a dump, Syd?"

"It wasn't me."

"It's always you," says Rafiq.

Syd is banging on the top of an old TV that has never worked, trying to get a signal. Taj is sitting on a sofa that is spilling foam. Rafiq keeps watch at the window. Through a half-inch gap in the curtains, he sees the Courier coming, moving along the walkway.

"He's here."

The young men take their places. Standing. Showing respect. Aware of how the atmosphere in the room changes whenever this man appears.

The Courier looks from face to face, stopping at Syd.

"Have you been talking to anyone?"

"No, not me, not a soul, nobody."

"I heard you were bragging to your mates."

"No fucking way."

"The next time you come in here, lock the door."

The Courier paces the room, checking the light fittings, power sockets, running his fingers under the edge of tables and along the underside of the windowsills. His lips are flat and thin against his teeth.

Satisfied, he returns to the table and opens the cardboard flaps of the box. He pulls out a canvas vest—a simple garment tailored to fit a man or a woman's body. Thick shoulder straps hold the midsection in place.

"Do you know what this is?" he asks.

Nobody answers.

"This large disc just under the breast area is filled with three-millimeter steel balls. Behind that, next to the skin, is a compartment filled with C-4 plastic explosive. Two detonators, one on either side, are rigged to timing devices or can be triggered manually or via a text message from a mobile phone. When that happens the vest becomes a bomb, killing or maiming anyone within a hundred-foot radius."

Syd looks like he might vomit.

The Courier tosses the vest towards him. "Here, try it on."

"We're not suicide bombers," says Taj.

The Courier breathes loudly through his nose, as though smelling the odor of fear rising from their armpits. "So you're not willing to die?"

"That's not what I'm saying."

"What *are* you saying?"

"You didn't say anything about suicide vests," says Rafiq.

The Courier shows his teeth in something approximating a smile. At the same moment he slips a vest over his arms, buckling it in place.

"You only have to wear the vests until you get inside. After that, you place them near the dance floor under tables or next to the bar. Crowded areas."

The Courier unfurls a map on the table, holding it down with broken bathroom tiles. On top he places the floorplan of a nightclub called Nirvana in Piccadilly, just off Regent Street. There are galleries on each of the three floors. The main dance area is on the ground level, while the loft level has a VIP area next to an open-air terrace. The basement has another dance area and bar.

"You park the van here," he says, pointing to a loading area a block away. "You'll be wearing the vests by then."

"How do we get inside?" asks Taj. "Most nightclubs have metal detectors at the doors."

The Courier produces a key from his pocket. "This is for a service entrance." He points to the floorplan. "It takes you into a storage area used for liquor deliveries. One door leads to the bar. The other into a storeroom used by the cleaners. It's dark. Noisy. Lights are flashing. On a good night they get a thousand people in Nirvana. Nobody is going to see you come out of the storeroom."

"What about the CCTV?"

"You wear baseball caps. Keep your heads down. Once you're inside you split up. Go to the toilet. Get a cubicle. Take off the vests. Once you plant them you leave as quickly as possible through the main door, without drawing attention. Don't talk to each other. Don't communicate at all."

Syd raises his hand, as though in a classroom. "Who's going to detonate them?"

"You'll each have a mobile phone that has been programmed with the number. The explosions must be synchronized. Two early. One later. The vest on the ground floor must be detonated after the police and fire brigade arrive." The Courier points at Taj. "You will detonate the last one."

"Why me?"

"Because God is giving you an opportunity to prove yourself."

Taj puts out his cigarette in an ashtray, mashing it methodically. His eyes go to the open box.

"What about the passports and tickets?"

"You'll have them."

"And the money?"

"Tomorrow."

The two men size each other up, their eyes like sharpened sticks. Taj is talking before he thinks. "What if the vests go off accidentally?"

The Courier drops a vest at Taj's feet and stamps down on it with his heel. Once…twice…three times. Then he picks it up and throws it to Taj, who catches it cautiously.

"If you are caught you must detonate the vests. I don't care if you're wearing them or not—it's better to die than rot inside a British prison for the rest of your lives. It will be fast. You will not feel a thing."

25

LONDON

Daniela and Luca have been up all night, fueled by machine coffee and the scent of something big. Both of them feel like college kids pulling an all-nighter, their heads tipped tensely forward, checking facts, comparing figures, picking apart the details of hundreds of transactions.

Often the numbers pose more questions than they answer. Luca has to console and cajole Daniela, pushing her to keep going. She circles the desk, scribbling numbers and tapping a calculator. Luca stares at her in awe. "Whoever said accountants were boring?"

"Are you saying I'm boring?"

"No…"

"What are you saying?"

"I'm saying you're brilliant, beautiful, intelligent, resourceful and amazing."

"And boring?"

"You are the sexiest actuary to ever run a ruler over the numbers and I would happily look at your spreadsheet every day."

"Was that so difficult?" she says.

They're working at Keith Gooding's desk while Ruiz dozes between two chairs. Holly and Joe are sleeping on sofas in the editor's office. The night sky is giving way to a yellow glow, and shadows lengthen across rooftops. Ruiz groans and arches his back, swinging his feet to the floor. He rubs his eyes, adjusts his crotch and looks out at the dawn.

Daniela lets out a soft yelp of triumph. Another number has fallen into place. Ruiz glances at the Moleskine notebook in her hands and wonders how something so small and ordinary and seemingly innocuous could have caused such mayhem—the deaths, the violence, the secrecy.

Keith Gooding has arrived with decent coffee, pastries and juice. Shortly after nine, Daniela and Luca emerge from their huddle. They eat a little and freshen up, before pulling chairs into a rough circle.

Daniela begins. "You're probably wondering about the notebook," she says, holding up a double page. "These are codes."

"Like account numbers?" asks Ruiz.

"Similar, but not quite the same," she says. "See this one here: No. 2075. That code belongs to Banco Internacional de Nassau Ltd in the Bahamas. No. 20966 is an account opened by the Banque Assandra in the Cayman Islands."

"So the codes are given to foreign banks?"

"Banks, companies, corporations, private individuals... They're non-published."

"What does that mean?"

"They're secret, off the books. In essence they are ghost accounts with no paperwork, just a number. Clients can transfer funds or buy stock or swap derivatives, but nobody knows who they are and Mersey Fidelity keeps no central record of the trades. Only the number is ever mentioned in the transaction."

Daniela turns her laptop to show Gooding. "Some of the biggest corporations in the UK have taken advantage of the scheme. Look at these names."

The journalist whistles through his teeth. "How many accounts?"

"Thousands."

"What did Mersey Fidelity get out of it?"

"Handling fees. It used a debit and credit system. Often the actual funds never left Syria or Jordan or Lebanon—they were just credited to the client's account as a paper transaction."

Daniela taps on the mouse. "With me so far?"

Everybody nods. She points and clicks. A new landscape of information unfolds before them.

"It's a brilliant system for doing dubious deals. It launders money. Avoids tax. It hides income or the ownership of assets..." Daniela points to a page of the notebook. "Look at this. There are twenty-three Colombian accounts, thirty-two from Syria, eighteen from Afghanistan and more than a hundred from Russia, but there are just as many from the US, Germany, France, Britain...Anybody could use the system, from legitimate corporations to crime gangs or drug cartels—there's no way of knowing who owns the accounts." Daniela calls up another list of accounts. "We looked at Syria and found twenty-eight ghost accounts linked to the same banks that secretly channeled money to Saddam Hussein. This time the transfers went the other way. Forty-six in the past three years."

"Going where?" Ruiz asks.

"Into Mersey Fidelity and then out again."

"How much?"

"Close to three billion dollars."

Gooding: "How could they keep amounts like that off the books? Surely it has to show up somewhere."

Daniela points to another note she's made. "Here is where it gets even more interesting. Most of these non-published accounts were opened in the morning, used for a transaction and closed in the afternoon. The only person who would know about that transaction is the guy who gave the order. The auditor won't see the account because it existed for less than twenty-four hours.

"Look at this unpublished account, No. 3625. The bank that opened it is in Lugarno, Switzerland, but the final destination of the funds was a company registered in the Bahamas. See the name:

Bellwether Construction. It was the company that won a contract to rebuild Jawad Stadium in Baghdad. The work was never done."

"Where does Richard North come into this?" asks Ruiz.

"He was the compliance officer," says Luca. "It was his job to report any suspicious transactions, no matter how small."

"Why would he risk keeping a notebook?"

"Someone had to have the codes. My guess is they weren't digitalized because that creates a record that is difficult to wipe from a computer hard drive."

Ruiz wants to be clear. "So this is money-laundering?"

"Money-laundering, tax evasion, insider trading...on a massive scale," says Daniela. "The notebook reveals more than two thousand ghost accounts in fifty countries."

"Can we see where the money was going?" asks Gooding.

Luca takes over. "We can trace the transfers to offshore banks, but we need more time to locate the end-user. I think Richard North was researching some of the transactions. Elizabeth North found a file that her husband had hidden. We've been matching some of the account numbers to the transactions he circled and grouped together. Once money has entered the European banking system it can be wired and withdrawn anywhere without any controls. Members of terrorist groups can be using ATM machines to access cash, just like the 9/11 hijackers did. It was the same in Bali and Madrid before the bombings.

"Look at this," Luca points to the computer screen. "North identified a bank in Madrid and another in Bali. They're the same banks the bombers withdrew funds from."

"Are they the same accounts?" asks Gooding.

"That's what we need to find out. We have to trace each transaction."

"Which could take us months."

Holly has woken and come looking for food. Ignoring the conversation, she picks up a croissant and pulls it apart with her fingers. Pastry sticks to her nails and she sucks them clean, almost purring like a cat.

She's watching the TV above her head, Sky News, a Bambi-eyed newsreader sternly reading an autocue. The headlines are running as a banner across the bottom of the screen.

"This is huge," says Gooding. "Money-laundering. Tax avoidance. Terrorism. Mersey Fidelity was being touted as the beacon of the new banking system. It's supposed to provide the Bank of England with a blueprint for new banking laws." He looks at Luca. "Who knew at the bank?"

"It could go right to the top."

"They'll deny it."

"Or destroy any incriminating evidence."

"We can't publish this without independent verification. We need someone from Mersey Fidelity to go on the record."

"Someone senior."

Ruiz marvels at the strange light in both the journalists' eyes, like they've discovered the Holy Grail or stumbled upon a fortune in gold.

"Maybe we should think about this more carefully," he says, letting his fingertips rest lightly on the pages of the notebook. "You don't have the resources to investigate something like this properly. The police can get warrants, tap phones and seize documents. SOCA specializes in this sort of thing."

Gooding scoffs. "We're not just handing this over to the police."

"Why not?"

"Because our exclusive won't be exclusive anymore."

"You're worried about a story."

"In case you haven't noticed—this is a newspaper office."

"This isn't just about the bank or a few big corporations," says Ruiz. "This notebook could expose organized crime gangs, terror groups, drug cartels... It's about terrorist funding. It's about the end-user. It's about thousands of transactions, every one of them a possible prosecution."

Gooding throws up his hands. "You know it doesn't work like that. The CPS will be happy with a handful of convictions. I say we publish first and then hand the dossier to police. Scotland Yard can share it with Interpol, the Iraqis, the Americans—it won't matter by then."

"It will matter if the money disappears," says Ruiz. "It will matter if Yahya Maluk and Mohammed Ibrahim flee the country and can't be extradited back here. Ibrahim is a wanted war criminal. He should be arrested. Prosecuted."

Daniela looks at Luca. "He's got a point. If you report this now they'll go to ground. Cover their tracks. Remember how this started. You were following the money."

She's talking about Baghdad. The insurgency. Someone is funding them.

Luca has been silent through the argument. It can't be a choice of one thing or the other. There has to be common ground.

"We make copies of everything. We hand everything to SOCA, but we keep investigating."

Gooding wants to continue arguing. Holly interrupts him. She's pointing at the TV screen, which has footage of police divers tumbling backwards from Zodiacs. A photograph appears of Richard North. A banner headline runs across the bottom of the screen. Some stories don't need sound.

26

LUTON

Taj is sitting at the small kitchen table pushing scrambled eggs around a plate. He looks at Aisha's hips moving beneath her long skirt as she goes about her chores. She put on weight during her pregnancy; hasn't lost it all, but he rarely sees her eat anything.

Barefoot and bare-chested, his jeans hang low on his hips.

"You should put on a shirt before you eat," she says.

Taj sniffs and says, "Fine," meaning something else. He fiddles with his watchband, opening and closing the clasp.

"You're very quiet. Is everything OK?" she asks.

He inhales. Exhales. "I have to go away for a while."

"Is it about that job? Why won't you tell me what it is?"

"It's in Pakistan."

"What do you mean?"

"I'm going to Pakistan for a few months."

She looks at him incredulously. "Why?"

"Work."

"What work?"

He makes a line on the tablecloth with a butter knife and wets his lips with his tongue.

"First I got to do something in London, then I fly out."

"When?"

"I'm leaving tonight."

"You can't just leave, Taj. Not without telling me."

"I *am* telling you."

"But we haven't talked about it. What am I supposed to do?"

Taj drives the handle of the knife into the center of the plate with his fist. It smashes, spraying eggs and baked beans on the wall.

"This is *my* business," he yells. "This is *me* looking after *my* family. You never stop wanting stuff. That baby never stops wanting stuff."

"I never ask you for anything, Taj."

"I babysit, don't I? A grown man shouldn't have to do that shit."

She can see he's angry. Hurt. She knows not to test his temper, but she wants to understand. For months he has been like this. Bitter. Resentful. Distant. Ever since his father died, ever since he lost his job. Mr. Farouk at the Laundromat said that Taj has stopped going to the mosque on Fridays.

The baked beans are leaking down the wall and on to the skirting board.

"This has something to do with that man, doesn't it?"

Taj doesn't answer. Aisha looks at the floor.

"What about Syd and Rafiq?"

"They are coming too. We'll be together. In a few months I'll send word to you. Money. Passports. You can join us."

"In Pakistan?"

"Yes."

"I don't want to live in Pakistan. I want to live here."

Taj pushes back his chair and goes to the bedroom where he takes an old suitcase from the top of a wardrobe and begins packing.

"What is it, Taj? We have to talk about this."

"You'll do as I say because I'm your husband."

"Why can't you get a job here?"

"Don't you think I've tried? I'm sick of this country, sick of begging, sick of being made to feel like a scrounger or a criminal."

"Most people don't treat us like that."

"We're discriminated against."

"We're just poor."

"What about my father, eh? He died because they discriminated against him."

"He died of heart disease."

"He was more than a year on that waiting list. He could have had a new heart, but they gave it to some white woman."

"She had three young children."

"She wasn't on the list as long as he was."

Taj is throwing socks and underwear into the bag, T-shirts, an extra pair of jeans. Aisha is standing in the doorway, her apron bunched in her fists. She can see his muscles flexing on either side of his spine.

"You don't have to go. You can pull out. Tell Syd and Rafiq."

"I'm committed."

"What about me . . . the baby?"

"You're going to wait for me."

Taj reaches into his pocket and produces a roll of cash in a rubber band. Aisha blinks twice, moves her mouth. She has never seen so much money. It scares her.

"What have you done?" she whispers, trembling now.

A silence. Taj isn't going to tell her. It's not what he's done but what's expected of him . . .

27

LONDON

Summer leaving. Autumn coming. On an ordinary morning full of ordinary things, Ruiz walks to clear his head, following the river, watching the sun ascend. He passes old Billingsgate Market and HMS Belfast reaching the shadows of Tower Bridge.

Six years ago, not far from here, he was pulled from the Thames with a bullet in his thigh and a missing ring finger. They found him clinging to a navigation buoy east of Tower Bridge. Less than a mile away, drifting on the tide, a boat looked like a floating abattoir. At first Ruiz had no memory of what had happened, but then it came back slowly in snapshots, dreams and shivers. He had been washed through London's famous sewers and been spat out into the Thames as he followed the ransom for a missing girl. He survived the river and the bullets, but his career couldn't be saved.

Richard North had been fished from a different river — a bullet hole in his head. He won't be coming home to meet his new daughter or watch his son grow up. Ruiz had almost surrendered that same chance with his own children.

At that moment a bird, black as polished onyx, tumbles from the sky and lands with a dull thud on the footpath. Neck broken and blood on its beak. Ruiz looks up and contemplates which window it dashed itself upon. In a split second shining air had turned to solid glass and the world had snapped shut. Not fair or unfair. Life.

He turns and begins retracing his steps. Joe O'Loughlin appears ahead of him.

"I thought I'd find you here."

"Why?"

"The river."

He has a large white envelope. "Luca wanted me to give you this. He said you'd know what to do with it."

"Where's Holly?"

"She's gone shopping. That girl can make twenty quid go a long way."

"Has she ever shown you the receipts?"

Joe's face drops. "Am I aiding and abetting a shoplifter?"

"Holly is a little more subtle than that."

The two men walk in silence, feeling a chill breeze blowing down the river, moving into the heart of the city.

"You want to tell me what's wrong?"

Ruiz takes his tin of boiled sweets from his pocket. Offers one. Makes his own selection.

"I still don't know who killed Zac Osborne and Colin Hackett. One died for the notebook, the other for the photographs. Same shooter. Same MO."

"You have a theory."

"Not really, but I keep coming back to the Americans. They've known about the notebook all along."

"Maybe they're investigating the money-laundering."

"Maybe they killed Zac Osborne and Colin Hackett and Richard North."

"You're talking about state-sponsored murder."

"You're right. Stupid idea. I'm sure they're all registered patriots."

"I'm being serious."

"So am I."

Joe falls silent. Ruiz fills the void. "Richard North told his secretary he'd done something terrible. He was investigating some of the transactions."

"Cold feet?"

"Maybe he developed a conscience." Ruiz pats his pockets. "You got any spare change? I got to make a call."

He taps the coins against the metal box, waiting for Capable Jones to answer.

"Been trying to reach you?"

"Problem?"

"That thing you wanted. Brendan Sobel has booked a restaurant for this evening at nine o'clock—a private dining room at Trellini's in Little Thames Street. You want me to make a booking?"

"A table for two."

28

LONDON

Owen Price, the editor of the *Financial Herald*, is an Australian who arrived in London in the eighties at the height of the Wapping dispute and hasn't smiled since Margaret Thatcher resigned in tears. The editorial meeting has been underway for twenty minutes. Luca and Gooding are pitching the story—the money trail from Baghdad to Mersey Fidelity, the ghost accounts, secret deals and tax evasion.

Price grunts occasionally, a bestial gesture that can be read as either positive or negative, depending upon a person's level of paranoia. "And you're saying this dead banker is involved?"

"Up to his eyeballs," says Gooding.

"It was his job to vet all new accounts and investigate any suspicious transactions," adds Luca.

"Now he's dead, which means he can't verify your story," says Price.

Gooding: "We don't need him to verify the story and dead men can't be libeled."

"How high does it go?" asks Price.

"Richard North is the brother-in-law of Mitchell Bach, the chief financial officer."

Price wrinkles his nose, not liking some hidden smell. "Call Legal and tell them to have a QC ready. I want the lawyers involved early. Keep this to a small team. Need-to-know only. You can have Spencer and Blaine."

The editor is pacing back and forth to the window, chewing on a biro. "They're going to shit bricks upstairs. Mersey Fidelity has a big advertising budget. Deep pockets."

"Is that a problem?" asks Luca.

"Not for you, Sunshine, unless this is a set-up." Price looks at the cracked plastic end of the biro and tosses it into the bin. "This is one of those stories you fuck up only once. Could cost us millions in a libel action. My job. Your job. Oh, right, you don't have one of those."

He picks up another pen and addresses Gooding. "You're in charge. Personalize the story. I want a full profile on Richard North—animal, vegetable and mineral—and get me the complete Bach family album. Where's the wife?"

"She had a baby last night," says Luca.

"Better and better. I want someone at the hospital. Send her flowers. A letter. Softly, softly…she could tell her side of the story…"

"Maybe we should go easy on her."

Price grins. "Don't go wobbly me on me, Terracini."

"I'm just saying that she's been through a lot."

The editor senses something more. "You know her?"

"I've met her."

"You've talked to her! Shit! Why don't we have quotes?"

"She doesn't know anything."

"There are no fucking friends in this story."

"Her husband is dead."

"That's the whole fucking point. I want quotes. Photographs. A sit-down interview."

A phone is ringing on Price's desk. He grunts in annoyance. Picks up. Listens. Puts the handset back in the cradle. Then he walks to the sofa and opens the vertical blinds. Three plain-clothes police officers are walking through the newsroom. With them is another man, overweight, dressed in a pinstriped double-breasted suit: a lawyer.

"Someone ratted on us. The bank just called in the police."

Gooding and Luca peer through the blinds.

"Where is the notebook?" asks Price.

"Not on the premises," says Luca. "I have copies."

"Right, you go in there." He points to a bathroom. "Gooding, you stay here. Let me do the talking."

Luca follows instructions, keeping the door ajar so he can listen. The detectives and lawyer introduce themselves, handshakes all round and a discussion about the weather. The British are so very polite.

The lawyer's name is Marcus Weil.

"This is a High Court injunction that prevents you publishing anything based upon statements made by, or materials belonging to, any employee of Mersey Fidelity."

"Materials?" asks Price. "You'll have to be a little more specific. I'm Australian. Slow on the uptake."

"We believe you are in possession of a notebook and other files that were obtained by theft, deception or false overtures. These materials were created by Richard North in the course of his employment at Mersey Fidelity and therefore remain the property of the bank."

Price has resumed his seat, leaning back in his expensive leather chair; his fingertips pressed together, a frown linking him to his inner world.

"What's in this notebook?"

"The paranoid ramblings of a disgruntled employee."

"Oh, so you've read it?"

Mr. Weil dismisses the question. "Should you disseminate inaccurate and malicious opinions based on false information and flawed interpretations, you will be sued." The lawyer then delivers an arrogant non sequitur by denying the bank is in any way suppressing or hiding information to avoid its corporate responsibilities.

"And what makes you so sure we have these materials?" asks the editor.

"I'm not at liberty to say."

"You're not at liberty? That sounds like scurrilous newspaper-speak. Surely you're not going to hide behind the defense of protecting your sources?"

"Richard North was an employee of—"

"Richard North is dead."

"His notes are covered by commercial and legal privilege."

Price repositions his long legs and tilts his head to one side in order to observe Weil from a different angle.

"Since you seem to know quite a lot about this notebook, perhaps you could tell me what I should be looking for?" The editor turns on a tape recorder. "Just for the record."

Blood has drained from the lawyer's face. He blusters and whines, threatening warrants, subpoenas and writs. He looks at the detectives, demanding they take action. The most senior of them speaks.

"Have you seen this notebook, Mr. Price?"

"No."

"Is any member of your staff in possession of such a notebook?"

"No member of my staff."

Mr. Weil interrupts. "What about Luca Terracini?"

Price raises an eyebrow and glances at Gooding. "That name sounds familiar."

"One of our foreign stringers—works mainly in Iraq," says Gooding.

"Yeah. Freelance. A hired gun." Price gets to his feet. "These stringers are always dreaming up conspiracies. We had one here the other day who accused a bank of laundering money out of Iraq and running a second set of books."

From Weil not a flicker.

"You should go back and tell your clients not to worry. The *Financial Herald* doesn't publish half-baked stories. When we go hunting for elephants we carry a big gun."

29

LONDON

Elizabeth has pillows propped behind her and bedclothes pulled across her lap. Despite the painkillers she feels as though someone has taken a baseball bat to her during the night. Everything below her waist hurts. Everything above the waist is numb. Claudia Rosaline North arrived just before midnight, weighing in at seven pounds with all the required fingers and toes: minus only a father.

There are two detectives waiting to see her. The older one looks like an undertaker. The younger one has blond, cropped hair and nice eyes, which he casts down deferentially, uncomfortable in her presence.

"We've got some bad news, Mrs. North," says the older officer.

"Is there something wrong with Claudia?"

"Who's Claudia?"

"My baby."

"No, I mean, we're not here about your baby."

Elizabeth can hear herself changing the subject. Making conversation.

"I thought it was a bit odd, them sending detectives instead of a doctor. This must be about my husband."

The younger officer takes a deep breath. He almost speaks but doesn't. He leaves it to his more senior colleague.

"Your husband's body was found last evening by police divers not far from where they recovered his car. This is now a murder investigation."

Silence.

Maybe he says more. Maybe he says nothing. The words go missing. All Elizabeth can think about is the cruel nature of the timing, to have lost a husband and gained a daughter on the same night.

The car. The river. The blood. Pausing for a moment, her head bowed, shoulders sagging, she braces herself for tears but they don't come. Instead an oddly comforting thought occurs to her.

Yes, North had been unfaithful, but he hadn't abandoned her. He was coming home. Maybe she would have listened to his excuses. Forgiven him. Taken him back.

How quickly her circumstances have changed. Ten days ago she had been a reasonably contented, stay-at-home mother with an enviable life. Not perfect — what marriage ever is? Now she can recognize the countless foretellings, the innumerable small breaks from normalcy, the telltale signs of disintegration and decay. North's chin unshaved, his long hours at the office, the second bottle of wine opened on a weekday night... One evening she found him in tears, but he wouldn't tell her why. "Just a sad day," he told her. "I'm allowed to have sad days."

Elizabeth's phone keeps beeping. Text messages. People are starting to send congratulations. Soon they'll be sending commiserations. There's an interesting dilemma: What card do you send a new mother and a widow?

The detectives apologize again and say they'll want to interview Elizabeth when she's out of hospital. It is all so very polite and civilized. No hysterics. No recriminations. They leave her alone and she stares at the ceiling, feeling divorced from herself, watching the scene rather than playing her part. From along the corridor she hears the scuttle of little feet. Rowan hurls himself into her arms.

"I saw Claudia," he announces excitedly. "She's got a squished-up face."

"All babies look a little squished."

"When can I play with her?"

"She's a bit small to play with, but she'll grow up quickly."

"Is mine Daddy here?" he asks.

"No."

"Doesn't he want to see Claudia?"

"I'm sure he does, but Daddy has gone away. He's in Heaven."

"Where's Heaven?"

"It's where people go when they die."

"Is mine Daddy dead?"

"Yes."

"Is he coming back soon?"

"No, sweetheart, people don't come back from Heaven."

"What about angels?"

Elizabeth doesn't know how to answer that question. She can see the complete trust in her son's eyes, wanting to learn and believe, every day a new adventure. At that moment something damaged inside her finally breaks.

Alistair Bach is standing in the doorway. Mitchell appears behind him, carrying flowers. Elizabeth speaks quietly and calmly.

"Get him out of here. I don't want to see him. I never want to see him."

Bach tries to intervene, but Elizabeth stops him. "Stay out of this, Daddy."

"I'm just saying that, whatever you think has happened, you should remember that Mitchell is family."

"Don't try to guilt me," she says sharply. "North is dead. I know he's involved."

Mitchell wants to defend himself but doesn't know how to begin. The look of contempt on Elizabeth's face is too much for him. He places the flowers on a chair and leaves without saying a word.

30

LONDON

Standing beneath the colonnaded arches, Ruiz watches the lift doors open and three men emerge. One of them is the driver of the blue Audi; the others are slightly older, dressed in suits, one with a black umbrella and the other wearing a light overcoat. Staying out of sight, Ruiz lets them pass.

They cross Fenchurch Street and turn into Mark Lane. Once they're around the corner, Ruiz doesn't alter his pace. He knows where they're going.

The restaurant is modern Italian with Polish waitresses, French kitchen staff and an English chef: a microcosm of the New Europe. The private dining room is in a mezzanine area, overlooking the main restaurant. Earlier Ruiz had watched two other men arrive and sweep the room for listening devices.

Luca and Daniela are sitting at a table by the window. Luca hands a camera to a waitress. It's their anniversary, he says. They pose. Behind them the door opens and the three men enter. The shutter blinks. Take another one just to be sure. It blinks again.

Moments later a cab pulls up outside. A fourth man has arrived, this one more surprising. Yahya Maluk hands his hat and coat to a waitress.

Ruiz enters a few minutes later, not making eye contact with Luca or Daniela.

"I'm with Mr. Sobel's party," he tells the maitre d'. "A late addition. Did someone call? No, not to worry."

Taking the narrow stairs, he arrives at the lone table.

"Sorry to keep you waiting, gentlemen. Bloody traffic. Grind to a standstill one day."

Bernard Sobel looks up from the menu. Ruiz takes a chair and shrugs off his coat.

Sobel: "Hey buddy, you're in the wrong place."

"This is a private dining room," echoes Artie Chalcott.

"But you guys know me." Ruiz opens his arms. Then he motions to the driver. "We're old friends. How's your mate? Sorry about his nose. Didn't know he was a bleeder."

The driver's first instinct is to reach inside his jacket. Ruiz fixes him with a stare. "I had you pegged as stupid, but not *that* stupid. Are we *really* going to compare weapons in a public place like this? Is yours bigger than mine? Is mine bigger than yours? I don't like to boast, but I think size does count and now isn't the time for you to grow a pair."

Ruiz reaches across the table to Brendan Sobel. "Brendan, nice to finally meet."

Sobel is so stunned he shakes his hand.

"And you must be Yahya Maluk. We haven't met," says Ruiz, "but I know you by reputation."

The banker looks completely nonplussed. He glances from face to face, waiting for an explanation.

Ruiz turns to Chalcott. "Another American. Welcome to our shores."

A waitress offers to take Ruiz's coat.

"Thanks, love, but I'll hold on to it. Can't be too careful. Thieves about. Don't want to put temptation in their way."

She looks at his shabby coat and frowns.

"I'll have a Peroni," he says, giving her a wink.

Chalcott is glaring at Sobel. "Who is this clown?"

"Vincent Ruiz."

"There you go—you *do* remember me," says Ruiz. He pours himself fizzy water from a green bottle. Sips. Then he picks up the menu. "I'm ravenous. Any recommendations?"

Sobel whispers something to the driver, who has gone quiet, touching nervously at his mouth with a napkin.

"Oh, and I'm sorry about your car. That broken window. Just to prove there are no hard feelings, I'll pay for the damage."

Ruiz pulls an envelope of cash from his jacket, tossing it on to the table where banknotes spill across the white linen. "You left that on the front seat of my car. It's all there—count it if you like."

Yahya Maluk pushes back his chair. "I didn't come here for this sideshow. Who is this man? What's he doing here?"

Chalcott tells Sobel to get Maluk out of the restaurant.

"You're leaving so soon? We've hardly had a chance to talk," says Ruiz. "I was going to ask you about Mohammed Ibrahim. He's looking very healthy for a man who died a few years ago and then escaped from jail. How was Ramsay's restaurant in Maida Vale?

I've heard good reports. The man has a potty mouth, but he can cook up a storm."

Blood has pooled in Maluk's cheeks like pink flowers. He wipes a film of perspiration from his top lip, stammering, "How does he know about Ibrahim? You said nobody…"

"Shut the fuck up!" says Chalcott.

The driver leads Maluk down the stairs. Luca and Daniela get another set of pictures as they leave.

The upstairs waitress has come to the table with Ruiz's beer. She is staring at the money.

"Don't get too excited," he tells her. "It's not your tip. This is what you call a bribe."

She hesitates and walks back to the kitchen.

Ruiz shakes out his serviette. "You're probably wondering how I found you, Brendan. You'll find my mobile phone on the floor of the car that you sent to my daughter's house. It was tracked to the garage beneath your offices. While on this subject—I'd like the phone back."

Chalcott is staring at Sobel, who is altering the position of his body, trying to disassociate himself from the conversation or to disappear sideways.

"What do you want, Mr. Ruiz?"

"Call me Vincent, please. And you are…?"

"I don't think that's important."

"No need to be so formal—I know all about Brendan and that office of yours. No listed telephone numbers or company tax returns."

"We're a communications company," says Chalcott.

"Not the CIA then?"

Chalcott is trying hard to look relaxed and sound perfectly natural. He doesn't like being embarrassed.

"Perhaps we could talk about this somewhere more private?"

"This is a *private* dining room."

"Just you and me."

"I'm happy if you want to invite Yahya. We can bring Ibrahim along. We can play twenty questions."

Ruiz slides his hand into his pocket again. This time he produces a small black notebook.

"That bribe was very clumsy. I thought you guys had moved beyond trying to buy people off with beads and trinkets. This is what you wanted: Richard North's notebook. Is this why you killed Zac Osborne?"

"We were not complicit in the murder of Zac Osborne," says Sobel.

"Complicit: such an old-fashioned term. What about Richard North and Colin Hackett?"

"Please keep your voice down, Mr. Ruiz."

"Explain it to me."

"You are not owed an explanation."

Ruiz taps the notebook against his cheek. "You have broken into my house, you have gate-crashed my daughter's wedding, bugged my phones, hounded my friends...I'm owed for that."

"You must think this is feeding time at the zoo," says Chalcott, who has folded his serviette and placed it neatly on the side of his plate. "I won't say that it's been a pleasure."

"I thought the CIA might be investigating a money-laundering operation," says Ruiz. "Or trying to track down a wanted terrorist. But then I saw Mr. Maluk arrive. You've known all along about the cash being laundered through Mersey Fidelity. The ghost accounts. Iraqi money. Reconstruction funds. Drug profits...Which begs the question—why would the CIA allow something like that to happen?"

"That is a question too far, Mr. Ruiz, but you are right about one thing—you are jeopardizing a major security operation."

"Oh, I see. There's a bigger plan. So what is Mohammed Ibrahim doing in London? Perhaps you organized his release from prison. Is he your monster?"

"Be careful, Mr. Ruiz."

"You know what they say about lying down with dogs?...You wake up with a career in the movies. No, that's not it. Fleas. You wake up with fleas."

Chalcott's eyes behind rimless glasses seem to be concentrated on burning a hole through Ruiz's forehead. "You do us a disservice, sir. You come in here, treating us like the Bumstead crowd, making outrageous allegations, getting in my face in a public place—that's not very intelligent behavior. We can go somewhere now and talk about this, or I can *find* you later."

It is a threat. Chalcott doesn't look like a dangerous man, but an unlined face can hide a myriad of sins. His thick brown hair is ruffled slightly by the currents from the air conditioner. Joe O'Loughlin has taught Ruiz that true narcissists become intensely angry if anyone suggests they are not perfect. They seek to destroy the messenger rather than admit their flawless image might be blemished.

"I thought you were a clever man," says Chalcott. "Clearly, I was misinformed. You come in here looking like you fell out of a laundry bag, making threats and baseless allegations, thinking you can rattle me. You think I give a fuck what some pissant, washed-up former detective is going to do?"

Ruiz looks at his hands and feet. He was wrong to come here; foolish to think they would tell him anything. By confronting them, by humiliating them publicly, by peeling away the carefully constructed façade of their work, Ruiz has inserted broken glass into the brains of dangerous men.

The manager has arrived. He is standing three feet away, his tongue wetting his lips.

"Perhaps you gentlemen could lower your voices."

Chalcott's eyes are filled with a black light. "Why don't you fuck off?"

The manager takes a step back.

"It's all right," says Ruiz. "I'll be leaving in a moment."

"Nice to hear it," says Sobel.

The driver leans down to whisper something in Ruiz's ear but doesn't finish the sentence.

In that moment something breaks inside Ruiz—not a clean snap like a bone or a branch splintering, but a moist sound like wet sheets flapping on a windy day. A kaleidoscope of images tumbles through his mind—Zac Osborne's tortured body, Elizabeth

North vomiting in the gutter, Holly Knight without a family, Richard North dragged from the stinking mud.

In the pause between heartbeats, Ruiz swings his elbow back in a short arc, connecting with the driver's throat, closing his windpipe. In the same motion, he drags him face-first on to the table sending plates and glasses crashing to the floor. The next blow is delivered with a pepper mill inside Ruiz's fist, hooking the driver under the left eye. He doesn't want to stop. He can feel the old wheels starting to turn and the cobwebs being blown out. It feels better than it should.

"That's enough," says Sobel, holding his hand inside his jacket.

Ruiz places the pepper mill back on the table and rights his upturned chair. The notebook has fallen on to the floor. Picking it up, he brushes beads of water from the cover.

"This is what you wanted. You can stop looking for Holly Knight and you can stop following me."

He presses it against Chalcott's chest.

"I realize that you're not going to tell me what's going on. Keeping secrets is how you guys get a hard-on. But just in case you think of coming after me or Holly, you should know that photographs were taken of you entering this restaurant. Time and date stamped. I might never learn the whole story, but I have enough to cause you some embarrassment."

No reaction. Ruiz walks down the stairs and out of the restaurant, listening to the soft scuff of his shoes on the pavement, trying to make his heart beat slower. Luca and Daniela have already gone. He moves quickly, knowing that someone will most likely be trying to follow him.

Reaching the junction, he turns south and ponders whether anything has been achieved. Not a lot, he suspects, but subtlety was never one of his strengths. He has just broken all his own rules about keeping a low profile and never revealing his full knowledge. It was a conscious, culpable, willful lapse and these men could make him pay.

Heading underground, he takes the escalator into the bowels of Tower Hill Station and pauses in the walkway between the west-

and eastbound platforms of the Circle Line, waiting for the first train to arrive.

He notices a man with a knapsack, a woman with a baby in a sling, a teenager carrying a skateboard with his wrist in plaster. Two men in bulky jackets and boots are jogging down the escalator, hearing the approaching train.

The carriage doors slide open. Ruiz steps inside. The men squeeze into an adjoining carriage. Ruiz squats out of sight and waits for the doors to start closing. At the last possible moment he steps off. Running up the stairs and over the tracks, he forces open the closing doors of a westbound train.

Nobody is following him.

31

LONDON

Holly opens her eyes, awake instantly, disturbed by something. She listens to the sounds of the city. Rubber on tarmac. Trains on tracks. Car horns and sirens.

Letting her heart slow, she turns back to the bed. The digital clock is glowing red: 2:47.

Lowering her head to the pillow, she stares at the water stains above her head and the cracked plaster rosette. For just a moment she remembers the night she waited for her father to return home from the pub to see the ruined ceiling and flooded room, her younger brother Albie cowering beneath the sheets.

Her father had a strange temper—placid one moment, explosive the next, with nothing in between; no safe ground or sanctuary or flashing light to warn her of the dangers ahead. She learned to read his moods by studying his face, discovering what lay behind his eyes where a fuse was always spluttering and hissing.

She hears the sound again—soft footsteps on the metal of the fire escape. Someone trying not to be heard. Awake this time. Her heart hammering. Certain.

The professor has the room next door. She moves to the interconnecting door and presses her head against it, the wood cool against the shell of her ear. No more sounds.

Opening the bedroom door, she peers along the corridor, left and right, deserted. There is a smell, something familiar yet disturbing. It filled her nostrils when Zac died. The man can't have found her. He doesn't know her name. She should wake Ruiz. He'll know what to do. Keep her safe.

She looks at her bare feet, her T-shirt and panties. She should have changed. Something moves in the corner of her eye at the far end of the corridor. It's gone. It might have been nothing. This is crazy. She needs Ruiz.

Moving in the opposite direction, towards the stairs, she can feel the worn carpet, the pattern faded long ago beneath her bare feet.

She knocks on his door. No answer. Knocks again.

It opens suddenly, pulling her inwards and she bounces off his chest. He grabs her by the hair and puts his hand over her mouth and nose. Not Ruiz, but a ghost who walks through locked doors. His lips brush against her ear. "Do you remember me?"

She inhales a breath.

"I am going to take my hand away. If you scream I shall kill you. Do you understand?"

He pushes her towards the bed and chains the door. He's wearing a suit and white shirt without a tie and his hair is shaved at the edges, longer on top. The only light is from the window, a faint glow that paints the contours of his face in monotones, but not with detail or depth.

Words have turned to bubbles in Holly's throat. She looks around the room, searching for Ruiz.

"Your friend is not here. He seems to have abandoned you."

His eyes drift down her body, hunger in them.

"Why did you kill Zac?" she asks defiantly. "He never did any-thing to you."

"He would not communicate."

"That's not a crime. He fought for his country."

"Maybe I am fighting for mine."

Holly looks at the bed. "Are you going to rape me?"

"I don't rape women unless they're whores. Are you a whore?"

"No."

"Are you a virgin?"

"That's none of your business."

He smiles. "You think I'm evil, but it was a woman who betrayed the first man. Women are the sinful sex. You come to a man's room in the middle of the night. Look at how you dress. You are like uncovered meat, and then you wonder why the dogs come and feed upon you."

Holly sits on the edge of the bed, her knees close together, one foot on top of the other. The Courier takes the chair by the win-dow. When he turns his head the light catches one side of his face. His eye is like an amber bead pressed into teak.

"Can you imagine all the germs that collect in a place like this," he says. "The acts that have been committed on that bed by women like you."

His eyes drop to Holly's loins as though drawn there.

"Come here."

"No."

"You need to, Holly. Sometimes in life we are given a choice. This isn't one of those times."

Holly crosses the room.

"Kneel."

"Please."

"Don't beg. Did you find the notebook?"

"Yesterday."

"Where is it?"

"The journalists have it."

Dropping to her knees in front of him, she can smell his strange odor. He takes the back of her head, pulling her closer. Running his fingers through her hair, he lets them trail down her face until his thumb brushes her lips and he pushes it against her teeth, smearing saliva across her cheek. Her eyes go in and out of focus.

His thumb passes her lips again and she opens them, taking his thumb inside her mouth, sucking it gently. He jerks his hand away.

"An offer like that is so typical of a woman like you. A manipulator. You claim victimhood, but you use your body and a man's desire to get what you want. You think that if you can get me between your lips or your thighs that you can take control."

"No."

He pushes her away. "Get dressed, my little liar."

"I don't have any clothes."

"I was going to wait here and kill your friend, but he has obviously found someone else to keep his feet warm."

"Where are you taking me?"

The Courier stands and checks the corridor. "First we are going to get your clothes. I am not going to tie your hands and cover your mouth, but this gun will be pressed against your back when we walk from the hotel. If you say anything, if you smile or nod or alert anyone, I will kill them first and you will be responsible for their death."

32

LONDON

Ruiz walks across the empty supermarket car park to a dark-colored limousine that soaks up the light from an overhead lamppost. The driver, young, begloved, opens a door for him. Douglas Evans is sitting in the back seat, his trouser cuffs rising up to reveal his pale ankles and black socks.

"This is an interesting choice of time and place, Mr. Ruiz, very cloak and dagger. We could have met at a more sociable hour."

"At your club, perhaps?"

"I doubt if my club would have allowed you in." His cultured accent is effortlessly condescending. "What can I do for you, Mr. Ruiz?"

"There is a man in this country—a wanted Iraqi war criminal called Mohammed Ibrahim Omar al-Muslit. He escaped from a prison outside of Baghdad four years ago. The Americans have him listed as having died in custody, but the Iraqis say he was accidentally released."

Evans blinks his droopy eyelids and runs a hand over his forehead, pale as a cue ball.

"What makes you think he's in the UK?"

"Elizabeth North identified him from a photograph. She saw him with Yahya Maluk, a banker on the board of Mersey Fidelity."

"I know who Mr. Maluk is. Is Mrs. North certain of who she saw?"

"Yes."

Evans tugs at his shirt-cuffs as though his arms have grown longer during the course of their conversation.

"You asked about the Americans," says Ruiz. "You wanted to know what they were up to. They know about Ibrahim and Maluk."

There is a flicker in the corner of Evans' mouth. Just as quickly, he resumes his requiem mode, a marvelous silence that borders on deafness.

Ruiz hands him a file.

"What's this?"

"A copy of a notebook belonging to Richard North and a file he collected. A forensic accountant will be able to explain what it means."

"Perhaps you could précis it for me."

"A banking scandal."

"Another one."

"This one is special. Iraq reconstruction funds, the proceeds of crime, tax avoidance, the sponsoring of terrorism—money that shouldn't be in a UK bank. I'm assuming that you'll pass this information on to the relevant authorities."

Evans rolls the information around in his cheeks as if sipping sherry. He opens the envelope and leafs through the pages.

"Where are the originals?"

"Safe."

"In the hands of your journalist friends?"

Ruiz has already reached for the door handle.

"They cannot publish," says Evans. "We need time to study this."

"Your problem, not mine."

33

LONDON

Arched like a bent bow, Joe O'Loughlin's head is pulled backwards by the noose around his neck that leads to his bound wrists and ankles. Curled on the floor of the hotel room, he cannot straighten his legs without tightening the noose.

Using his hands, he tries to relieve the pressure on his neck, but eventually he gets tired and his legs drop, cutting off his air supply.

He endures on the edge of consciousness, picturing his own funeral, imagining the eulogies, putting words in people's mouths. Julianne inconsolable. Wanting him back.

"You will not see the morning," the man had said when he pressed the gun to Joe's forehead, waking him from a dream. A good dream, Julianne had been in it. They were reconciled. Getting physical. Oxygen deprivation is supposed to heighten sexual pleasure.

Joe rolls on to his stomach feeling four gospels and two testaments of pain. He rolls again, resting his head against the inside of the door. If he loses consciousness he'll suffocate. Raising his head an inch, he takes a breath and brings it down against the door. It rattles with a dull *thunk*. Back and forth he rolls, his bruises like burning charcoal.

The night manager is complained to. Summoned. The door unlocked. Ropes untied. Tape cut away. An ambulance called. The journey to the hospital made in a haze of opiates and questions. His voice box has been bruised. He can't make them understand.

Later he wakes in hospital, his neck smothered in ointment where the nylon rope chaffed and broke his skin. Ruiz is outside his room, bellowing something at an unfortunate nurse.

"This is me calm, OK. You don't want to see me upset."

The door seems to narrow as he enters with the nurse hanging on to his left arm, but not in a romantic way.

Joe looks at him for the single longest second of his life. Tries to speak. The sound is a strangled croak.

"What's wrong with his voice?" Ruiz asks the nurse.

"His voice box was damaged."

"Is he going to be able to talk?"

"In a few days."

Ruiz pulls up a chair and reaches across the sheet, taking Joe's hand in both of his. Squeezes. It's the most intimate physical contact they've ever shared.

Joe tries to speak, mouthing the word "Holly."

"She's gone. I'm going to get her back. How many?"

Joe raises one finger.

"Recognize him?"

He shakes his head.

"If he hurts her I'll kill him. I'll rip out his arsehole and stitch it into his mouth."

A police officer appears, puffing, having run down the corridor. Uniformed. Nervous at the sight of Ruiz, he has one hand on his radio.

"Step back from the bed, sir. No visitors are allowed."

Ruiz asks for a moment longer. Joe is trying to say something. "Where were you?"

"I fucked up. I'm sorry."

He's about to stand. Joe pulls him closer, mouthing words.

"Find her."

"I will."

Ruiz nods to the police officer and apologizes to the nurse. Then he takes the corridor and the stairs. Crossing the foyer, he passes Campbell Smith, who is dressed in full uniform, marching like he's on parade. Ruiz doesn't stop.

"Where are you going?"

No answer.

"What are you, Vincent? Not a police officer. Not a private detective. All you do is make things worse."

Still no response. The doors are closing. Campbell again.

"This is your fault. We could have protected her."

34

LONDON

Luca and Daniela are waiting for Ruiz at the hotel, fear hanging over them like a curse. Nothing they say can make him feel any less responsible. His fault. His guilt.

They take a table at a café. The morning well advanced.

"This should have been over," says Ruiz. "People got what they wanted."

"Ibrahim didn't," says Daniela.

"Nor did the bank," adds Luca.

Studying his scarred hands, Ruiz closes his eyes, warding off a fresh wave of hurt. He should call Julianne, Joe's estranged wife. Explain. Apologies. What would he say? If Julianne had her way, Joe would never be friends with someone like Ruiz. She'd have him wrapped in cotton wool, safely tenured at some university, disconnected from the real world.

Daniela and Luca are talking about the money-laundering investigation. They have spent the past twenty-four hours tracing some of the transactions, following the money trail between various accounts. They are so comfortable together they're starting to finish each other's sentences.

"We're concentrating on the Middle East," says Daniela. "We've linked twelve accounts to Saudi Arabia, eight to Syria, five to Pakistan, fourteen to Iran and six to Indonesia. We've found an indirect link between one of the accounts and the militant group responsible for the Bali bombing in 2002. ATM withdrawals."

"What about accounts linked to UK addresses?" Ruiz asks.

"Not so much," says Daniela. "There's an address in Luton, but that looks like a dead end. We're looking at others in Italy and Germany."

Ruiz is staring back at her. "What did you say?"

"About Italy and Germany?"

"Before that."

"Luton. There were money transfers to a private postbox in Luton. A hundred thousand pounds."

"Who owns the postbox?"

"A Muslim charity, but it looks legitimate."

Ruiz is holding his breath. Exhales. "When Colin Hackett was following Richard North he went to a postbox in Luton. He mentioned a charity. When I talked to Hackett's niece she told me that her uncle was in Luton looking for the missing banker on the day she called him and he came back to London. That was the day he died."

Ruiz is already moving.

Luca has grabbed his coat. "Where are you going?"

"To find a car."

Charlton Car Impound looks like a World War II prison camp with razor wire atop an eight-foot-high perimeter fence. Spread over nearly four acres, the compound is covered by tarmac and a series of brick warehouses with iron roofs and roller doors.

This is where vehicles are towed if they're involved in serious accidents, or abandoned, or used in crimes, or seized by the police or the courts.

The office has a staff of three, hardened souls with a thankless job—a twelve-hour shift full of abuse and insults from members of the public who find their cars have been towed from red routes or double-yellow lines; or because they are unlicensed, uninsured, untaxed or being driven by a drunk. Thank you, sir/madam, that's two hundred pounds—we accept cash or credit cards. No American Express.

The guy behind the counter is black, six-two, and has granny glasses perched on the edge of his nose. It's like seeing Mike Tyson wearing a pinafore.

"I need to look at a car," says Ruiz.

"You got the plate number?"

"No."

"Was it towed under your name?"

"No."

"Registration paper or owner's license?"

"It's not my car."

His eyes move from Ruiz to Luca. "Are you guys taking the piss?"

"It was towed here two days ago from Earls Court. It belonged to a Colin Hackett."

"Are you a copper?"

"Not anymore," says Ruiz.

"A private detective?"

"Not as such."

"Can't help you. You're not authorized. Move aside. I got people in the queue."

Ruiz can hear a scraping sound inside his head like a blade being sharpened on a stone. Holly has been missing for nearly eight hours. Getting further away. There must be four hundred cars on the lot—each with a number and grid reference. Even if they could get past the security, it could take them hours to find Hackett's car.

Through a reinforced window, he notices a mud-streaked truck pull up at the boom gate. The driver jumps down from his cab to sign paperwork. He tucks the pen behind his ear.

Ruiz tells Luca to wait in the Merc. "I won't be long."

He leaps a low fence and walks towards the gates.

"How's the Pekingese?"

Dave looks up from the clipboard.

"Shitting all over my carpets, but it's still better company than my wife. What are you doing here?"

"I'm looking for a car, but the lads behind the counter aren't being very helpful. I don't have any paperwork."

"Not official business."

"Just as important."

Dave glances across the lot where cars are lined up in neat rows. "Is this going to get me into trouble?"

"It could save someone's life."

He makes a decision. "Jump in the cab. Stay out of sight until we get inside."

The truck passes beneath the raised boom and then through a sliding electronic gate. Dave takes a series of turns before stopping in a warehouse. He leads Ruiz to an outer office where the drivers have a tearoom with a jug and chest fridge. Page Three girls with arched backs and melon-like breasts gaze down from the walls, some of them yellowed by age and aged even further by their hairstyles.

Dave makes a call. Asks about a car towed in from Earls Court. Moments later they're walking between rows of vehicles. Colin Hackett's Renault is at the back of the lot parked against a brick wall. A common make, a common color, it was chosen to blend in with the traffic when Hackett was tailing unfaithful husbands or insurance cheats. There are fast-food wrappers on the floor, along with separate bottles—one for water, the other for urine—clearly marked to avoid confusion on long stakeouts.

"You got the keys?" asks Ruiz.

"It's already unlocked."

"Can you hotwire it?"

Dave is shaking his head, holding up his hands. "You wanted to see the car — you've seen it."

"I'm not going to steal it, Dave — I need to see the satnav."

The driver squeezes his hands against his temples, unsure of what to do next.

"A young woman was abducted a little while ago," says Ruiz. "I was supposed to be looking after her. If I don't find her in the next few hours I don't know what could happen to her."

"Abducted?"

"Yeah."

Dave scratches his jaw and finds a pimple to squeeze. He takes a pen-torch from his pocket. "Here, hold this."

Opening the door, he leans into the footwell of the Renault and reaches beneath the dashboard, pulling out the electrics. The engine starts on the third touching of the wires. Dave pumps the accelerator with his hand, revving the engine until it idles smoothly. Ruiz taps the screen of the satnav, which lights up with a welcome message. He looks for the last known destination. Bury Park. Luton. He jots down the street name. No number.

Dave takes him out through a side gate on to waste ground between the motorway and a set of newer factories. Following the fence, Ruiz turns the corner and crosses a forecourt before reaching the Mercedes. Sliding behind the wheel, he borrows Luca's mobile.

"Campbell?"

"Yeah, who's this?"

"Ruiz. I've got a lead on Holly Knight — an address in Luton. Colin Hackett had it programmed into his satnav when he was following Richard North."

Campbell seems preoccupied. Ruiz wants him to listen. "Hackett and North were both killed by the same caliber pistol. They both went to Luton and both of them finished up dead."

"Jesus, Ruiz, I told you to stay out of this."

"I might need some local backup."

"I can't spare anyone. We're pulling warm bodies into London."

"Why? What's wrong?"

"Counter terrorism just raised the threat level to critical. An emergency call: a woman called 999 and said something about an attack on London tonight. Pakistani accent. She hung up before we could get details."

"A verified threat?"

"We're tracing the call."

Campbell has a phone ringing in the background. "Go home, Vincent, and stop acting like some third-rate vigilante. We'll follow your lead tomorrow."

Ruiz hangs up and looks at the sky, the trees bending in the wind. A storm coming.

35

LUTON

The rain starts falling just north of Watford, a few spits at first, mixing with dust on the windscreen and bleeding down the wipers. Then the clouds break and sheets of rain are swept across the motorway as if the air has turned to water. Ruiz drives with both hands on the wheel; his head canted forward, wanting the traffic to part. He stays in the overtaking lane, flashing his lights at any slow vehicles.

Luca is next to him, still trying to fathom how quickly the euphoria of yesterday has turned to this. Ruiz didn't ask him to come, but some decisions have all the momentum and certainty of gravity. Nicola had once accused him of sitting on the sidelines, unwilling to get involved, watching and reporting while sharing none of the pain. Maybe she was right. Maybe this is his moment.

"Do you believe in God?" asks Ruiz.

The question is so unexpected that all Luca does is stare at him. "I have a Catholic father and a Muslim mother. I call myself confused."

Ruiz drums his fingers on the wheel and they drive another mile in silence.

"But it's the same God, right? Muslim. Christian. Jewish."

"Yeah."

"I've been in two churches in the past week. I couldn't remember a single prayer."

"They say it's just a conversation with God."

"Guess I'm not much of a talker."

Luca doesn't doubt the statement.

Ruiz can hear the tone of his voice thickening. "I've never asked for much or felt entitled. Low expectations, less to be disappointed about. Some people talk about fate or karma or say that luck evens out, a little here or a little there, floating around and falling randomly on people like it's a raincloud. Holly Knight has been swimming in shit her entire life. She lost a brother, both her parents and a boyfriend—violently, pointlessly. When is Lady Luck going to smile on her?"

"Maybe today," says Luca.

Ruiz nods. "Yeah, maybe today."

It's still pouring when they arrive in Luton, the satnav directing them along Airport Way into Windmill Road, taking the Merc through a series of roundabouts that are threaded together like beads on a string.

"In two hundred yards you will have reached your destination."

Ruiz parks across the street from an abandoned motel in a neighborhood of warehouses, factories, garages and workshops. The two-storey, red-tiled motel is a leftover from the sixties, built around an asphalt forecourt that glitters with shattered glass. Most of the windows are barred or boarded up. The doors padlocked. Raindrops are bouncing off the windscreen.

"What do you think?" asks Ruiz.

"I think maybe Norman Bates had a British cousin," replies Luca, peering through the gloom.

Ruiz zips up his waterproof jacket and flips the hood.

"Where are you going?"

"To get a closer look."

"That's not a very good plan."

"You got a better one?"

"I haven't thought of it yet."

Instantly wet, Ruiz stays in the shadows, moving across the road and into the forecourt, which is empty except for a van parked near the rear fence. The rooms have numbers. He counts them down and slips his right hand into his jacket. Checks the Glock.

Room 12 has light leaking from behind the curtains. Voices. Accents. For a full minute he listens, trying to pick up the words. He's twenty yards away without any cover. If anyone walks out of the room they'll see him immediately. Backing away, he crosses the forecourt in a crouching run and squats beside the stairs.

The door opens. Three men emerge, silhouetted by the light inside. Young. Fit. They walk towards the van and open the rear doors. Ruiz can't see the interior, but one of the men has something in his hands: a machine pistol. He pulls back the slide mechanism and gazes down the barrel, aiming it at Ruiz, who is invisible in the darkness. More weapons are checked.

Having seen enough, Ruiz turns into a walkway that takes him behind the hotel, where he follows a chain-link fence back to the road. Luca sees him coming and opens the door.

"So what is it? What did you see?"

"Trouble."

He turns on Luca's mobile and calls Campbell, who's in the middle of a briefing.

"I've been trying to reach you. Where are you?"

"Luton."

"Shit!"

"What's wrong?"

"We traced that 999 call to a Homebase store in Bury Park, Luton. One of the female employees, Aisha Iqbal, is married to a man on a watchlist. Her husband is booked on a flight to Cairo first thing tomorrow."

Ruiz rubs a hole in the fogged glass. "I'm looking at a white van. Three up. Pakistani extraction. Heavily armed."

The van is pulling out of the forecourt. No headlights. Luca cranes forward and reads the number plate. Ruiz relays the information.

"If the van is heading for London it's going to reach the M1 in about fifteen minutes. You'll need to do a mobile intercept. In the meantime I need backup."

"Don't fuck around, Ruiz. Get out of there."

"Holly Knight could be inside."

"No, no, no. You listening? Stand down."

"You're breaking up."

Ruiz hears Campbell bang something hard. "All right, I'm sending a fucking army. You sit tight. They'll be there in fifteen."

"What about the van?"

"My problem. Don't you move."

The windscreen has fogged again. Ruiz wipes a circle on his side and sees a dark figure emerge from Room 12, a fourth man. He's carrying something in his right hand—a plastic jerrycan. He crosses the forecourt and disappears from view. Several minutes later he returns.

Ruiz opens the car door.

"Where are you going?"

"Want a closer look."

"He told us to wait."

"You wait."

Retracing his steps along the fence, Ruiz reaches the rear of the motel, keeping an eye on Room 12. The walkway is ahead of him, the rooms in darkness... all but one of them. Room 17 has a padlock hanging on a latch, uncoupled. He slides the bolt and nudges the door.

Disarray inside. Broken furniture. Cardboard boxes. Larger bins of old curtains... sodden. Petrol fumes catch in his throat and he fights the urge to cough.

The door to an adjoining room is partially open. He moves along the wall, holding the Glock at an upward angle. Peering through the opening he can see a table, a sofa spilling foam, chairs, a bed...

He hears a sound like a trapped animal and sees a shadow across the table. Someone sitting in a chair.

The situation is all wrong. He has to move through the door without cover, with his right arm extended at an awkward angle around the doorjamb. If there is someone on the other side, he won't have time to sight the target before firing. He should wait for backup. All he can do from here is hold someone, he can't take them out. He hears feet scraping on the floor.

"I'm armed. Come out now and you won't get hurt."

He listens. There is another muffled cry. Someone captive. He kicks open the door and crouches, pivoting and swinging the gun towards the chest of a seated figure. Muddy-eyed, he yells at the figure to put up his hands before realizing that *she* can't. Her arms are bound. Her legs. Her mouth covered by masking tape.

Holly.

Luca is resting his forearms on the dashboard, occasionally wiping the fogged window. He lost sight of Ruiz a few minutes ago. It seems longer.

At times working in Iraq he had been scared—at checkpoints or during firefights or when he was arrested in Baghdad—but over there he'd felt somehow better equipped. It was a war zone. He was doing a job. He had colleagues. Accreditation. Here he's an outsider. He's like an extra or an understudy who has wandered into the wrong play.

Ruiz is a different personality. He acts instinctively, unburdened by doubts or refusing to succumb to them. Luca shouldn't have let him go. They should have waited for the police. What's taking him so long?

He sees something moving at the periphery of his vision, near the back door of the Merc. Ruiz returning. He turns his head and frowns momentarily at the man squatting in a shooting position, his eyes alive with the thought of killing. The side window shatters and a round strikes Luca's shoulder like a fist wrapped in nails. Two more shots, fired with a silencer, punch into the metal of the doors, searching for his prone body. But the doors on the Mercedes 280 are built with a German Panzer in mind.

Luca lies very still as the pain drills through the bones of his shoulder. The longest minute passes. The kill shot doesn't come.

———

Ruiz rips the tape away from Holly's mouth. Her lips are cracked and bleeding and her body streaked with dirt and sweat. She's wearing some sort of vest over her thin dress. Putting the Glock on the floor, he runs his fingers around the edges of the heavy fabric, feeling the metal disc on the breastplate and the ball bearings packed tightly around the plastic explosives. His eyes follow the wires to the detonators.

"Please get it off me."

"Shush! Let me concentrate."

He looks for switches or pressure pads, feeling a rectangular outline beneath the material, two of them, detonators. Holly is handcuffed to the chair. He can't remove the suicide vest without first freeing her hands. Unless...? He needs a knife, shears, something sharp to cut the fabric.

"Get it off! Get it off!" whispers Holly.

Ruiz holds a finger to his lips and looks around the room, lifting boxes, opening cupboards, fumes in his head. He tries the bathroom. The sink is broken. A cascade of water runs across the broken ceramics. The mirror—it would take him too long. He has bolt cutters in the car.

Re-entering the bedroom, he catches a glimpse of the Courier at the last moment and pivots to take the first blow on his shoulder. The second comes down on the side of his head. The third crushes his scrotum, sending pain to the center of his brain. The Glock was on the floor next to Holly. He can't see it. Where has it gone?

He rolls on to his side and puts his hands on the floor, trying to rise but the floor won't let him up. The butt of a pistol thuds into the side of his head. Barely conscious, he feels himself being dragged across the room. Something closes around his wrists. So this is how it ends, he thinks, a victim of his own stupidity, a sucker for a sob story. One door too many—that's what they say when someone dies in the Armed Response Group. "One door too many."

Ruiz opens his eyes. Blood is trickling from his forehead down his nose and over his lips and chin. He is handcuffed to a radiator. Holly is standing in the corner, her thin dress clinging to her frame, the suicide vest still buckled around her torso. Ruiz jerks at the metal cuffs.

"I wouldn't trouble yourself. It's a done deal," says the Courier, who turns a chair backwards. Sits. Legs akimbo. He has a face now, real features. Dressed in black with razor-rimmed hair. Not handsome. Not ugly. Ordinary.

Ruiz has seen him before; he was in the crowd outside Colin Hackett's office when Ruiz was talking to Gerard Noonan. Now he's holding a mobile phone in his hand, spinning it like a six-gun.

"In case you're wondering, that vest contains ball bearings packed around plastic explosive—enough to blow this room apart. When I send a text message it will detonate. The wearer will not have a choice. That's one of the fail-safes I build into a project like this. I plan for cowardice."

Ruiz glances at Holly. She nods her head. He's telling the truth.

"They're not going to reach London. The police are following the van."

"I don't believe you, Mr. Ruiz. If the police were coming, they'd be here by now."

"Suit yourself."

The Courier is annoyed by his nonchalance, his lack of respect. The girl knows how to fear him. She knows what he's capable of.

"I am leaving now," he says. "Perhaps I shall have to take a hostage as insurance. Who shall it be?"

"Take me," says Ruiz. "Let her go."

"Are you begging?"

"I'm asking."

"Perhaps you should beg."

"I beg you."

He glances at Holly and smiles. "This one is in love with you."

"Maybe I just want a chance to rip out your throat," says Ruiz.

The Courier laughs. "Oh, you sound so courageous, so heroic, but it's not bravery if you're lying on a floor, chained to a radiator. All I hear are empty threats from a hollow man. I know all about you, Mr. Ruiz, and there's nothing heroic about your history. Your daughter. Your son. Three wives. A failed career. Did you really think you could come in here, without a weapon, and hope to succeed?"

He doesn't know about the Glock. Holly must have hidden it. Ruiz follows her eyes. She glances at the bed.

The Courier raises his hand. Listens. Sirens. He looks at Ruiz with loathing. Then he grabs Holly and pushes her out the door, pausing to strike the wheel of a cigarette lighter. He crouches and touches the flame to the carpet and a thin blue film shimmers across the floor. Liquid fire. Feeding. Growing.

The door closes. A padlock clicks into place.

Ruiz tries to pull his hand through the cuff. Ripping one arm back, he almost dislocates his wrist. He gets to his feet, leans backwards, arms outstretched and jerks against the chain, bellowing in pain. He lies on his back, kicking at the radiator, and then hooks his fingers over the top, rocking it back and forth.

The fire has spread from the floor to boxes of curtains in the next room and the bedding. Smoke is filling the ceiling space. Toxic fumes.

He yells for help. Screams in frustration. Someone is rattling the padlock on the door. He yells again, but fire whooshes across a mattress, drowning out the sound.

Then he hears a car engine, a familiar rumbling. Someone is revving the Merc, letting off the clutch, taking aim. The front wall of the room explodes inwards and part of the ceiling collapses on to the bonnet. Luca is sitting behind the fractured windscreen, slumped sideways with blood pooling in his lap.

The impact shakes the entire building. Plaster crumbles and

pipes bend. Ruiz rocks the radiator again and this time pulls it clear off the wall. His wrists are still cuffed, but he's free.

Luca puts the Merc into reverse and spins the wheels, pulling over broken bricks and plaster, using one arm to drive. Ruiz scrambles across the room and reaches beneath the bed, feeling blindly for the Glock. His fingers close around the grip.

Climbing over the debris he tries to open Luca's door, but the impact has bent the frame, trapping him inside. Ruiz sees the blood.

"I'll be fine. Just go," Luca yells. "They went through the back fence."

Ruiz crosses the forecourt and runs along the chain-link fence, looking for a gate or a hole. He peers into the freight yard to where spotlights create pools of light between rows of containers. He can hear them moving across the screed. The Courier is yelling at Holly to hurry up. Cursing her.

Ruiz aims the Glock with both hands, bracing the barrel in the diamond of the mesh fence. They are visible for a moment as they pass between rows of containers. Silhouettes. Two figures, Holly the smallest, being dragged along behind him. Squeezing the trigger, Ruiz fires six rounds in a row, the brass casings flicking past his eyes. He releases the empty magazine and shoves in a fresh one.

The Courier has never been in the military. He's never been taught to stay off the crest of hills and embankments and never to run in a straight line when someone is aiming a gun at you.

Ruiz waits, scanning the broken edge of the horizon. There they are. Aim. Squeeze. Fire. The Courier spins sideways and falls. Holly goes down with him, disappearing from sight.

Police cars are screeching to a halt outside the motel, bathing the windows in blue and white. The first officers are wearing body armor and carrying weapons. One of them yells at Ruiz to drop his gun.

Ruiz is scanning the fence line, looking for a way through.

"Drop your weapon, or I'll shoot," the officer shouts.

Ruiz raises his arms and throws the Glock to the ground.

"They're getting away! He's got a hostage!"

Finally he sees where the wire has been cut and peeled back from the metal posts. Dropping to his hands and knees, he crawls through, ignoring the orders of the policeman. Up again, running, he crosses the trolley tracks, heading towards the freight yard.

The motel is eighty yards behind him when he reaches the ridge where he last saw Holly. He notices blood on the rocks and weeds, a dark stain like fungus or rust.

Ruiz doesn't stay on top of the ridge. He drops down and scans the rows of metal boxes, stacked four and five units high. The Courier is hiding somewhere among them. Wounded. Bleeding. He's still with Holly.

The next fifty yards is open ground. Ruiz decides to run for it, huffing air in his nostrils, feeling like an elephant rather than a gazelle.

Someone like the Courier is trained for this. His reflexes. His instincts. No conscience. No guilt. What will he do if he's cornered... if he can't run? He'll fight. He'll die. He'll take Holly with him.

That's when he sees her. Running. Legs pumping. Chin tilting back. She's still wearing the vest. Still handcuffed.

Ruiz reaches her in moments, lifting her like a rag doll. She fights at his arms. Squirming. Screaming.

"Get it off! Get it off!"

Ruiz drags at the vest, pulling it over Holly's head, turning her in a somersault, wrenching the fabric to the end of her arms, where it can go no further.

"Please. Help me!"

The Courier is slumped against the wheel arch of a rusting freight trailer; his head is tilted back and lips parted as though drinking in the sky. He's drowning in his own saliva from a sucking chest wound. Dying.

Opening his eyes, he watches Ruiz and the girl. Then he glances at the mobile phone in his hand. The screen lights up. This thumb presses "send." A two-word message: **Allahu Akbar.** God is great.

Kicking open the heavy metal door of an empty container, Ruiz carries Holly inside and lays her on the floor with her arms stretched in front of her. Then he drags the door closed, trapping the vest on the outside of the door, still attached to Holly's handcuffs. He pulls at her hands, holding them a few inches inside the closing door. The vest is looped over the chain of the handcuffs and the double door won't shut completely. He braces his feet against the frame, holding the handles, pulling with all his strength, shielding her body with his.

That's when the prayer comes to him—the one from his childhood—the one he couldn't remember in the church.

Matthew, Mark, Luke and John,
Bless the bed that I lie on.
There are four corners to my bed,
Four angels round my head,
One to watch, and one to pray,
And two to bear my soul away.
Now I lay me down to sleep,
I pray the Lord my soul to keep.
If I should die before I wake,
I pray the Lord my soul to take.

Taj is driving the van, keeping to the middle lane, using the cruise control to keep a constant speed. Being stopped by the cops would be silly. Stolen van. Bombs on board. Syd is in a playful mood. Poking his head between the front seats. Ketchup stains around his mouth.

"Did you see that girl? Do you think he was going to fuck her? I would have fucked her. She was fit. I mean, wow, she made Jenny Cruikshank look like a slag. Do you think he's going to do it?"

Rafiq tells him to shut up. "Put your seat belt on. We don't want to get picked up."

Syd giggles. "You think they're going to worry about my sodding seat belt, when they see the hardware we got in here." He picks up one of the guns.

"Put that away!" says Taj. "What if someone sees you waving that thing about? They'll call the cops. We'll never get to London."

Syd puts down the gun and leans back in his seat, sipping on a can of Red Bull. It's raining. The wipers are slapping against the bottom of the windscreen, air blasting on the inside of the glass. Taj has to crane forward, trying to see the electric red smears of brake lights. London is still an hour away but already the traffic is building.

Syd leans forward again. "A thousand fucking people—how cool is that? The place is going to be packed. I feel like a fucking soldier. What are you going to do with the money? They reckon fifty grand will buy you a palace in Pakistan. That's what I'm gonna do. Then I'll bring my mum and dad over. Show them my palace. Tell my old man he can shove his fish-and-chip shop up his arse." He crushes the can. "Are you going to bring Aisha over, Taj? Did you tell her? What did you say?"

Taj doesn't want to talk about Aisha. Their last words had been harsh. He had never seen her in such a temper, so adamant that he was wrong. She had thrown the money at him. Spat on it. Tried to tear it into pieces. She would change her mind, he reasoned. She knows her place.

There's a three-ton truck in front of him that has slowed right down and another in the left lane, side by side like the drivers are talking to each other. Taj indicates to overtake, but another truck cuts him off. Slows down.

What are these tossers doing, he thinks. He looks in the rear mirrors. The road is clear. The nearest cars are a hundred yards behind. That's odd, he thinks. Then he notices the opposite carriageway is empty. Deserted.

"Something's wrong," he says.

"What?" asks Rafiq.

"The traffic."

"Just go round these guys."

"I can't get past."

"Hit the horn." Rafiq turns and looks through the rear window. "Where has everyone gone?"

"They're on to us."

"What do you mean?" says Syd. "I can't see anyone."

"They're fucking on to us!"

"Settle down," says Rafiq. "Maybe there's an accident."

The three trucks in front have slowed almost to a halt. A fourth passes on the verge, squeezing against the safety rail. They all have roller doors at the back. Taj nudges the brakes and stops thirty yards from the nearest truck. Then they notice the police cars on the other carriageway. A military chopper is overhead.

"Go back!" says Rafiq. "Reverse."

Taj struggles with the gears. Where's reverse? There it is. Pedal down. The roller doors have rattled up. A dozen men in black body armor are crouched in firing positions. Taj spins the wheel, sending the van into a slide. It's facing in the opposite direction, driving the wrong way. Ahead, a row of police cars. Lights flashing. Armed men behind the open doors. Guns drawn.

"Ram them!" says Rafiq.

"They've got guns."

"Go back!" says Syd, wiping the fogged windows, looking for some means of escape.

"We're fucked!" says Taj.

"We got the guns," says Syd. "We can shoot our way out."

"They're going to kill us."

"I'm not going to prison," says Rafiq. "You heard what the Courier said. A week is going to feel like a lifetime."

Taj has stopped the van a hundred yards away from the police cars.

"You want to run, you run," says Taj. "I've had enough."

"We made a pact," says Syd.

"We're not the three musketeers."

Taj opens the door. Steps out. Holds his hands above his head. Walks slowly down the middle lane, watching his shadow in the beams of the headlights. Rain pours down his face, into his eyes and mouth. He can't hear Syd and Rafiq arguing any more.

In the next instant he's flying. Falling. The explosion blows out the window of the van and covers every surface in a film of pink. Ball bearings punch through the seats and the thinner metal in the roof, letting the rain pour in.

Glass showers across the tarmac, landing in his hair and on the back of his neck. Fragments of metal have torn his coat, but he can't feel any pain. Lying on the motorway, eyes closed, arms spread like a crucifix, he sucks in the oily water like a breath and feels the residual heat of the day warm against his cheek.

———

Ruiz's life doesn't flash before his eyes in a conventional or chronological sense. Events run backwards like in that movie where Brad Pitt is born as an old man and grows younger every year. All of Ruiz's accumulated knowledge is disappearing, along with his anger and weariness. Things are being unlearned. Discoveries are being undiscovered. Painful memories are being wiped clean.

Eventually all his grey hairs and fine lines are filled in and he's a young man again, dancing with Laura at the twilight ball in Hertfordshire. The clock keeps rolling backwards. Soon she'll be a stranger, who could pass him on the street with no recollection of the life they're going to share or the children they are going to raise, but for the moment they keep dancing.

These are his final conscious thoughts before the pressure wave of the explosion buckles the door of the container and blows him backwards, slamming his head against the far wall. His eardrums are bleeding. He cannot hear the paramedics shouting for bandages and plasma, or feel the needle sliding into his arm or the mask covering his face.

Someone is getting blankets to keep him warm.

"Any head injuries?"

"That's negative. Christ, look at his hands!"

"You look after the girl."

Ruiz can't feel anything; instead he's floating on a cloud of opiates, still imagining himself as a young man, spinning Laura across the dance floor, her head beneath his chin, her soft hair against his lips.

"Ready?"

"Yeah."

"One, two, three."

"Watch the IV lines. Watch the IV lines."

"I got it."

"Bag a couple of times."

"OK."

Laura smiles at him. She's standing near the entrance, waiting for the buses to take guests back to London. She points and summons him with her finger. Ruiz looks over his shoulder to make sure.

"What's your name?"

"Vincent."

"I'm Laura. This is my phone number. If you don't call me within two days, Vincent, you lose your chance. I'm a good girl. I don't sleep with men on the first date or the second or the third. You have to woo me, but I'm worth the effort."

Then she kisses him on the cheek and she's gone.

36

LONDON

Awake now. Eyelids fluttering. Ruiz turns his head. Orange dials come into focus on a machine near the bed and a green blip of light slides across a liquid crystal window.

A nurse says something to him. She's mouthing words.

"I need to make a call," says Ruiz.

She shakes her head.

"If I don't call Laura she won't go out with me."

The nurse mouths a question. "Who's Laura?"

She presses the button above his head. "We were very worried about you."

"Sorry?"

"Your hands. They're going to be fine," she says, still mouthing words.

Ruiz notices the bandages. They look like white stumps.

He points to his ears. "I can't hear you. What's wrong with me?"

"Ruptured eardrums," she mouths. "You may need surgery."

"Holly?"

The nurse laughs. "I thought you wanted Laura. Holly is down the way."

"What?"

"Holly is OK. She's fine."

Ruiz tries to get out of bed, but the nurse puts a strong hand on his chest, digging her knuckles into his breastbone.

"They warned me about you. Said you'd be a difficult patient."

He doesn't understand.

"Your friends." She straightens his pillow. "They've been waiting outside all night."

"Luca?"

"Oh, he's here. They pulled a bullet out of his shoulder, but he's out of surgery."

Ruiz shakes his head, not understanding.

The nurse uses a pad on the bedside table and writes:

He's fine. Bullet removed. Recuperating.

The door opens. Joe O'Loughlin is wearing a cravat and looks even more like a professor than usual. He stands beside the bed and the two men communicate wordlessly in a language that only dogs and men can understand. He takes the notepad from the nurse, who tells them both to behave as she leaves.

Joe writes: *You can't hear. I can't speak. We're like two of the wise monkeys.*

"You're a monkey. I'm a gorilla," says Ruiz, shouting at him. "I want to see Holly."

Joe writes: *Can you walk?*

"Yeah."

Joe helps Ruiz to sit and then stand. He's wearing a hospital gown with ties at the back. Ruiz can't hold it together with his bandaged hands, so Joe does it for him, clearly not enamored of the task.

"I could get used to you not talking," says Ruiz, as they shuffle down the corridor. Joe pinches him on the arse, making him jump.

They reach Holly's room, which is full of flowers and get-well cards. Holly is sitting on the edge of her bed while a doctor peers into her ears with a torch-like contraption. She's chewing gum. Looking bored. There are marks on her wrists where the handcuffs tore at her skin.

"How come you get proper pajamas?" says Ruiz. "Your legs are better than mine—you should be wearing a gown."

Her face lights up and she's on him in a heartbeat, throwing her arms around his shoulders, her legs around his hips.

"This is the not the way a young lady should greet a man of my age and in my condition."

He doesn't hear what Holly says. Maybe she says nothing at all.

37

LONDON

Throughout Monday, Luca sits in the High Court listening to opposing lawyers make grand speeches about press freedom and commercial confidentiality. It has been almost a week since the thwarted terrorist attack and two days since he left hospital with his arm in a sling and the bullet in a small glass jar that is nestled in his pocket. A souvenir. Proof that he doesn't always sit on the sidelines.

The *Financial Herald* is trying to overturn the High Court injunction preventing publication. Mersey Fidelity's lawyers are doing verbal and linguistic somersaults as they argue that commercial privacy should outweigh public interest. The judge is not having a bar of it. The lawyers lodge an immediate appeal. He dismisses it. Luca steps from the court and calls Daniela with the news.

"We're going to celebrate."

"You're not supposed to be drinking."

"I'm going to watch you get drunk and then take advantage of you."

"But you're an invalid."

"We're not going to arm wrestle."

Daniela laughs and it sounds like music. Luca ends the call and steps outside, looking for a cab. He has a story to write, but there are still questions to be answered. Dialing a new number, he listens to the call being rerouted through different internet servers until Luca's new best friend answers.

"Capable?"

"Mr. Terracini."

"Call me Luca."

"Thank you, Mr. Terracini."

"Any news?"

"They're on the move. A van arrived this morning."

The address in Cartwright Street is an old bank building with an ornate iron door and arched entrance. A removal van is parked in the narrow side alley in front of two identical black Pathfinders. What a world these people live in, thinks Luca, as he pays the cab driver. Taking a table across the road, he nurses a coffee and watches boxes and computers being loaded into the van.

Another Pathfinder shows up, this one disgorging a set of beefy passengers in suits and dark glasses. One of the occupants he recognizes. Older. Grey-haired. Giving orders.

Luca waits until he disappears inside. He pays for his coffee and crosses the street, following a removal man into the lift and rising through the floors. The doors open. Boxes are stacked in the corridors. A shredding machine lets out a long whine. Industrial-

sized. Worm-like mounds of confetti are spilling from plastic
sacks.

Soft footsteps. Somebody yells at him to stop. He is gripped
from behind and pushed into an office where Artie Chalcott and
Brendan Sobel are deep in conversation.

Chalcott looks up. His face reddens. Luca notices that his eyes
are very small. Perhaps they are the standard size and his head is
overly large. Maybe they shrink when he's angry.

"You got a nerve, coming here."

"I just want to ask you a few questions."

"Get him out of here."

"We're publishing tomorrow," says Luca. "I'm giving you a
chance to comment on the story."

"No comment."

Brendan Sobel is walking Luca towards the lift. The journalist
yells over his shoulder. "You can't cover this one up. You can't
shred it or bury it. It's going to come out."

Chalcott laughs. "You really think you can make this one fly—
some fatuous conspiracy theory about Iraqi robberies and a British
bank? A week from now nobody is going to care."

"You will."

"No, that's where you're wrong. I'll have moved on."

Luca fights at Sobel's arms. "I'm giving you a chance to explain."

"Patriots don't have to explain. It's pacifists and apologists like
you who need to justify what you do."

"I took a bullet."

"And you've cost the lives of countless people."

Chalcott is angry now. On his feet, storming down the corridor.
For a moment Luca expects a punch.

"You think you're a fucking hero, Mr. Terracini? You think
you're the people's champion? I hope you have nightmares about
what you've done... the deaths you're going to cause."

"What deaths? What are you talking about?"

"Why do you think Mohammed Ibrahim was released from
prison? Why do you think we let him re-establish the network of
accounts?"

Luca's gaze falters and his self-possession deserts him for a moment. "What are you talking about?"

Chalcott finds the question amusing. "How did you begin investigating this story?"

"I followed the money."

"Exactly."

"I still don't understand."

"My job is to stop the bad shit before it happens—to catch the mad mullahs and the bomb makers and locate their training camps. Smash the fuckers. Bring them to their knees. But we can't defeat these people militarily. And we can't bomb them back to the Dark Ages because they live in caves already. But they're not cavemen. They're cleverer than that. They use our own systems against us. Our technology. Our markets. Our banks.

"People make the mistake of thinking this is an ideological battle. It's not about religion or faith, it's about power. It's about politics. It's about control. We set this up, Mr. Terracini. *I set this up.* Mersey Fidelity has been breaking the law for years, laundering money through ghost accounts. All I did was introduce a new client."

"Ibrahim."

"And then I followed the money—just like you. Ironic, isn't it? But while you were looking for a headline, I was looking for terror cells and training camps and secret hideouts."

The last statement is spat out like he's swallowed an insect.

"Where is Mohammed Ibrahim?" asks Luca.

"We've taken his toys away. He's out of the race."

"They were going to blow up a nightclub."

Chalcott waves his hand dismissively. "A few dozen lives to save thousands."

"You think the end justifies the means."

"I think it *should* be a factor."

"Who chooses?"

"Pardon?"

"Who makes that choice?"

"People like *me*. Because people like you don't have the stomach for it."

Chalcott signals to Sobel and the lift doors slide open.

"Enjoy your fifteen minutes, Mr. Terracini. I hope it was worth it."

38

LONDON

It has been six weeks since Ruiz left hospital. His hands have healed, adding to his scars, and his hearing is almost fully returned, apart from a persistent buzzing in his ears that sounds like a bee trapped behind glass. It's no more annoying than his second wife, he tells people, not entirely joking.

The story about Mersey Fidelity is almost old news but Luca Terracini is still bathing in the glory—he's been profiled in the Sunday supplements and interviewed on morning TV. He and Daniela were photographed on a weekend break in Paris— the globetrotting foreign correspondent and the glamorous US auditor who uncovered the biggest financial scandal since the meltdown.

Ruiz stayed out of the spotlight, barely mentioned in reports of the terrorist blast that closed the M1 for twelve hours on 1 September. Two of the bombers died when cornered by officers from the anti-terrorism branch. A third, Taj Iqbal, unemployed of Luton, is in Belmarsh Prison, London, awaiting trial. The *Daily Mail* published a photograph of his wife and baby son arriving at the prison. She wore a Muslim veil and didn't talk to reporters. Something in her eyes reminded Ruiz of the moment he first met Elizabeth North, her emotions held in check, defenses raised, a child to protect.

Elizabeth has visited him three times, once in hospital and twice at home. She brings Rowan and Claudia and soon his living room is covered with toys and tinkling with the sound of children's TV shows.

"Mitchell jumped before he was pushed," she says. "There's been a boardroom reshuffle and half the directors have gone."

"Any news of Maluk?"

"They think he's in Syria or Egypt."

Elizabeth unbuttons her blouse to feed Claudia, her breast swollen and pale, lined with the faintest of blue veins. Ruiz looks at the feeding infant, her tiny mouth pressed hard against the nipple, eyes closed in concentration.

"What about the bank?" he asks.

"I had a man come to see me: Douglas Evans."

"I've met him."

"Doesn't he remind you of someone out of a le Carré novel?" Elizabeth does his accent. "Confidence is the key. As much as I would like to see those responsible punished for this abomination. Publicly flogged. Humiliated. There are greater issues to consider. Three years ago our banking system suffered a heart attack. It has been on life support ever since. Nobody wants to turn off that life support system."

Elizabeth laughs and Rowan looks up from the floor. "What's so funny, Mummy?"

"People who talk with posh accents," she says, smiling at him and continuing. "They say they're going to prosecute executives, but nobody has been charged. Mitchell has hired a QC. We haven't spoken. He's cut himself off from the family."

"I'm sorry."

Elizabeth starts cleaning up the mess, putting lids on Tupperware containers and packing her changing bag. "That girl—the one who went home with North."

"Holly Knight?"

"How is she?"

"She's good. She got a call back for a play and she's looking for part-time work."

Elizabeth nods. "If you see her..." She hesitates. "Tell her I don't blame her for anything and I'm sorry about what happened."

"If you hang around she'll be home soon."

"She's staying here?"

"Yes."

"Are you two...?"

"Christ no, but I need a lock on my bedroom door."

Elizabeth shakes her head. Her pram is packed and Claudia strapped inside. Rowan rides on a platform at the back, standing between the handles. They're going to walk over Hammersmith Bridge and along the river to Barnes.

Pausing at the front gate, she turns. "About Holly," she says. "Is she any good with children?"

After she's gone, Ruiz tidies the sitting room, sweeping up crumbs and straightening pillows. Among the "get well" cards on the mantelpiece he comes across one from Capable Jones. Unsigned. Capable is paranoid about people forging his signature. The message is typed and printed, wishing him a speedy recovery, with a postscript tacked on to the end:

That nanny you wanted to find. Do you still want her address?

Ruiz puts on his jacket and goes out, walking the river path where autumn is decorating the trees before winter strips them bare. He doesn't have the Mercedes anymore and will do without a car for a while. He doesn't need one in London, where every business seems to deliver, even the off licenses.

Polina Dulsanya lives on the fourth floor of a block of flats in Fulham, just off the high street. Ruiz climbs the stairs slowly, his body still depleted. Knocks on the door.

A woman answers, barely out of her teens, with a gymnast's body and dark bobbed hair. She's wearing jeans and a short T-shirt that barely covers her torso. Flesh is the new season's color.

"Can I help you?" she asks with a confused smile, pronouncing the English words perfectly. She sounds Russian or maybe Polish.

"Can I come in?"

"Why?"

"I want to talk to you about Richard North."

"Vincent, how did you get through the gates?"

"Your wife let me in."

Alistair Bach shakes his head. "Sometimes I wonder why I installed a security system. People buzz and Jacinta just opens the gate. She's far too trusting."

He's pruning rose bushes at the rear of the property, where the northern sun hits the stone wall and reflects the heat back on to the flowerbeds.

"It was *your* bank."

"Pardon?"

"Mersey Fidelity—you built it."

"Oh, I can't take all the credit."

"And it was your scheme. You set up the ghost accounts and recruited Richard North to carry on your work."

Bach's shoulders tighten beneath his cotton shirt. For a moment Ruiz braces for a confrontation, but the older man gazes at the secateurs in his hand and seems to reach a different decision.

Ruiz continues. "Mitchell had no idea when he took control. You couldn't be sure how he'd react, so you hired someone to infiltrate his household, someone to seduce him just in case you needed leverage. You were willing to blackmail your own son. Once you succeeded in gaining his co-operation, you sent Polina to your daughter's house to seduce your son-in-law."

"That's a fanciful story, Vincent. You've been hanging around with journalists for too long."

"I've talked to Polina. She told me."

"And you believe the word of a prostitute?"

"She has no reason to lie anymore."

Bach continues to prune, holding the branches with a gloved hand to avoid the thorns.

"Do you know why roses have thorns, Vincent? It's to prevent grazing animals from eating them. The sweetest-smelling roses have the sharpest thorns, because their scents attract the most animals. We all need defense mechanisms ... even banks."

"You broke the law."

Bach chuckles with delight. "The law! Where have you been, Vincent? The law doesn't apply to banks. We're too big to fail."

Shaking his head, he grows circumspect. "I didn't mean for any of this to happen. Things got out of hand. It began with a few accounts. Major corporations. We helped hide their assets or shift profits between territories to avoid tax or arrange a hostile take-over. Over time our client base expanded and became less than savory, but we couldn't say no because they could expose us."

"You were blackmailed," says Ruiz.

Bach gives him a pained smile. "The system was working. It was brilliant really. Almost foolproof ..."

"Until the global financial crisis came along."

"Mersey Fidelity was hemorrhaging money like all the others. People were closing their positions, selling investments, withdrawing their money. We had a liquidity crisis and needed funds to stay solvent. Mitchell panicked and tapped into some of the ghost accounts."

"That's why North was so concerned with the audit."

"He came to see me. Begged me to intervene."

"When?"

"On the Saturday he disappeared. He said he'd been robbed the night before — picked up by some girl in a bar and drugged. I thought he was bluffing when he told me about the notebook.

"Nobody was supposed to have a complete list. That's how we protected the bank — nothing in writing, nothing on file, nothing on computer. Numbers, not names on the accounts."

"North began piecing it together."

"Yes."

"Did you tell Ibrahim about the photographs or was it Maluk?"

"I have no control over Yahya. I'm not the chairman anymore."

"You signed Hackett's death warrant."

"I don't even know who you're talking about."

"The private detective ... Ibrahim had him killed."

"You can't hold me responsible for his actions."

"Why not? You're a part of this. Did you have North killed?"

"Of course not! Now you're being ridiculous."

"North was trying to find out where the money was going."

"He was foolish. He fell for the lifestyle and then developed a conscience. I told him not to go looking for trouble."

"When?"

"That Saturday he came here. He said that he'd traced some of the money to a postbox in Luton ... something about a Muslim charity. And he was prattling about earlier transactions in Madrid. The Spanish police had contacted him about some ATM withdrawals prior to the train bombing in 2004. North managed to fob them off by saying the accounts didn't exist at Mersey Fidelity, but he knew where the money had come from."

Bach stands, straightening his back, gazing across the pond towards the house, which is wreathed in ivy. A castle fit for a king.

"He should have kept his mouth shut. The audit would have blown over."

"Don't you feel any responsibility?"

"What's done is done."

"I'm going to tell the authorities."

Bach laughs. "Good luck with that. Nothing is going to happen. They know already. Why do you think I haven't been charged? I'm an old man. They're not going to prosecute me. They can't risk damaging confidence in the banking system."

There's no hint of triumphalism in Bach's voice, yet he was right all along, thinks Ruiz. People might hate him or question his morals, but when the economy picks up and the banks grow strong again, they'll envy his wealth and his power. They'll want to be just like him.

"Can I ask you one favor, please, Vincent?"

"What's that?"

"I'd appreciate it if you didn't tell Lizzie about Polina. She's been through so much. Family is all she has left."

His arrogance is astonishing; hubris on a grand scale. Ruiz can feel the skin tighten across his face.

"If it's a question of money," says Bach, "I'm sure I can find some honey in the pot to sweeten your medicine."

The buzzing in Ruiz's ears has grown louder. "I'm not the only person who knows."

"Polina won't say anything. She's been too well paid."

Ruiz has already turned away, in sudden need of fresher air. After several steps, he stops and spins.

"By the way, Elizabeth has a new nanny who knows all about dysfunctional families and their secrets. She can even tell when someone is lying."

"My sins have been confessed."

"But they haven't been forgiven."

Ruiz leaves, walking up the slope towards the house, the turf soft beneath his worn leather shoes. Beneath the canopy of a fig tree he notices a rope swing dangling from a lower branch and can picture Elizabeth as a young girl, her hair flying, pushing herself from the shadows into the sunshine.

Although reality can sometimes corrupt the fairytale and alter our ambitions, some things remain unalterable. From richest to poorest, we start and end with family.

ACKNOWLEDGMENTS

The Wreckage is based on many real-life events and documents but the characters are entirely fictitious. I am indebted to many fine journalists and authors who have written about the global financial crisis and about Iraq. I have drawn upon their experiences and wisdom to hopefully create fiction that reads like the truth.

As always, I wish to thank my agents Mark Lucas, Richard Pine, Nicki Kennedy and Sam Edenborough, as well as my editors David Shelley and John Schoenfelder.

For their hospitality, friendship and advice I thank Mark and Sara Derry, Martyn Forrester, Peter Temple, Jonathan Margolis and Scott Dalton.

Last, but by no means least, I am indebted as always to my beloved wife Vivien, who has suffered more than usual during the birth of this particular baby. My daughters have also endured my mercurial mood swings and many absences. One day I'll make it up to them.

I love you guys.

ABOUT THE AUTHOR

Before writing full-time, Michael Robotham was an investigative journalist in Britain, Australia and the US. He is the pseudonymous author of ten best-selling non-fiction titles, involving prominent figures in the military, the arts, sport and science. He lives in Sydney with his wife and three daughters.